1st Edition

Ciby Emrie
Pipe Dreams

A NOVEL

STERLING MONOGRAM PUBLICATIONS

Sterling Monogram Publications
Chatham, Virginia 24531

Copyright © 2011 E. Ciby Emrie
All rights reserved. No part of this book may be reproduced in any form or by any means without prior written consent of the publisher, excepting brief quotes in reviews.

This is a work of fiction. Names, characters, places and incidents either are the product of the author's imagination or are used fictitiously, and any resemblance to actual persons, living or dead, events or locales is entirely coincidental.

ISBN: 0982786204
ISBN-13: 9780982786208

Design by Ms. Jenny Givner
Edited by Ms. Carol Givner
Printed in the United States of America
Paperback Edited by Createspace Staff

Chapter 1

October 1992

Gloria

"What is that?"
 The phone.
2:22 a.m.
"Hello," I squeak.
"I'm so sorry to wake you, Gloria, but—"
We were suddenly interrupted and placed on hold by an operator. My caller searches for more change to extend her pay phone minutes.

While waiting, I grope for my robe and search with my right big toe, finding one scuff under my bed and another beneath a chair. *How had my right slipper ended up all the way over there? Who knows?*

Scratching my head I pad to my French doors. I'm drawn by habit from other middle-of-the-night

awakenings, to just gaze into a black sky, sprinkled with stars like sugar crystals; thinking about nothing, really, and hoping for a quick return to sleep. Other times, like now, I'd study this crystalled expanse more intently. Tonight, for whatever reason, I'm reminded of sequins on that old, velvet dress.

As a little girl, I'd play dress-ups in a discarded gown, with time-dulled sparklies, as I called them. I coupled it with a broad-brimmed, crimson hat, formal gloves pulled to my armpits, and emerald satin, spike-heels. Gazing at my mirrored reflection, I'd dream of being all grown up. I'd imagine how perfect my life would be—then.

Fast forward roughly fifteen years to my wedding rehearsal dinner. I'd worn a dark satin sheath—the exact shade of that old gown. I copied its new design from a magazine, picturing one of Jackie Kennedy's dresses—shiny sequins accenting an empire waist.

I loved wearing that dress, in anticipation of my next day's wedding, which would be perfect, too, of course—just like Jackie's. My dazzling sequin-dotted gown was a Priscilla creation—same as Tricia Nixon's—complete with full, cathedral train; eight bridesmaids in blush; and Julia, my maid of honor, in rose; all with flickering sparklies, too.

I'd been sure my Cinderella wedding would deliver me into a glittering fairy tale life.

Unfortunately, like Jackie Kennedy's, my life didn't exactly turn out to be a happily-ever-after fairy tale. (I don't remember hearing how Tricia Nixon's life turned out.) My Camelot-husband wasn't as Cameloty as

Jackie's appeared, although we'd both married Irish-American lawyers and our less-than-perfect marriages lasted close to the same number of years. Parallels ended there—abruptly. Sparkly dreams dissolved with tears into dark reality, much like sugar crystals dissolving in bitter, too-strong coffee.

Pipe dreams; much of my life had been chasing after the wind.

Something about darkness, spoken by someone, maybe Chambers, I think, pushed among my dangling thoughts while I waited to hear multiple dings from deposited coins: "...song birds are taught to sing in the dark..."

My life has certainly been made up of more than enough dark times—probably more dark ones, than light, if you really want to know the truth. I'm not talking about night skies or dark, sequined dresses, either.

But, yes, I've learned to sing in the dark, and I'd witnessed other birds learning to warble in their dismal times, too. A hard school, for sure.

"Yes, operator, I'll accept remaining charges."

"Glory, sorry, I ran out of change."

"Are you packed?" I whisper.

"Yes. I never could've imagined myself driving a U-haul, but I rented one. Can you believe it. . .me, driving a truck? I've crammed my most important things in it, but I've left a lot of stuff behind and said my goodbyes. I'm scared, but I'm kind of excited, too. Now, tell me again: I turn right at the second mountain and go to the very top. There'll be a light, right?"

Late August, 1991

"Help," I say weakly.

It has come to this: I, Gloria Harris, ne: Holland, am sitting in an ancient chair, resurrected from my parents' basement, in a decrepit house in Baltimore. Actually, it's not my house. It's one in which I find myself residing temporarily. I must emphasize to you—just temporarily. But I said that three months ago, didn't I?

True enough. I nodded with an unwanted sense of resign.

This house is one of several rental properties left from my father's estate, eight years ago. It's been vacant since then—until my arrival.

I gaze passed my cup of tepid tea, poised, and ready to tip at any moment. I scrutinize this place I presently call home.

Pleeze. I shake my head slowly in utter dismay.

My part-Himalayan cat, Purrfect, prunes herself on her claimed sofa cushion. She hasn't done well in her adjustment to our temporary move back from country to city, either. Street noise, although somewhat muffled by a rattling air conditioner Mr. Wilson installed, still causes us to jump. The unit was placed not, primarily, for its cooling capacity, (whose output of cold air is barely measurable), but for noise-filtering qualities, which help me and my cat to sleep.

The idea was one I dreamed up, after sirens and trucks traveling this Hampden end of Roland Avenue, day and night, have set Purrfect tearing around as if

demon-possessed. I used similar logic, as in if you stub your toe, your headache doesn't hurt as badly.

I shake my head with a sick feeling. This time last year, I couldn't have imagined sitting in this house, pondering what issues have become my life.

Purrfect has found mice; mice, and their rodent relatives, which colonize amidst us. (Creatures I don't even want to think about, not now, not ever.) Uncounted numbers reside here.

Mice, it seems are the least of my problems—except, when Purrfect is full or loses interest in her prey, and leaves her half-consumed snack somewhere my toes discover on a middle-of-a-night bathroom trek. I shudder, recalling that other night. I'll spare you those details.

Well, it can't be much longer, can it? I take a deep breath and blow it out slowly.

I close my eyes and think back to last year, basking on my little porch in western North Carolina. Life, although never easy, was gently quiet. Air was clean. I was finally able to relax, and experience a sample of hospitality which so characterizes the South.

My small inheritance allowed me to escape pressures of this hectic city and my stress-filled position as a hospital social worker, and enjoy a small-town, health-department position. My only son, Tad, had left for college. For all intents and purposes, I was happily settled into life in a lazy hollow, looking forward to time for me.

I met Bill.

I miss Bill, I do. He's the best friend anyone could ever want.

Swallowing, with a slight twinge of guilt, and an uncontrolled grimace, I'm aware I have to make a decision about that.

About Bill.

Bill is my neighbor, and my boss, actually: the County Health Department Director. We did everything together. I miss him. I miss him a lot.

There's the rub. He wants more than just friendship.

And what's wrong with that? It's reasonable. We've been working together and living near one another for how long? Four, no six, could it be seven years? Surely not.

He wants a committed relationship. He keeps saying we're not getting any younger.

Well, that's true, but I'm only 42…or is it 43? I counted my fingers. No, it couldn't be. *I couldn't be 47, could I?* Well, it's not important. It's not like either of us wants children. My only son is nearly 21, and his daughter is 30ish, I think. He doesn't often speak of her, but I think she's about 30.

I'm just not ready for anything serious. I need more time to heal and process my life.

Bill was right, of course. It's been nearly fifteen years since my marriage ended. He was nice when he tactfully asked, "Can you estimate how much more time of actual healing you need before you can go to the next level?"

I know it sounds obsessive. It does to me, too, when I choose to think about it. It's just—I'm afraid, kind of.

I shake my head. How can I possibly consider another change in my life?

I peruse chipped plaster walls and ceiling cracks. If that's not bad enough, cracks line toilets and sinks, badly stained with rainbow colors of copper, turquoise blue, and whatever that disgusting shade of yellow-green is.

My life is an absolute mess right now. Although thinking about it, it has been for some time: months ... years? Maybe decades.

Then there's the whole reason why I came back—to Baltimore.

Mother: my mother suffers from dementia.

Lucille, our long-time housekeeper called me last June. I recall that life-altering phone call:

'Honey, your mama ain't doin' so good,' she'd said and sighed.

Alarmed, I'd reacted, "What's happened, Lucille? Has she fallen? Oh, my, she hasn't fallen, has she?" There were several flights of stairs in that sprawling house, any of which would cripple the sturdiest of walkers.

"Honey, it ain't like that. It's jes yo' mama don't know thin's she used to. She ask 'bout where yo' daddy be and why he not be home. She forgets reg'lar thin's an' don't know many a' her friends. I worry 'bout leavin' her t' go t' market."

"Don't worry, Lucille. I'll come up this weekend. Are you all right?"

"Yes, Honey, ya don't need t' worry none 'bout me. Jes yo mama. She poorly. Law, law, she poorly."

Upon my arrival, I realized things were far worse than Lucille described. It was not unusual for Mother to call me by my sisters' names. After all, there were fo

girls, and she never could get us all straight. I could see she'd really declined from even six months before.

After having been back for less than two weeks, Lucille's mid-night call alerted me to Mother's fall. A frantic trip to Midtown Memorial forced me to realize I needed to stay in Baltimore much longer than I'd thought, or wanted to contemplate.

I recall the day I'd informed my brothers and sisters about Mother's accident. They all descended on our family house that Sunday. No one had guessed the severity of her problem, and they were as shocked as I'd been. After a rather brief visit to the hospital and drawing our own conclusions, we regrouped at our family home on St. Edmonds Road. That meeting, and its conclusions, although memorable from my standpoint, should have come as no surprise.

My brother, Richard, the stock broker, launched that discussion. "First of all, I'm open to any suggestions as to how we can proceed. Obviously, this has gotten much more than poor Lucille can handle. We need to diversify our plans. We must consider nursing care, or at least a regular companion to see to both their needs; someone to clean and prepare meals, at least. We need to find out what her doctors advise."

Sheila interrupted, "I've spoken to her doctor. As a nurse, qualified in this type of situation, determining a diagnosis is not easy. She's nearly seventy-three, after all, so few tests can be performed. It's dementia, of some sort. Whether it's Alzheimer's, there's no real way of being sure. That, of course, is complicated by the fact she

might have had a small stroke which could have caused her fall. And then, of course, if she hit her head, that would add to her confusion—"

George, the lawyer, spoke up, running his fingers through his hair, "What difference does it make what we call it? The bottom line is, we need to come up with a plan for her care and the legalities of this estate. Is there enough money to afford private nursing? What about power of attorney? Do we need to consider residential care? What about this house? Well, someone needs to answer these questions, and I need to catch a train to Connecticut. Flo, what can you do?"

"George, you know I'm teaching in Annapolis, and our kids are active in sports. There's nothing I can do. Margie, how about you? "

"You know I can't take time away from our children, and I'm working part-time. Jimmy's going to night school at Wharton, finishing his MBA. There's nothing we can do either. I mean, I'm certainly willing to do what I can, but, I just don't know how much time I can commit. Philadelphia is two hours away—an hour by train. I can't be here at the drop of a hat, you know."

Heads turned and eyes riveted on me.

"Glory, you're single and Tad's in college. It seems only natural you come back—at least for a little while—and tend to Mother's needs."

I looked up suddenly at the mention of my name.

"Have you forgotten? I live twelve hours away. I have a job as a social worker, a house to maintain, and no one with whom to share responsibilities. Is there nothin anyone else is willing to do?" Even as I said it, I knew the die had been cast.

Five sets of eyes darted around nervously.

Flo interjected, "Well, I really must get back. Glory, give me a call if you need to talk. Bye, everyone, great to see you. We mustn't let so much time slip between us. Kiss, Kiss."

Sheila stood abruptly and followed Flo, not even taking a quick glance back.

Richard and Margie stood, almost in tandem, "Glory, you're a doll. You always were the capable one. Let us know what you decide— got to run."

George called, "I'm out the door. Glory; call me, when you have a plan. I'll be sure to look it over."

I sat for twenty minutes after the door slammed, and voices could no longer be heard. What had just happened? I hadn't been able to get a word in edgewise. This was a family conference? As a social worker, wasn't it my job to moderate such a meeting and take a problem to resolution—a fair and just resolution?

My family had done it again. We all knew each sibling's weaknesses. The babies scampered when work or trouble came—just like when we were children. I was the responsible one—the one who picked up details, rescued younger ones, and ultimately, faced the final music, as it were. Again, I had capitulated.

The first week of my return, I decided if I were to function and have time to make calls, set up schedules, and take care of details surrounding Mother's care, our house, and all the other houses, rental and my own, and search for care arrangements, I could not stay at

St. Edmonds with Mother and Lucille. I needed to be away from that house. I remembered one rental house in Hampden was vacant, and had been for years. I could stay there... temporarily.

I had my choice of any number of furnishings lodged in basement and attic of our huge family house, under tarps and otherwise. Plenty from which to choose, dating back nearly seventy-five years, not only from our immediate family, but grandparents, aunts and uncles, you name it. A creative endeavor, I concluded, trying to choose a positive slant.

At first, I thought this long-vacant rental just needed a good cleaning and airing. I hadn't seen this actual building, however. After only a cursory inspection, I realized it needed more than I could've ever imagined—more cleaning, more renovation, more work, more money, more time, and surely, more patience.

Now, as I gaze at this hodge-podge, I close my eyes. Too much, the mish-mash of patterns and fabrics bombard my visual field and remind me, continuously, of my life's mayhem. Musty odors have left me with itchy eyes, a chronic headache and debilitating fatigue.

The issues seem massive. Even now, as I recall that afternoon, I feel as overwhelmed as I did then. How could I possibly take it on, all by myself? Plus, PLUS, how was I going to make necessary changes Mother neither wanted nor, at present, understood? What about my home, and my life in North Carolina?

Well, if I had to coordinate it all, then I'd do it, help or no help. I recalled that childhood tale of <u>Little Red Hen</u>, who asked her friends to assist in making bread.

They were too busy. I surrender. I am the Hen. After running in circles for three months on waning adrenaline, I'm too tired to make bread—or anything else, for that matter. Few answers and little help would likely remain unchanged.

I'd longed to be away from the hectic pace of this city, away from memories—good and not so good—away from control of expectations which could never be realized. I longed for the anonymity of another place, with no traffic, and no crime. I long for home, my friends, and Bill. Well, I'm back, but, surely, it can't be any longer than October, *can it*?

I'm jarred from my mental rehash by my ringing phone. I've been pacing, circuitously about this diminutive kitchen, for how long? The caller ID reads North Carolina. I grab the receiver.

"Bill? Is it you? How's our little neighborhood?"

I sounded like Mr. Rogers. *Why had I said that?* A long-ago memorized theme-song from that children's TV show began its play from memory. ". . . Please won't you be my neighbor."

"Glory, is that all you can say to me, 'How's our neighborhood?' How about this person on the other end of your phone? I miss seeing your house lights. Yes, I've forwarded your mail, pulled weeds around your garden, and replaced a burned-out porch light, so it looks like someone's home. I wish."

"Bill, you know I appreciate all you do. You're the best friend anyone could ever want. Thanks so much."

"I'm still just called friend?"

He thought they'd progressed beyond this friend point. Just when he hoped their relationship was proceeding toward commitment, some stressful circumstance would present itself. Bingo—back to just friends, again.

"What's better than a best friend, anyway?'

"Well, I could think of a lot of things, but, you keep coming back to friend. I miss you"

"I miss you, too, but I won't be here much longer, I hope. I thought I'd be home by now, surely. You can't imagine how overwhelmed I am."

"How's your house?"

"Well, Purrfect's taking care of mice. That's the only thing she seems to like about this place. The air conditioner rattle filters street noises pretty well and helps us sleep. I don't know what we'll do when temperatures drop. We still have a couple of weeks before that becomes an issue."

If only he could see this place. Something like a scene from a Charles Dickens tale—complete with dangling shutters and litter-strewn walk-ways comes to mind; the only thing missing is half-starved dogs milling around. Most days, I half expected to hear shouts of "Bastille" chorused from our street. Perhaps there were, but I was unable to hear these chants above roars of traffic.

I close my eyes and shake my head. Dismay.

"Not your dream house, huh? Thinking about coming down some weekend to check on your house, your clients, and your friend?"

How I wish.

"As I said, I can't imagine I'll be here much longer. I should have someone hired in the next couple of weeks. I've put ads in <u>Towson Times</u> and <u>Baltimore Sun</u> for nursing assistants. Certainly, I should find someone soon."

No time would be soon enough, as far as I'm concerned. I tried to remember when I'd last felt this way; perhaps my final week of pregnancy, already overdue by two weeks.

My voice cracks and I feel tears brim my lids. "I so wish I could be back at home, talking with you face to face. It's not much fun here, without you."

"I know, Sweetheart. I wish it could be face to face, too. No, more like cheek to cheek, but we won't go there. You know, it's been three months."

"Yes, and it isn't over yet. I guess I need to contact our health department about holding my position. I hate to beg for another extension."

Bill laughs. "I'll take care of that, too. Call it a job perk, if you wish."

Bill is really the dearest man in the whole world. Why couldn't I think about more? I just can't bring anyone else along on this roller coaster ride. If only he knew how chaotic my life was, he'd run in the opposite direction. He didn't know I was protecting him. Friends it was and friends it would remain. I really did miss him, though—lots.

Enough.

"Bill, I've got to run. I'll call you this weekend, OK?"

"Do I have to wait that long? It's lonesome here without you."

"For heaven's sake, it's only the day after tomorrow. Saturday night, around 9:00?"

He didn't know how lonely I felt. I couldn't think about that now.

"OK. You know I care about you, Glory."

"Thank you, Bill; I care about you, too. Take care, Bye."

I sigh deeply, choking back a sob. I missed my home, my friends, and yes, Bill. Well, that's an incentive to get moving on details.

I feel exhausted and achy. I hope I'm not coming down with something—probably dust and mold allergy. Maybe flu—maybe even pandemic flu.

Chapter 2

Back in Baltimore, Un-convent-ionally

So far this Friday morning, I'd called Lucille to check on things. I'd called the hospital to check on Mother. Status quo: same. Little has changed since I'd last called, but calling helped me feel I was being attentive and relieved some vague guilt at not physically being at either place. It also served as a huge reminder of things left undone, with more looming on my horizon.

My stomach feels tight or something. Maybe it's an ulcer. . . or worse. Maybe that mysterious digestive disorder I'd heard about on public radio. I rubbed my middle soothingly. Maybe I needed lunch—chocolate sounded better.

To break out of my doldrums, I decide to walk eight or so blocks north to the grocery. It was a place of community, sort of.

This city is one of those places where you could be among lots of people but still be alone, somehow. After eight years away, I just didn't fit in, anymore.

You and your problems were an entity all your own, like a coat you wore. You'd pass others in their coats. No one ever offers to help you with your coat, and you never help others with theirs. You just walk around and belt your coat tightly. You might bump into others, maybe, but nothing more—like balls on a billiard table. Sometimes this separateness felt comfortable. Certainly, it was familiar.

The goal was to wander through crowded, city life and avoid entering another's space. Reactions could be unpredictable and harsh, most times.

Inside the grocery, I wander to its seafood case, absent-mindedly tossing items from streamlined isles into my basket. I've got that cart with the bent, front wheel again. I groan and sigh, using all my strength to advance the thing in a forward, albeit zigzag movement.

A posted sign announces *Crab cakes—Sale today only.*

"Crab cakes? I don't think so." I muse.

I gaze toward a wall menu, and consider what I do want. I automatically join the queue of a growing crowd, observing necks stretched, eyes squinting, mouths gaping, but lining in an orderly and customary fashion. A digital machine clicks a set number of seconds.

Miriam's situated behind the case. I don't know her personally, if you're wondering. Her name's embroidered on her shirt. She plants herself like a catcher ready for a pitch. This formidable woman dons vinyl gloves and

thrusts her hands into an evaporation-streaked container of crushed ice. Her fingers scoop scallops, kind of like the metal thing at an amusement park. You know, the pincher-thing that drops into a glass case of stuffed animals, grasps an ear and jerks it to the top. My eyes widen as her hand mechanically flings them into a waiting plastic container.

Confirming an order with a gentleman in a seersucker shirt, she yanks off her vinyl glove and deftly pushes numbers on her scale. With hammering noises, a printed label slides from the machine like a paper tongue. She rips it with exaggerated fanfare, and slaps it onto his plastic container, bellowing "137". With a flourish, she drags the back of her hand across her perspiring brow, looks at her colleague, rolls her eyes, and yells, "Next." Again, she resumes her catcher's stance.

(I can't believe I'm even commenting to you about this. I must truly be in need of diversion.)

Number 138 flashes on a lighted panel. All heads jerk toward this panel and quickly down at their black and white tickets. Although I know it's not my number, I automatically study mine once more, each time a new number flashes. Bobbing heads in my peripheral vision confirm others are doing the same.

Suddenly, a harried woman forces her way through our crowd, now at least three deep, four in some places. All heads sharply turn toward her.

"Any salmon?" she shouts, assuming Miriam is deaf.

Undaunted, Miriam answers curtly, "Take a number, Hon, and go to the end of the line. Next," she barks.

A balding, self-appointed spokesman for this group, glares at this woman. "Can you believe her?" He surveys his fellow crowd members and shakes his head, deliberately. "We have a schedule 'ere. Some of us have t' get back t' work," he snarls, with a strong, east Bal'merese accent. Commiserating mumbling of ascent can be heard amongst this disgruntled crowd.

I eye a shelf directly in front of this seafood case. There must be twenty or more different types and sizes of rolls and biscuits. I hastily decide to count while waiting my turn. I dare not look at others in this crowd. I don't want to upset anyone.

I'd learned that lesson on my journeys around the inner and outer loops of 1695 beltway. Neither loop was a place where you looked at people; no, indeed. People tend to be edgy when they're stressed and hungry. The goal was to be oblivious. Try to blend in. Be a non-person in a coat. I'd read ingredients on packages, if need be.

"145." Miriam's roar, ever-increasing in resonance, causes me to jump. I'd forgotten my number, again, after I'd begun counting breads.

I un-crumple my tag, trying to do it quickly, not wanting to disrupt progress and upset this crowd. They seemed so uptight.

I'd read about mob reactions. My mind jumped to a scene from an ancient, black and white movie about Marie Antoinette, with a hungry mob yelling, "Guillotine, guillotine." My fingers tremble.

As edges of my stamped number reveal themselves, I squeal, "Yes, it's mine. I have 145." I called out like it was a winning Bingo number.

Blushing with sudden acknowledgement of my exaggerated enthusiasm, I wonder, again, about my sanity.

After receiving my plastic container of chicken salad, now fastened and labeled, I inch my basket, forcing its front, skewed wheel backward against the flow of this crowd, and head toward check-out counters and finally the exit.

With the close of an automatic door behind me, I'm greeted by honking horns, screeching brakes, and shifting gears from city buses belching smoky exhaust. Shrieking children dismissed from surrounding schools call to waiting mothers.

Coughing, I lower my head, heave my bags, and try to assume a comfortable position to walk the distance.

North Carolina: no traffic, no smoke. Don't even think about it, I warn myself.

Keep walking.

My bags are slipping and their plastic straps are making deep creases on my hands and wrists. Only a few more blocks, I mumble. My wrists are starting to smart.

"Hey lady, watch where yer goin'. Ya' wan' t' get run over 'er somethin'?"

"Sorry," I reply to a now-passed cab. My words cling only to dust and debris his back tires blew at me as he careened by, racing to who knows where, unhearing.

I must remember to move faster. Not a time for an afternoon stroll, packages or not, to be sure. Life seemed so fast-paced and uncaring in Baltimore—even at that store. Although I'd been raised here, I'd somehow forgotten. I seemed out of rhythm, or something: out of touch, out of sync.

I recalled a conversation with Mr. Wilson: "Can't sleep at night, these days, 'specially if you watch th' 11:00 news. Things aren't th' same as th' ole days, that's fer sure. Most 'a th' boys at Beth'lem Steel think it all started t' go bad when our Colts left town, or maybe even when Johnny Unitas retar-ed. Things jes kinda' went down-hill after that." He nodded his head knowingly. "Yeah, thin's are diff'rent in Bal'mer."

I'd nodded, respectfully, with his insight.

Panting as if I'd just run a marathon, I rearrange my packages. Just a few more steps, I encourage myself. I can do it. Wiping an errant hair from across my eyes and mouth, I shift my head, and notice Mr. Wilson across the street.

He returns my "hi" enthusiastically.

Thank goodness for Mr. Wilson. Since I'm not the least bit talented with handy-woman things, he's offered his fix-it services whenever I'm in need—almost daily. I've avoided calling him, as I don't want to impose. After all, an emergency might present in my future. I didn't want to wear out my welcome with incidentals.

I shift my bags to push an old wrought-iron gate. I stumble toward my house, my marathon goal. It truly is in dire need of repair, but considering mine is a most

temporary stay, I could only do so much. I'd try to ready it for another tenant with some light cleaning and small repairs. This property, as well as the others, is probably my responsibility now, but that was all I could do. It was all I had energy to consider.

This old house, Mr. Wilson said, had marked a strong and long-term friendship between his family and my father. Harry had helped Dad with upkeep and general managing of all his properties. Although Harry Wilson had been employed at Bethlehem Steel since the 60's (after Hampden-area mills closed), he and his sons put in long hours to help my father for a little extra cash to bridge rough times.

"Your father was one a' th' mos' depen'ble and honest people, I knew," he acknowledged. "If somethin' weren't right 'round here, he'd do all he could t' make it right. People knew he was a man 'a his word. People don't know much about a man's word no more. It's a daggon shame. An' many 'a th' folks from further down th' ole neighborhood would know, if times were tight, your dad would help' em out a lil': a dollar or two t' hold'em over 'til their next pay checks. Yep, your dad was a good 'un. Since you was a lil' girl, Doris and I always say yer jes like 'im when it comes t' helpin' folk. We always say that. We felt we lost fam'ly, wen th' Lord took 'im," he said, shaking his head, having removed his Orioles cap to show respect.

Since Dad's death, nothing had been done with any of his rental properties. Some had been sold over past years. Others just remained with renters—no

rent increase, but no improvements either. Their care and upkeep was a job, in itself, and Mother was in no condition to do it. She'd never been involved in any of it. In honor of Dad's memory, most renters just cared for things themselves. Mother left the care of our huge family house to Lucille as she'd always done. That was another responsibility I hadn't even begun to consider.

Hurrying toward my door, I fumble with its rusted skeleton key, which continues spinning in its old cylinder, increasing my growing frustration. I must get this door open, fast. This lock would be one of the first things I'd fix. I made a mental note.

I scolded myself for not using the grocery store's restroom before leaving.

I hear my phone ringing as I continue to fumble with this lock, while dancing now. My answering machine would have to pick up. I must heed Nature's call.

I manage to lug my bags onto a counter, and race to my hall bathroom. With a quick flush, I skid to the kitchen in hopes of reaching my phone before its final ring.

Nope. Not this time. Sorry. Lunch first. Messages could wait.

I spoon a huge bite of chicken salad with my plastic fork. "Yes-s, I'm so hungry," I sing. I dance a few steps around my kitchen, while chewing, and bounce onto a slip-covered chair to sort mail. Dust escapes in a cloud as I settle onto its cushion. I sneeze three times, and rub my nose and watering eyes.

Spooning more chicken salad into my mouth, I unfold the morning news. I don't know why I even want to read it. At home, that weekly news, arriving Thursday with mail, contained such simple but happy events as 50th anniversary celebrations, and local bake sales. Although stunned with its simplicity when I first arrived, I now longed to be transported back to its old-fashioned ways.

In abrupt contrast, I skim the front page of the <u>Sun</u>, through election debates and Middle-East tensions, murders and robberies.

A headline catches my eye: "Local church minister pleads no contest in homosexual affair with male prostitute." A picture of a well-dressed, strikingly handsome man, extending his hands in front to fend off press, was emblazoned across the lower quarter of this front page.

I have to read this.

Apparently this pastor of 4th Evangelical Church in Baltimore County had frequented Baltimore Street's infamous XXX- rated *The Block*. (The most openly indecent street in this city. . . in any city, I'd think.) His liaison was angry about a bad check written at his place of business. He decided to report his loss to media.

"He treated me unfairly," the man said. (Actual words were inappropriate for print.)

The pastor replied, "No comment," to press. Last night, however, he'd confessed openly to his shocked fifteen hundred-member congregation near Towson, and presented a letter of resignation to its board. His community is stunned, as he had been active in its Boy Scout organization, and was described as a kind and compassionate neighbor by those who knew him. He has a wife and young son. His family could not be reached for comment, according to this paper.

What could this man have been thinking? Didn't he realize a time would come when it would all catch up with him? What about his poor wife and son? What would this do to them? That poor woman would be left to pick up broken pieces, all by herself, no doubt, and take care of her son, alone. Kind and compassionate? Well, not to his wife and son.

I forced my tea from a bent straw in my carry-out cup, spooned remaining chicken salad into my waiting mouth, and let the remaining paper fall to the floor. I scanned coupon advertisements that had dropped into my lap, before tossing the lot. Domino Pizza, Food Center Grocery, Auto Mart. Nothing of interest.

Gathering my trash, I slip on flip-flops before re-entering the kitchen. I'd learned with a waning rodent population, I must know where my feet were sliding. Flip-flops were open, so I could see where and on what my toes rested.

Back to business; time to check messages. I slurp the last of my tea, crunch a Frito, and push play.

"Four new messages," a voice pronounced, reminiscent of an older Nun in elementary school; who by her very tone, commanded her small audience to answer, "Yes, Ma'am," and sit at attention.

Where did they GET these recordings anyway? I wiggled my nose in a grimace, and prepared to hear from my callers:

First message: "Hey Mom, it's me. Chapel Hill's great. I made first cut for Carolina's Lacrosse team—is that not cool? Classes are tough, though. I decided to pledge a fraternity, but I need money. I know. I'm trying to make it stretch. Love you and Purrfect." BEEP.

A smile crept over my face. "I love you, too, Honey," I spoke to air.

Second message: "Ms. Harris, Sylvia from the salon. A final reminder of your 10:00 appointment, and be prompt. Remember, I'm fitting you in." Click. BEEP.

Third message: "Just a friend missing a friend. Call me tonight. I miss you. In case you don't remember, this is your friend, Bill." BEEP.

My smile widened, "Miss you, too."

Fourth new message: "Glory, how are you, girl? Sorry I haven't had a moment until now to welcome you back. Things are wild here at our college. You remember, summers and early fall are our busiest. Listen, if you don't have plans, let's grab lunch tomorrow to catch up. Besides, I have something important to share with you. Call me around 7:00 tonight. 555-2559. BEEP.

"No new messages. Five saved messages."

I'd saved messages containing phone numbers for mother's doctor's office, the beauty salon, Mr. Wilson, the grocery's order department, and Tad's ever-changing residence numbers. It was easier to punch save than write them down. I shake my head in disbelief at my laziness. Oh, well.

I glance at my reflection in my blurred hall mirror as I pass. Obviously its cloudiness is from gilt, scraped off the back of its glass . . . NOT my eyes.

Even without my glasses, though, I look awful.

It's no wonder. I've been living off Nabs and soda from hospital vending machines, and mostly junk, here. It's sickening to think about cooking in this grimy kitchen. I'm amazed paint can still peel, amidst so many layers of grease. That certainly did not help my fatigue or negative attitude of late, I'm sure. *Goodness. Could there be lead chips falling in my food—a slow poison, do you think?*

Maybe I needed to visit a health food store. Maybe just being around better food might motivate me to get healthy. *Café Hon* and the grocery store I'd just visited failed to inspire me to cook, beyond what they could prepare for me. Yes, maybe a trip to a health food store.

Someone told me of an unusual one in Mount Washington, full of all kinds of delicacies virtually unknown by most of the common horde, including me—just the other day. I needed healthful food. Maybe I needed a more healthful lifestyle, in general.

I was facing the unthinkable 48 in October. My reading glasses revealed new worry lines.

Oh, to heck with glasses. *What are they good for anyway—certainly not for acquiring information from that newspaper.*

But while they were on my face, I peer at my naturally, reddish-blond hair, which I'd lately only pulled back with a clip. I lift a few strands of the dulled stuff. My blond is not blond, at all, but, gasp, is that gray? Certainly not! Bite your tongue. I squint to steady my focus. It's platinum. *Keep telling yourself that, Glory: it's platinum.*

If I couldn't do anything to change my life, right now, I could do something to take care of me—obvi-

ously long overdue from what I'd just seen in my mirror, distorted as it was. Thank goodness it was cloudy. I had enough reality from what I'd just seen.

My sisters certainly took time for themselves—weekly manicures and pedicures, spas and body wraps—whatever was new and fashionable. I giggled recalling a quote by Ambrose Bierce, defining fashion as "a despot whom the wise ridicule and obey."

It was time to update me. I'd make a plan.

Bill told me I didn't need anything at all—I was beautiful. I grinned recalling it.

However, he used those words—when? Last year or was it the year before? Well, no need to go completely au naturel; and at this point, I needed help for even au naturel. A little—just a little something might make me feel better. Yes, I'd have something more than my usual dry trim at that salon tomorrow.

Yes, that's what I need: purpose, a plan—something positive to distract me from homesick musings. I glance at my watch. Yes, I still have time to visit that health food store. I'm excited—a path to better days.

I look at Purrfect, meowing again for more gourmet cat food I'd bought her as a treat when we moved. That was a mistake. Now she refuses anything else—except mice, of course. Whenever you set a precedent. . . wasn't that what my lawyer/ex-husband used to say? No need to go there.

Perhaps Purrfect might need some grooming, too. She's beginning to have a bedraggled look of an alley cat. I must do something about her alley associates. Bad company corrupts good morals and my cat would

be . . . would be what? Different? Better? I'd call a groomer for her, too. Could a cat be a reflection of her mistress? I'd read some psychological journal articles about pets and their owners. . . . enough, already.

I pull my hair up with my tortoise-shell clip. Its color was fading and chipping off, as the hair it held. I dab on a little foundation, blush and touch of coral lipstick (an item someone years ago said blended nicely with my spring color palette). I grab my brown leather bag, and throw open my car door.

Onward to Mount Washington.

Creeping through traffic, I turn left onto Northern Parkway. The sun sits flat at the bottom of the western sky, reminding me of a sunny side-up egg I had for breakfast at *Café Hon*. Days were getting shorter.

Although afternoon, it resembled dusk. Street lights flickered on. Temperatures were dropping. It'd be cool enough for heavy sweaters, soon. Maybe I could convince Bill to meet me next weekend, for a picnic in western Maryland. I'd mention it tonight.

I turn onto Falls Road, left onto Kelly Avenue Bridge. I'm taken aback by its quaintness. The old military academy had long closed its doors to little cadets due to lack of funds and decreasing student enrollment from anti-war bias of the late 60's and 70's, I'd heard. The parish church was still alive and well, however, and stood proudly on its hill as a last bastion to tradition, juxtaposing artsy-craftsy stores that comprise a new Mt. Washington. A couple of times around narrow streets and I spot a parking place.

The health food store nestled cozily between a rare book store and a New Age crystal emporium. Rather curious.

With the tinkling of a small bell dangling above its door, I'd entered another world. Incense and chili bombarded my sinuses. Barrels held dried figs and dates, imported from the Middle East. Plexiglas containers brimmed with cumin, saffron, and other spices, probably from the Far East.

Kosher foods lined one wall, with a prominent display for Rosh Hashanah. Oddly, across the aisle were items suitable for non-fasting times of Ramadan. Jars were labeled in languages I could only guess as Slavic, Russian or Arabic. Garnished hummus lay artistically displayed in a refrigerated case surrounded by hard-boiled eggs, Gefilte fish, blintzes, egg salad, tuna, and cheese–lots of cheese. No ham.

I'd almost forgotten the wonderful variety of food in Baltimore—a reflection of the ethnic diversity which makes Baltimore, Baltimore.

A welcoming voice, (friendlier than most I'd heard, lately) comes from the vicinity of a cash register.

"Can I help you?" a woman called and smiled. Her long, auburn braid swung as she moved.

"About one of everything, I think," I reply, giggling, "I'm starving."

This young woman laughs easily, but her amber eyes reveal sadness.

"I could make you a sandwich—roast beef, maybe? Or are you vegan?" She glances at me for a sign.

Her accent was not native Baltimorean; Boston, most assuredly.

"No," I shake my head, "roast beef will be fine."

I waddle to my car, with arms loaded with all manner of goodies, plus their recommended cookbook, <u>Baltimore's Natural Kitchen</u>; a Pikesville Hadassah group's community fund-raising project.

It's nearly 5:00. My trip home would not be short, as stacked cars indicated—heavy traffic. WBAL lists accidents along I695 and Jones Falls Expressway. Helicopter blades whirred in the background.

Were these sound effects recorded and played in a radio studio or were brave souls cruising above me in the real thing? Obviously someone had to relay information. Stopped at an interminable light at Falls Road, I peered through my windshield to see if I could spot a copter. If there were any, they were noticeably absent from this location. No whirring noises, just angry drivers cursing other cars who dared to break into line—not an action one wanted to attempt without considering dire consequences involving life and limb.

Ah, Baltimore at rush hour.

Saturday

"Y-e-s," I beam, sitting up in bed.

I'm getting my hair done, and going out for lunch. What fun. I might even go shopping at the mall where <u>Saks</u> recently opened. I had to remember to visit the grocery, too—on my way back— for a few staples; a must.

I refuse to let myself dwell on any problems. Not today.

I'd be seeing Jules again. It's been ages. She's been my closest friend since Cathedral School. Our friendship continued to grow while we attended a boarding school specifically designed for young women aspiring to be Nuns. Our paths briefly separated when Jules left after two years and graduated from Institute of Notre Dame (*or was it Notre Dame Prep*—I could never remember) leaving me alone to prepare to be a novitiate after graduation.

After only one post-high school year, though, it was decided that particular life of service would not be an option for me. Just thinking about that time brings shame—even now. My cheeks burned.

I remember my private meeting with Mother Superior. After some pointed questions (Mother Superior always had a way of helping someone come to grips with a problem,) she'd concluded a Nun's life was not for me. Had I thought about college, perhaps being a wife and a mother? After all, I was only nineteen.

She'd gently dropped into conversation, although she loved me as a daughter, she was not convinced it was God's will I join the group taking their final vows. Tactfully, she said she'd had a dream. (*Boy, I could relate to dreams, for sure.*)

"You are to do other things—take another direction for your life of service. One I'm sure will bring you much joy, as well as sorrow, as the mother of our Lord, Mary, also had to take. It will be with you as the Holy

Scripture says, ". . . a sword will pierce your very soul." Mother crossed herself, ending her comments.

What an odd thing to tell a 19-year-old girl. *Was that supposed to encourage me?* I felt embarrassed and vastly disappointed. *Wasn't I good enough to be a Nun like the rest of my classmates?*

Mother Superior simply nodded and responded, lovingly, "It isn't what you're not, it is who you are. You have certain gifts. You are to return to a life of service outside these walls. My child, you will learn more lessons through joy and through sorrow, no doubt touching more lives than you could ever do here."

What shame. What would people think? Would they view me as a failure? How would I face my family's disappointment at not being ALLOWED to finish something I'd thought was my life's plan? It's not like I changed my mind. Oh, the humiliation of it.

In an Irish-Catholic home, it was considered a special honor for a son or a daughter to enter a life of service within the church. I'd always wanted to please God and please my family. After all, I was the first-born daughter: the responsible one, the compassionate one, the sensitive one.

I'd always pictured myself as the nun Audrey Hepburn played in <u>The Nun's Story</u>. I'd seen that movie at least three times as a little girl. . . or maybe Sophia Loren in another movie about a Nun—I don't remember its name. . . Yes, certainly Sophia Loren.

That was spring of 1965—so many years ago. I'd returned to a Catholic women's college close to home and reestablished my friendship with Julia over the next

four years. By college end, I'd been her maid-of-honor, and she, mine. We married two Loyola College grads who were law students at University of Baltimore. Julia and I completed graduate degrees while our husbands buried themselves in their studies.

Tragedy struck when Jules's husband died in an automobile accident, only days after their bar exam. Not long after, I found myself expecting my first son, who died at the tender age of one week. We were again bound, this time by grief.

As time passed, I was thrilled to become Tad's mother. Although Jules was his Godmother, our friendship drifted for a time. Her disappointment for not having been the mother she'd longed to be, and the obvious fact I had a husband, when hers had been taken. It was painful.

When Tad was nearly four, Charles announced he was leaving me for someone else. He'd see we were provided for, and left me our house. (How could I pay its mortgage without a job?) I sold my house out of necessity, with its proceeds paying my attorney. I had little to live on, in that final arrangement. (*What did I expect, confronting two lawyers?*)

Jules, who remained unmarried, continued at the college as an administrator. She offered me a job, albeit part-time, as a counselor for new students. Tad and I moved into a small carriage-house apartment on its grounds. Although barely two rooms, a kitchen and bath, it was a lifeline. I'll never forget Jules's kindness during those dark and tremulous times. I'd missed her.

I glance at my watch. I can't be late for this hair appointment. I'd been warned by Sylvia and again by Pierre.

Who's my stylist? I had no idea.

Chapter 3

New (s) To Me

Glory

Goodness, I didn't think to ask about my stylist. Now considering possibilities, it was a rather important bit of information, wasn't it? Perhaps I should've gotten a referral.

Too late, now.

In North Carolina, I trusted a woman who trimmed and brightened my locks in her basement studio, to be close to her baby. She answered her phone, shampooed, performed waxes and manicures—ran the whole show. It was a homey sort of place, where one could smell bacon and eggs from breakfast or fried chicken and collards from last night's dinner.

I could see this salon would not offer quite the same experience; no indeed.

Pierre assists with hanging my coat, and offers me a cup of Chai tea. He escorts me to an upholstered chair. Soft music, certainly not Dolly Parton, is piped through rooms: Mozart. I sip my tea and enjoy this ambience. I cuddle against soft cushions.

Ummm. I could get used to this.

9:55. I relaxed my breathing, relieved I'd arrived early. I sense if I'd arrived one minute late, demerits would've been dispensed or something. I do not want to upset any stylist. My hair's future depended on scissors in his or her hands.

Several women settled in surrounding chairs. None of whom looked particularly eager to converse. Someone exits a hallway door in a terry robe, asking which way to the sauna. Another woman hobbles down the hall, cotton balls between each of her freshly polished toes. I witness some poor soul in only a towel and turban stumble from a massage room, looking disoriented; not knowing where to find her clothes, no doubt.

I momentarily wonder what my appointment will bring. *Had I remembered to bring my charge card, recalling the advertisement, "Don't leave home without it."* I grinned.

Since ten minutes had passed, and I had not been summoned, I decided to read one of many magazines, displayed on a coffee table. The choices were New Yorker, Architectural Digest, Town and Country, and Baltimore Magazine. Maybe I'd catch up on what's happening in my old home town—who's who and all that.

I casually open the most recent volume of Baltimore Magazine, dated spring of this past year. I page slowly past ads for an exclusive jewelry store, department stores, designer clothes, and Rolex watches.

I regard an article about a charity function held at Meyerhoff symphony hall to raise funds for a new wing at Kennedy Institute. I study each displayed picture of smiling couples scattered over two pages, noting by-lines to see if I recognized any of these people.

Oh, look. There's Ginny. She hasn't aged a day. There's Lil. She's lost a lot of weight since I last saw her. Oh, Sue looks striking in that gown. In these photos, everyone appeared to be having the time of their lives (I'd attended my share of these events—dry as dust, from my experience.) Who were they kidding?

Maybe I should call Lil. She and Sue might like to do lunch.

Scratch that, I reminded myself, mid-thought. I remembered the last time I'd joined them: not good. When a girl-friend transitions from Mrs. to Ms, things change. Women often feel threatened with a *divorcee* coming into a *wives-only* group; disappointing, but true.

Back to my magazine.

My eyes rest on a picture of a couple, toasting their champagne flutes. I didn't recognize either of them. The blond woman was tiny in comparison to her athletic-looking husband. He was a prominent periodontist in north Baltimore County. She was secretary of Junior League, one of several sponsors of this event (type beneath their photo read). Although certainly an attractive couple, something was unsettling about their expressions. Even while smiling, her eyes looked like those of a frightened animal. (I'm reminded of Purrfect, when she's alarmed from street noise.) His demeanor looked dark. . . his eyes or expression. . .something.

I scold myself and giggle. This is silly. I don't even know these people. I'm simply passing time until I'm called back to the inner sanctum of this salon. I glance again at this photo, and shiver. *What am I sensing?*

Sylvia calls with her clipped combination of Baltimore and New York accents. I gently set the magazine in its place, and make myself forget those troubling faces. *Don't I have enough to be concerned about? Do I need to make up problems for people I don't even know—people in a magazine, no less?*

Two hours later, after having been colored, rinsed, dried, glossed, trimmed and sprayed, spun from side to side, whisked from room to room (posing for before and after photos), and made-over with samples from a new Scandinavian line of natural cosmetics, I dizzily wander from this salon. *Did I really spend over $200 plus tips today on just my hair?*

I do look a lot better, though, I must admit.

As I mentioned earlier, I'd done little for my appearance since my return, other than twist my shoulder-length hair in a clip, dab on foundation and a little coral lipstick. I now proudly sport mascara, liner, taupe shadow, pencil, blush, lip gloss; instead of my coral lipstick, a soft rose, which the make-up artist said brought out my green eyes. (*Really? Who knew?*)

I felt good. I felt pretty. I've never considered myself pretty. Flo was the beauty—long legs, long lashes, long list of beaus, long arms which could reach into my closet and borrow my best and most favorite outfits, and my boyfriends. I laugh.

I feel new. Maybe I'll follow lunch with a shopping trip for a whole new outfit—with shoes.

Chapter 4

A Little Arm-Twisting

Stop, look and listen.
I nod to no one but myself, and prepare to step from my safe place at this corner curb onto the street. A green light is no consolation.

Cautiously maneuvering Roland Avenue, I move quickly, careful to dodge careening vehicles trying to beat the light. I'd learned my lesson about strolling in front of cab drivers. If you value your life in this city, you'd better move fast, or else.

Lunch at the new *Morgan* and *Millard* restaurant promised to be a treat. Everyone was talking about its transformation. All I could envision was that old drugstore landmark in Roland Park, built even before I was born. This new restaurant is bright and sunny; charming. I immediately become so consumed with studying vintage photos, I almost miss Jules, waving her arm.

"Glory? " Julia's cheerful call gently rights me to present. "Glory, you look wonderful. I feel like I'm meeting fashion-model Glory."

I feel like she's describing the newest Barbie: Beach Barbie, Tennis Barbie, Sports-Car Barbie. *Do they even make those dolls anymore?* I quickly conclude they'll probably never stop making Barbie for little girls.

Jules looks just the same, although a few no-color strands surround her warm, brown eyes. Those platinum strands had decorated my own temples, too, but at present were disguised beneath a soft henna permanent rinse, highlighted with strawberry blond. We giggle like 13-year-olds, and follow our maitre d' to a window table to bask in the warmth of sunshine.

I'm so hungry after my morning of exertion. (Being shuffled from chair to chair to washbowl could be called exercise of sorts, couldn't it?) I drool as I smell Old Bay seasoning from sizzling platters just delivered to the next table. September's an R month, so it's safe to order oyster stew; a small bowl—just enough to taste. Then I'll dig into a platter of crab cakes.

Our server looks so familiar. *Where have I seen this woman?* Long auburn braid, small freckled-nose...something recognizable about her sad eyes.

Hmmm. *Who knew?*

"All right, tell me everything. I want to know about your mother, Tad, and your new life in North Carolina—everything." Julia leans forward, expectantly, a cup of tea cradled between both hands, eager as any child for a gift of exciting news.

A brief, somewhat clipped recount of the past four months spills from my mouth, like so much ice tumbling from a pitcher into a glass.

Julia leans back with a huff.

"You sound like an announcer giving a fifteen-second news cap—no details, no voice inflection, devoid of emotion you know I crave."

That was the Jules I knew: loving details, as if each syllable were a chocolate truffle—delicate and brimming with flavor. She loved to savor each word. Of the two of us, I was more reserved. She often accused me of being secretive, depriving her of the joy and excitement of particulars.

A more devoted friend no one could ever hope to find, though. She'd come to my rescue more than once. She also had a way of drawing me out—forcing me to see truth about myself, I was likely to cover or avoid, altogether.

Jules continues "What's your mother's prognosis? What, if anything, are your brothers and sisters contributing?"

"Well, they're busy with their lives—children and jobs, you know. Mother has dementia, and with her broken wrist, and Lucille's arthritis. . . . Not a pretty picture, at present."

Julia interrupts, "So, Glory is taking care of everything, as usual?"

(There she goes again—getting right to the heart of a matter.)

"Well, not really."

"Really," she chides.

She's right. She knew our family dynamics. As I'd long recognized, as a social worker, I needed to set boundaries, be assertive with my feelings, open in my communication with my siblings. Somehow, it was a lot easier to suggest this to clients than put theory into practice in my own life.

I could not make them help. I could not change them. I was weary of even trying to alter these facts, or face them, either. It was simply easier to bite the bullet and do it myself. I'd make plans, and hire necessary help. I love my mother. It's a small sacrifice. After all, her years are numbered.

"I don't mean to be tough on you, Honey," Julia soothes, 'I just know you must be tired, with no one to share burdens. You may look like a beauty queen today—I do love your hair—but your dark circles are a dead giveaway you're exhausted."

I sigh, "Jules, I'm really not; just weary. There's a difference. Days are piled upon days of checking on Mother and Lucille, and living in that awful house. I can't tell you how much I've been looking forward to this lunch, getting my hair done, and going shopping—just for me. I'm even thinking about a weekend back in North Carolina—to get clothes, of course."

"Of course," A suddenly smiling Julia leans forward, "What about your man-friend?"

(There she goes again, truth time.)

I sigh before answering. *What is Bill anyway? Yes, he is more than a friend, but could I call him a lover? If not, what then?* I'd lived a single life for fifteen years. A life I could handle. At present, I'm sandwiched between my son, who's still dependant on me, at least financially; a senile mother, who's becoming more and more dependent on me; plus multiple houses and a cat. I couldn't consider another relationship. I say as much to Julia.

The oyster stew is served, with dime-sized oyster crackers. We eagerly eye oysters hiding beneath its bubbly surface.

Julia reaches across our table and grasps my hands. "Let's bless our food and our company." A replay of how we started meals at convent school. Beginning with our customary blessing, "Bless us, O Lord, for these thy gifts. . . ." We silently cross ourselves, in established Catholic tradition, shared from childhood.

We chase oysters around our bowl, like prized hockey pucks in a championship game; trying to capture them with our sticks, or in this case, spoons. Laughing, we settle back in our chairs. Jules tosses oyster crackers high in the air, only to catch them in her mouth. What a clown.

Waiting for our crab cakes, she leans forward and declares, "OK, time to tell. I want to know all about Bill. Do you have a picture?"

I shake my head. Then recalling I'd picked up pictures from a photo mart just a couple of days before, I rummage through my old brown bag. Voila. Fumbling to open my package, I sort through the stack, fan them like a hand of cards and choose one for Julia.

"O-o-h, pictures."

"First, here's Tad in his 1983 Honda Prelude, fire-engine red, with what we used to call, four-on-the-floor."

"I can't believe how much he's grown, Glory. He has your sparkling green eyes. That dark wavy hair—where did he get that? Look at that tan. He sure didn't get that from you." She's teased about my freckled forearms which looked like cocoa splattered on a scrubbed white cup.

I laugh. Being with Jules is just what I need. I've gotten too wrapped up in me lately.

I pass a photo of Bill and me, surrounded by wild flowers and Rhododendron buds. Julia studies its image.

"He's gorgeous. You left him alone in North Carolina?"

I shrug. "We're only friends, really"

Bewilderedly, she gasps, "I knew you were crazy, but are you blind, too?"

Thankfully, our server brings our platters. We agree to more Earl Grey, and dessert. When our server hesitated, I ask, "I feel like I've seen you before, but I can't place it."

She smiles. "I also work at the natural food store in Mt. Washington, where you shopped yesterday."

"Yes, of course," I say, "and I might add, I loved your store."

She shyly adds, "Thank you. I'm glad you enjoyed your purchases." She excuses herself.

Jules looks questioning again. "Glory, how much longer do you plan to be in Baltimore?"

I shake my head, and reply, "It may be longer than I originally anticipated or wanted. No prospects for Mother's nursing schedule, as yet. Plus, her doctor thinks it's prudent to research residential facilities, specializing in Alzheimer's. Most facilities have extensive waiting lists."

Another job to consider. The list keeps growing by the minute, it seems.

"I'm overwhelmed with what lies ahead. I may need to resign my position in North Carolina, which saddens me. I miss Bill, and I do care about him. He's a wonderful man, but he's aware of my constraints. . . not happy, but aware."

Jules nods. After a lengthy pause, she speaks, "Gloria, I must discuss something with you."

I note her serious expression. It alarms me that she used Gloria, as opposed to my nickname, Glory. I gulp. *What's coming?*

Jules pauses as our server places Crème Brule and peach cobbler before us. After refilling our tea, she quietly excuses herself.

Jules slowly picks up her dessert fork and cuts a small portion of cobbler, and then gently drops it. "Gloria," she begins again, "may I present something for your consideration?"

I smiled, recalling how Rod Sterling introduced vintage episodes of <u>Twilight</u> <u>Zone</u> on television with those same words, years ago. I stifled my urge to laugh.

"I realize your life's in a quandary now. Something has come up, though, and I must not let this lunch end without discussing it."

I hesitate, wanting to allay my fears, "Jules, are you all right? Your health?"

She nods, yes, "No, it's nothing like that. Our college has been authorized to sponsor a six-week, pilot program, focusing on displaced homemakers. Its anonymous donor wants our school as its main sponsor."

Puzzled, I ask, "What do you mean by displaced homemaker?"

I'd never heard that term. Not surprising. So many abbreviated names for things and politically-correct titles, one could never be current enough.

"Divorced or widowed women who are suddenly on their own after having been at-home wives and mothers for an extended time. Numbers are rising and statistics concerning problems relating to them are staggering in this north Baltimore area alone. Many care for children alone, without help from extended families. Some older women have no marketable skills, and have never worked outside their homes. Some don't even have a driver's license.

"Numbers show, in their first year following divorce, a man's income doubles; for women, many with children and expenses of homes, incomes drop by half or more. These women have no credit in their own names. They can't rent an apartment or apply for a car or school loan, as their credit record, if they ever had any as a single, is researched by their married names. Past copies of utility bills are required, even to rent an apartment. Many women and children become homeless.

"Those who are alone as a result of domestic violence have fled to shelters, but these facilities are underfunded and over-crowded. Most shelters depend upon private donations because of limited resources. Many women give up and are forced to return to situations they've left, because they can't make it. Tragedy often results, and even death."

"It's so sad," I answer, softly.

As she speaks, I recall my own divorce. A corner of my memory I do not relish revisiting. I'd gotten through that horrible time with God's help. Memories of pain of rejection, fear for my future, and a continuing struggle with anger were what I fought daily. The constant worry of not being able to pay bills or to even buy food haunted me. I often allowed myself one meal a day so I could provide for Tad's medical or clothing expenses. We shopped at thrift stores because my child support allocation was simply not enough, with Baltimore's cost of living exponentially increasing, almost daily. *Why is Jules telling me this?*

"This free seminar will direct these women to housing solutions, food, child care, jobs and job training, to assist their getting on their feet."

Julia hesitates, "Gloria, I'd like you to consider leading this group. This project calls for a licensed social worker as a moderator. Only six weeks."

She raises her hand as if to stop refuting reasons why I could not do this. "You have a compassionate gift without measure, Glory. More than that, you've been there. Our college is a Catholic institution. We have no one on staff who's been divorced or separated. We still have several Nuns, who have never been married. Their security is the church. They have no idea of difficulties involved in finding a place to live or wondering from where a meal will come. Most of them have never even conceived of the betrayal and fear you've shared with me over the years."

How I remember. Jules had pulled strings, secured a part-time counseling position and arranged a home for Tad and me on campus. After my first year, it was also Jules who'd been chosen by a new board to inform me about changed policy: I could not continue to be employed, even on a part-time basis. A board member had voted against my being in any position to mentor young women. Single motherhood and divorce were not things our college could condone.

A shock. Julia had been furious, but was powerless to change the board's decision. It was hard.

My family had distanced themselves. No one in our family had ever been divorced. It was considered my fault—somehow. I'd failed as a wife. They'd been shocked when I'd left the novitiate program. Divorce was yet another blow. Rather than try to understand, they separated themselves from me and Tad. I was too embarrassed to ask for help, but I don't think any of them would've helped me anyway, sadly.

Tad and I stayed with Jules until I could find other employment and an affordable place to live. We rented an efficiency in an old, inner-city building. Fairly safe, certainly reasonable, but not exactly what I'd been accustomed to or wanted for my son.

I was appreciative of anything, though. God protected us even in that awful place.

I wasn't completely comfortable or welcome as a divorcee in my church, either. I sought solace in a small Episcopal church. (After all, wasn't divorce what separated Anglicans from Catholicism in the first place; recalling Henry VIII and his unique solution for his displaced wives.) This small congregation offered me comfort and anonymity I needed so desperately to heal. A lot of pain, and I'm not sure I've completely recovered from it yet.

Counseling helped me discover that forgiveness is key to healing—forgiveness of those who'd hurt me, and then, forgiveness of myself. Forgiveness defined NOT as excusing hurtful behavior but giving up the offense's hold over me—both the hurt and the hurter.

Someone said to forgive is divine. I surely needed supernatural help to do it. I'd moved on, but was I ready to help others in their pain? I don't even want to think about it.

I racked my brain for any excuse Jules might buy. I did not want to be a leader of anything—especially a group of displaced homemakers. I answered with the first thing that came to mind.

"Jules, I don't know whether I'll be here that long."

"You just said it could take months to find a nursing facility, "she quickly countered.

I blushed and grimaced, only confirming what she'd just said.

She's got me. What made me think I could out-reason Jules? She's a master of persuasion. Besides, she knows my weak spots and how to bend my arm just enough to make me say yes.

"What could I possibly do to help these women?" I stammer. "I'm still trying to mend . . . myself."

"All it would involve is to moderate six sessions, one per week, and determine the most urgent needs of these women. Connect them to resources we now have. All you have to do is keep meeting-records, and give those women love and understanding that's your God-given gift. Promise me you'll at least pray about it?"

There she goes, bringing God into it. She's baited and hooked me. My options were eternal guilt with a refusal or to just say yes now and get it over with.

"Oh, Jules, I'd do anything for you, but my life is full of uncertainty. I'm more than a little fearful about re-addressing my own past. I'll promise to pray about it, if only because you asked. You've been my only friend during my darkest times. I'll get back to you by Monday, I promise."

Julia extends her hand across our table, and squeezes my closed fist. "Just promise you'll consider it," she whispers, barely audibly.

She ended her plea with just the right amount of gentle coaxing.

How did she learn to be so effective? Was there some kind of course available for this type of thing? If so, I desperately needed to enroll so I could at least try to take a defensive stance. Who am I kidding? I'd still lose. She's an expert.

I silently nod—an unspoken punctuation to our conversation.

We finish our desserts in silence, both lost in our own thought-worlds.

Jules signals to our waitress for our check, while I stared at my half-eaten dessert, and dangled my spoon, mid-air.

"Would you like more tea or maybe sherry?" our waitress asked.

Julia answered "We couldn't eat another bite—delicious. Please compliment your chef, won't you?" She quickly grabs our check.

"OK, Jules, but I'll leave the tip. Check's mine next time." I concede.

Jules smiles, and answers, "Race you to the ladies room."

Something urges me to leave a large tip for this young waitress: so kind, so sad, and having to work two jobs—a story there, I know. A tip is such an insignificant offering, but maybe it'll help a little.

Leaving the restaurant, Jules heads toward her SUV. I slowly walk toward my house, lost in thought and deciding to forego any shopping trip—even the grocery I'd earlier deemed an essential errand for today.

Chapter 5

To Do Or Not To Do

Today had not gone as I wanted or planned.
I'd left this morning excited about having a day to escape unpleasant aspects of my life. I'd have my hair and make-up done, and enjoy lunch. I looked forward to shopping for a new outfit: a carefree day.

Well.

I hadn't felt like shopping. Lunch was yummy. It was fun seeing Jules. I just didn't feel so cheerful after hearing her plans for that displaced homemakers thing, or whatever it's called.

Don't get me wrong. It's a remarkable project. Certainly it's needed—more on top of that, actually. I applaud any donor who wants to help these women. A traditional Catholic college is just where it's needed, with numbers of divorced couples rising more than ever, within Catholic and non-Catholic communities, across the board—not to mention widows—sounds wonderful.

I wish there'd been such a program when I was in the midst of my struggles.

Why was I feeling so—I don't know—edgy now? I couldn't isolate my feelings to describe them. I wandered around my house, trying not to think but thinking, none-the-less.

Diversion. . . I needed diversion. The library had closed at noon today. My professional literature bored me; nothing on TV. I scanned titles of abandoned books someone had left behind on a shelf. A yellowed, dog-eared copy of <u>Love Story</u> by Eric Segal lay on its binding on a bottom shelf.

Thirty pages into it, I find my mood darkening. In fact, parts of its story simply remind me of uncomfortable parts of my own life.

I'm tired.

Although fully dressed, I grab my hypoallergenic, alternative-down comforter and decide to nap. It's only afternoon, but maybe, if I'm lucky, I can sleep all night.

I yawn.

———————

"Mommy! Mommy!"

"Yes, Tad, Mommy's here." I stumbled through palpable darkness to Tad's room.

I knelt beside his little youth bed, and lifted his small frame onto my lap. His hair dripped with perspiration and his pajamas were soaked through—another wet bed.

"Honey, did you have another bad dream?" I pushed wet curls from his eyes.

"Mommy, I'm scared," he started to cry again.

"What are you afraid of, Honey? Mommy's here."

"A huge monster took our house away, and took Daddy, and my toys and you, and . . . and it was chasing me. It was trying to catch me."

"Oh, Sweetie, see, there's no monster here. It was just a bad dream."

I felt as frightened as he did, but I could not confess that, even to myself. I must be strong. I was the mother, after all. I must be his protector. I had to help him feel safe. How could I do that?

He slid his thumb into his mouth. Odd, that habit has re-emerged, after having been eliminated almost a year ago.

He removed his thumb to play with a tendril of my hair. "Mommy, can't we go back to our house, and live with Daddy?"

Tad replayed this question numerous times each day in past weeks. Bless his heart. What comforting answer could ease his hurt that was so profound?

I took a deep breath, "You miss Daddy, don't you?"

"Uh-huh. I miss my playroom, too. Can't we go back?"

His tears were breaking my heart. I'd do anything to take away his pain, but I was powerless to change things. How could Charles have been so hateful? I wish he could be here, night after night, and witness what his thoughtlessness and lack of sensitivity has done to his son.

"Honey, Daddy moved someplace else, like we did. He didn't want to live with Mommy. He loves you very much, though. You'll be seeing him in his new house next weekend, remember?"

'I don't like it there. I want my old house." He sobbed

I wanted my old house and my old life, too. Who had been so cruel as to have captured his heart and broken mine? Some nights I ran through names of people from our neighborhood who might give me her name. I thought of a girl next door. No, she'd moved away right before I left. No way to contact her. What would she know anyway?

There was always Karen who lived across the street. She seemed to be everywhere I went—church events, community activities. She had a reputation of knowing everything about everybody: a busybody: her nose always in someone else's business, as if bored with her own life. Whenever I'd tried to talk with her, she'd always seemed so distant or cold; shifty eyes. I wouldn't feel comfortable asking her. I didn't trust her, anyway.

It was probably better I didn't know the third party. I could only deal with so much information and pain. Not knowing a name made my pain less personal, but no less agonizing.

I rocked him. "I know. It makes you sad, doesn't it? I feel sad, too."

How could I help this little one understand when, as an adult, I could make no sense of what had happened? I wondered how much longer we'd feel this loss so acutely. Hopefully we were through the worst. I had this nagging feeling this could go on for a while. Could it get worse? I shudder with the thought.

"Listen, let's get these wet pj's off and find some milk and cookies. Then we'll go back to sleep, OK?"

After dressing him in fresh pj's, we stepped into our drafty little kitchen. I opened our cupboard. Uh-oh, only one cookie left in its box. I searched other shelves, but found no more boxes, anywhere.

I must go grocery shopping tomorrow, but I was down to my last dollar. How would we make it? God would have to do a miracle.

Handing Tad the last cookie, I carried wet sheets and clothes to our washer. I looked up. As far as I could see was dirty laundry—a mountain of soiled clothes piled to the ceiling. Beside it was a huge pile of bills, with envelopes coming from every direction —bills and more bills.

Charles's booming voice shouted from somewhere in the room "You're a terrible wife and mother. I don't love you anymore."

Another voice called, "You're a divorcee and a Nun-reject. You're a failure, a miserable failure."

"No, no, no." My screams awaken me.

Oh, what a frightening dream. *Why were my memories and emotions weaving themselves in my dreams? So real. Was there a message in this one? Something I needed to think about?*

I untangle my feet from bunched covers and get some water. I was trembling.

Most dreams I didn't remember.

This was startling, and significant, I feared.

Sunday Evening

It's been a miserable day. My mood's been foul.

8:30. I'm ending this day and going to bed. I fluff cold pillows, and grope for my warm comforter. It's only 35 degrees outside, and the wind's howling.

I can feel a draft pushing through that old, bow window, and hear its vibrating whistle around old panes. I must see about re-caulking before winter sets in. This wretched house needs insulation desperately. Winter could be bitter in Baltimore, although the worst was not generally until January. I intend to be long gone by then.

Long gone, I repeat to myself, to give encouraging finality. I tuck my covers as tightly around my limbs as I can.

But what if I'm still here? Finding a residential facility for Mother might take a while, I've concluded, recalling multiple responses in yesterday's mail. Even when she resides elsewhere, what shall I do with our family house? What about Lucille?

I gulped down a lump in my throat. *Will I ever be able to go home?* I hadn't really acknowledged that fear until now. I lift my comforter around my head so only my nose braved frigid air.

Maybe that's why this project bothered me so much. Maybe by accepting this position, I'd be acknowledging I'd stay—long enough to take a job, of sorts. Was that it? Fear of being stuck here?

I want to go home. . my home, not take a job—here.

Well, I'm feeling kind of angry, too, at my siblings for not wanting to share some of this responsibility. Whose problem was it, after all, if I expected them to help and to care? I'd taught them not to take responsibility by simply doing everything, myself. I'm tired of all of it, all the time.

I resented my family. I now realize that's probably why I dreamed of a convent: an ideal escape.

The idea of a cloistered existence—without my mother, brothers or sisters—a quiet and controlled life of service sounded like heaven on earth. Appease my conscience, too. Secretly, I could leave it all. Do something I wanted to do; by myself without burdens of my dysfunctional family—or its shame.

Mother Superior had been a loving but firm mother-model I so needed. As an adult, I could see she must've seen through my deluded reasons for coming. Not God's call, but a selfish escape. She knew of my lost childhood and my lack of parental guidance; my need to be away to develop into my own person.

Because I never knew actual reasons for my not being accepted, I felt like a failure. My return home to re-enter a life I had not missed was even more dispiriting than falling short as a nun wannabe. My escape attempt had been thwarted.

Was this present irritation simply a replay of past emotions? I didn't want to come back to Baltimore—then or now?

Maybe.

Or, perhaps it was helping women in need. I was spent. I had needs, didn't I? I didn't want to take on anyone else's problems, any more.

My recent life has not been entirely selfish. I worked part-time as a social worker. It was professional, though and I could counsel from behind my desk; separate myself from my clients. I could guide, but not get involved. *Was that such a sin*? Do I have to keep doing for others and continuing to be vulnerable to pain?

I punched my pillow. Then, sensing cold air, I withdrew my fist back under my covers.

All of the above, I guess. But perhaps it was the focus of this particular task: helping women who've been displaced from their homes, their husbands and, in some cases, their very existences. I'd been there. Jules was right. No one was more qualified to know the panic, the pain, and the betrayal of that whole dreadful thing.

I kept my painful memories carefully hidden—and locked— in a corner of my mind.

I was trying to move on. I did not want to look back. *Was that it*?

Maybe—probably.

I hated thinking about this stuff.

Enough. I'm going to sleep.

I adjust my pillow, arrange covers over my shoulders as close to my chin as possible, lift my knees and hug them to my chest. I will for sleep to come.

12:05. Is it too late to call Bill? I really need to talk with someone I trust. I lift my cordless receiver.

After four rings, a sleepy Bill, alarm in his cracking voice, answers, "Glory, are you all right?"

"Bill, I'm sorry it's so late. I just wanted to hear your voice."

"Now, I'm glad you woke me for that. Do you miss me?"

"You know I do. I miss your voice, your hugs, your kisses and your wisdom." I was whining now, I knew it.

I also missed his touch and his strong arms around me, comforting me in my distress as he'd done so many times before. I tried to dismiss those longings. It would only make things worse. He was so far away. I sighed audibly.

"When can I see you, Glory? I miss you so much."

"How about next weekend? I can't get home, but I could meet you in Cumberland or Hagerstown. We could see changing leaves. We could spend some hours together. Maybe we could have a picnic?"

"I'll see if I can steal away. My schedule's stacked with meetings, but I'd much rather be meeting you."

"Me, too." I feel a sob rising. "Go back to sleep. We can talk more tomorrow. Maybe see you next weekend? Oh, I hope so."

"Me, too. Night Glory, love you."

"Night, love you, too." I push end.

Tears escape. I want him with me, as before. I'd taken him for granted, I suddenly realized. Selfish is what I've been—with Bill and other people, too. My cheeks flamed, despite the cold, and I grimaced with my acknowledgement. I'm not going there tonight.

I hate this. Focusing on Bill's absence was not helping me sleep.

I'm no closer to a decision about this job of Jules's. She'd call tomorrow, if I didn't call her first.

"Julia," I say out loud, "What are you doing to me?"

I lie here, ruminating. I glance at my clock. 1:00. I'm no closer to sleep than I was four hours ago, although my body aches with fatigue.

Could it be God had placed this position in my lap for a reason? I don't want to consider that. I really don't want to do this. Why does everyone always want me to do something? Couldn't I be left alone?

I roll over on my other side, and punch my pillow again. *Where is this anger coming from?*

I have reasons I didn't want to do this thing, or that I couldn't do it or why doing it would make me even more resentful. Good reasons. I'd just refuse. No big deal; over and done with.

2:00 and I'm still awake. No peace. I should pray about this. Why hadn't I just prayed earlier? Maybe because I didn't really want to know what God wanted. Maybe I want to run from God right now. I grimace. That's not good. I was beginning to understand how Jonah felt inside that whale or big fish, or whatever it was.

OK. OK. OK.

I swing my bare legs over the side of my bed, pull my gown over my knees and kneel to pray, as I'd practiced those five years at convent school. "Lord, I really need your help right now. I've got this position to consider. . . ."

"I have been driven many times upon my knees by the overwhelming conviction that I had
nowhere else to go. My own wisdom and that of all about me seemed insufficient for that day."
Abraham Lincoln

Monday Morning

8:00 a.m. Would Jules be in her office now? It's a school day, isn't it? Of course she'd be there. I might as well get this over with.

Dial-tone. . .8-2-5—

"Jules, this is Glory. Can we meet for coffee? Yes, yes. I know. An hour? Your office? Fine. I'll be there. Sure, Styrofoam cups.

"Life's disappointments are veiled love's appointments."

C.A. Fox

Chapter 6

Coffee, Tea, Or Me~ In Styrofoam

"Did you decide?" Jules bounced.

I nodded.

She clapped, "Glory, you'll be wonderful; the perfect one for this position."

I thrust my palms forward. "Jules, please, slow down. It's a resignation, you know that."

"I know, but I'm convinced you'll be blessed as you help these poor women."

"Yeah, yeah, only six weeks, right? Just show up?"

Julia pours watery coffee, stirs in powdered creamer substitute, and displays a package of sugar stand-in, as well. "It helps this stuff taste, well, you know, less bitter."

"No, less like mud," I add with a forced smile, eyeing the chemicals suspiciously.

She settles on the edge of her chair. "Here are the details: Flyers have already been distributed around a five-mile radius, taking us west, as far as Mt. Washington, north into Baltimore County, east as far as Loch Raven Boulevard, and south as far as Guilford, with the southern-most boundary being Johns Hopkins, main campus. Women in this area will be close to public transportation and of a similar demographic."

Listening to all the names of streets and potential people from various neighborhoods was making my head swim. I couldn't think of anything to say. *Why had I agreed to this again?*

"Uh-huh" I answered, trying to sound engaged.

"A list of volunteers offering temporary rooms for shelter and child care has been compiled. With your background in our counseling department, here, you know appropriate tests for identifying personality profiles for career paths."

"I guess."

Please. The more I hear, the more anxious I feel. Were my eyes crossing?

"It'll be easy for you, Glory. Only two hours each week—tops—just enough to give you a time-out from responsibilities, which are really dragging you down."

For sure—my eyes are crossing.

"Jul-i-a," I exaggerate her name to get a word in, "your ever-loving enthusiasm has always been enthralling to me. Our whole friendship has been my following your zeal into the unknown, only to find it was not e-x-a-ct-l-y as you described."

She waves her hand, dismissively, "Nonsense."

"No," I blurt out, "I must know exactly what I need to do."

I'm passed nervous. Panic mode, definitely.

"Oh, Glory, all you have to do is come to conference room C, near our auditorium. Coffee machine, napkins, coffee, sugar, and stirrers are in that hall closet. I'll give you a key each day."

"Is that it?"

Just tell me that's it, please. I parted fingers covering my eyes and dared to look.

"Just welcome the women as they arrive. Children over age six will watch a video across the hall. Younger children will report to our early childhood-education playroom."

She continued, "You'll have sign-up sheets for health care, child care, whatever, and their names and contact information. Some may be reluctant to give their names. That's OK. You'll help them feel secure. You're great at that. Then, you can plan each week as needs dictate. Easy, right?"

Please, let that be all. I had a feeling, this was not all. There was more. I closed my eyes to wait for the inevitable: the final shoe to drop, as it were. I need an aspirin.

"And when is this intended to begin?" I squinted, thinking this sounded far too simple.

Julia looked away, mouthing, "This Tuesday?" coordinating her words with shrug.

There it is. I knew it, yet I could not believe it.

"Julia." I snapped, more forcefully than I intended, "Tomorrow?"

She waved her hand again, as if it were a minor issue. Perhaps it was, in the whole scheme of things, but it remained huge for me.

Julia answered with a nervous laugh, "Oh, Glory, I love it when you get mad. Really, it'll be nothing. It'll be fun, you'll see."

"Jules, what have you gotten me into?" I shrieked, "Tomorrow, really?"

Julia arose, glancing at her clock. "Oh, Glory, I have a meeting in eight minutes."

She shifted papers on her desk.

Why am I surprised? I thought, as she pushed me toward her door.

"It'll be perfect, you'll see. You'll just see." She thrust her door open and ushered me out.

"Call you later tonight."

She threw up her hand in a quick wave, and bounced onto the sidewalk.

"What have I agreed to?" I muttered, following in a daze.

". . . Do you truly love me?". . . Jesus said,
"Take care of my sheep."
John 21:16, (Bible, NIV)

Chapter 7

First Night

Tuesday

I must consider practicalities of this thing. Time is short.

Since returning to Baltimore, my life had been catch-as catch can, between hospital trips, converting that rental house into a temporary home, and righting things at St. Edmonds: days upon days of unscheduled chaos. Go with the flow had been my motto. A few minutes or hours here or there hardly made a difference, as long as the urgent was addressed. Now I'm being forced into a different mode.

What about clothes? I need something to wear. My fall transition-wear amounted to a pair of jeans, a couple of turtlenecks, and a gray cardigan sweater. No professional clothes.

I'd found nothing that looked even slightly close to being appropriate on my shopping trip yesterday. What really would be suitable, though? A professional suit would be best, probably. A skirt, gray flannel or navy, and a soft blouse with pearls could be a good substitute. After all, my role as a professional moderator and a social worker demanded I look as if I could help these people. I must look believable.

The truth was, could I? Be believable, that is. Was there really a lot I could offer? I'd been through a divorce. I'd raised a child alone. I'd struggled to make ends meet and somehow create a stable life for Tad and myself amidst a cruel world. *Had I done it right? Had I done it well enough?*

Who even set the standard? When it came right down to it, who really cared about a single mother or her overwhelming life of pressures, coming from all sides? Who cared about these souls when their children cried, or when they, the women, cried? When pain from divorce or widowhood was more than anyone could bear? I surely didn't know. What could I possibly do to help?

It was best to remain cold, professional and stick to the script. Stick to the bottom line of housing, job training, child-care. I could do this.

Yes, definitely a suit.

I'd visited the St. Edmonds house and rummaged through my old closet. There, practically hidden under eaves, was a 70's something blazer and A-line skirt. Burgundy. It certainly needed to be aired. No time to dry-clean. *Would it even fit?*

I peeled off my jeans and stepped into the skirt. Its waist didn't quite meet its button and hole alignment. A safety pin or two might close the gap. It's a bit short, with horizontal pleats pulling across my hips, but they'd be covered by a jacket, surely.

The blazer barely stretched over my shoulders, though. Fine, I'd just drape it over a chair and deal with pleats.

I visited other closets. Alas, my sisters had taken all that had ever remained. Probably why this is still left in my closet; no one else wanted it. Too late, now. . . almost time to leave.

At least my hair still looked decent. I shuddered as I examined my nails. Dry cuticles surround poorly manicured stubs—too late for help there.

Shoes? My taupe summer flats would work. After all, the only other options were flip-flops or clogs. A beige blouse topped a pile set aside for Salvation Army—a color-coordinated match for my shoes. Mother's dark-toned panty hose would have to do. Something had to be better than nothing.

I passed Lucille in the hallway. She studied my outfit and Mother's drooping panty hose gathering at my ankles and knees.

"Law, law," she muttered under her breath.

Thanks for your vote of confidence. Well, it would soon be over.

6:45. I raced to the college, wondering if the folds in my hose were flapping in the breeze. Both stocking legs seemed to move independently of my legs.

The sun had already set and dark shadows cast from street lights made me shiver. I felt as if I were re-entering a time of darkness from my own life. Something like re-reading Edgar Allen Poe's "Tell Tale Heart".

Keys? I searched my pocketbook and found the manila envelope, with a number scrawled in red ink. Apparently conference room C was reserved for another purpose. Our group would gather in a classroom next door.

Light revealed a rather large classroom. Student chairs with arm-extended writing surfaces, embellished with carved initials and ink-drawn hearts, were arranged in even rows, facing forward, awaiting a lecture. I recalled my years here, both as a student and as a professor—so long ago—another life-time, at least. I glazed my fingers over one of the scarred extensions, remembering.

I located the coffee machine, et. al, on a gray metal push cart in a hall closet (the kind that once held a movie projector or slide cassette when I was a student.) It advanced much like the same cart that kept choosing me at the grocery store—the one whose wheel had a resistant mind of its own.

I filled the urn with as much water as I could carry without spilling, and placed it, splashing, on its stand. Once the oversized container was plugged into an outlet, it began chugging, increasing in sound with time. I placed opened boxes of Sweet and Low, sugar, creamer, and Styrofoam cups next to this now whistling, dancing urn. The noise was almost deafening, but maybe it offered a welcoming touch to this unwelcoming place. I hoped.

Three women entered the back door of our designated room.

"Sit anywhere you'd like, Ladies."

Each chose isolated seats, mostly in the back, as far from one another as possible. A few more filtered in and took equally distant seats.

By 7:15, twelve women sat in silence. All eyes stared at desk tops, as if something more interesting than graffiti had been engraved into their scarred surfaces. Perhaps answers to a test they were convinced they'd fail.

I introduced myself, and spoke briefly about what we'd be covering. I was stumbling through this. With no eye contact, I was not convinced I was even being heard or understood.

I decided on another tactic. "Please help yourself to coffee."

Silence ensued.

A couple of women glanced longingly at the pot, which was now wildly dancing what could almost be a "buck and wing" to "Happy Days Are Here Again," around the table top; musical repertoire for our evening, I suppressed an urge to laugh.

I decided the best way to start the ball rolling would be by announcing I was getting a cup of coffee. I extended another invitation to join me.

"The coffee urn is demanding we take a cup, Ladies. We'd better hop to before it starts doing other things to capture our attention."

One or two women smiled, but most remained rigid, heads bowed, hugging themselves. I remembered doing that.

When I first separated from my husband, I felt an uncontrollable urge to clasp my arms around myself and hug tightly. An unconscious gesture which gave confidence of my not crumbling into pieces, I later realized.

I looked around at this non-speaking group. Getting their attention was going to be harder than I thought. Why had I agreed to this?

Well, I was here, so think, Gloria, think. Pray, Gloria, pray.

I know. I'd eliminate these parallel rows of chairs which seemed to encourage isolation. Enough isolation, I was not going to lecture, for heaven's sake.

"Ladies," I motioned, "let's arrange our chairs in a circle. You can bring your cups with you (although I knew I was the only one who had a cup)."

I moved the first two chairs. Slowly, others joined. The cacophony of chair legs scuffing against floor tile and shoes against chairs ensued, then halted as suddenly as it had begun. Bodies quickly fell back into seats, aligning themselves in positions they'd once occupied: something like the rush at the end of a game of musical chairs.

I distributed generic name labels with "Hello" stamped on top, along with a black magic marker; in hopes someone would share a name. Only a few felt comfortable with identification, as if forbidden. Those who placed labels over their broken hearts looked as if they were prisoners preparing for a mug shot ID. I gazed from face to face, eyes to eyes, slumped shoulders to slumped shoulders and realized they were—prisoners of excruciating pain and fear.

I didn't expect this. I was suddenly moved to tears. *Control yourself,* I silently scolded. I reached for my reading glasses to disguise my eyes.

"Ladies, I'd like to go around our circle and let each of you share your reasons for coming."

More silence. Within minutes, though, the door opened. The tall, young woman who I quickly recognized as the *Morgan and Millard* waitress entered—perfect timing. I motioned her to take a seat, and offered her coffee and a name label.

She smiled, peeled paper-backing from her label, and placed "Sarah" on her olive-green, leotard top that paired a mid-calf peasant-style skirt and Birkenstock sandals. Her long, auburn braid hung gracefully down her back, nearly to her waist. Her expression looked nonchalant, but her eyes betrayed conflicting feelings—stress, anger, perhaps? Hard to ascertain; certainly, fatigue.

"I was just asking each of our guests if they'd like to share their particular reason for coming tonight."

Just as my words were out, the door flew open again, and a petite, young woman burst into our room, clearly out of breath. She apologized profusely, as the door closed behind her.

"So sorry I'm late." She smiled and shrugged her shoulders. "Babysitter," she added.

Women nodded, in sympathy. They knew all too well, what that was like. I nodded too. I remembered the stress of trying to find someone to watch my son, and coordinating this with an impossibly tight schedule of a single mother. Under time pressure, nothing ever seemed to go as planned.

I offered this young woman coffee.

Giggling, she said, "It's so cold, and coffee sounds so-o good. Thank you. I never have time to sit and enjoy a cup of coffee anymore."

Several women nodded again and looked at one another in agreement.

Katie, as we were to learn from her name tag (large, flourishing print, ending in a curlicue E), may be just the one who can get a discussion flowing. Her contagious joie de vivre and laugh lines conflicted with . . . was it sadness or fear her eyes betrayed?

Unlike others, she chose a middle chair, purposely surrounded by the group. *Was this for acceptance . . . or protection a group might offer?*

Prominent collarbones and shoulder joints revealed her thin frame, as she removed her jacket. Her wispy, blondish hair was caught in a thin ponytail, and her blue eyes, circled with dark shadows, contrasted with her fair complexion. We waited, transfixed, as she settled in her chair, grabbed a pen and paper from her monogrammed bag, and announced she would not interrupt again.

The women smiled and some giggled. We could all relate to the disorganization which comes with being newly alone.

"Katie" I asked, "why don't you start? From what neighborhood do you come? Do you have children? Why did you come tonight?"

"Hi, everyone, I live in Baltimore County. I have two sons, three and fourteen. My life is in transition." Her face saddened a bit. "My husband and I have separated." She stumbled with this truth. "I'm not doing so well, trying to adjust. I'm not working yet. I guess I'm here because I need to find some direction for my life, which seems to be falling apart."

Others nodded in sympathy, realizing this woman was speaking for them all, when she spoke of her pain—a pain that many were still unwilling to share beyond a nod of agreement.

"Thank you, Katie. I appreciate your honesty. I know many of these ladies can relate to the same adjustment frustrations to which you've alluded."

Poor girl, behind this cheerfulness was a vulnerability I couldn't read. "Anyone else. . . Sarah?"

Sarah uncrossed her legs and leaned slightly forward, clasping her hands, as if that gesture would keep her from falling.

"I'm from Mt. Washington. I have a 15-year-old daughter who presently attends Country Day School. . ." She trailed off. "It remains to be seen how long she'll be able to attend."

Several women nodded their heads, understanding.

"I'm most recently from Massachusetts, but I was raised in upstate New York. I came here with, you know, my husband. We've separated. I work at a health food store during the week and as a waitress on weekends. I don't know whether I can keep my house. I have no family here. I'm tired." She stopped talking, leaned back in her chair, and lowered her head, trying to gain composure.

As if on cue, a woman from across the room, left her seat and placed her hand gently on Sarah's shoulder, reassuringly. Rather than return to her seat, this woman drew up a seat behind Sarah. Her label read, "Ruth."

I smiled at Ruth, approvingly nodding my head. She'd be an anchor for this group, I could see. I needed to know more about this woman.

I coaxed, "Ruth, thank you for that kind gesture toward Sarah. This is uncomfortable for all of us. Your action helps us feel safe. Can you tell us a little about yourself?"

Ruth, in contrast to Katie's thin frame, was slightly overweight, with a gently curved, almost angelic face and expressive brown eyes. Her cheeks blushed strong pink with unexpected attention.

She answered, "I've been living in Rodgers Forge since my husband and I moved here five years ago. I'm originally from Iowa. I have a son whom I teach at home. I don't have a job. I really don't have any job skills, as I've been an at-home mom since I married and left college." Her voice cracked, "I don't know where I'll live or how I'll provide for my son. . .since. . .my husband. . . ." She did not continue.

I nodded. No one said anything. Sarah placed a hand on Ruth's shoulder, but didn't make eye contact; an unspoken understanding that this action would have violated the privacy of each of them. Just a touch that said, *I understand.*

Another woman sitting to the right of Sarah scooted her chair a little closer to Ruth and Sarah. She was gracefully tall, with straight, black, shoulder-length hair accenting large blue-violet eyes. Both contrasted with her pale, flawless skin. Unlike others, who were casually dressed, she wore an elegant gray cashmere sweater and matching wool skirt, *Ferragamo* pumps and matching bag. She looked as if she'd floated off a page of Town and Country magazine. An understated gold necklace circled her neck, but she wore no other jewelry except for a family-crest embossed ring on her right pinkie. Her label read, "M. Carroll."

I nodded in her direction. Without looking up, M. Carroll recited in a strong, Southern accent, "My name is Mari Carroll. I live in Guilford, not far from here. I have a 17-year-old son who's a junior at Hilton Academy. I also have a son in heaven. I don't have a job nor do I have any marketable skills. I have no family in this area, and . . ." she hesitated, "as we speak, my house is scheduled for auction. We need a place to live." She straightened her back and looked to me and the group and said, clearly, and firmly, "It will be all right."

I nodded, "Yes, it will be all right."

As she'd been speaking, the door opened quietly. A woman (I assumed), dressed in a drab brown hat and scarf, dragging coat and humongous sunglasses slipped into a chair. After Mari Carroll had finished, I signaled this visitor to come in. She shook her head firmly and darted back through the door. She looked so troubled.

Why had she come and then dashed out so quickly?

Chapter 8

Furthermore

"Is there anyone else who'd like to share?" I scanned the circle, clearing my voice.

I tried to dismiss my bewilderment, and re-focus my attention away from the closing door, and back to this class.

Several other women recounted their stories. Some were older women whose husbands had left them for younger women. They were without money, had mortgages to pay, grown children and no working skills. Tears flowed. It was painful to listen.

One woman guardedly interjected her need to share.

She began, while twisting a strand of hair. "My husband is a financial analyst. I've been aware of his having affairs for some time. I'd confronted him once or twice, but he flatly denied it, even in the face of indisputable evidence: lipstick on clothes, tawdry perfume scents, receipts for unexplained purchases, even articles of female clothing not belonging to me. I'd threatened separation a year ago, which slowed him down, I think, but I've been too exhausted to pursue any action toward that end."

She hesitated, looking down at her fingers.

"I've been an at-home mom with three children: four-years, two-years and eight-months. Most days, I don't even have time to shower. The thought of responsibilities of being a single mother were too much to consider."

Heads nodded from around our circle.

"I've lost a lot of weight. When I look at my wedding picture beside my bed, I realize it'd been a long time since I resembled the attractive coed to whom my husband had proposed. I've been desperately tired and depressed; I've felt lonely and unloved.

"Because there were no grounds for divorce my husband could hold against me, his obsession became discovering something which would make me appear guilty, to protect his financial resources, I know now. I was totally unaware of what was being planned to deceive me."

She took a deep breath, and released it, slowly.

"One night, "she recounted," my husband, holding a beautiful bouquet of roses, vowed he loved me. He apologized for his transgressions. He wanted to be a more loving husband. He'd show me by taking me away for the weekend. A formal dinner party was planned with clients in Philadelphia, Friday night. We could make a weekend of it—just the two of us. He'd arrange a sitter for our children. We'd stay at a beautiful Inn, downtown. I could buy a formal gown, get my hair done, manicure, whatever I wanted. . . a dream-come-true. I was thrilled.

"When we arrived, I dressed in my new gown. I almost looked as pretty as I had ten years before. No, I could not disguise under-eye circles, bony arms and shoulders, or several gray strands which appeared at my right temple. Maybe they weren't that noticeable.

"At the party, while sipping my second glass of champagne, I noticed a handsome gentleman lifting his glass to me. I blushed, and giggled. I felt giddy."

"'Yes,' my husband answered the waiter, 'she'll have another glass.'"

"I didn't protest. After all, I'd left bottles of my breast milk in our freezer for our baby. I didn't have to worry about alcohol tonight. It was a romantic evening, just me and my husband. Besides, it was an especially fine sparkling wine; French, I'd bet. It would be a long time before I enjoyed something this good, I'm sure.

"Not long after that, my husband insisted on introducing me to one of his colleagues. We strode across the room and stopped at the same handsome man I'd noticed earlier. After a brief introduction, this man began to draw me out with a discussion about the background music. I was mesmerized."

She smiled slightly, lost in recollection.

Silence reigned in our classroom. Eyes widened.

"You see, music had been my college major. It was amazing. He loved Chopin, as I did. It was fantastic conversing with an adult about music instead of financial prospects with my husband, diapers with my neighbor or Sesame Street with my children. He'd love for me to listen to a recording of a concert he'd attended in Moscow. Would I come to his room—just a few doors down? I could listen to his tape. He was eager to share it with someone who appreciated exquisite music as he did.

"I'd felt uncomfortable. I'd looked for my husband, but he'd disappeared, bored by our conversation, I guessed."

She hesitated, her voice straining.

"The man said, 'Look, it'll only take a few minutes. We can be back in ten, for dinner. Your husband won't mind.'"

"My head was spinning from champagne. I couldn't think clearly. He eased my elbow in his hand, and scurried me down the hall and into his room. I felt dizzy. His arms supported me gently as I settled onto his sofa.

"The recorded music was a quality I'd never heard. I closed my eyes to concentrate on the dual-piano arrangement. Its notes resonated in my very soul. My skin prickled with each musical crescendo. Glorious.

"This gentleman, which he was not, drew me close. My head buzzed with music coming from several speakers and the large quantity of champagne I'd had. My tongue and lips felt numb. I was unable to consider actions or consequences."

She sighed deeply before continuing her saga.

"He started telling me how beautiful I was. I guess I needed to hear that from someone. He began kissing me."

Her down-turned lips reversed their direction, glimpsing a hesitant smile which vanished as quickly as it had manifested.

"I felt powerless to do anything. Suddenly, coming down from my high and grasping what was left of my rational mind, I ran from his room, trying to re-zip my gown as I exited. I was sober then, but sick, from guilt and hunger, but mostly guilt. I whimpered as I stumbled down the hall, my ankles turning in my pumps. *What have I done, what have I done?*

"I raced back to find my husband. I feared my hair was wildly disheveled. I just hoped I'd fastened my dress so it looked together."

"I'm sick," I stammered. "I need to return to our hotel room, immediately."

Women in our room covered their eyes and mouths, sensing a disastrous ending.

"He called a cab and agreed to meet me there later. We cut our weekend short, which had been his plan all along. The next week, I received separation papers, with pictures of my kissing this man in his room. My husband pretended to be appalled by such behavior, which he could only presume had been typical and going on for a long time. What kind of woman was I? What kind of wife was I, and I had the nerve to accuse him?"

Gasps escaped from some of the women.

She hesitated before continuing, in an effort to compose herself. Choking back sobs and wiping her eyes with a Kleenex, she said, "Now, after our lawyers are through, I've been told I may take my children, but I've lost my home. I have nothing, and as soon as our house sells, I must move back to Georgia, and promise never to return."

"What in the world am I going to do?" She dissolved in sobs.

I looked at the women in this circle. Most of them hid their faces behind their hands. Others looked as if they were going to be sick. It was time I intervened.

"First of all, I want to thank this woman for her courage to disclose her painful situation and make her appeal for help. You, Dear, are safe, among those of us who have experienced horrors of divorce. Yes, I've been divorced. Each of our experiences has been different, but our pain is the same. It can be a devastating experience, unfair and hurtful to all involved."

I walked to this sobbing woman. I rested my hand on her shoulder.

"This program is being sponsored by a Catholic college. Although I am no longer Catholic, the only way I know to deal with the difficulties all of you have shared is with prayer. In my divorce, and problems that grew from difficulties of being a single mother, I've found God is the only person who could help me through each day."

I circled our room, looking into faces of each woman, "Is there anyone here who would object to my praying for this woman? Is there anyone here who is not a believer?"

Alone, Sarah weakly raised her hand. She spoke softly, "I was raised in a church, but I gave up my beliefs long before I married. My husband is Jewish in heritage, but atheistic in his position. Since my marriage, I assumed I was too educated to believe in God—kind of like realizing there's no Santa Claus. Now that I'm alone,

I just don't know what I believe. So I don't object to your reference to God or to your prayers."

I smiled at Sarah, and said with compassion, "It's all right to have doubts and questions."

I looked down at this woman on whose shoulder my hand was resting. "Do you want me to pray for you? Do you want others in this room to pray?"

She nodded in affirmation, still trying to control sobbing spasms.

At that moment, Ruth rose from her chair and joined me. She asked, "Why don't those who do believe, support her with our own prayers."

One woman arose; then another. Some chose to stay seated, but bowed their heads, respectfully. Those who rose joined hands—Mari Carroll, Katie, and several other unidentified women.

What have I just done? This was to be a secular, resource-giving meeting. *Here I am leading prayer?* Was this what Jules had in mind when this seminar was being planned? *But what else could I do?*

After a simple prayer, not recalling what I'd even said, I walked to the front.

"On these chairs, I've placed forms for those of you who need information on housing, job training, and child care. There is a blank form for those who have other needs—medical, spiritual, or whatever."

"This is a new program. I've never moderated anything like this. I'm a professional social worker, and although I've been connected with this college in my past, I have no connection with it now. All conversations within this room are confidential, and I will back that up with standards of my profession. I would ask all participants to keep in confidence any information and names you've heard tonight."

I approached the blackboard and picked up a fraction of a piece of chalk left on its ledge. I printed my full name and office phone number. "You may contact me at this college. Leave a message. I'll return your call."

Sounds of chairs shuffling and shifting belongings commenced as women found pen and paper and copied the number.

"You'll be safe here. Your concerns will be confidential. Please fill out our forms.

Include any suggestions you'd like to see addressed in future meetings."

I noticed women who had isolated themselves in their pain at the beginning of this class, now chatted together. Their troubled expressions had been transformed into smiles. Peace had replaced fear.

"If I can ease one person's journey along life's path, I will not have lived in vain."
Emily Dickinson

Chapter 9

At Best... Disappointments

For Pete's Sake

Mari

Tonight I attended a self-help group.
Unbelievable.

Why didn't I see any of this coming? Why didn't I recognize Pete had problems before I married him? Yes, he drank when we were in college, especially at his fraternity house, and at football games, but who didn't? Even my father said 'Nothin' at all wrong with a little <u>Wild</u> <u>Turkey</u>, from time to time.'"

The <u>Wild</u> <u>Turkey</u> had gone south.

Once Pete's corporate success established, his personal standards grew lax, and his work grew careless. His lunch-meeting drinking started as early as 11a.m, sometimes. Numbers of evening cocktails increased exponentially. *Even so, what could he have been thinking?*

I shuddered as I remembered last month, cruising down my street, mid-afternoon, after having dropped Tyler at lacrosse practice. My concerned neighbor flagged me down.

"Hi. What's up?" I grinned.

She thrust a folded newspaper through my window. She'd circled an auction notice.

"You didn't tell me your house was up for auction." Her eyes looked questioning.

Assuming she was teasing, I grabbed her paper, laughing.

My house. My house number. Auction? My face burned.

"There must be some mistake." I snapped, and sped away.

Even from a distance, I recognized a garishly large auction sign, centered among my English boxwoods. My husband's 280 SL classic Mercedes blocked our driveway.

I pushed our cracked door far enough to enter. Tightly drawn draperies created purposeful darkness. Inebriated Pete sat, forearms on his knees, clutching an almost-empty bottle.

"What is the meaning of this?' I screeched, waving my newspaper.

He stared back at me, eyes glassy and squinted. "Well," he slurred, "my investments went belly up, I lost my job and—"

"And what more, dare I ask?"

"The government's begun an investigation. Our company's being audited for accounting practices. I'm responsible."

"What?" I backed against the door, placing my hand to my forehead.

"But how could you auction our house without consulting me?"

He shrugged, and downed remaining liquid, visibly straining to swallow.

"We owe, big time, an' I wan' out."

I could hardly believe what I was hearing. I felt my very breath sucked from me. My knees buckled. I sank to the floor, my back pinned against the wall.

I ventured, "Out of what, exactly?"

"I don't wan' this house. I don't wan' this marriage. I don't wan' any of this anymore," and he drunkenly swung his arm in a half circle.

'You can't be serious, Pete. We can get through this."

"Nope, not a chance" He said, slobbering.

I was numb. Laws had been broken. Obviously there was no money. How would we survive?

Somehow I managed to return to Tyler's lacrosse field. I pulled close to where Tyler's friend's mother stood.

"Mari, what's happened?" she asked, covering her mouth, sensing my alarm.

"Please take Tyler home with you. Please, Sally, don't ask me anything. I can't talk about anything right now."

I reversed and drove, unseeing, through residential streets. *Where could I go? Who could help me?* I wanted to call Mama, but I hadn't talked with her in years. *What could she do, anyway?*

I needed sleep. Maybe if I could sleep, I'd find this had all been a nightmare.

Back home, Pete's car was absent from its place in our driveway. Goodness, where was he? (Knowing it was anything but goodness.) He was so drunk. *Where could he have gone?*

My mind couldn't consider another thing. I dragged myself upstairs. I'd be able to sort through this after I slept.

It was dark when I awakened. My door bell had been ringing for a long time. *Why had I been napping anyway?*

I stumbled downstairs in a sleep-induced stupor.

"Mrs. McGuire? Police. There's been an accident—"

Pete had been taken to Midtown Memorial hospital: dead on arrival. I stood in its emergency room, dressed only in my robe. The room grew dark and close. My vision faded. A buzzing in my ears prevented my hearing what these people were saying.

Smelling-salts and questioning nurses focused me.

"Who can be called? Which funeral home will arrange for his body?"

That was nearly a month ago.

Newspapers had been mercifully brief about his accident. Thankfully no one else was hurt. Tyler and I survived his funeral.

I needed to meet with our attorney to go through papers. Our house is to be auctioned at the end of next week. We still have no place to live.

How could episodes of my life have brought me to this point? I review the path my life had taken.

Plans for my young life, as ordered by my parents, would include my being a polished coed at a fine university, hold a Tri-Delta sorority legacy and according to Daddy, find a suitable husband. It was still customary among prominent Mississippi families for a young lady to be presented to society as a debutante. After which, she'd attend a women's junior college, as a kind of finishing school, and acquire a degree if she had not found an acceptable marriage partner, approved by her father and her community. She'd then be a charming wife and behind the scenes support for her future business executive, health professional, law firm partner, or political figure her husband would certainly become.

My father was a man of investments, having been on the boards of several banks in New Orleans. My family had moved inland into Mississippi, after my birth, to escape bad influences which had seemingly taken over that city. In Mississippi, Daddy had established several bank branches. He was also close to Memphis, near his political contacts.

I'd been sent to a girls Episcopalian prep school near Nashville. I'd made my social debut in N' Orleans, which my mother had decreed was essential for my being included in proper society. After attending a small women's college, I transferred to University of North Carolina my junior year.

My father was disappointed with that choice. His first choice for me was 'Ole Miss or maybe Baylor or Auburn. Sons of his business colleagues were attending each of these.

"Some interesting matches could be made." He sparkled.

When I countered I wanted to marry for love, he growled and laughed crustily.

"Oh, yes, I forgot. Lo-o-ve! Just remember, Honey, I love you and I've provided well for my girl. It's a manner to which you've become accustomed." He dramatically drew out his syllables with his deep southern drawl.

Mother interrupted, having heard our conversation from the hallway. Sensing the direction of our discussion, she waved me out.

"Come, Ma Cherie, your papa just wants you to be happy." She pinched my cheeks. "Let's drive to Memphis, and go shopping. I heard about a darling little boutique with some precious things, por tu, Ma Cherie."

It was understood I'd marry someone with money—Old Southern money. This meant status as well as actual money, itself. Au contraire, I'd met and fallen in love with a young man who was an accounting major; a whirlwind romance.

When I introduced him to my family, my father stubbornly refused to see me again if I married him. I considered him to be bright, promising and handsome, but his family was without social standing. He was also a Yankee. In reaction, we eloped and moved to Baltimore after graduation. It was my life. I wanted to be in control.

I did not see Daddy again. He died eight years ago, never having met his grandson, his namesake. I had not returned for his funeral. I was too ashamed.

He'd been right, you see. My choice of marriage partners had been a huge mistake. To call our relationship rocky was an understatement. I was determined not to let anyone guess the biggest mistake I'd ever made.

My grandmother once said about marriage, "You make your bed and you lie in it."

Well, I'd done that. Was that right?

I stayed in my marriage because, why? Because I loved Tyler and I didn't want him raised in a broken home. I loved my home, even without my husband most of the time.

Alone, I made most decisions, to cover for my husband's lapses. I made things look perfect, to justify my decision to marry Pete. I'd make this marriage work. That would become my mantra.

I had not been employed outside my home. Pete had wanted me at home, especially after Tyler's birth. I enjoyed being at home.

We'd moved from a small townhouse near Johns Hopkins main campus to a second home in Homeland. Several years ago, I'd embraced the restoration of our huge, federal-styled home in Guilford.

We loved this city. Problematic areas surrounding our community were of no concern to me or Pete. We had a lovely house for entertaining and enjoying. The city was exciting. My days were filled with volunteering at Baltimore Art Museum, being on planning committees for charity events at Meyerhoff Symphony Hall,

Lyric Opera House and Center Stage Theater. I'd also been active in Tyler's Hilton Academy since he started pre-first. I'd cared for our house and coordinated Tyler's school, sports, camps and extra-curricular activities, and our family's social calendar. It was a good life, as long as we all kept busy, blindly busy.

Life had moved along rather uneventfully for years. Then problems beneath the surface began to rise to the top, bubbling more furiously each day.

I knew my marriage had been dead for years. There had been other women, especially on business trips. I remember finding panties in his suitcase after returning from one such business trip. My stomach wrenched. My father's voice replayed.

"Mark my words, you'll be sorry if you marry that loser."

My pride won out. I simply threw that evidence in the trash and held my head high. I'd make this thing work if it was the last thing I'd do.

At least, our marriage appeared made-in-heaven, though—to final minutes of his funeral. Yes, we'd been living a lie. Just like my husband's eulogy: . . . good father . . . loving husband. . . upstanding in the community and his company."

I guess being a widow was better than being divorced.

Who was I kidding? The walls had come crashing down, and I didn't know the half of it, I feared.

For this past month, I could hardly function. Pete's death left us in shock; numb with the reality of it. I'd barely completed daily routines. Mostly, with Tyler at school, I sat in my dark curtain-drawn living room contemplating my never-ending nightmare. I should've been packing boxes, but I could not. It was all beyond my energy. I simply could not focus my concentration.

Well, tonight, at least, I'd found a place to start. Somehow, when I prayed with those women who had no idea of my circumstances, I felt hope.

I heard tragic stories tonight. It'd been sadly comfortable, though. Hearing that woman's awful story of betrayal helped me see I wasn't alone. Others had disappointments, too. Gloria helped me feel safe with my shame—safe among strangers. I'd found a haven, of sorts, among friends.

Now, I'd face Tyler, with his share of anger. If as an adult, I could not make sense of this mess I called life, how could a 17-year-old?

Thankfully his school was paid through first semester. Could he graduate, though? Would Hilton Academy give us a break for the rest of this year? For all the tuition we'd paid over these last twelve years, I would hope so.

Tyler's dream had been to apply to Princeton for early acceptance next year. He was an excellent student, and captain of his lacrosse team. He deserved a chance, didn't he? How could I think of Princeton, for Pete's sake, when after this month, we'd have no place to live?

Maybe our lawyer and accountant knew something I didn't. I hoped. I had an appointment with our lawyer tomorrow. Joy.

I had not even met this man. My husband had always taken care of legal and financial aspects of our life. I'd trusted his judgment. After all, he was the accountant.

Finances had never been of interest to me. Tomorrow I'd be forced to look at those dismal facts. I didn't want to know facts.

There was a temptation to escape—to run somewhere, anywhere. I had not been a drinker, having watched Pete ruin his life, mine and Tyler's. That type of escape was not something I could even consider. My doctor had offered a prescription for anti-depressants and sleeping pills. I refused. I had to be in control for Tyler. Neither medications, nor alcohol, could be an option for me.

I'd witnessed an acquaintance go downhill rapidly with medication prescribed to ease peri-menopause symptoms. Her dependence had escalated, and eventually, she was committed to a drug rehabilitation facility, according to some. She simply could not stop, with her need increasing for more and more. Tragic. No one spoke of it, really, but when her name was mentioned in conversation, eyebrows raised and heads shook from side to side. We all realized, "There go I but by the grace of God."

No, Mama had taught me to be strong. I would survive. I'd heard stories of my ancestors, weathering epidemic illnesses like yellow fever and cholera in New Orleans, standing firm with loss of husbands, and sons, as well as property, during the Civil War and before. My widowed grandmother had held it together during The Great Depression in 1929. My own mother had been strong, with the sudden loss of my baby sister. "Be poised in face of adversity." That was our rule—our unwritten commandment.

What was poised, anyway? It was standing tall with chin held high. It was facing life's mountains and valleys with strength and determination. That was what being a Southern Lady was about, *right?*

How was I going to do that, exactly? But what choice did I have? I needed to care for Tyler. I'd focus my energy on him and his dreams, as I had since he'd been born. His well-being was priority.

Maybe Gloria could identify some avenues for housing. Perhaps Pete's life insurance policy would help, or money we'd get from selling our house. Something had to come through.

I started my car, backed out of the lot, and swiped at a tear which had dropped onto my cheek.

"I also tried to find meaning in building huge homes for myself and by planting beautiful vineyards. . . But this too was meaningless—like chasing after the wind;"
Ecclesiastes 2:4, 11 (Bible, TLB)

Sam the Sham

Ruth

Walking quickly to the parking lot, I was surprised it had gotten so cold. I shivered, and pulled my sweater close. For weeks, I'd avoided any news reports, even weather broadcasts.

Not since Sam's confession.

I tried to digest all I'd heard tonight: so much pain. My heart just broke to see those women melt down and share their accounts. My situation was still worse than any other story I heard tonight, but pain was pain. Nothing any of us could do. We were all in the same boat, I guess.

My mind jumped from tonight to memories of my own heart break. Incredulous, still, as I recall that day.

My husband, Sam, had asked if Sam, Jr. might be occupied elsewhere. Noting his apparent stress, I assured him Sam, Jr. was playing with neighborhood children. We could speak openly. I could see his straining to speak.

"Ruth, I must confess something. It's probably the hardest thing I've ever had to do."

Was he ill? Had someone died?

He continued. There had been an indiscretion. He'd been unfaithful, not with another woman, but in a homosexual affair he'd been so careful to hide. It had leaked to media. Now known by his church elders, it necessitated his tendering his resignation immediately. He understood I'd be upset, and he hoped at some point I could forgive him. I was not to worry, as he intended to leave.

I replayed his words without responding. Time stood still. I couldn't grasp his meaning.

When his actual implication suddenly dawned in my stunned mind, I screamed. The rest is a blur. I remember throwing one of Sam, Junior's *G.I. Joe* figures, as if his toy soldier could fight for me, somehow.

He walked out and drove away. *Who knew where?* I didn't care.

I'd called a neighbor boy's mother. Could she keep Sam, Jr. for the night?

Emergency.

I locked myself in our bathroom and heaved for what seemed like hours. In between episodes, I lay on bare tile, cooling my hot face.

I wanted to talk to Mom, but she and Dad were in China and unreachable by phone. This was NOT the kind of news I could paragraph in a letter.

Surely, I must've misunderstood what Sam said. But, no, I wouldn't have ever imagined anything like this.

How could he have betrayed me so thoughtlessly? It was one thing to be unfaithful with another woman. That would've been terrible enough, but to have had an affair with a *man*?

I studied myself in my full-length mirror, wondering if I was such an awful wife that my husband was attracted to a man over me. I'd never refused sex. *Was it because I'd put on weight over the years?*

I hugged my toilet and heaved again. The pictures in my mind were nauseating.

My thoughts drifted to my health. Could I have HIV or some other deadly disease he could've given me—something which could shorten my life—my life as little Sam's mother?

I remember screaming, "I wish I were dead. God, where are you? How could you let him do this to me and little Sam?"

The next days—or maybe weeks—blurred. I refused any newspapers to enter our home, or TV. I had to protect Sam, Jr. He was too young to know any of this. How could he understand? *How could I?*

I knew we shouldn't have come to Baltimore. If we'd stayed in Iowa this wouldn't have happened.

I loved Sam so much. I would've done anything to please him. The only time I'd ever fought any of his decisions was when he'd announced he'd been called to a new location. A new flock, he said. I'd bristled when he mentioned Baltimore.

My family was in Iowa. Sam, Jr. was close to his grandparents and cousins. I wanted our life to stay the same. I knew the final decision was his. It was his work and his call, but I felt it was all wrong, from the beginning. Sam was dead set on an immediate move from Iowa, though.

We'd been so happy in Iowa. That's where we received Sam, Jr.

We'd been childless for years, but happily we were able to adopt little Sam when he was 18 months old. After a year of what seemed an endless stream of red tape, we became parents. I thought that our trials of home studies, worrying about state approval, and its endless paper work, had brought us closer.

At least I'd been happy.

I'll never forget that precious blond toddler in short pants who came complete with Pooh bear and pacifier. I smile when I recall those adorable chubby legs. It had been a wonderful year.

Then Sam started traveling to Baltimore. I couldn't guess why he'd ever choose a big city, back East. He said

God called him to this particular congregation. I begged him to reconsider. I had no peace about this move at all.

It was a step up, he assured me. A bigger congregation would mean more money to give Sam, Jr. what he needed. I'd see. Things would be better.

I refused to go, at first. I'd miss my family and friends. I'd miss our small congregation with which I'd become so close. They were family. We'd shared so much. I believed their prayers brought Sam, Jr. to our home.

Why this urgent move? God had not spoken to me about this whole thing. I finally gave in, reluctantly.

Our decision seemed to be a catalyst setting an irreversible chain reaction into motion. In days, my home and garden belonged to someone else. Mom and Dad took a missionary position and moved across the world to China, of all places. My only sister vacated her house across our street and was packing a moving van for Kansas. We'd attended our farewell party at church, and our friends had gone on with their daily tasks, without us.

All chances of staying or returning were gone. All doors once open for me to change my mind and remain with family were closed. I must go. No more options. My hands were tied. I felt numb, as if a backhoe had scooped up everything I held dear and dropped me into a life in another world, so foreign to me in every respect.

We were given a small town-house in Rodgers Forge as our manse. It was OK, but I missed our little Iowa house. There I could see for miles out my kitchen window. I had a flower garden and raised vegetables, and my neighbor taught me to can and preserve. Sam, Jr. could play safely outside for hours. There was no crime and we trusted everyone.

All gone. Even after five years, I missed it all so much. Tears slid toward my nose, recalling it.

My mind shot back to years before that. I smile as I recall meeting Sam at college.

He was the most handsome man I'd ever seen. He dressed smartly, and had the most gorgeous smile. He had a sense of direction for his life, making him seem wiser than his years.

He was an upperclassman when I met him in Speech class. I was amazed he even noticed me. I'd always considered myself to be a plain Jane, but he walked me to my dorm and we shared lunch daily. He was my first serious boyfriend, and by the end of my sophomore year, upon his graduation, we married.

Things were so happy then. *What happened? I thought Sam loved me.*

Hadn't I tried to be a good wife and mother? I'd been faithful, I'd taken care of our son, and home-schooled. I sensed his destiny.

I volunteered for everything at church, from singing solos to directing cars from its parking lot, and a whole lot more, besides. I thought if I worked really hard helping him with his dreams of eventually administering a mega-church—if I did everything to help him succeed, he'd love me more. The only real dreams I had were for Sam and me to have a perfect marriage—be a perfect couple—create a perfect dream.

I loved him.

*"I even {tried to} find pleasure in hard work, a reward for
all my labors.
But as I looked at everything I had worked so hard to accomplish,
it was all so meaningless—like chasing after the wind."
Ecclesiastes 2:10-11 (Bible, TLB)*

Woodstock Revisited or Life at the Kibbutz

Sarah

I drag myself to my old Volvo station wagon, rusted and badly in need of repair. I hope it'd make it—for how long? Forever: that's about as long as I needed it to last. *How could I make it?* Like my car, I'm in need of repair and updating—I guess Joel thought so.

I'm so tired.

I started working at the health food store about three years ago, just because it looked like fun—just because I loved to cook, not because I needed money.

My husband was a fully-tenured professor at Johns Hopkins. His area of concentration was Israeli history. Some said no one knew more and cared more about that subject than Joel. He was passionate about it, and it was contagious.

That's what brought us together. I'd been attending Boston College, and he'd been pursuing his doctorate at Harvard.

I was young, and it was the late 60's: time of anti-war demonstrations, communes, burning bras, free love, Jimmy Hendrix and Janice Joplin. It was a passionate time in our country then—a "Purple Haze", if you will.

Joel and I'd met at a rally. He'd spoken about his love for Israel. He still spoke of her great victory in 1967, when Israel was victorious against her enemies, against all odds. A modern-day miracle no one could deny.

He'd never actually been there, although it was his aspiration. He'd been raised in a reformed Jewish home in the Bronx, but his dream was Israel.

I'd been raised in a middle-class, close-knit family in upstate New York, not far from Massachusetts. It was a small community near the Catskills. We were close to friends and neighbors.

We belonged to a small Congregational Church, but were not what you'd call devout by any stretch. It was simply what you did as a part of our community. Church was the center—the hub of the wheel, so to speak. Life centered there—socials, baptisms, funerals, picnics, dances, day-camp, whatever. It was our town—life in a small town.

I'd grown restless in middle school. I'd read about anti-war demonstrations, civil rights struggles, and big concerts like Woodstock, in school copies of <u>Time</u> and <u>Newsweek.</u> My dream was to leave this place—to see the world, because the world was not happening here.

I'd gone to school with the same kids and known the same people (those who had known my grandmother's second cousin's nephew, or whatever), since I'd been born. I was bored with it. A huge world was waiting to be experienced, and I could not wait.

I dreamed of enrolling in a big city college—maybe New York or Washington or Boston, but, to be sure, it'd be a big city. There'd be lots to do, things to learn, places to go, and parties to attend.

A phase, my family described it. My friends, as well as my sister, thought I was weird. That was OK. I'd leave and never come back. My goal was to leave this little town behind.

My grades were excellent. In fact, I'd been valedictorian of my senior class. Of course, there were only fifty of us. Still, the honor made my parents proud. It made other kids jealous, which was fine, too. I didn't care.

I won a full scholarship to Boston College. It was in the big city of Boston, and I was on my way. *Go Sox!*

When I met Joel, after his speech in Harvard square, I was barely twenty years old. I thought he was the most handsome man I'd ever seen. I adored his passion, and his zeal for Israel made him captivating. I knew nothing about Israel, except what I heard in Sunday school, which amounted to nearly nothing. But this man—I could not get him out of my mind.

Imagine my amazement when I discovered he was teaching a class at Boston College. I had to get into that class. I enrolled, and was bound and determined to read everything I could about Israel. I'd show him I could be passionate about Israel, too. And, he did notice me.

During summer break, he organized a two-month trip to Israel, where students would live in a kibbutz and see the REAL Israel. Of course, I had to go.

My parents were puzzled about this new interest. "Israel, of all places," they laughed.

My mother said only, "Please, be careful."

She told her friends and our relatives, "Just a phase."

The trip to Israel and our two-month stay were a dream adventure for me. Joel and I became more than friends. We decided not to return to our respective colleges, fall semester, but instead, stay and work at our kibbutz. He'd prepare to be an Israeli soldier. It did not matter that I was not Jewish. I caught the fever and excitement for all that was happening in this new, blossoming country.

Although most of its inhabitants were Jewish, they were not necessarily religious Jews. Since I was not a religious non-Jew, our passion was shared for this country, not for the God of Israel.

That year brought hard work, long hours and romance for Joel and me. We were married at our kibbutz, without benefit of family on either side or clergy.

Needless to say, neither family was happy about this arrangement. My parents were appalled that their daughter had not at least asked for their blessing; and married outside a church, in a kibbutz, no less? What kind of marriage was that—to a Jewish man from the Bronx? What could the two of them have in common?

That would be a question which would come back to bite me.

Joel's family was heartbroken, refusing to even see me, for years. His father even threatened to disown him, upon our return from Israel—even contemplating a funeral for their 'dead' son. His mother could not go that far. She loved her only son, married to a non-Jew or not.

However, the way we looked when we returned was not a welcome sight to any traditional family, Jewish or not. We wore heads of long untamed hair. Joel had a full beard, and we dressed in Israeli military fatigues from our two-year stay.

Joel finished his doctorate and I left college, two years before graduation, with the birth of our daughter.

Now when I look at pictures, with our daughter, Becky, we giggle. It was serious then, though. We were in love with each other, with our adventure and with the passion of those radical times.

Becky brought such happiness for us. Her birth united our extended families—not without conflict, however. All agreed, reluctantly, peace was best for our little Rebecca. She'd have the best of everything as the only grandchild then, and would ever be, for both families.

Joel's first assignment was a full professorship at Johns Hopkins University. Neither of us knew anything about Baltimore. It was a big city. That was all I needed to know.

His family was concerned as to whether there was a strong Jewish community. I heard the first American synagogue was built there. Certainly that must show there's a strong Jewish community.

I'd never converted, and didn't see the point in it, since both of us were avowed agnostics. We struck a compromise: we'd live in a mixed community of Mt. Washington, where Jews and non-Jews lived and worked peacefully among themselves. When his parents visited, we celebrated with Jewish customs and a Kosher table. When my parents came, we swung to a Christian theme and cuisine. It didn't really matter. For Rebecca, we were all united toward peace.

As Becky grew, she had the best education we could afford. In preschool, she was enrolled in Montessori School, with Suzuki Violin, piano, and ballet. Since elementary school, she'd attended Country Day School, where students of diverse backgrounds were enrolled. It offered a liberal learning environment, and was considered by many as academically challenging. It'd certainly help her to be accepted at her daddy's alma mater, Harvard.

We were so proud of Becky. She was our joy. She was an excellent student, active in school politics, student council president her freshman year, and outspoken in issues of the environment and civil rights, as her father had been before her. The grandparents on both sides adored her.

I'd been a stay-at-home mother. I coordinated all extra-curricular activities of an a busy young lady—sports, dance, whatever, and of course, clothes—buying what was needed or current for all occasions.

I prided myself in gourmet cooking. I'd mastered Kosher cuisine, but loved international cooking and natural foods, which I'd learned to prepare in Israel. I had a small garden in my Mt. Washington yard, where I grew whatever small vegetables I could. I dried veggies and herbs throughout the year. Cooking was my passion.

In addition to our already decent-sized house, I designed an addition just for my kitchen. It included a large window wall with boxes to grow fresh herbs in year-round sunshine. My orange, French Le Creuset pots hung decoratively over a large island. I even had a hearth where I could roast meats on a rotisserie.

I dreamed of having my own TV cooking show. It was fun dreaming, but I was much too shy for something like that.

As Rebecca became busy with school and extra-curricular activities, and Joel was constantly gone with cross-country teaching assignments, (I rarely saw him without a suitcase) I decided to take a part-time job at a nearby health food store. I could get the best gourmet items from all over the world, but especially the Middle East. I could order goat's milk yogurt and hummus, as well as figs, dates or imported olives—anything I could imagine. As an employee, I could make sure our store offered the best.

By age of forty, I rarely saw my husband. I noticed he was distracted when he was home, more often than not; jet-lag, of course. It had to be. Besides, Joel had always been moody. He was a passionate man. Ups and downs were part of that type of personality. One couldn't be up all the time, right? Some distance just came with familiarity in a long marriage, I'd concluded.

I had noticed questionable expenses on Visa statements, and multiple calls to Israel on phone bills. Israel was his job, of course; nothing unusual about that, right? Sometimes I did wonder about inconsistencies, but I chose more important and happy things to focus on.

We were, for all intents and purposes, happy, I thought. I was happy. Rebecca was happy. The grandparents were happy. It was all well and very well.

Now I see I'd been oblivious to glaring signs of our disintegrating relationship. Who knew for how long? After a few weeks back in Israel, where Joel had taken a few-month sabbatical, his love and excitement rekindled, as it had in our early months in that kibbutz. He'd returned to his first love, his real love.

In a November letter, he'd penned news of not being able to return in December. Research responsibilities would keep him a few more months. Then he'd be back.

Late spring, we received a final letter from Joel. He intended to resign from his professorship to remain in Israel. Although older than most, their armed forces could still use him in their military. He described the excitement of his espionage position.

His other excitement was his lovely assistant, a young Israeli officer, who shared his love for Israel. He would not be coming home. *Please tell Rebecca her Daddy loves her. I love you, too, but I must ask you for a divorce. Clearly my life is here with Katura. You understand my passion for Israel. Thank you for all the years. PS. You can keep the house and car.*

Thank you for all the years? Is that all he could say? I had a daughter I'd now be providing for myself, private-school tuition, and future college costs, and I was only an at-home Mom.

My two years at Boston College didn't amount to anything employable. I'd been a political science major. Not a whole lot of demand for that, for goodness sake. Now I had a mortgage, an old car, a 15-year-old daughter and a part-time job at a health food store. Plus, I had to begin divorce proceedings with almost no savings.

I called both sets of flabbergasted parents. Even his own parents, never having been keen on our marriage in the first place, were astounded by their son's irresponsibility. No, they had not heard a word from Joel.

They extended an invitation for Becky and me to stay with them. We could share their spare-room bed and take care of their house when they vacationed in Florida. After that, extended family could put us up, somewhere. Perhaps Aunt Ethel and Uncle Sol would have room. Then again, their only son recently moved back with his full-sized pool table. Not to worry. Something would come up. Maybe I could help out at their deli.

My parents were equally shocked. Daddy bellowed, recalling his warning to me about Joel from the beginning. He'd give him a piece of his mind for deserting his baby girl. Mom called him a cad (whatever that meant. Given her emotional tone, it must be bad—*go Mom!*)

She told me to pack our things and come home. We could squeeze in their guest room. Somehow they'd rearrange boxes of memorabilia, out-of-season clothes, ski equipment, tennis rackets, a mini-tramp, (good for her arthritis, you know), some gardening tools,(hand-driven and motorized), Dad's new treadmill and a fake Christmas tree, complete with assorted decorations stored in there. Oh, and also an old freezer, she remembered.

Both sets of parents were retired, and in failing health. Neither could help financially. Both of them ached for Rebecca.

To live in New York would be more expensive than Baltimore, and still, I had no job skills. Even though

I loved to cook, working at a deli was not something I relished doing, nor did I want to live with Aunt Ethel.

If I went home, it'd be less expensive, for sure. I could live in my family house, but where would they store all that stuff now housed in that junk room? My mind pictured all that filled their room. *How in the world did they get all that in one room, anyway?* Still, the question remained: where would I work?

I'd have to take Rebecca out of school at a critical time in her education. If we had no money, what did it matter? It mattered because one of us had to have a career. I'd sacrificed my education for my husband. Rebecca shouldn't have to, though.

So unfair. *How could he do this?*

Joel was passionate, all right. He was also crazy. What's a 50-something man doing fighting in the Israeli army doing espionage, with a soon-to-be, 16-year-old daughter at home? It made no sense at all. Again, though, it did. He was the same, hot-headed man he'd always been.

I'd been passionate once, when I met him, but mine was fueled by his. Left to my own devices, I was the happy, down-to-earth, country girl who'd grown out of her adolescent hormones, thank goodness. Yes, more sophisticated. Yes, more educated and worldly, but content to be at home, being a mom, as my mother had been—happy in my garden and in my kitchen. *But I still loved my husband.*

Both of us had decided to settle in Baltimore. We'd been married for eighteen years. He'd been happy, hadn't he? He said he was happy. He loved his work. He loved Baltimore. He loved his family. He loved Rebecca.

How could he do this to me, to Rebecca, to his family? Just desert us, for what... the Israeli army?

I was trying to keep up with bills, by taking another job as a waitress at *Morgan* and *Millard*, but it was not enough. What could I do?

If I didn't pay our $1500/ month mortgage payment, our bank would foreclose. I knew that much. Plus, I had utilities to pay. I could take a loan out for Country Day, but I shudder to think how much $15,000 for two years, plus expenses could be at 7% interest, variable, at a minimum.

Joel hadn't died, so there was no life insurance. There might be some retirement from his years of teaching at Johns Hopkins, but there'd be a severe penalty for withdrawing funds now. Were there any stocks or mutual funds? *Who knew?*

If I sold our house, what could I get for it? It'd be good if I could get enough to pay for the last two years at Country Day, but where would we live? How could we eat? What about our other bills?

I might be able to get the health food store owner to sell me food at wholesale prices, especially if I'd agree to work longer hours. I could work for food. I could creatively budget my food costs, since it was only Rebecca and me. I could eat at work. We would at least eat, but food costs were not all I had to budget, sadly. I looked at my car again.

It's now been twenty weeks. I have not heard from Joel. He could at least send child support—certainly the

Israeli army gave him some compensation for his work. But how could I have legal recourse when he was residing on a kibbutz in the middle of nowhere? It's just best I forget Joel, altogether.

I was tired, though. I'd been working seven days a week, and had barely seen Rebecca. In passing, I'd noticed she'd lost weight.

Becky was not a heavy child, and to lose weight when she needed it during a key growth period could not be good. She needed counseling, I conceded. Rebecca missed her Daddy, and didn't understand. I didn't understand, I missed him, and I needed counseling, too. No money, no time.

I stopped my car, and let tears fall.

I had to stop. I must go home to Rebecca, and I couldn't let her see me cry. I had to be strong. But . . . I . . .am. . . so. . . tired.

Having gone to this group tonight was a help. I don't know what possessed me to even go. I just happened onto a flyer as I passed a community bulletin board outside the restaurant, next to that real estate office. Its pink paper attracted my attention and sparked my interest. It offered hope, with the words: Help, Housing, Job training, Displaced, Widowhood, Divorced.

Maybe I should go. Maybe I could get some ideas. Maybe I could get help.

It was at Our Lady of Grace College, though. I wondered if you had to be Catholic to go. But how many Catholics are divorced anyway? I didn't know, but it used to be, when I was in college, if you were Catholic and divorced, you couldn't be a member of their church anymore, right? But I didn't know. I was not Catholic and did not know anyone who was. I didn't know anyone who even went to any church, for that matter.

Maybe things had changed. Maybe it didn't matter anymore. Maybe it'd be OK if I went. What's the worst thing that could happen? Maybe someone would invite me to classes to become Catholic. I could politely refuse. But could they refuse to give me help? I was as needy as anyone, right now. Certainly, they would not refuse me because I was not Catholic.

And they hadn't. In fact, it wasn't clear whether anyone there was Catholic. Gloria had been raised Catholic, she said, but was now Protestant. The divorce, I guess. But she was holding this meeting in a Catholic college, so there must not be any hard feelings from her side or that of the college, obviously.

They'd been kind. In fact, I felt welcomed. Gloria seemed to be so genuine all three times I'd seen her.

Three: I tried to recall from Sunday school, didn't three have significance in the Bible? I couldn't remember. Do you think God planned for me to meet Gloria? But wait, I don't believe in God. But maybe I do, but I don't understand it. But why would God let this happen? But... what had I done for God, anyway? I'd denied he existed for years. If I ignored him, perhaps he was ignoring me, in return.

Silly banter; I think I'm cracking up.

Whatever. I think I'll call Gloria. Ruth was sweet, too. She really seemed like she cared, and she didn't even know me. She obviously had problems, too, or she wouldn't have been there, right? Maybe Gloria could offer solutions for my house. . . my jobs. . .my daughter.

Maybe she'd pray for me—again.

"I said to myself: let's try pleasure. Let's look to the good things in life. But I found that this, too, was meaningless. . . What good does it do to seek only pleasure?"
Ecclesiastes 2:1-2 (Bible, TLB)

Don Juan—NOT

Katie

"Hey, Sweetheart—did my boy have fun tonight?"

Timmy padded toward me; his tired eyes were circled, his thumb in his mouth and his tattered blanket, or what was left of it (also tired) was in his left fist.

"Did you have fun with these nice ladies?"

One of the students dropped to one knee and softly inquired,

'Timmy? You had a good time tonight, didn't you? We played with blocks, read stories, and had juice and crackers, Mrs. Ward. He seemed tired, but it's late for a 3-year- old. Next time, I'll have cots out, so he can rest. Will you be returning next week?"

I scooped Timmy in my arms and drew his little head close to mine,

"Of course, we wouldn't miss it for anything. You want to come back and see Megan and Jessica, don't you, Darling?"

I couldn't tell them that, lately, the only time he slept or I slept was when he was snuggled beside me. No, I couldn't say that.

Timmy sucked harder on his thumb. He rested his head on my shoulder, twirling my hair.

I smiled at these students. I must act like everything's fine at home. Everything's fine with Timmy. Of course, I am an attentive, responsible mother. It's what I wanted to be, needed to be, tried to be—that's for sure. Could these students sense differently?

"He's tired. We'll see you next week, OK?"

Megan and Jessica chorused, "Night, Timmy, see you next week."

"Can you say goodnight to these nice ladies, Timmy?"

He weakly raised his fist and blanket scrap, and mumbled, "Night."

Ambling as fast as I could with a 35-pound child, I made my way down the dark sidewalk to the parking lot. An uneasy feeling replaced the almost happiness I felt only minutes ago.

To be out of my house and in a safe place with other women who cared for one another was freedom—almost like my college sorority. It felt like a lifetime ago since I had friends, since I could be carefree, since I had dreams.

Waving tree branches shadowed by moonlight, gave an eerie backdrop to my jangled emotions. I held Timmy close to my chest, as I checked from side to side. It was OK. I was alone.

Although no other cars remained in this lot, I could see Gloria leave a house across the street. She was talking with someone. If I could get Timmy strapped into his car seat quickly, maybe I could leave behind her.

I kept my keys close at hand, in my warm-up jacket pocket, as was my practice, lately. Just in case I had to get away quickly. A small suitcase for me and Timmy were hidden in my trunk, just in case. It was hard for me to acknowledge the peril that could erupt at any time. I must be prepared, and cautious. For Timmy's sake, I must be alert at all times.

"Timmy, help Mommy with your car seat. Lift up your arms under the straps, Dear, please."

Timmy began to cry. He hated his car seat. He needed to be asleep in his bed. Oh well. Nothing was as it should be, lately.

After strapping him securely, and draping him with a blanket I kept folded on my back seat, I climbed into the driver's side, barely settled, and quickly turned my key. I glanced to where I'd seen Gloria. Good. She was just getting into her car, probably to go home.

She obviously didn't live at this college or at that house across the street. I needed to follow her. I don't know where that thought came from, but it seemed like an urgent one; one I needed to heed.

I followed her car at a distance, at first, as I didn't want to frighten her. I just needed to know where she lived—just in case. I stopped at a red light at Charles and Cold Spring. Gloria's car turned right. I'd catch up to her.

I glanced in the back seat. *Bless his heart.* Timmy was already asleep, with his whistling breathing as music to my ears. It calmed my heart.

At the same time, I glanced further into the rearview mirror to make sure I was not being followed. I suspected Don was at his office, or wherever he went when he left our house, but I couldn't take a chance.

Since separation papers had been filed, I didn't know what to expect anymore, as if I ever did. I'd tried to be such a perfect mother and wife, but perfection was way out of sight, now, and had been for quite some time. Now, it was make do and survive.

I shouldn't even be staying in my house. It wasn't safe. But my older son, Jeremy, was there. He was only fourteen. I had to try to make his transition as easy as possible. After all he'd seen and experienced in his young life, I wanted to show him I loved him. The other reason I stayed was I simply had no place to go and no money.

I'd been a stay-at-home mom since I became pregnant with Jeremy. Don had wanted that. Although I'd been a dental hygienist, and he, a periodontist, he said my place was in our home. He'd manage our practice.

OUR practice. . .right. What a joke. He'd told me close to eighteen months ago, well before talk of legal separation, he and his staff had voted me out of our practice. Locks were changed so I could not go in.

I was shocked. Could someone do that to a wife of eighteen years? Well, whether or not, he and they had done it. I suspect the other staff member who joined him in this action was more than a friend, or staff member, but I had no proof.

Things were getting bad. *Why had I been such an ostrich with my head in the sand for so long* ? Stupid, but it was for my children, for my marriage, and for our future. As I had come to realize now, it was in my dreams. I had no marriage or future, and at present, my safety was in question, as well.

After turning right onto Cold Spring, I could see Gloria's car ahead of me. I rubbed my hands together, glad that warm air had started to heat my car. Again, I checked Timmy to make sure he was covered.

Streets were empty, except for one obviously drunk man on that corner. I quickly checked my door locks. Although this area was safe, one could not be too sure. I'd thought my house was a place of safety and security.

That's the biggest fantasy I've ever invented. Yes, invented; too many Walt Disney stories at a young age. One must be careful of literature one allows children to read. A bitter laugh emanated from a place deep within me.

Okay, turn left onto Roland Avenue, down several blocks. I see Gloria slow and turn right, another right and enter an alley, presumably behind her house. Most houses in this north Baltimore area had an access alley behind them with a parking pad or small garage. I'd just stay until I saw which house lights went on. There she is, and that's her house.

Now, time to go home. I'd take a chance Don would not be there. He was rarely home at this hour. Usually, I could count on his being home for dinner, and then he'd nap for a half hour or so.

He slept so soundly, even when our kids were making noise; it was as if he was hearing-impaired. He'd then return to his office and stay until 2-3 a.m.

The only reason I knew his time of return is when our boys were babies, I'd be feeding them about this time. Often, he'd just walk passed me as if he didn't see me, climb into bed and pass out. He'd have no recollection of when he returned or what he'd done, apparently. At least he never answered any of my questions.

If he were home, tonight, it'd be a bad sign. Something was out of pattern. When he was out of his routine, he paced the floor a lot, looked anxious, and usually left— a good thing. Sometimes, he'd scream at Jeremy, unmercifully.

If I went to Jeremy's defense, he'd sometimes strike me. He kept saying I asked for it for making him so mad.

This didn't happen often, so sometimes I could forget it'd ever happened. The first time he hit me was when I was pregnant with Jeremy. I was shocked. He said I asked for it. I remember replaying that incident over and over.

What could I have done to upset him so much? What could I have done differently?

I'd tried to change aspects of my personality I guessed might bother him, but found if I just stayed away as much as possible, with Jeremy's sports and school events, and preschool programs for Timmy, we could have a reasonable amount of peace—as long as he stayed at our office; where he gladly preferred being, anyway.

His mood swings had become more frequent and more intense, lately. Not long ago I was collecting dirty laundry from his closet, when I noticed plastic medication bottles hidden in shoes on a back shelf. I checked their labels: controlled substances—two read Vicodin, a third read Lomotil, a fourth read Valium, and the last, Percocet.

"Don, why are these in your closet? Are you taking all this medicine?" I questioned.

He forced his bottles from my hands.

"These are for backaches, headaches, and my nerves; good drugs. You stay away from them, you hear? "He squeezed my arm, tight enough to leave marks.

"Of course," I muttered.

He left our room in a huff and left our house, slamming our front door behind him.

Timmy cried, "I'm scared."

I soothed and rocked him. Once he quieted, I read his favorite book, Dr. Seuss's 500 Hats of Bartholomew Cubbins (which I felt, at that moment, I was trying to pile on my own head—or maybe I was trying to walk on 500 . . . no, more like 500,000 egg-shells without breaking any.)

I'd waited a couple of days, until Don's schedule normalized. After our boys were in bed, I checked the PDR (Physician's Desk Reference). I'd sneaked this old copy from the trash when his new one arrived last year—before he changed office locks. I carefully read about each drug I'd found. Each, by itself, was more than potentially addictive, psychologically and physically, after a short time of usage. One warned of side-effects which included hallucinations, paranoia, and anxiety.

I'd taken pharmacology in college. What was the potential effect of all of these together? How long had he been taking these pills? For years, I feared.

I closed my eyes and a chill crept over my entire body. That explained a lot—perhaps even his periodic, episodic violence, if you considered he'd used these meds for at least eight years. He'd visited so many different doctors for stress-related disorders for nerves, digestive issues, headaches and backaches, and who knew what else. He never shared any information with me about any of his appointments.

Had it been longer than that? Had it been since I'd been pregnant with Jeremy, when his violence started? The characteristic mood swings, the long hours by himself at his office, deep sleeps that could not even be aroused by a crying baby right next to his ears.

This was bad. But what could I do? I had a toddler to care for, and a teen to cater to. I had to be a good mother. I had to try to hold this family together, for all our sakes.

My Bible had been my solace after all the trouble in our home had escalated, since our separation. I needed help. I could trust no one with my secrets, but I knew my prayers were safe with God.

Don had not been a believer. After graduating from college, which was hardly a conservative Christian school, I was filled with curiosity for all kinds of religions. There had been representatives of Hare Krishna, Transcendental Meditation, Buddhism, Hinduism, and other less known spiritual groups, like Baha'i camped out on campus.

Although I'd been raised in a Methodist church, growing up outside of Raleigh, I could hardly call myself of that persuasion when I married Don. It didn't matter that he was an atheist, and Irish-Catholic (He saw no inconsistency with that—strange. I guess he and his family regarded Catholicism as a genetically-segregated club with life-time membership, rather than a belief system.)

I wanted to marry and have children. We were older when we met, and I was tired of being a bridesmaid and never a bride. Although he was not exactly what I dreamed of, our relationship was close enough, I reasoned. We had our future occupations in common. We could make it work.

He reasoned a successful dentist, especially a specialist, needed to have a wife and preferably 2.2 sons, or something like that, he said. A hygienist at home had to be good for business, right? He'd never have manpower issues with a hygienist at home.

After our second year, I realized we had big problems, but I was already expecting our first baby. That's when the abuse—physical that is—began. Verbal insults and unrelenting criticism seemed to begin almost the week after we returned from our honeymoon. I was shocked. He was always so polite and charming when we dated, and never got angry—or at least he covered it well.

I headed north on Roland Avenue, turned right onto Northern Parkway, left onto Charles, down winding streets and roads, home.

"Lord, please let him be away tonight," I whispered. Timmy and I really need a good night's sleep. I just can't deal with any changes tonight.

A good sign: our house was dark except for a light shining from Jeremy's room. I could hear rock music emanating from a slightly open window.

Good. Safe.

We could all sleep tonight.

A Reflective Perspective

Gloria

It was late, but I had to make notes about tonight's meeting, before details slipped my mind; specifically insights concerning Ruth, Katie, Sarah and M. Carroll, who seemed to be pivotal people. If this class continued, they'd likely hold positions of support. What about that woman who came and abruptly left? Odd.

I'm eager to get to know more about all these women in coming weeks—should they decide to return. If this program met the goals for which it was designed—but what were its real objectives? *What was the donor's original intent?* I wish I knew this donor. It would be nice to question him or her about their desired outcome for their financial outlay.

What had really happened tonight? I'd wanted to be professional, objective, sterile and matter of fact: a moderator, no more, no less. I did not want to be involved. I was doing this as a favor to Jules. My goal was to just get through that hour and get it behind me.

Instead, I felt excitement I hadn't dared feel in years. Rather than being overwhelmed, I felt motivated. A small flame lit inside me—like the pop when a match and gas ignite its pilot light on my ancient gas stove.

Now. . .what about next week?

Chapter 10

Good News...
And Bad News

Wednesday Morning

Gloria

"Hello?" I croak, trying to shield my eyes from bright, morning sunlight.

"Glory, you did it."

"Jules, did what?" I yawn hugely.

"This morning, I had voicemail messages saying how much they needed our program."

"How could they?" I yawn again, not trying to hide it. "I put lists out—for housing and training, but I haven't even looked at them. I did nothing for them."

Julia laughed, "Silly, you did what you do best. God works through you to love. That's your gift and your mission. It's time for you to come out of that cave you've been hiding in this last decade; time for God to use you—not as a Nun, but as a Nun-reject, a divorcee, a single mother, a friend. The wonderful friend you've been to me. Remember what Mother Superior told you? Your calling is not as a Nun, but service in life-trenches outside convent walls."

"No, you're the one who's silly. I don't know if I presented what was needed. I don't even know what I said, exactly."

"Well, this is the first of its kind, so there are no set expectations. You're a Columbus of this new world . . . Lewis and Clark of The Old West. Keep going. Five weeks left. Want to return to *Morgan* and *Millard* Saturday?"

"Yes. Want to go shopping, too? I desperately need winter clothes."

"Early lunch, then? See you at 11:30."

Wednesday

Ruth

My soft knock alerted a church elder to open their door.

A conference table was surrounded with men who'd been our friends, but their collective faces were not the welcoming ones I'd come to trust. Their grave expressions made me feel as if I were coming to trial.

Perhaps I was.

Wordless nods greeted me. Some wore sheepish expressions, as if fearing I'd overheard a comment outside their door.

I smiled and waved timidly. "Hi."

One of them pulled a chair for me, which I accepted. I couldn't stand by myself—I didn't trust my knees. After asking how I was holding up, and dismissing my OK, the spokesman announced that issues needed to be discussed:

They understood I must be as shocked as they'd been by Sam's news (Really? I hardly think they could've been as shocked as I, his wife, had been—pleeze.) His scandal had placed our church in an exceedingly vulnerable position. Some mentioned withdrawing their membership. Worse, some dialogued of a church split.

In view of an overwhelming desire to return to a stable position and rid themselves of all vestiges of my husband's term as pastor, these elders had voted to obtain an interim pastor as soon as one could be secured. Because of its severe drain on their church budget (after all, their most prominent families had threatened to withdraw and transfer memberships to other congregations), the church had voted on the future of the manse. It must be vacated as soon as possible for preparation for an interim pastor and his family.

All eyes slowly drifted toward me.

My jaw dropped. No words would emerge.

"Now we know you need time to find suitable living quarters and move your household. We'd be glad to help remove your belongings."

I stammered, as tears flowed freely, now.

"But where can I go? I have no job, I have no family here. I have a son. What can I do?"

The men lowered their heads and gazed at either the table top or tops of their fingernails.

"Are you saying because my husband has left his church, his wife and his son, that we are to be evicted from our home, even though we've done nothing to deserve this injustice?"

"Of course not," someone countered. "Ruth, we simply don't know what to do. We cannot afford to allow you to stay in that house when we expect another pastor and his family. Surely, you understand."

"How about a church's responsibility to care for needs of widows and orphans? I've worked hard in this church, as you know. I've taught your children in Sunday school. I've chaperoned your teens on retreats, camps and mission trips. I've cared for your crying infants in your nursery so you could go to services. Aren't I entitled to something?"

"Now, Ruth, we know how faithful you've been to our church. Your help has been invaluable. We all agree on that. However, technically, you are not a widow, and your son is not an orphan. We have no precedent for this type of situation. Nothing like this has ever happened. We'd like to help you both, certainly, but we don't dare ask our congregation for assistance. Our church is still in shock from your husband's admission. To continue to give you and your son aid, well, it might cause a great deal more dissension than we already have."

I could not contain my sobs.

Did any of these men consider how I must feel? They'd never been faced with a sudden loss of their homes, their spouses or their livelihood. I wanted my overwhelming pain to be heard and my desperation felt by each and every one of them. I wanted to rub it in so their guilt would keep them awake at night, like fear was doing to me.

A box of tissues was passed to me. I threw it back at them, a little more forcefully than I should have, perhaps.

"How can you do this to me?"

Silence reigned for what seemed a long time. Glancing from one person to another, the leader said, "Well, Ruth, it's getting late, and we have to get back to our families." His face reddened realizing his wording was not exactly the most diplomatic and changed his phrasing. "I mean, we need to leave. The committee and I will discuss your particular concerns and get back to you about details. Thank you for coming."

The room emptied. One neighbor, standing, said, apologetically, "Ruth, Jill and I are so sorry. I don't know what to do or say, really. Can I walk you to your car?"

I truly wanted to be alone, but this church building was no longer my home. I allowed him to assist me with my coat. My car seemed miles away.

Within minutes, I'd arrived home. When I was able, I gathered my son. Together, we descended one set of steps and up another, to our adjoining row-house—our present, but obviously temporary residence.

In bed that night, I curled in a fetal position: the only position possible for sleep. I wondered where I could go. I had no money. I was sure Sam had taken our savings for an attorney. My parents were in China. My only sister now resided in Kansas, but she had no room in her tiny bungalow.

I'd call Gloria. Certainly, she'd have other people to help but who did I have?

Hot tears flowed again. Would I ever be able to stop crying? It hurt to cry, but it hurt not to. I hugged myself.

Where were my friends? Where was God? Where was my husband, who promised before God and everybody to love, honor and cherish me? Is this what he called cherish?

Sunday

It's Sunday. I need the peace of church. I need to be in the company of people who care. Sam, Jr. can return to the normalcy of Sunday school. I'll feel better after this service.

I chose my usual seat—middle, on the left. I smiled at friends, but received disappointing responses. Some grabbed hymnals and studied musical notes. Some covered their faces with their bulletins, in an attempt to appear severely far-sighted.

Whispers. *Was my slip was showing? Had toilet paper stuck to my shoe?*

I was grateful for the solitude of my empty pew. As minutes elapsed, my row remained empty, although the rest of our sanctuary filled. I tried to concentrate on the organ prelude, as hushed comments reached my ears. I noticed some teens pointing, giggling. An older couple abruptly turned their heads, after glaring. The man shook his head, grimacing. His wife lifted her nose high.

Why was I being treated with such contempt? Sam's indiscretion was not mine.

One of the ushers approached, and looking from side to side, red-faced, whispered, "Wouldn't you be more comfortable in the back?"

Outrageous.

Fighting intense embarrassment, I grabbed my handbag, threw down my bulletin and walked back up the aisle, interrupting the choir processional. Heads turned and eyes followed.

Silence. The organist even stopped playing the opening hymn.

Although tears betrayed me, I held my head high and repeated what Mari Carroll had said, "It will be OK." I signaled to Sam, Jr.

His friends laughed as he slowly gathered his things. One boy actually pushed him toward the isle. Another boy—the choir director's son—actually kicked Sam from behind as he struggled to cross over extended stiffened legs blocking his passage. Another crumbled a bulletin and threw it at us as we stumbled toward the door.

Disgraceful. I will never set foot in this building again.

What had Sam done to us? Anger consumed me. I grabbed Sam, Junior's hand, a little more brusquely than I intended, and raced toward our car.

Sliding my key in the ignition, I hesitated. Where could we go? Not home, that's for sure. MacDonald's for breakfast? Yes. Sam, Jr. could enjoy its playroom.

Where did people go on Sunday mornings when they didn't go to church? Who knew? I'd heard jokes about finding God on the golf course. Other options had to be available. I hated golf.

My son sat teary-eyed in our back seat. Sniffling, "Mom, the kids said Daddy is a fag or something. What does that mean? Why is everyone mad at us?"

"Honey, I don't know exactly. Your daddy made a big mistake that hurt our church. We remind them of his hurt, I guess. It's hard for everyone."

How could Sam have done this to us? How could he?

As Sam, Jr. wandered through climbing tunnels, I grasped my cooled, bitter coffee, unconsciously tearing bits of Styrofoam from my cup's edge, numb.

Who could've imagined any of this? It was beyond imagination. After experiencing unspeakable pain, my church shuns me. How could people be so insensitive, after all I've done? How could they allow their children to be so hateful to Sam, Jr.? Insufferable lot.

Sam, Jr. ran from the play area with one of his neighborhood friends. His mother approached both boys at the same time.

Sam, Jr. asked, "Can Evan come play and stay for dinner?" Sam, Jr. bobbed.

The woman embraced her son, wordless and wide-eyed.

"Certainly, that would be fun." Sensing her hesitancy, I added, "Of course, I'd be with them all afternoon. He'd be well-supervised."

She shielded her other two sons, both of whom I'd taught in Sunday school, still wide-eyed. Silence awkwardly extended, pregnant with unexpressed meaning.

My face grew hot and my mouth dry. I gripped the table top for support.

"I understand," I stammered.

She gathered her brood, commanding, "Come, boys. We need to go, NOW."

I slid onto our bench, and dropped my face to my hands. It's one thing for me to face ostracism, but my son?

I felt as if she'd punched me in my solar plexus with all the force of a locomotive. *Didn't she remember all I'd done for her sons? Sunday after Sunday, wiping their noses and tying their shoes?*

So unfair.

How could I salvage my reputation if there was nothing I'd done to lose it, but be a wife of a wayward husband, who just happened to be her pastor or former pastor, as the case was? I had to distract Sam from his huge disappointment somehow, and conceal mine.

"Honey, have some French fries. You love fries."

He hung his head, silent and unmoving.

"I know, let's rent some movies. I'll pop popcorn. Doesn't that sound like fun?'

I grabbed our remaining food and paper, tossed it into the trash; witnessing our mess spiral downward, erratically.

Monday

We dozed, off and on, throughout the night, watching Disney classics over and over and over again. Neither of us realized we'd forgotten dinner. Food didn't matter.

Sunlight peeked through blinds now. Sam, Jr. needed breakfast, even if I didn't.

I padded into our kitchen in my nylon-stocking feet, still dressed in my skirt and blouse, crumpled from a night on the couch. Dull light from our refrigerator revealed dwindling rations.

I must conserve cash. I was unaware of our account balance. Sam had his checkbook, and I had mine: joint account, no income.

We needed to eat, though. Sam had that obligation. He needed to take responsibility for something. How to contact him was the question. His whereabouts were anyone's guess.

Phone rings jolted me.

"Hello?" I answered, my voice lacking its usual upbeat cheerfulness. I couldn't fake it this morning.

The male voice was that of a chosen representative from the elders. Sam's personal effects and related books and papers, had been boxed. Would I retrieve them? Things needed to be tidy for the interim pastor. Someone was being sent imminently, to rid memories and proceed toward a brighter future. You understand. Click.

This would be the last time I'd be returning, for sure. As it was early, few people would be there now. As soon as I changed clothes, I'd get this thing behind me.

Who would watch Sam? One little boy lived down the street who sometimes played with him. The family liked Sam, Jr.

They were strict about a natural life—no TV, no radios, no newspapers. Mother Earth types: very nice, actually, although I'd only spoken with them once or twice. Sam could probably visit while I trekked to church.

I hesitated and then smiled. Under the circumstances, they'd be a god-send. Unaware of media hype, and home-schooling, as well, their lack of current events actually offered safe haven for my boy, right now. They might welcome Sam, Jr. to play this morning. Sam, Jr. would be thrilled to be with someone his own age; someone other than Mom.

We walked to their house, finding the mother reaping wheat and corn in their postage stamp-sized yard. Word was she made bread and pasta from her gleanings It was also reported she used a harvester and other noisy farm equipment.

Where could they store all those things? No, couldn't be. Our houses hardly had closet room for out-of- season clothes.

I'd heard rumors of our community's largely ignoring this family, who relocated from the west, somewhere. Weird, was the word on the street. Some community residents wanted zoning restrictions for their unusual gardening.

Now, reflecting on gossip, I now considered their existence appealing. I felt an enormous amount of compassion for their rejection.

I hurried to the pastor's office for Sam's effects, as they'd been called. The secretary pointed toward three boxes.

She added, "Additional books are on that shelf, but since they don't interfere with the order of this office, you can get them later."

Yeah, right, I thought. This was my first and last trip, you can be assured.

After my returning for his last box, the secretary raised her eyes over her reading glasses. She stated, matter-of-factly. "How are things going with you and your son?"

I felt relieved. Someone actually cared enough to inquire.

"It's been rough, especially for Sam, Jr." I confessed.

She raised her nose in the direction of the ceiling,

"No doubt. Divorce is always hardest on children and yours is especially . . . public. Maybe you should've considered that earlier."

I dropped the box,

"What? How can you say that? This was not my idea, you know."

Raising her brows, she punctuated, "Well, you know what they say. If a wife does what she's supposed to at home, her man has no reason to wander."

"Are you saying this is my fault?" I asked.

How dare she imply such a thing. Was that the word that was spreading in gossip circles, or perhaps the prayer chain—which often seemed a justifiable label for tale-bearing in this particular church?

"Well...," she paused, "if the shoe fits." She lowered her head and purposely returned to typing on her Smith Corona electric.

Fighting tears, I lifted the box and headed for the door.

"Insufferable woman" I mumbled, stumbling down the hall.

Her words hit me hard. *Was this because I hadn't been a good wife?* I stormed toward my car.

"God, is this true? Where are you, God?"

"All who see me mock me. They hurl insults, shaking their heads."
Psalm 22:7 (Bible, NIV)

M. Carroll

I straightened my skirt, fastened my jacket and walked toward an elevator. With a ding, I filed into a small chrome space joining other information seekers. I avoided eye contact, focusing on floor numbers as they lit. To be invisible was my desire.

In another hour, this would be over. I just had to get through it. Hopefully, there'd be good news I could embrace.

The '12' lit, doors parted, and I squeezed between other oblivious occupants, whose eyes fixed on numbers and concerns of their own.

I sipped water from a fountain before I entered the office. I coaxed, *'Shoulders back, head high, slow breathing.'*

The sparsely furnished reception area was unwelcoming. Stark, faded gray-green walls canvassed photographs in dusty bronze-colored frames, showcasing decades-old Baltimore. No color from view through this high-rise window, either: pale concrete-colored sky with an occasional stream of rising black smoke. No sun.

The secretary's expression signaled me to approach.

"Mr. Williams, please…."

She nodded, handing me a legal pad on which to sign.

"Thank you," I smiled.

She nodded without interest.

I returned to my seat. Reading material included <u>New York Times</u>, <u>Wall Street Journal,</u> and a publication, entitled, <u>Success</u>, which, dog-eared and tattered, lay askew on a table. My thoughts needed diverting, so I chose the <u>Times</u>.

Within minutes, a gentleman wearing a gray button-down shirt, and smoke-colored tie, off-centered at his neck, led me to a large office. His desk juxtaposed its only window; different view, but same sunless chimney-scape and same dingy paint. The rug was Aubusson, but thread-bare; whose once rich hues paled indistinguishable.

"Mrs. McGuire, my condolences on the passing of your husband."

He extended his hand across his expansive desk, unceremoniously abrupt.

"I trust you and your son are holding up?"

More of a statement than a question—a monotonous question I'd been receiving a lot lately. Polite concern; answers were not expected nor wanted.

I nodded with an implied "Thank you".

"Let's get down to business. We'll start with assets, as I've best been able to assess them."

I took a deep breath and crossed my ankles.

"My records are not completely current, as it's been some time since I met with your late husband. You have a home in Guilford, correct?"

I told of its scheduled auction. "I don't know why he felt it had to be handled this way."

"Well, we might as well jump in. Your husband's debts were—or—," clearing his throat, "—are presently, quite large. He was delinquent with IRS payments for the past three years, at least, that I can see. I don't have his full accountant's report, but I should be receiving it in several days. I imagine his reason for auction is debt."

"How much do we owe the government?" I cleared my throat. My voice strained with this surprise revelation.

"From what I can see, well over $100,000; maybe more, with accrued interest. You have three cars and a boat, none of which is paid for. Outstanding credit card balances amount to over $50,000. Selling your house should cover much of that, but you have a mortgage to be satisfied."

"Didn't Pete have a life insurance policy?"

"He did. He borrowed against it some time ago."

Panic.

"What do my son and I have to live on?"

He sat back in his chair, palms extended. "Not too much."

"My advice is to sell your house. The auction can be cancelled, but it may take significant time to sell it in a conventional manner. Some people may have concerns about city-living: crime, you know. A large house like yours, impressive as it is, may have a limited sample of interested buyers with means to support such an expansive property."

I looked down, trying, in vain to stop my lip from quivering.

"Contact a realtor, familiar with that area, to estimate time it could take to liquidate your property. Do you have enough money to cover mortgage payments and expenses while you wait?"

I stumbled with words catching in my throat.

"We've used most of it this past month. What can we do?" I asked.

"I'd proceed with auction. Are its contents of a quality, if sold, might provide income? Are you aware of any stocks or bonds I don't know about?"

"I deferred to him. He was the accountant."

Silence.

'Well, I must ask about your training. You've been a stay-at-home mother, correct?"

I nodded, grabbing a tissue he passed.

"Do you have a degree?"

"B.A. in art history."

"Any specific skills?"

I sat silent.

"I'd advise you to investigate some type of work. Try the art museum or put your name on the substitute teaching list for the public schools. You might apply at a furniture or jewelry store. Check the community college. You might qualify for a scholarship for some training to put food on the table. Any family help? Do you have somewhere to live after the sale of your home?"

I shook my head no, to all the above.

"When I receive paperwork from your husband's firm, I can better advise you. I'm sorry my news is not better. I wish you and your son well. I knew your husband. I believe he was a good man."

He held the door. "I'll contact you when I receive news."

I stumbled through the colorless reception area. I could no longer control my tears, nor could I hold my head high, nor could I be poised.

I wandered to the elevator, blindly pushing a button with a black arrow pointing down.

Chapter 11

City Rose?

Saturday

Gloria

I glanced at my fingertips, as I finished my morning tea. Disgusting.

I decided, day before yesterday, to schedule a manicure this morning—a splurge I rarely, if ever, made. My cuticles looked a sight, hardly professional. Even if most people wouldn't notice, I would.

Sylvia warned again, if I did not show up, a twenty-five dollar fine would be imposed. If I was even a little late, I must reschedule. Hair stylists and nail techs were deserving of respect.

"Yes, ma'am," I answered automatically as I'd always done, addressing a Nun.

Maybe a detention room, of sorts, was located at the end of that hall. I could picture detainees who were late or, heaven forbid, did not show up or pay their twenty-five dollars, being housed in there. Maybe as a punishment, they'd apply wrong color product on your hair, so your flaxen locks were raven, or orange, even.

I giggled, enjoying silly imaginings.

I arrived, wind-blown from October breezes nearly knocking me off the sidewalk. Pierre greeted me.

"Please come in, Madam Gloria."

He assisted me with my coat, reached for a handful of my hair, let it fall, slowly, rolled his eyes, shook his head, and walked away.

It couldn't be that bad. It's been only a week since I had it styled—here. *Could I have ruined it in less than a week? After having thought about it, I guess I could.*

After declining a Latte and mini-bagel, I settled in a cushy chair. No magazine updates since last week. Let's have a go at Baltimore Magazine again. Maybe an article I'd missed or one I could re-read. Maybe I'd scan classified ads.

As I held the magazine with my left hand and paged with my right, it slipped and fell open to that Meyerhoff-picture again. Bored, I scanned this same page, once more, and that troubling picture caught my eye. I adjusted my reading glasses and focused.

I dropped the volume and closed my eyes. It was Katie, and that man must be her husband.

She looks so, what? I looked more closely. Fearful, was that it, fear? She sported her darling smile and her gorgeous gown, but fear was what I sensed. Although debonair, her husband wore a dark expression as he gripped her arm . . . a little too tightly. Alarming.

Perhaps it was nothing. I turned to its cover. This issue was eight months old. Certainly, my eyes and imagination were playing tricks on me.

I closed the magazine and exchanged it with Town and Country. I stared at a jewelry ad displaying a six-carat diamond on a model's hand (as if I'd ever wear something that large—if I could afford it, in the first place.) Anything to divert my attention from the troubling sensation I was feeling about Katie.

Why had she really come to our meeting? Her name was noticeably absent from lists for job training, and testing. She left quickly after her exchange with M. Carroll to retrieve her little boy, I suppose.

My thoughts were interrupted as Pierre glided into the room, waving his hand.

"Ms. Gloria, please come quickly; your manicurist awaits."

I smiled. This whole experience, Pierre included, was such fun. I followed close behind. The music, wind chimes and bongs of unidentifiable percussion instruments, somewhere, made my steps feel so klutzy. I couldn't get the beat.

Audrey, the nail tech, was a woman of decided tastes. Today, her hair was multi-streaked gold, brown and green, for an autumn theme. Last week's pink steaks were "too-too summer", she'd announced.

My usually natural, no-polish nails were now dressed in 'City Rose'. The color appeared pink or orange or gold, depending upon the direction of light hitting their surface–interesting, really.

I'd declined her offer to dot my nails with teeny falling leaves. Maybe next time, I'd offered, trying to sound appreciative.

I hope it didn't chip too quickly. I guess if it did, I'd have to return to face scolding with Pierre's look of condescension or Audrey's scorn.

After leaving a lot of cash in Sylvia's palm, I held my hands high, and strode across the street to *Morgan* and *Millard*. So what if I looked strange. After this beauty salon experience, I should fit right in. Pierre would approve.

Someone was kind enough to open the front door for me, in deference to my nails, certainly. I pranced through the pond of lily pad tables to our usual spot. (I can't believe I even think this—too much time at the beauty shop, definitely.)

I feared Jules would tumble from her chair, laughing. She dabbed her eyes with a napkin.

The maitre d' held my chair. A knowledgeable woman, certainly, or at least one who'd enjoyed a recent manicure.

Jules croaked, "You're too much. Let me see those nails."

As I displayed them, she howled more. I was beginning to feel self-conscious. All eyes zeroed in on our table. This was certainly not luncheon decorum.

"Calm down, Jules. It's just a manicure for heaven's sake."

Wiping her eyes, again, "Glory, you beat all." Her laughter continued, "Who'd ever believe the two of us once considered becoming nuns, spending our lives in a convent?"

Sarah approached our table. "Great to have you back. Do you ladies want the same as last week? Let's see . . . Oyster stew, two spoons, Maryland-beaten biscuits, oyster crackers and crab cakes, right?"

"Wow, how can you remember that?" Jules gaped.

"Shall I bring Earl Grey?"

Julia answered with her hand gracefully lifted in the air, "Bring on the Earl Grey."

Sarah laughed and headed for the kitchen.

"Jules," I nodded, "Sarah's one of our displaced homemakers."

Julia leaned forward, "Really?"

"Really" I answered, knowing Julia wanted to know all about Tuesday night.

I wanted to share details, but I had to be careful not to divulge anything within Sarah's earshot. I must avoid any information which might be taken as personal.

Jules caught my drift.

"But you couldn't have known last week—"

"No, of course not."

"So, feedback time," Jules words sailed out like tennis serves, "Tell all."

"Sad. Such pain, and I expect to hear more this week, as people feel more comfortable about opening up. That's the important thing. They were beginning to feel safe."

"That's good."

"Several leaders emerged in the group dynamics, mostly because of their strength in the midst of their sorrow, and their compassion, in the midst of another's pain. This group will gel. It may even continue on its own after I'm gone in five weeks. I hope it'll prove to be a support network for these women and others who may join, long after this formal group dissolves."

Julia was quiet. I could see she was thinking. Her eyes were dancing with delight, but she said nothing for a long time. "Do you think you'll handle this week's class the same way you did last week?"

She was fishing for information again. I knew this woman. She'd get what she wanted either directly, or between the lines. She was brilliant about obtaining details.

"I've thought about it all week. You see, I wore this suit to look professional—circa 1970's. The only reason I found it at St. Edmonds, was because no one else wanted it."

Julia laughed, "I remember it. Glory, You didn't wear that awful Burgundy thing, did you?"

"I did. I had no fall clothes. After I found nothing at stores on Monday, I had no choice."

I laughed and continued, "I wore some of Mom's over-sized, cinnamon-toned panty hose with gathers collecting at my knees and ankles. I paired it all with an old beige blouse I dug out of a give-away pile. Matched with my summer beige flats, it was a winner."

Jules howled, spitting out her water. "How could anyone keep a straight face? I'm amazed it even fit you. That suit must be at least twenty years old, isn't it?"

"I've worn older than that, actually, but it did. I hooked two safety pins together to hold the waist and donned my trusty old panty girdle."

She wiped her eyes with her napkin, "Oh, Glory, I don't know when I've had such fun."

"At my expense, I might add."

Ever since we were children, Jules has always found something about me to laugh at. I really should say, laugh with. I knew her well enough to know she wouldn't hurt me for the world. The humor we shared kept me from melancholy moments, I was often prone to. Our times of laughing—yes, even and most importantly, about me—had been balm.

"Please, please no more. My stomach can't take anymore. Just answer me: Did anyone say anything?"

"Of course not, who could even care what I wore when their life issues were so huge?"

Julia stopped laughing, "It's tragic, Glory. Do you have any ideas?"

"Well, I have contacts for child care and housing. I've made several appointments for job skill testing. That doesn't seem to be what most of them want, though, or need, oddly enough."

"What more do they really want beyond getting basic needs met?"

"Given all their problems concerning lack of money, grief over lost homes and in some cases children, what they want most is to know someone cares about them and their pain. Even if it's a stranger—and maybe that's the best thing."

I wanted to elaborate about what I saw and heard, and share it. I'd wait for a private time. Jules's strength in keeping confidences was beyond reproach, but I couldn't risk Sarah—or anyone else—overhearing anything. There may be women in this restaurant—now–who may consider joining our group.

"Each person sat isolated from others, at first. Something happened when one woman reached out to comfort another in her distress. That single gesture seemed to convey: you are loveable even if your husband doesn't love you, even if you have no money, or you are homeless. Someone loves you—here, and God loves you when you leave."

Julia sat back in her chair and closed her eyes.

Sarah placed our oyster stew in the table center, filled our empty cups to the brim with tea, and excused herself.

Julia leaned forward in her chair and squeezed my open hand. "Glory, that's what we're all about, you and me, in our life's plan. We're to show others love is real. Not what TV or movies say it is, but acceptance, forgiveness, and compassion, when the world screams the opposite; especially in grief, when pain and discouragement seem all encompassing. Love, kindness and God's mercy is what it's all about."

"Man is never nearer the Divine than in his compassionate moments."
Joseph H. Hertz

Chapter 12

A Break In Routine

Monday

Saturday's shopping trip yielded a few sweaters, two skirts and a shiny necklace Jules said added pizzazz. Add gold earrings and I could pull together some nice outfits for the next couple of weeks.

However, the thought did occur to me: maybe I should wear jeans. After all, I wanted these women to be free to open up, share their problems and feel comfortable asking for help. If I dressed too professionally, would I be encouraging them to be open or closed? An interesting thought I must consider.

I deliberated about coffee. I hated Styrofoam cups. These ladies are guests. If I had guests at my house would I offer them Styrofoam? I think not. I thought of my china cups. I could probably piece together twenty cups and saucers from St. Edmonds. Perhaps I might offer tea, rather than institutional coffee.

I'd call Jules.

"Hi," she answered.

"I'm considering cups, saucers and tea, tomorrow night. These ladies deserve more than institutional stuff. They deserve a tea party."

"How lovely, but how will you clean and transport cups?"

Hmm, I hadn't thought about that. Disposables would certainly be easier.

"That's a problem, for sure. Maybe pastel paper cups would be a pretty alternative and more practical—with tea. Maybe some cheese cubes, with decorative napkins.

My mind was painting a picture on how it would look and be received.

"These ladies have been through so much. They've taken care of children, family, and husbands who have deserted them. It's time someone did something special for them."

Yes, they definitely deserved a party.

"Great idea, they need something. What can I do besides pray?"

"Well, that's the most important thing. If you think of anything before tomorrow, call."

"Will do." Jules punctuated our brief tete-a-tete with an audible yawn.

Second Tuesday Night Session

Nearly time. I decided on a T-neck, pearls and jeans with a pair of suede clogs. Maybe my nails dressed in

"City Rose" were a bit over the top, but it was too late to change.

I entered the room with eagerness markedly absent last week. I placed cookies, yellow napkins, cups, cheese and some interesting crackers on a tray, with green grapes, to add color; plus I offered tea. I could do nothing about the urn, so I filled it with water and let it go.

The urn started its whistle and dance routine as if screaming for help. . . or maybe calling to celebrate. My attitude was changing. Let's call this a celebration—a tea party.

I circled chairs, dropping name tags on each seat; again, knowing few would wear them.

A box of pink tissues, for dabbing noses or eyes, would occupy a center chair.

Footsteps clicked down the hallway. "Oohs" and "aahs" lighted air like soap bubbles.

Smiles and giggles flourished.

One older lady commented, "I haven't been to a party in years. I love parties."

It worked. Although technically not a party, candles and classical music playing from an old Am/Fm transistor radio from St. Edmonds, made it so. Our room was transformed from a drab classroom to an EVENT for these suffering souls who appreciated it more than anyone could imagine.

Tonight, instead of isolating themselves as they had last week, they huddled like 7th grade girls at a dance, giggling.

Sarah entered a little later, with Katie trailing close behind. She squeezed behind some of the women and sat in an empty chair on the far side of our circle. Katie, profuse with apologies, chose a chair closer to the middle.

I decided to start the discussion with Ruth.

Ruth did not look herself tonight. Dark circles eclipsed her eyes. Her expression was harried, to say the least.

"Ruth? Would you like to begin with a recap from last week, for those joining us for the first time? Can you share why you came?"

Tears welled in her red-rimmed eyes. "For those who weren't here last week, I'm from Iowa. Presently, I live in Rogers Forge, but not for long." Her voice quavered. "I'd like to share more, but I just can't, yet. It's so awful. Please, someone else start."

I passed her tissues. "It's OK." I mouthed.

"Is there anyone who would like to share? Katie?"

Katie looked unwell tonight, too. Maybe she was worried about her little boy. Something was not the same.

"Presently, I live in Baltimore County." Katie studied her feet.

"Like Ruth, it may not be for long. I'm presently an at-home mom. That may not be for long, either. Nothing seems to be permanent anymore. I'm in need of a lot of things (heads nodded in agreement), but for this one moment, I just need a friend. I need to be around people who say I'm OK—not because of what I do, who my husband is, what degree or job I have. My life is a mess and I don't know what to do anymore."

Tears started to overflow onto her cheeks now, although she desperately tried to smile. "I don't want to cry, because that seems to be where one goes to give up. I need to keep fighting for my sons, if I can no longer fight for my marriage, my future or my home."

She hesitated, softly adding, "My life is in utter shambles, and I don't know which way to turn."

Others lowered their eyes, each identifying with her pain. Tissues were passed. No one spoke.

I purposely stood behind the circle, waiting for this process to unfold as it was meant to. Rachmaninoff's prelude in C sharp minor, a fitting backdrop, played softly on WMPR.

Katie, who'd last week rallied everyone with her enthusiasm, was in a pivotal position. Her words were courageous. She admitted she could not control her life or solve her problems, and yet she wanted to fight for her children. She asked for friendship and help. I'd wait this out.

Tension hung heavily in the air.

Ruth tried again, strengthened by Katie's courage to speak. "Last week, I was optimistic. I'd hoped things would improve, but they've worsened. I may as well say it. My husband is the minister," she stumbled, "you've read about in the paper."

She should've added TV, radio—maybe even billboards, for all she knew.

She cried. "I'm so ashamed. I've been asked to vacate my house, without any place to go. I've worked in a church my whole married life. I only finished two years of college before marrying. I have no skills. I have no friends. I have no family. I'm homeless and helpless, and my reputation is shot. Like Katie, I don't know what to do."

She lowered her head and rested on the scarred extension.

Who would help her in her grief as she'd helped others last week? I waited.

Mari Carroll arose, as did Sarah and Katie. They embraced her.

Quiet.

Katie said, "If you'll be a friend to me, one who has no one either, I'll certainly be a friend to you. Friendship is all I have to offer."

Mari extended her hands, reached for one of Ruth's hands and extended her other to Katie. Katie grabbed Sarah's hand. I arose and grabbed the last adjoining hands to form a circle.

I heard a noise and saw last week's mystery girl, again wrapped in hat, dark glasses and scarf, enter and then bolt from our room. So peculiar.

What was she afraid of? Was it because our group was larger than her comfort level could allow? Could there be someone here she didn't want to see or share with? The area from which these women came is relatively small. She might recognize someone. A puzzle, for sure, and that outfit? She obviously did not want to be recognized.

I began, "This is a safe place. Anything shared, stays within these walls. Please promise confidentiality. People may be here, who, unbeknownst to us, may be in danger if information was to leave this room. Women may feel threatened in their own homes."

Why had I added that? I didn't say anything about domestic violence before, but for some reason, I had a strong urgency to say it tonight. Maybe I was being overly sensitive, but tonight's atmosphere was different. Tension penetrated the air that had been absent before.

Katie looked at me quizzically, then, suddenly dropped her head.

"I would like to pray for those of you who do not object to prayer. For all of you, who are without a home, have lost a marriage, lost a child, who have no money, or who are without a support system on this earth. You are welcome here, and God loves you. For those who are fighting a court battle, which is anything but fair, I pray for you and your strength in on-going months. I pray you will find gratifying work to establish new homes. I pray you will find rest for your souls and friendship from those around you tonight who desperately need a friend; someone to call in time of emergency or intense sorrow; someone who will support you in prayer to our Heavenly Father."

I paused. "If anyone wishes to add to this prayer, before I close, just call it out. You needn't be embarrassed. God loves you and has brought you to this place to bring you to His heart. He is friend to the friendless and father to the fatherless."

Someone called out, "Pray for me about a custody hearing for my daughter."

I nodded.

Another voice called out, "Please pray my house will sell quickly."

I nodded.

"Please pray my car repairs will be affordable."

I nodded.

Concluding, I said, "Tonight, tell God about your impossible situations, and your need for His help. He promises to hear your prayers if you ask. 'Ask and it shall be given, seek and you shall find, knock and the door will be opened unto you'."

"If there is anything you wish to discuss, I'll be in front. You'll find sign-up sheets for housing, job training, or child care. Please have some fruit and cheese. If you are hungry, eat. It was prepared just for you."

Women slowly filed out. Some stopped to eat cheese, as if they hadn't eaten in days. Perhaps they hadn't. All whispered kind words to both Katie and Ruth as they left.

Ruth, Katie, Mari Carroll, and Sarah remained behind. I pulled a chair close to Ruth.

"What seems to be your most pressing need, Ruth?"

"When the church finds an interim pastor to replace my husband, I'll have no place to go."

This poor girl, I remember feeling just as panicky when Tad and I were forced to leave our carriage house apartment with no place to go. The horrifying thought of homelessness seems more intense when a woman must care for a child.

"Ruth," I said, "if there is nowhere else, you can stay with me. I live in a tiny house but I do have two other small bedrooms."

"Do you mean it?"

Her eyes brightened, her brow relaxed and I could see tension drain from her face. Color returned to her normally pink cheeks which had appeared ashen moments ago.

"Of course, you may stay as long as you need."

I thought Ruth would leap for joy.

"Oh, Gloria, I can clean for you. I can take care of things for you, you'll see. I can do whatever you need done, I promise. Sam, Jr. is quiet. We'll stay in our room. You won't know we're there, promise."

I insisted on someone taking our remaining cheese. Whoever had the greatest need. Mari Carroll? Well, she'd share her story when she was ready.

As women returned to their cars, I replaced coffee urn, candles and other supplies, rearranged chairs, and grabbed my radio with the rest of my paraphernalia. I managed to flick light switches, and lock doors while awkwardly clutching my stuff.

I scuffed along but wooden-soled clogs proved more difficult to navigate on this slick surface than my beige flats. Balancing was difficult as temperatures had dropped and thin, invisible ice glazed the pavement. Walking was treacherous. Quickening my pace toward my car, I overcorrected, slipped on undetected ice and slammed onto blacktop.

Awakening from lost consciousness, I see Mari Carroll, Ruth and Sarah circling me, warning me to remain still. An ambulance was coming.

"This is silly," I argued. When I tried to move, though, I found I could not.

"My leg," I moaned. My head hurt, too.

Ruth knelt and supported my head in her lap. She gently stroked my head, soothingly, repeating, "It'll be all right."

After who knew how long, I lay on a gurney in Midtown Memorial Hospital's hallway. I knew immediately where I was parked. I'd spent hours here with Mother.

Mother's doctor approached, "One fall isn't enough for your family? Your mother only fractured her wrist, but you've fractured your tibia, and sustained a concussion. What were you trying to do?"

A good question, *what had I been trying to do anyway?* I couldn't remember.

"I've called an orthopedic surgeon to set and cast it."

"Cast it?" I moaned.

"You'll need a cast and to be off that leg for at least a week. Is there anyone who can help you at home?"

Ruth quickly interjected, "I can."

"Are you family?"

"Close enough," she answered, and clasped my hand.

I closed my eyes, and let grateful tears flow. I recalled one of Julia's favorite sayings, "Whatever you freely give will freely come back to you."

After my doctor left, she said, "Looks like you'll be getting house-help a little sooner than you thought. Since your car has a clutch, you'll need a chauffeur, as well— at your service."

Sarah added, "I can cook for you."

"That would be wonderful. You must promise to share it."

"Really?" she answered.

My mind was alert. Is it possible this woman and her daughter needed food? I could not assume, but she had not shared her need, either. Waitresses only earned a dollar or so an hour, and were totally dependent on tips for their living, unrecognized by most restaurant patrons.

Sarah said, "I love to cook and my daughter could help. We'd be so appreciative." She lowered her head. "We have no money for food, right now," she whispered.

What else? I closed my eyes, marveling at the pain of these women.

"Who are the helpers, the comforters for the times when we're bleeding and need a transfusion of love?"
Billy Graham

Chapter 13

Help...I Need Somebody...Help.

Tuesday Night

Katie

Maybe I shouldn't have gone to that meeting at all. I didn't mean to cry. I feel so foolish, but why? Were my problems any different from the others?

Look at Ruth, poor girl. At least my problems weren't blasted, over front pages of newspapers. There was something to be said for that. If I feel like a failure, think how she must feel.

What about that woman last week whose husband set her up, all for selfish gain?

What was wrong with people? There's something terribly wrong with a society where relationships were throw-away, like a discarded Hardee's fry wrapper.

Should I have stayed home? Perhaps, but it's a relief to be with other women who are also going through tough times. I needed to share my enormous burden, which seems to grow larger each day; like a balloon continually being filled with air, and finally, unpredictably, just pops, spewing its contents from here to everywhere.

I guess that's how Ruth feels. I have a sick feeling my balloon is ready to pop any time now. Would I be in any better position than Ruth? It couldn't be good, that's for sure. I could do nothing but hold onto my balloon until it or I crashed.

I mounted steps to the child-care building, two at a time. *Bless his heart*; I hope he's Ok. I stoop and call, "Timmy, where's my boy?" in a sing-song voice I used playing hide and seek.

His bare feet slapped the tile floor as he ran toward me. He clutched his blankey in his left hand, and managed a grin with his thumb still wedged between his teeth.

"There he is," I sing with glee.

Megan followed, smiling, "Ms. Katie, he's so adorable. I could eat him up. We had such fun tonight. We worked puzzles and read books. He's really bright. It shows you spend a lot of time with him."

I scooped him in my arms, and smiled, "He and I are best buddies, aren't we, Sweetheart?"

How long would I be able to stay at home with him? It was my dream to stay home with my children. My mom had stayed with us. My parents were happy. We had a happy family. Neither of my parents took drugs.

Megan commented, "He had one wet diaper. I tried to persuade him to tell me, so I could teach him to use a potty. He didn't seem interested. Is he afraid of the potty seat at home?"

It was a perfectly reasonable question, of course. Jeremy had trained himself at two years and two months. But Jeremy started out in a different home with a different mommy.

Timmy was well over three, and I had tried everything. All manner of potty seats resided at home: a red, white and blue one with a ladder, a floor model with a little rubber ducky; one shaped like a car, among our lot. Timmy refused them all. I had bought any number of big boy pants. Not interested. He wet them all.

Born pre-maturely, his doctor seemed to think perhaps, developmentally, he wasn't ready. "Well, don't worry. He won't need diapers when he goes to college." He laughed like it was the funniest thing he'd ever said.

Yeah, easy for you to say, Buddy, he's not your child.

No one could believe Timmy still wore diapers. If anyone really knew the turmoil we called home, it'd be no surprise.

Ditto with his thumb. As a dental hygienist, I knew thumb-sucking affects teeth. Somehow, straight teeth were the least of my concerns, right now. So he'd need braces. *What's the big deal? Who didn't need them these days, anyway?* If my son needed his thumb for comfort and defense against his world, so be it. Let it go.

Megan asked, "Can we expect you next week? I'll try to bring activities Timmy might like."

She knelt to his level. "Bye, Sport, we really enjoyed having you. Please come back."

His head rested on my shoulder, now. He waved a blanketed fist, good-bye.

I glanced at their wall clock. Goodness. We need to run. Hopefully, Don is out.

Then there's Jeremy. I wonder about his unpredictable mood. Lately, he'd been surly. Of course, he was fourteen. That had to be it. I remember fourteen as being hard. Life's tough for everyone at fourteen, right?

Last night was scary, though. Strapping Timmy into his seat, I replayed last night's incident—unwillingly.

Dinner time and Jeremy was anxious and hungry. As he hunted refrigerator shelves, Timmy joined him, crying "I want to see, too. . .see, too."

"Fifteen minutes," I'd announced.

Jeremy's impatience darkened his eyes. His mouth scowled and fists clenched. Then, before my eyes, Jeremy forcefully grabbed the juice and kicked Timmy across our floor, eight feet to a wall.

Horrified, I declared this inexcusable behavior. "The baby could've been hurt. Go to your room and reconsider your behavior."

Jeremy turned to me. "You can't make me."

He grabbed each of my shoulders and shoved me across to the other side of the room.

Astounded, I retorted, "Don't ever do that again."

He repeated his shove, grabbed the juice and thundered upstairs.

I stood stunned and shaking. Timmy embraced my knees, crying. As minutes passed, my whole-body trembling became uncontrollable.

Switching my stove dial off, grabbing our coats, and stroller, Timmy and I left our house.

I ran, pushing his stroller. I felt as if a blind had just lifted from my eyes.

I'd stayed all these years with my abusive husband, for the love of my sons. A whole, sick family was better than a broken family, I reasoned. What had I done?

I'd stayed long enough for my older son to model himself after his father's behavior. I shared my house with two monsters, now, instead of one. Horrified with that reality, I continued pushing the stroller faster.

Timmy interrupted my thoughts. "Mommy, I'm hungry."

Of course he was, but I couldn't return. What could I do? This is a living nightmare, getting worse each day.

I fished in the undercarriage bag and found animal crackers and *Cheezits*.

"Sweetheart, we're taking an extra long ride, tonight. *Cheezits* and animal crackers, which do you, want?"

He screamed, as a full-blown, temper tantrum erupted, "I want dinner and juice like Jeremy got."

He was hungry and tired. Maybe he'd cry himself to sleep while I tried to think what to do.

I continued running behind his stroller. *Would it be safe to return at all tonight? If I could just arrive after Timmy falls asleep, sneak into his room and lock the door, I'd stay until morning—all day, if necessary.*

I sobbed, now, overwhelmed with fear. My head throbbed. Ice formed on the road with freezing temperatures. My hands were raw and my fingers numb around the icy metal handle.

Oh, please, Timmy, go to sleep, I said to myself.

Finally, I entered a darkened house, not knowing whether Don or Jeremy was there.

I couldn't take a chance.

I shed my shoes at our back door. I balanced a sleeping Timmy over my shoulder, grabbed my cordless phone, and noiselessly mounted steps, one at a time. *If it took me all night, I'd get to that room in silence, not even disturbing a squeaking floor board.*

I gently lay Timmy onto his bed. I locked his door, but not before removing an extra key above its exterior molding; one I kept to unlock his door from our hallway, in case he locked himself in his room.

I joined him on his youth bed, barely enough room to stay on, and pulled covers over us both. I welcomed fitful sleep.

Well, that was last night. I felt my throat constrict. I could only imagine what I'd find tonight.

Wednesday Morning

While Timmy joined *Sesame Street* actors singing their opening jingle, I walked to our adjoining laundry room and dialed my attorney's office.

"Connie, I need to see Mark. Urgent."

"He's at Towson courthouse until 11:00. Only fifteen minutes are open."

"I'll be there." I released a breath.

Timmy was counting to ten in Spanish with Muppets. Good.

Now call directory assistance.

"May I please have the number for House of Ruth? Yes, Baltimore County. Yes, hot-line. Yes, ma'am. Thank you." I clicked end.

Timmy was still entertained. Thanks, Elmo. *What would I do without Elmo?*

Backing further away from my singing son, I dialed 8-1-2-. . . . *Come on, come on, come on . . .someone. . . anyone answer. . .*

"Oh, yes, hello. Can you help me?"

Sobs erupted from some deep place in my soul. Flood-gates spilled onto that poor woman on the other end of my phone.

"Are you in danger?" the voice asked.

"Not right now."

"Do you wish to speak with a counselor?"

"Please," I choked.

"Go to a safe place. A counselor will return your call."

"Soon?" I spoke quietly to avoid disturbing Timmy's concentration.

I could hear Oscar the Grouch now. I didn't want to arouse Timmy's curiosity if he knew I was on the phone.

"Yes, soon. Stay safe, Ok?"

"OK," I stammered, trying to compose myself.

Clicking end, again, I skipped to Timmy. "Hey, Honey, what's Elmo up to? Oh, is it Big Bird now? I'm sorry. I missed a few minutes." My trembling hand clutched my cordless.

A ring interrupted Oscar the grouch. Timmy glared, "I can't hear."

I re-entered my laundry room "Yes?"

A voice queried, "I'm a counselor from House of Ruth. How can I help you? Are you all right? Is this a good time?"

"Yes," I said, "but I'm afraid."

"Tell me your circumstances."

I scripted my last weeks, summarizing in a few sentences.

"Do you have a safety plan mapped out? Are suitcases in your car? Do you have an extra set of car keys if you must leave quickly?"

"I have a few things—"

"After we hang up, put essentials in your car. Do you have a safe place to go?"

"No, not really" I swallowed a sob.

Who in this world could I trust with my secrets? My family's in North Carolina, and they know nothing about what's going on. I doubt if they'd believe me anyway. I have no real friends. Even if I did, I'd be mortified to ask if Timmy and I could stay. It's so embarrassing. How could anyone understand that my own husband and first-born son were trying to hurt me—no one who was close enough to trust and share that humbling confidence.

"Can we meet this afternoon? We can talk then. If you're in an urgent predicament, call our hotline, understand?"

"Yes, ma'am" I whispered.

"Call at 1:30 for directions. You're going to be fine—and Katie?"

"Yes?"

"You may have saved your life and perhaps even lives of others. You do know what you've done is right?"

"I guess."

I felt humiliated at having had to make this call. My face burned just thinking about my stupidity at having arrived at this place in my life.

"Katie, you're a smart and courageous woman. I'm proud of you. Now take care of your little boy. He needs you."

"Thank you for speaking with me."

"That's why I'm here. Goodbye, Katie."

I slowly returned to our TV. I had to calm down—for Timmy.

At 10:30, I checked Timmy in 'mother's day out' at our local YMCA. He hated it. He said there was a mean girl there. This mean girl was a year younger, but obviously had learned how to defend herself. (Apparently, I had not had an opportunity to acquire that skill, growing up.) Poor Timmy.

"Just a little while, Honey, I promise. I love you." I planted a kiss on his tear-dampened cheek and departed.

I checked a wall clock. If I hurried, I could just make my appointment.

I needed something to pass time while I waited in Mark's reception area: a dated copy of Baltimore Magazine would do. I quickly paged passed Rolex watches, recipes from Maryland's Eastern shore, department store ads, and Coach Bags, not taking in or caring what I saw. Suddenly my breath caught in my throat. That's a picture of Don and me at that Meyerhoff fundraiser last year. I had no idea someone had snapped our photo.

We certainly looked like a happy couple, I must say. Less stressed and a little heavier than I appeared lately. Although active in Junior League then, I hadn't attended a meeting since . . . well, since things started to really go downhill.

Don hadn't wanted to go that night. We hadn't attended a social event in years. He didn't want to be seen with me, I supposed. It was OK. I couldn't afford a sitter very often, anyway. (Don kept tight control of our money—my every expenditure needed his approval.)

Where was all our money going anyway? Since he'd been in practice for nearly eighteen years, he had to be earning a lot more than what he doled out to me for a home allowance, surely.

He refused to allow me to accompany him to accountant meetings or see his books—as if I had time to do either, anyway. Even our tax returns were shoved in my face for signing while I was fixing dinner. He'd claim to be rushed, and forms needed to be mailed immediately. No time for me to look them over—ever. I was never permitted to see anything.

I closed the magazine. I couldn't bear to look at it. I'd focus on something else while waiting.

Mark blew in and signaled me to follow. His desk was piled high with files, books, yellow stick-on memos, and legal pads; cluttered, like my conscious mind now, and both hidden from public view.

"What's up, Katie?"

I explained finding medication bottles in Don's closet.

Mark asked, "What doctor prescribed these pills?"

I answered, "He prescribed them for a staff member."

Mark leaned back in his chair and dragged his palm across his mouth. "Go on."

I described satanic symbols on Jeremy's room walls, following with that kitchen episode.

"Go on."

"I'm fearful I may have contributed to this awful mess by staying in our marriage so long—long enough for Jeremy to model his father's behavior."

Mark hammered a pencil on his desktop, without speaking.

"Your husband has broken laws, and he knows it. If he asked his staff member to purchase meds for him with her insurance card, we have insurance fraud, as well as other professional illegalities to consider. However, if you pursue this, you'll need to present evidence in court. Not only is your safety at risk, but there would be ramifications for you and your children.

"Your older son is already exhibiting significant problems. Damaging publicity would hurt your whole family's reputation, not to mention your business viability. It could also affect your ability to be employed later."

I looked down at my finger whose cuticle Id been picking. I released a desperate breath.

"If I were you, I'd stay in your house a little longer—just until your first separation hearing; just until your support and temporary custody is determined. Try to stick with it until three weeks before that hearing. After all, you have no money and no job. You have no place to go. Let's just closet this meds thing, for now. It's not going to help you to bring it up now. Later, it may, but much later."

"But I'm afraid for my safety." I whined, ashamedly, but I couldn't help it.

"Well, I think he's trying to frighten you into stopping these proceedings. He's got a lot on the line, here. You know your situation better than I do, though. If you feel threatened by either your son or your husband, get out and call police."

He rose and extended his hand, "Keep in touch, and keep safe."

Everyone today was telling me to keep safe. How exactly was I to do that?

1:17 p.m. I spooned yogurt and munched a cookie. I wasn't hungry, but I was losing weight—a lot more than I knew was healthy. *I'd been eating normally, hadn't I?* I don't even know.

Food was the least of my concerns. I was eating a healthy lunch now, right? Reconsidering, it wasn't so healthy, after all. I couldn't even swallow this little bit. In recent weeks, my stomach closed down after only a fraction of a normal meal. Stress, I suppose.

I shut myself inside a corner phone booth, stretching my jacket-hood to conceal my face. I dialed the number scrawled on my torn piece of scratch paper.

"Hi, this is Katie, from this morning?" I squeaked, clearing my voice.

"Hi, Katie; are you safe?"

"Yes, ma'am, so far."

As I said these words, I looked back over my shoulder for the n-th time.

"Can you write directions?"

As I confirmed that I could, I fished into my pocketbook for my chewed pencil stub.

She dispensed detailed information.

"Katie, if you suspect you're being followed, drive passed the woman I'm sending as an escort. Do not stop. Return my call when you can. We'll send help."

"I'm leaving now."

I walked stiffly to my car, trying to gain control of trembling limbs.

Just talking with this woman seemed, in some way, clandestine.

I kept trying to second guess myself. *Maybe this is stupid. Nothing is going to happen to me. I'm just over-reacting. Jeremy's just a hormonal teenager, certainly.*

I repeated my unspoken words to convince my mind to release doubts.

I'd felt frightened that night, though. *What could it hurt to talk with this woman?* Maybe it won't help, but perhaps it will. *Who else do I have to talk with, after all?*

In fifteen minutes, I met my designated escort. She waved and pulled her car away slowly, and I followed.

After another twenty minutes, we slowed at a gated area. A security guard compared my license plates to their receptionist's relayed information, and I entered. We drove another mile or so.

Secure here. It would really be hard to find if you didn't know where you were going. That must make a lot of women feel safe.

Right now, though, I was feeling like the only woman ever to be in this situation. *How stupid could I have been?*

I felt pulled between two polarized options: I felt paralyzing shame, urging me to run; while I knew, beyond a shadow of a doubt, I must proceed. Perspiration dampened my hairline. Although cold, I felt sweat slowly slide between my breasts.

I parked about fifty feet from the entrance. Approaching its secure door, a buzz welcomed my approach. I cautiously entered, still checking over my shoulder, as had been my unconscious habit lately.

A young woman smiled. "You must be Katie. Please sign in and your counselor will arrive momentarily."

Another buzzer.

I was concerned about signing my real name. *What if someone I knew recognized my name on this form?* Reluctantly, I signed—first name only. *After all, it could be any Katie, right?*

As I set the pen back on their counter, I heard heels clicking on tile. I looked up, startled to see a woman about my age, walking toward me, hand extended in a welcoming gesture.

"Katie? I'm Cathy, and I'm so glad you came. Your calling took a lot of courage. You made an excellent decision to come. Let's go to my private office, shall we?"

I was glad she mentioned private. Again, I turned and glanced over my shoulder to make sure I hadn't been followed.

We arrived at a cozy room where she assured me we'd be undisturbed. After I cautiously entered, she offered a rose, slip-covered chair in front of her desk for me to take. I felt soothed, allowing myself to be cuddled by its fluffy padding. Blush walls surrounded us, and pink silk flowers graced a table beside me.

The ambience was welcoming and forgiving; merciful not censorious like that psychologist's office I'd visited with my boys, or any other professional office I'd visited lately—ever, in fact. I'd read that this shade of baby pink promoted calm. For sure.

I made my story sound as commonplace as possible: *run of the mill-stuff, humdrum, like a trip to the grocery store. No big deal. Maybe she'd dismiss me, saying it was nothing out of the ordinary; normal everyday life. Not to worry. Certainly, other women lived with worse situations than mine.* I skimmed episodes with Jeremy, my husband's medications, and my lawyer's advice.

Her expression was grave. "Katie, has your husband ever belittled you?"

"Sure, lots of times."

She handed me multiple, stapled papers. "Would you please read this first page?"

A list of characteristics describing the abusive temperament covered its first page and spilled over several. Astonishing, each characteristic described my husband. *How could she have known? Could everyone recognize an abuser but me? Was there some kind of class I missed in school explaining this phenomenon?* I'd taken multiple Psych courses in college, and never had I seen a list like this.

I suddenly felt hot, almost faint. "May I have a glass of water, please? I don't feel so well…"

"Certainly", she answered, looking concerned.

She brought me a cone-shaped paper cup from their water cooler.

"Katie, has your husband ever struck you?"

I covered my face with clammy hands. *I didn't want to think about that. I didn't want to talk about it. I wanted it all to go away.* Suddenly, for no reason, I screamed at her.

"Yes, all right, yes." Then, embarrassed by my reaction, I started to cry. "Please, I need someone to help me. I'm so frightened. I don't know what to do."

Cathy draped a fuzzy pink blanket around my shoulders. Oddly, that blanket made me feel secure. *I guess she knew the effect it would have on me. Even Timmy would know that, remembering his blanket scrap.*

"Katie, you're safe, here. We'll give you any help you need. Please tell me exactly what you left behind today, and to what you'll be retuning."

She handed me paper and a pen, and slowly, but deliberately, spoke about a safe plan of escape. She encouraged me to write her words, because when I needed them, I might be too upset to remember what she said.

I needed a safe place to go. This meant telling someone I trust about my circumstances.

I shook my head "I'm too ashamed."

"What if a friend came to you for safe haven? Would you deny them or laugh at them? Would you refuse their admittance? Of course not—not if she were a friend."

True enough.

She recommended I contact police about Jeremy's actions and what I might need to do in that regard. She further recommended I meet with a counselor like herself; someone with whom to talk during times of distress. It was my decision to stay in my house for another six weeks, but she deemed that unadvisable. She handed me a package of printed material and encouraged me to call their center any time.

I thanked her and left, even more troubled than I'd been on my arrival.

Too much.

I felt blind-folded in the midst of a mine field. Any step in a wrong direction could bring disaster.

I must remain at my house until I could save money to make a run for it: $10 a week out of my grocery allowance.

That's all I could manage without looking obvious.

Chapter 14

Taking Care Of Business

Late Tuesday night

Mari Carroll

I need a plan. I'd organized charitable events, art gallery exhibits, club functions, parties, wedding and baby showers. Now I'm faced with ordering an unknown person's life—at midnight, no less.

The goal was to get Gloria settled in her house. I had to evaluate her present needs, and determine care needed for the next x-number of days.

I surveyed her small house through its windows. I could not move Gloria by myself. I'd have to wait for either Sarah or Ruth to help. Ruth was retrieving necessities from her house, enough to last three to four days. Her son would come tomorrow. Sarah should arrive with Gloria's car soon. Once Gloria was settled, I'd drive Sarah back to the college for her car. We'd return in the morning to coordinate schedules.

Sarah would arrange menus and food shopping, I suppose. I'd call a pharmacy to reserve a hospital-bed, porta-potty, and perhaps a wheelchair, also. A bedroom, of sorts, would have to be set up in that little alcove off her living room. We can do this if we all work together.

I shined my car lights into her garage. Garden tools, lawn mower, trash-cans, and wait—a wheelbarrow. Pretty dirty, but definitely an answer to transporting her into her house.

"Gloria, that wheelbarrow may be the best way to move you. Is there anything out here to line it?"

Gloria's mouth gaped and something like terror filled her now wide eyes.

"The wheelbarrow? Goodness, I have no idea. What if you get me in there and I can't get out? Promise me, you'll check for rodents and wipe out any spider webs. I may have left the hospital in one piece, but I'd have a heart attack if I felt a mouse, or spider or something worse crawling on me." Gloria gulped audibly.

I giggled. *What would've happened to this girl if we hadn't stayed in that parking lot?* There's a lesson to be learned from this: never leave these meetings alone. The buddy system is always best. I'd given that very warning at Tyler's Boy Scout meetings and sports events, time and again: stick together.

As chaotic as our lives were, some preparedness was needed. It was looking like we were a chosen team, of sorts. Holding hands in support of one another, tonight, I recalled the huddle at Tyler's lacrosse games.

I knew little of sports; just not my thing. I did know players and coach had to have a plan, though.

We seemed so different—diverse life styles and personalities. But, like a team, we were being joined together . . .to do what? Certainly not to win any game; just survive, is more like it.

Maybe we'd be like a relay team. We'd pool our resources and keep handing off a baton to whoever could carry it at the moment, until our race was over.

I was realizing after these two weeks, none of us could do anything without God's intervention. We had nothing else.

I knew little about God. I certainly didn't know him personally. Religion held little importance in my family. My mother's family, being of Creole and French descent, were largely Catholic, by faith, but hardly devout by any stretch of imagination.

In New Orleans tradition, a first-born daughter would be named Marie, or Mary, in English, for the mother of Jesus; hence my name, Marie Carroll. That was the only vestige of Mother's family's religious influence. (I shortened it to Mari in high school: unique. . . artistic).

My father's Protestant roots originated in England; he boasted of a long line of honorable descendants. Under no circumstance, would he consider Catholicism. (More of an allegiance issue, from historic battles between Anglicans and Catholics for the once coveted Anglo-Saxon crown, I guess.) Although his family was Presbyterian, Anglican seemed an acceptable compromise for both sides.

I was raised with some Biblical truth, but its facts mixed with myths and embellished century-old stories from New Orleans culture. Most people knew nothing about truth. Few cared, either. It interfered with the festival setting of N' Orleans, whose carnival atmosphere led my father to move inland.

Although I attended Episcopalian boarding schools, and was taught to pray, I never really understood who God was. No real assurance of God while in college; my faith-life amounted to nothing more than a quick prayer before an exam.

The religious scene in Chapel Hill during the late 60's resembled that carnival scene in New Orleans. Anything anyone could imagine or want. You could try one, or not. If you didn't like it, there were lots of other choices. It didn't matter.

Was God in our midst? Certainly the Anglican *Book of Common Prayer* spoke of that. Could He care about me—would He? If there was any time when I truly needed Him, it was now. Could He accept my prayers after all the years I'd ignored Him and thought only of myself?

Although I considered myself educated, I knew next to nothing about the Bible. I knew it as literature, the Psalms as poetry, and Bible stories as subject-matter portrayed in Renaissance art. Since the rest of my education was not helping in this crisis, I'd better do some quick learning. Life was crashing before my very eyes—for me and Tyler.

Tyler had been baptized as an infant, but we'd never attended church as a family—ever. Suddenly, I felt ashamed of that.

Sounds of Sarah's car wheels crunching gravel, interrupted my thoughts.

Together we loaded Gloria and each grabbed a handle to push her to her front door. A bumpy ride, I'm sure. Nothing she'd wish to do again, any time soon, but she giggled between moans like a good sport.

I passed her skeleton key to Sarah, as I couldn't figure how to make it work. Ten minutes of fumbling, and it clicked, finally.

Ruth arrived with the click of the lock. She proceeded to mount stairs, two at a time, to Gloria's room, remove sheets, comforter and pillow, and make a bed for her on the sofa for what was left of this night. She fluffed Gloria's pillows, and wrapped her in her comforter, with incredible speed and efficiency. She then dashed to her car, lugged in her own sheets, pillow, and blanket, and made a bedroll, of sorts, close by.

Amazing. Sarah and I marveled to see Ruth in action. I was glad she was on my team, for sure. Little Sam is lucky to have such a caring mommy. Probably she was a great wife, too. How mean of her husband to have left her.

I offered to call Bill and Julia. Although it was late, I felt obliged.

I scanned the directory from Gloria's caller ID. I'd call Bill first. I tentatively pushed buttons, having glanced at her kitchen clock. I grimaced. *It was awfully late, but he needed to know.*

After a number of rings, Bill groggily syllabled, "Hello." He alerted to my serious tone. Assured that Glory was being taken care of, he promised to be here tomorrow, ASAP. I clicked end.

I dialed Julia. After identifying myself, I relayed my news.

"Glory. . . my God, is she all right? I'll be right there," she screeched. Click. Dial tone.

Twenty minutes later, Julia charged through Gloria's back door, wearing a coffee-stained terry robe, toed-out slippers and spoolie-curlers.

Do they even make spoolie-curlers anymore? My memories wandered back to when I'd last seen them . . .?

"Where is she?" she bellowed.

Gloria mumbled, "Jules, I'm fine."

Julia hovered over the side of the couch and peered down with her reading glasses, as if Gloria was a research specimen. Suddenly, overcome with laughter, she managed to speak.

"What have you done to yourself? Can't I trust you for a minute not to get into trouble?"

Noticing our wringing hands, she added, "And who are these lovely ladies who have come to your rescue?"

Smiling warmly, she extended her hand with her introduction. We relaxed with her gracious manner.

Ruth turned to Sarah and me, "Look, I've got it covered for tonight. Go home to your children."

Sarah called behind her that she'd return in the morning to fix breakfast and give Ruth a chance to rest.

I added I'd be here most of the morning, and available for evening. I also said I'd order necessities from a pharmacy in the morning.

Julia argued, "Nonsense. I can place that order. I know a place that delivers. You ladies get some sleep. I'll see you in the morning. Now, Glory, be nice to these young ladies."

She glanced around and winked at us. "I know how she can be. I've known her for years."

Wednesday Morning

Gloria

"What are those heavenly scents coming from my kitchen?" Was it dill, nutmeg and cinnamon? I'm starving.

At my stirring, Ruth was at my side. "Are you all right? How are you managing your pain? It's not quite time for your next meds."

"Goodness, Ruth, have you slept, at all?"

I gazed, groggily, from my too brief, medication-induced sleep. It seemed barely minutes since we'd all arrived last night.

"A little, but I'm here to take care of you. Do you need to use the bathroom?"

Indeed, I did. I hadn't considered this predicament. No way could I get to my bathroom lugging this huge cast. Even if I could get there, how would I manage what I had to manage?

"Julia's having a potty delivered, but it hasn't arrived yet." She shrugged and grinned.

"We'll have to improvise or you'll be mighty uncomfortable if you wait. How about using a dish pan?"

I gasped, dumbstruck, my mouth agape. "A dish pan?"

I moaned, hiding my face behind a sofa pillow. So humiliating.

Jules frequently teased me about my out-dated convent modesty, but never in my wildest dreams could I have imagined discussing bathroom issues with a stranger, kind as she was.

Sarah quipped with amusement. "Gloria, remember your pregnancy? We lost all dignity then."

Retrieving an old shower curtain from my hall closet, Ruth pushed it under me, in case I missed the pan. Dropping T.P. in my lap, she joined Sarah in my kitchen, giggling.

After having produced results for Ruth's satisfaction, I indulged in a sponge bath, and freshened my hair with baby powder. I did feel more revived.

Sarah set a tray across my lap, arranged with a fresh herb and feta cheese omelet, frothy Chai tea, a butter-topped croissant, lace-edged napkin, and a small yellow mum. I marveled.

What had happened to me? Had I ever been treated like this? Maybe, as a measled little girl when Lucille'd babied me.

Noticing Sarah preparing to leave for work, I called, "Sarah, you'll need to grocery shop. Bring me my checkbook, please. Take this check as far as it goes, but remember you're feeding a family of five now, plus Purrfect. I hate to admit she only eats gourmet." I scribbled an almost illegible date and signature.

My cat meowed hungrily. The word gourmet always sparked her attention. I should've spelled it.

Sarah laughed. "Thank you so much. I've been cooking only for Rebecca recently, but she hasn't been eating at all lately." Her voice trailed off and her countenance changed visibly. "Maybe eating with others will perk her appetite." She waved her hand to dismiss her concern.

She didn't want to focus on Rebecca's weight—a matter she tried to dismiss with her life's frantic pace. Worries for Becky were beginning to haunt her, day and night, though. She would not go there. Not now.

"I'll drop off lunch." She answered, barely audibly, closing the door behind her.

Ruth motioned me to lie down. "Rest, you'll want to be at your best for a special visitor later." She winked.

Taking her advice, I relaxed on my narrow couch. After having just closed my eyes, it seemed, wild commotion caused me to suddenly jerk awake.

"What!" I cried out, my eyes wide.

Jules marched in, shouting orders like a drill sergeant to an army squad. Bed, wheelchair, and yes, a potty-on-a-stand were being conveyed by a delivery-team, with all the noise of stampeding buffalo.

Another stranger, bewildered and unaware of where to place his oversized floral arrangement, soon joined this melee. He side-stepped– first to his right, then left, then back again–looking wide-eyed, and somewhat delirious. Drops of sweat dotted his pale brow.

Ruth grabbed his vase, while Julia fought for its card. Victoriously, Jules extended it out-of-reach, pronouncing its message aloud for benefit of all—especially me and these delivery men, I'm horrified to say.

She enunciated slowly, in a sing-song voice for dramatic effect." Be there soon. L-o-v-e, Bill."

They hooted, in chorus, "Love, Bill?" Their response was punctuated with backslapping and guffaws.

My face burned, which was, of course, their desired response.

After brief merriment, Julia quickly organized her team and headed out my back door.

She bellowed, "Hop to, gentlemen, forward march."

Squeezing through this procession and looking around dazedly at its wake of confusion, Mari interrupted Ruth's bed-making and shouted over clamor, "Ruth, get your son. I can stay until noon."

Without argument, Ruth grabbed her pocketbook and coat, and waved, while Mari eased through a bottleneck of new furnishings. She pressed her legal pad to her chest.

"Wow" she muttered, almost as a release of breath. Mari seemed at a loss for words, gazing slowly from side to side.

I nodded, wide-eyed, still groggy from medication and my too-sudden awakening.

My heart thundered. *What exactly had just happened, anyway?*

Smiling, noticing my arrangement of blossoms, Mari turned to business at hand.

"Lovely. Now, I've made a list of things you'll need. With some schedule-juggling, one of us can be with you every minute. Don't worry about anything. Now, can I get you some tea, maybe?"

"Thanks, Mari." I mumbled, grasping my pillow for support.

Something to clear brain-fog was clearly needed: Earl Grey, certainly.

I longed for peace and quiet—neither attainable this morning, I concluded.

Sleep would not be an option any time soon. I strained to push myself to a sitting position in my new bed. I could hardly move under tightly swaddled sheets Ruth'd tucked around me. No need to worry about falling out of bed, that's for sure.

Goodness, this mattress was hard. *Wouldn't you think hospital-bed makers might consider the needs of a convalescent by creating a comfy mattress?* I didn't dare complain, though. I don't think I could survive another episode like this morning's.

After sipping tea, I welcomed its caffeine kick-in. *Whew.* I shook my head to clear it. *Were my eyes crossed?*

I must divert conversation from my confusion. I'd zero in on Mari. After savoring a few welcome minutes of heavenly solitude, I started,

"Now that we're alone, do you feel comfortable sharing some of your concerns, Mari? You've been so kind to Katie, Ruth, Sarah and now, me, but what about your needs?"

I struggled to widen my eyes, making a serious attempt to appear focused.

Suddenly I was sorry I'd brought it up. I noticed her head lower and shoulders drop. I was glad we were alone, so she could feel safe sharing her worries.

She took a deep breath before speaking. Words describing her background, her family and her son tumbled out. As she described her marriage, tears, the first I'd seen, filled her eyes. She pictured her last days—the night of her husband's death, her loss of financial stability, the soon auctioning of her house, and the uncertainty of her future.

So sad. More painful revelations. I shut my eyes to better concentrate.

"In fact," she closed, "I must meet with an auctioneer this afternoon about that event on Saturday. I dread trying to sort through what can be kept and what must be sold."

Mari could feel her stomach tighten, simply recalling her afternoon appointment.

She sighed. "My loss is so public, and my lack of privacy so distressing. It's like show- casing my entire life on an auction block. I can almost imagine how humiliating it must've been for slaves, last century, having all they had—children, husbands, everything—on display for all to see and pick over. Vultures hovering over carrion on the side of a road, inspecting, rejecting, and haggling for a bargain, without regard for anyone's feelings. No say over any of it."

She gazed into space. Her expression looked as if she was describing a movie she was viewing.

"What troubles you most right now?" I gingerly inquired, not wanting to appear intrusive.

"I hold a degree but I've never worked outside my home. I've participated in clubs, charity events, and Hilton Academy mothers club, but no employment." She shrugged.

I looked away as she spoke, to somehow ease her embarrassment. It was all too familiar.

"I have no job skills or work history. I've given my energies to decorating and remodeling my house, tending my gardens and being a mother to Tyler. I've loved that. With the auctioning of my house and its contents, it's all gone. After Saturday, we'll be on the street."

An errant tear streamed down her porcelain-like skin. She swiped at it with obvious embarrassment, as she would an annoying gnat.

She sank in my chair. "I'd appreciate any ideas you might have. I'm willing to try anything."

She couldn't believe she'd bared her soul to this woman, but who else did she have to talk with? She was desperate now, and there was no one—no-one at all—to help.

I ventured, "Mari, I experienced severe financial difficulties when I divorced. Like you, I had nothing, but Julia helped me find a job and a place to live. God and my friend, Julia, were all I had; no one else."

Mari gazed at me. Her expression was expectant, but she said nothing.

"This house is my family's rental property. When I returned to Baltimore to care for my mother, it was vacant. I'll be here until her situation is resolved. You and Tyler are welcome to stay, but with Ruth and Sam,

Jr., it'll be crowded. Tyler could use my finished basement as his room. It's pretty bad, but it's yours."

Mari's eyes widened, "If this is a rental property, you'll need to fix it up for renting it again, right?" She scooted toward the edge of her seat, while her hands gently clapped together with renewed excitement.

"Yes," I acknowledged. I winced, recalling other things needing my attention. I visualized endless lists of needed repairs for this house and all the others.

"Suppose I decorate it in lieu of rent each month?" Mari quickly added.

She could hardly believe it: a place to live. She had no money for rent, but maybe Gloria would consider barter in exchange for her generous offer of hospitality.

"That would be a huge relief", I said, feeling part of my burden lift. "No one would rent this place without a lot of work."

Mari looked eager enough, but she had no idea what might be involved in fixing this place. From her desperate standpoint, she thinks it's a great deal. *How long would it take for her to feel as overwhelmed as I felt?* I wonder. Well, I could do nothing to disguise its flaws from anyone now. In my present condition, I could do nothing about anything. Inevitably, she'd see what a nightmare it really is.

Mari added, "I interned for six weeks in the restoration of a storm-damaged house. That historic property needed to be refurbished from foundation up. I could help you plan what to do, while Tyler and I have a place to live. Let me check your basement to see what we have to work with. Gloria, are you comfortable with so many people in your house, though?"

"We'll just have to see. Right now, I'm stuck in one place for who knows how long. I have little say over what goes on with anything here."

Mari beamed. "This will be wonderful. I have left-over paint, wallpaper and supplies at my house. Whatever doesn't sell this weekend, I'll use to decorate."

She was thrilled. Not only would she and Tyler have a place to live, but she could use her love for decorating to return her favor; a creative way to vent her fears and frustrations, as well. Painting and beautifying always helped her relax.

"Bring whatever you like. All this," pointing to odd pieces of furniture, "is just borrowed from Mother's basement."

Mari appeared happier than I'd ever seen her. Light entered her tired eyes, and I could see her facial muscles relax.

"This'll be like sharing my first apartment with sorority sisters." Mari grinned, recalling a much happier time.

Ruth stumbled in, arms draped with clothes and linens. Her son, Sam, Jr., trailed behind her. He was slender, with flaxen hair, large aqua eyes, and his mother's contagious smile.

"Sam, Jr., this will be our new home for a while. We need to take care of Ms. Gloria." Ruth explained, feigning enthusiasm.

Although showing signs of fatigue, Ruth wanted little Sam to see this as an adventure, not a last resort. She hoped to be convincing.

Sam slowly peered from wall to wall. "Where can I sleep?" he asked his mother in hushed tones. He reached down to pet Purrfect.

"Let's go upstairs and see." Ruth answered reassuringly.

Mari bent to Sam's level. "Guess what, Sam? My boy, Tyler, and I are moving in also. He's in high school."

She recalled Tyler at his age. So innocent. She smiled with fleeting memories.

Ruth grinned, "Really? What fun."

"I have a meeting in less than an hour, so I must run." Mari added.

Little Sam nodded, saying, "I'm used to meetings. Mommy and Daddy go to a lot of meetings."

We smiled. *Poor little boy*.

Ruth grabbed Sam's hand, "Let's find our room, shall we?

"When they . . . become impoverished through oppression, trouble and sorrow, He rescues the poor from trouble and increases their families like vast flocks of sheep. . ."
Psalm 107:39-41 (Bible)

Chapter 15

House Plans

The Wilsons

Doris Wilson scooped cabbage onto their plates. Corned beef had been simmering in a slow oven all afternoon. Her mother often said a slow oven was the secret to tender, juicy meat, even cheapest cuts. This was one of Harry's favorites, but she was in no mood to cook today. She couldn't calm herself.

"Harry, Harry, do you hear me? Come and get dinner 'fore it gets cold." She didn't mean to sound so cross, but the sooner this meal was over, the sooner she could get on with the rest of her day. "Harry? Didn't you hear me call?"

She wiped her wet hands on her apron which was more hole than apron. *How old was this thing, anyway?* She shook her head. *Who knew?*

Harry had been dozing while watching the 5:00 news on WBAL. He slid his right hand down to crank the wooden handle of his recliner chair. It jerked him to an upright position, and he struggled to stand.

"UMPH, man-a-live" he groaned, straightened his back and arched it again, his hands supporting his low back. "Comin', Hon—smells good, as always." He stumbled toward the kitchen, tossing the sports section of his evening <u>Sun</u> onto a lamp table.

"My leg's asleep," he mentioned, limping to their table.

"Well, do a dance or shake it a lil' bit, and come sit down."

She thumped onto her thread-bare printed cushion and adjusted her plate, centering it between red and white checks designed in their oil-cloth table cover. Chipped paint on her chair arms caught her attention. These chairs could tell a lot of tales.

Though these chairs were green now, chips revealed yellow—when her first son was born. She felt sunny then. The next coat had been during her pink mood. She guessed she was feeling kind 'a left out, after her last son was born— being th' only girl in th' house, and all. Then it was beige, when she needed quiet and no color seemed to be best then. But when beige showed four sets of fingerprints, she decided on green. But this green was, was what? Gettin' kinda' sorry. She re-focused on her husband.

She smiled, and rested her hand on his calloused fingers. Harry was a good man. She patted his hand.

She'd been a lucky woman and she knew it. He was a hard-worker, and a good provider. Beth'lem Steel had been good t' them, and Harry was a loyal employee. He'd been foreman for the las' coupl'a years, and it promised a comfortable retirement when th' time came. He was faithful, and a good father. He was good to her, and she loved him.

"Harry, bless our food, so we can eat while it's still warm."

Harry scooted his chair a few inches closer to the table, and raised his callused hands in front of him. He noticed his wife's fingers, so gnarled with arthritis.

Maybe he could save a lil' more t' take her t' Florida when they reta-red. He was ta-red a' Bal'mer snows. Although he'd never left th' ole neighborhood where he'd been born, he knew Florida was th' ticket. He and Doris could get a nice lil' single-wide on a coupl'a acres, with some ar'nge trees. Maybe some apricot trees, too. It'd be nice to have some apricot trees. Maybe they didn't grow down 'ere, though. Heck, everythin' grew in Florida, he'd heard.

He bowed his head, "Lord, bless this fine food and my Hon." He grinned, as his wife squeezed his hand.

He carefully ventured out, "Hon, you seem a bit antsy t'night. Ever' thin' all right?" He knew better 'n t' bring up somethin' that'd upset her at dinner. Nothin'could toughen meat faster'n a disagreement at th' table. He'd learned his lesson a time or two o'er th' years.

Doris put her fork down and lifted her napkin to her mouth. "I jes feel so bad. I looked out th' winda' a lil' while ago. I haven't bin over to even welcome lil' Gloria back home. I don't know what's gotten into me, lately. I just keep puttin' off what needs t' be done. When she first moved in over there, I thought about droppin' by, but I knew she was busy with her mama an' all. I thought she'd only be there maybe a week, at most. It's bin months now, and th' poor girl's been all by herself. I haven't even bin over to give her a 'welcome back' or even a pie. Nothin' and I feel really bad 'bout it. I've looked out, and all I've ever seen was her lil' car out back and her light on nights. That's th' way it's always bin. She's taken care of ever'thin' and her hotsy-totsy brothers and sisters, livin' who knows where, not carin' what happens to their mama and poor Lucille. I'm jes sick of what I haven't done." She crumpled her napkin and stuffed it in her hip pocket, attached to her apron with a series of safety pins.

Harry finished a mouth-full of meat and potatoes, and lowered his fork. "Yes, I feel jes as bad. Her daddy made me promise t' look after thins'— rental prop'ties and all— 'specially Gloria, 'cause she's all by he'self. He always made good on his promises in all our bi'ness. After he passed. . . well, I haven't made good on my end of th' deal. No I haven't. I know those prop'ties are in sorry shape—always were. I should've kept up with 'em. I should've looked aroun' when I installed that winda unit. I feel bad, cause I jes didn't and no 'scuse for it neither." He threw his napkin down.

Doris jumped up and grabbed both plates, although neither was finished.

"Doris, I want more 'tate-as."

She replaced his plate, and made her way to the kitchen window above the sink. She raised the ragged, yellowed, paper roller-blind at the window, by jerking its stained crocheted pull. She should get rid of this ole thing. But what was the rush? The only time she ever pulled it down was when the sun was in the west and it was too bright to see each other's face at the table. She studied the house across the street.

"Lands, Harry, there's a lot'a activity over there right now. I hope everythin's O.K. Do you think somethin's happened? Maybe someone died or somethin'?"

Their gold-toned wall-phone rang. Harry made his way to the wall on the other side of their kitchen. He was always glad he added that twenty-foot cord. It allowed him to take a call pretty 'nere wherever he was. Now he needed t' get back t his 'tate-as 'afore Doris threw 'em out.

"Wilson, here." he answered. "Hello, Lucille? Everythin' all right?" Lucille sounded upset, if ever he'd heard her.

"Mr. Harry, I jes' worried sick 'bout Ms. Glory. She fell in the street out front las' evnin' and broke her leg. She spent mos' th' night at Midtown. Her friends stayed with her, as I ain't bin able to leave this house much. You know her mama in Midtown, too, and she don't know, and law, who knows what'd happen if she find out. She hadn't bin he'self in some time, y'know. I'd be obliged if you and Ms. Doris look in on her. She be like my own chile—and if anythin' happin' t' her—well, it's hard to tell what would happin' to any of us."

He'd never heard Lucille in such a tizzy. What she said was true, fer sure. There'd be a lot 'a hurtin' people 'round if somethin' was to happen t' lil' Glory.

"Lucille, I'm on it now. I'll let you know jes what's what, as soon as I find out. Now don't worry. Doris and I'll take care a' thin's, jes like we promised. Yes, yes, I'll call you back. Now you rest. It'll be all right."

At that, Harry jumped up and bellowed, "Time to git over there."

Gloria

"I can't get comfortable," I mumbled.

It seemed impossible to turn my body so I could reach my covers, hold onto my pillow, and not cause some muscle, somewhere, to hurt. I'd learn to do this. I certainly would not call Ruth to help me. Poor Ruth has to be exhausted from all of it. *Why did I have to do such a stupid thing?*

As if by my just thinking about her, Ruth popped in carrying cups of Earl Grey decaf with a sugar cookie on each saucer.

"Sarah bought cookies—day old, and a bargain."

We giggled. It was fun being able to laugh at our difficult circumstances. I realized, suddenly, how miserable I'd been, living alone and not being able to share with anyone. I'd been taking myself far too seriously. It's odd how we hold onto familiar circumstances and and defend them, even—not because they're good, happy, or have any merit whatsoever ,but merely because we're used to them. Perhaps it's the thought of change and risking more pain, that keeps us entrenched in misery.

Wow. Where had that thought come from? Certainly worthy of further consideration. I wonder if that's a universal with our human condition, or, as Jules would say, my melancholy again? Hmmm.

"Mind if I rest for a minute?"

Ruth settled in a chair scrunched in my make-do bedroom.

"Please. I'd love to have a spot of tea with a friend."

Ruth's eyes were underscored with dark half moons, and her usually rosy cheeks looked drained of color.

Ruth stretched her legs, sighing deeply. "Sorry, I'm a little tired."

"I guess so, and I want to apologize. You don't need to be running around for me when you're under such stress. I'm sorry. I must say, though, I would never have survived without you and the other girls. I can't thank you enough."

"I'm the one who needs to thank you. When I'm busy helping others, I can't focus on my own troubles. Right now, that's a gift. Thank you for that, but also coming to our rescue with a place to stay, food, and friendship when Sam, Jr. and I have absolutely nothing."

"Ruth," I started after a purposeful pause, having bitten off a bite of cookie and taking a gulp of tea. I pretended to wipe imaginary crumbs from my blanket to take my focus off her for a minute.

"I don't know too much more about your situation other than what you shared Tuesday night. We're alone for a few minutes. Do you feel comfortable sharing with me now?"

Ruth looked down, twiddling her spoon. "I think I'd be more comfortable talking about someone else's problems. When I look at my own, I realize no one can help me but God, and He seems really far away right now."

I nodded.

"My life's been wrapped up in my husband's ministry since I left college to marry. His mission became mine. I was sure that was God's will."

She continued. "I dedicated myself to what was important to Sam. I had no separate life, but isn't that the way it should be? Well, I see it was Sam and Sam, alone, now. I was just there to make it go smoothly."

"I know"

Bless her heart. I remember feeling much the same way when I was married to Charles. I was there to make his home-life, his professional life, and the life of our child go more smoothly. Wasn't that the role of a wife and mother? It certainly was the norm when I was growing up. A wife dedicated her life to managing her home and family–at least other families I'd observed—certainly not my own. My cues were taken from Lucille and June Cleaver, (mom on *Leave it to Beaver)*, I guess—apron and all.

Now, young women held careers, primarily—their homes often an afterthought. They held an identity all their own. In some ways, I guess it gives women more choices, but I couldn't help think it's a lot more frantic work, also. What happened when hectic home schedules and work responsibilities collided into twenty-four hours?

What happens to Mom, when she's expected to rise early to make lunches and get everyone, including herself, off to work, school, day-care, whatever. Often accomplishing this having been up all night with a sick or teething child, maybe washing soiled sheets and cleaning bathrooms during pre-dawn hours. Then, coming home from work, facing dinner preparation, dirty dishes, laundry, homework, crying children, and a husband who's feeling amorous when she didn't have an ounce of energy left to spare.

Having lived both ways, the new life of super mom was exhausting and at best thankless by husbands, children, employers, and largely by society—who often expected all-doing Mom to do even more, plus be responsible for results.

Like Ruth, myself and other newly single women, when the old way suddenly ends, all identity supports disappear, and one's left in a kind of limbo–often not knowing which way is up; where solid ground was to place a foothold.

"Gloria, I just don't understand. I did everything I knew to do. I sacrificed all my desires, for what? Did it make him better or make him love me more? No. I've been deserted by him, by friends, and at times, I feel even by God."

She looked at me with pleading eyes, indicating she needed to share more.

"I feel so stupid not to have seen this coming. I'm embarrassed because he left me for a man. I wonder about my own value as a wife, even a woman."

Her head dropped in her hands.

The pain of this poor girl was almost more than I could bear to hear. I hesitated before answering; looking into my tea cup as if some script might be written there. I silently prayed for insight or something worthwhile.

"Ruth," I started out, "God gives each of us free choice. You chose to do right. Sam chose to do wrong. No one can make someone do right or wrong—no matter how much you care. Only God can change a heart."

She just looked at me, or maybe through me was more accurate. I was suddenly aware of the refrigerator motor droning, almost like a commiserating moaning.

"I don't believe anyone has chosen to hurt you. How could anyone think of hurting you? Your husband simply wanted what he wanted. He's choosing to be blind to consequences of his actions, like a spoiled child wanting his own way. It's horribly unfair that you and little Sam are taking the brunt of it. It's got to be terribly painful for you, but you did nothing to cause it."

"You think so?"

"During my divorce, like you, I lost my home. I lost my job, I lost my church. I lost my reputation and friends, from false rumors. My son and I have been reeling for the past fifteen years. I understand a little of your pain."

Ruth's head remained in her hands. Through sobs, she confided, "I'm in the middle of a whirlwind of emotions I can't sort out. I want to be strong, but all I can do is cry." She wiped her eyes.

"Yes, I remember feeling like that. You're grieving over tremendous loss in nearly every area of your life and dreams. Just remember, others may have deserted you, but God promises he never will. We have to latch onto that promise."

Ruth arose, "Yes, but it's so hard." She sniffed and murmured, "Well, you need rest. Sometime when you're feeling better, I need to sign up for work training. Sam, Jr. is growing and will need new clothes for winter. Who knows what other bills I'll have?"

"Ruth, I need to say something else. You need legal advice. I'll talk with Julia to see if our program offers any help."

At that moment, my doorbell rang, which is amazing, since its wiring is loose. It rarely worked even as much as the skeleton key worked in its lock.

My mind was swimming again. I could relate to Ruth's overwhelming confusion more than she knew. This pain medication was miserable.

Ruth stuck her head back into my alcove after answering my door. "Feel like more company?"

Mr. and Mrs. Wilson skidded in and stood next to my bed. Mrs. Wilson sang my name, gently,

"Glor-y, Hon, Harry and I are jes sick at what's happened to you. Lucille jes told us about your leg. I'm jes beside myself that Harry and I've not bin over here to take care a' things ourselves."

She stood penitent, wringing her hands. Her husband stood beside her, holding his Oriole cap in his hands. He studied ceiling and walls.

"Gloria, Hon, why didn't you call me 'bout fixin' this place. Aren't you cole in here? It's worse'n I ever 'magined."

"Well, Mr. Wilson, it hasn't been that bad, but since you mentioned it, I do need help, and rather quickly. If it were just me, it wouldn't matter, but a friend and her little boy have moved upstairs to help me. Another friend will be moving in this week, with her teenage son living in the basement."

At this, Harry darted to my basement. Minutes later, he returned, and asked permission to look upstairs. Returning to my bedside, he reported,

"It's not fit fer man ner beast t' live in this place, upstairs or down. Leaks in yer basement, and yer roof, an' that's th' good part. Ya got rotten boards, and I don't know what all. I had no idea thin's were as bad as they are, Hon. If yer goin' t' be livin' here with yer friends, we've got t'get busy—fast. I'll get th' boys from Beth'lem Steel t' help. They owe me big time. It's 'bout time I called it in."

He left to check out my bathroom, as his wife called, "Harry, come and look at this bowl. It's got cracks a mile wide, and this floor's disgusting."

He returned, hat in hand.

"Hon, we'll be leavin' now. I've got a lot a' calls t' put in. I've bin lax, that's what I've bin, but we'll make it up t' you. This place'll be lookin' better 'fore th' week's out. Now you figger what color you want fer fixtures, and me'n th' boys'll take care o' th' rest. What color paint you want?"

Goodness. My mind is spinning with this medicine. I can barely remember my own name. *Paint color, fixtures? I have no idea. I had to think . . . wait a minute. Mari's arranging the decorating and renovation in exchange for room and board. Yes. It's time to delegate.*

"My friend is bringing leftover paint from her last house. Whether it'll be enough, I don't know. She can talk with you about that. Her son is the one who will be in the basement."

"Law, nothing alive should live down 'ere. We'll start down 'ere first. How ole is he?"

"17 years old, I think."

"Well, maybe he'd like t' help us, tell us what he needs down 'ere, and all. Be a part a' th' fixin'."

"Sounds good. This move is largely unexpected, and he's not handling it too well, I don't believe."

"Well, if he's seen 'at basement, it's no doubt." Mr. Wilson shook his head.

Poor child, his whole life has been turned upside down with losing his home and his father. What would his reaction be when he sees where he has to live? I had no idea what was down there, but I wouldn't want to stay down there, myself, or have my son stay down there either.

Doris grabbed his hands, "We didn't mean t' stay so and talk on and on, when you need rest. You take care a' yourself, and be sure t' call us, hear?" At that, they exited my front door.

My mind was at ease with the Wilson's helping. He'd see things were done right, as my father used to say. One less thing I had to worry about . . . but it only made a small dent in the number of issues on my mind.

I needed sleep. I fell back against my pillow and closed my eyes.

"When the poor and needy search for water and there is none; their tongues are parched from thirst, then I, the Lord, will answer them. I, the God of Israel will never forsake them." Isaiah 41:17 (Bible, NIV).

Wednesday afternoon—late

I awoke with what felt like a kiss. Opening my eyes, with a start, I recognized Bill, leaning over my hospital-style bed.

"Hey, Sleeping Beauty." He grinned.

"Bill, I can't believe it's you. I've missed you so much." I pulled his head down with a hug.

"I've looked forward to this for months. It took a fractured tibia to finally stop you dead in your tracks, so I could catch you."

He glanced around and winced.

"If I'd known my girl was living in this Yankee city and in this broken-down hovel, I would've been up here much sooner. Why didn't you tell me it was this bad? No, don't tell me. But now I'll worry about you all the more when I leave."

"Oh, it's so good to see you—am I still dreaming?"

Umm, to touch his face and smell his scent—I'd forgotten what comfort it always brings. I decide to sneak another kiss.

"No, but I intend to take you out of this dream and into another. Who is this lovely lady who answered your door?" He looked toward my kitchen.

"Ruth." I answered.

"Ruth?" he called.

Ruth bobbed in, blurting out, "Sorry, I let someone in and didn't ask your permission first. Somehow, I didn't think you'd mind." She grinned broadly.

"Ruth", Bill continued, "I need to go back to Cross Roads Inn, and I want to take Sleeping Beauty with me.

Would you mind gathering a few belongings for a four-day break for our girl, please?"

Ruth giggled and said, "It'll only take a few minutes."

I heard her scamper up stairs, two at a time.

"Bill, I really can't leave. People are coming this week to renovate, and two other people are moving in . . ."

How could he possibly know how many details needed to be attended to here? On the other hand, I really did not want to let go of his hug. Feeling his strong arms around me prodded my mind to slide out of responsibility mode into—do I dare think it—desire?

"Nonsense, what can you do but get in the way, and who, may I ask, would even want to move into this place," Again, scanning this room and shaking his head.

It's true. I really can do nothing here. After all, I'd be with My doctor, not my Doctor (I grinned with this play on words). 24-hour, around-the-clock care. I could certainly use a vacation. After all, I'd worked hard. I need a change of pace to get a fresh perspective, right?

"Look, I have rooms reserved for you and me—I know, I know. I remember. You need to have your own room. I've arranged for a nursing assistant through the hotel, who will help you bathe and dress. Come on. We have so much to catch up on."

We do have a lot to catch up on. After all, he has come all this way—just for me. But, I feel so unattractive—this old nightgown and robe—clean, but gross looking.

"Bill, I don't know. I haven't been able to dress with this cast, and I'm supposed to be off it for a week."

I really don't imagine he'd care about what I wore—or didn't wear, right? After all, nice clothes can be highly overrated, can't they?

He'd seen me in nice clothes for years. He knew what I looked like in nice clothes.

"Well, a few days at Cross Roads Inn are just what this doctor orders. As for clothes, I'll wrap you in a coat and blanket. Who cares who's watching? I'll just carry you through the lobby and up the elevator. No one will notice and who cares if they do?"

Bill kissed me lightly on my lips and nuzzled my neck. I giggled.

Maybe I could convince him to make sure I was concealed under this blanket as we paraded through that lobby. *Suppose someone I know sees us? Enjoying his nuzzle, I thought, who cares if they do.*

"You've convinced me."

Bill kissed my fingertips and whispered, "You won't be sorry."

At that, Bill lifted my dead weight plus cast and stumbled toward my back door.

Ruth ran down my stairs with a bulging grocery bag in hand.

"I've packed toiletries, night gown, robe and some sweet-smelling talc and perfume, pain meds, hair stuff, toothbrush, floss, and cosmetics. I don't want to hear from you until Sunday morning, all right?"

"But," I protested, "Ruth, what about the men who are coming?"

I had to do some protesting. After all, I had to act like I was being responsible, right? I do hope she found my nice nightgown—the one I always kept with me, recalling Mother's admonition about hav-

ing a nice gown in case of a hospital stay—along with nice undies. But, my cast wouldn't allow undies. . . .

Ruth shrugged, grinning.

"Tell them white bathroom fixtures, and ask Mari Carroll about other decorating details, as she's bringing paint and furniture."

"Will do" and she scooted Bill out with the slamming of the door.

Mari

A tinkling bell signaled my entrance into this Charles Street antique shop. A clerk, busy tagging a stack of oriental rugs, raised his head with the sound of an overhead bell.

"Can I be of assistance?" Tony (identified by his name tag) asked, with a raspy voice.

I shivered, seeing his expression. *Something decidedly unsavory about his appearance—somehow, he didn't look like he belonged among the lovely things in this showroom.*

Hoping he didn't notice my hesitancy, I quickly proceeded to inform him of my appointment with the auctioneer. As he strode toward the back and approached a door labeled, employees only, I called, "My name is Mrs. McGuire."

I dreaded this. I'd felt much the same way when I'd planned Pete's funeral. But, then again, this was different. That was kind of a surrendered loathing—I could do nothing but allow that process to happen, like being swept away in a flood. I simply had to endure that. Besides, the funeral home staff was so kind and comforting.

Now, in contrast, I wanted to fight this with every ounce of strength I had, to protect myself and my home. This dread was more like anticipating a robbery or assault or something.

He raised his hand to signal he'd heard me. With that action, I noticed a unique ring with a large, black stone in an almost too-high setting for a man's ring; sinister, like his persona.

I dismissed my discomfort as silly. This room, filled with old dark furniture, fed an emotion-charged imagination like mine was today. Too many Alfred Hitchcock movies from my past, I reasoned.

I averted my thoughts and determined to focus on fine period pieces arranged on this showroom floor. Burled mahogany secretaries and highboys gleamed with dancing light from sparkling crystal chandeliers, hanging from a reflective ceiling. Silver hollowware, shining with rich patina, sat, tastefully arranged among shimmering crystal pieces on several sideboards. This store had some impressive items, with similarly remarkable prices, as well.

I encouraged myself I had chosen the right place to maximize prices for my possessions which would be liquidated along with my house. Of course, this auctioneer's fee would be steep also, I knew.

Returning to his tagging, the clerk called, "Mr. Snyder will be with you shortly. Please, look around while you wait."

"Thank you. I shall." I answered, more to myself than to anyone.

I chose to study a large oil painting on the wall closest to me. A fine reproduction of an old master, I concluded, examining brush-stokes.

My concentration was interrupted by the owner's voice.

"Ms. McGuire, I'm Mr. Snyder, store owner and auctioneer. I'm trying to recall your phone message. You have some items you want to consign?"

"Sir, I have an estate auction scheduled for this Saturday. I'd spoken with you about my antiques some time ago." I was suddenly alert to the fact he'd forgotten.

"Oh, yes. Yes, of course. You'd mentioned pieces of particular value you did not want to be auctioned, in order to capitalize on their value by a private sale, later. I remember our conversation now. Have you arranged for your house auction?"

"My late husband arranged for that. It's also scheduled for Saturday."

If it had been up to me, I'd cancel both in a minute.

He called the clerk.

"Tony, check that we have Saturday down for Mrs. McGuire. Make sure our equipment will be available for an estate auction."

Tony's leering gaze traveled from my face and focused on my body parts, far longer than was appropriate. He was sleezy. His expression, greasy hair and beady eyes made my skin crawl. I willed this meeting to be over soon.

Mr. Snyder closed his calendar. "When can I see the items to be auctioned?"

This is it, I guess. I was forced to allow these vultures to ogle my house, my furniture, my life. My lip quivered. I hated this. I hated everything about this. I coached myself to be civil and appear gracious, before I spoke.

"I could take you to my house now, if it's convenient."

He glanced at his watch, "Tony, would you bring the van around to the front, please?"

He grabbed his jacket from a coat tree, and breezed out the door, turning the hanging sign from "Open" to "Out to lunch."

Walking toward my house, Mr. Snyder asked, "Mrs. McGuire, you don't sound like you're from here originally?"

"You are correct, Sir. I'm originally from the N'Orleans area." I managed to say through clenched teeth and a forced smile.

"Ah," he nodded. Noting my cool response, he studied his notebook, with no further attempted conversation.

Approaching my front door, Mr. Snyder whistled, "Great house, Mrs. McGuire. You don't see many like this anymore."

Yes, great house, all right. A white elephant and I knew it. I loved this house with its twelve-foot ceilings, handsome millwork, decorative moldings in every room and its view of Sherwood gardens. As exquisite as it was, my house was a relic. The market for such a property was exceedingly small, I knew.

It cost a fortune to heat and cool. Its grounds, with their ornamental shrubbery, required a full-time gardener. No, there would not be many who would want it, but auction it was, and auction it would be. I was resigned. No other choice.

Mr. Snyder, Tony, and I visited each room. I indicated which pieces would stay, which ones would be offered for auction, and which ones would be sold separately, later.

Mr. Snyder commented "You do know your antiques."

No comment was called for, I decided.

As we spoke, Tony made notes describing each piece, organizing a written inventory. Large placard numbers were placed on items to be auctioned to minimize confusion on Saturday.

He seemed to gape as lewdly at my possessions as he'd leered at me earlier.

I wanted to chase both of them, but especially Tony, out of my house as I would chase a rodent from attacking a baby: my baby, my things. Me.

My grandfather clock, positioned on the landing and acting as my sentinel, began its hour chime, signaling a multi-dong goodbye.

"Now, before I leave, let me confirm the time. 10:00, Saturday, correct? We'll arrive by 8:00 a.m. I'll call your Realtor directly to coordinate details. Mrs. McGuire, I'd advise your separating items you do not want sold, before Saturday. Did you want to be present for your auction?" he asked, finally.

"No thank you, Sir."

I could barely restrain abhorrence from my voice. My whole being repulsed with the these interlopers.

"Well, suit yourself, "he mumbled.

Moving toward my door, and rudely pushing passed me, Mr. Snyder called out, "Tony, make haste with that vehicle. We have another appointment."

He bounded stoop steps, allowing my storm door to slam behind him, not bothering to say even a civil goodbye.

Chapter 16

Reality Strikes Again

Saturday Morning Auction

Mari

"Bzzz, bzzz, bzzz, bzzz."

Odious and needless, I determined, trying to ignore that offensive noise.

I stirred in pre-dawn hours without reminders. A video of past events—garish auction sign, his last words, the police, and his funeral—played for the millionth time, to alert me—hours before my alarm ever sounded.

This morning was the same. I'd lain awake, putting off what was ahead. I wanted to enjoy my bed, my room, my house for a last time. I needed to prepare for yet another funeral, of memories and dreams. Errant tears escaped, slipped into my ears and dampened hair at my temples.

I repeated, out loud, "I must be strong for Tyler. I have to pretend to be in control."

Pretending required carrying an enormous weight, something like a 150-pound backpack. It was harder and harder to square my shoulders, as I'd been taught.

Mother's words played, "Mari, hold your head high. You are a lady. A lady must be poised, n'est pas? Problems must not alter your beauty."

She'd kiss my cheek and with a flutter of her hand, she'd flitter away, diaphanous and moth-like.

But it was just too hard. I fear I might just dissolve into the ground if I'm not careful. I pulled my covers around my neck. Just a few more minutes. . .*God, please help me.*

"Ok, allons. It's a new day, n'est pas?" I wiped my eyes and threw back covers.

I wandered unsteadily to our bathroom, tunneling through a narrow path of labeled boxes. I'd shower, dress, and then awaken Tyler. Only 5:00, but I needed a quiet breakfast with my son—private time before life as we'd known it came to an end. We needed time.

My line of vision rested unwillingly on large numbers which singled items to be auctioned. We were sitting, not in our home, but in a showroom. Surreal. My stomach shut down, not allowing me to swallow even milk-sodden cereal.

6:00. Tyler poured remaining juice, and emptied crumbs from our last box of cereal. I encouraged him to finish leftover milk, as well.

He sat, wordless, staring into his bowl. Suddenly, silence shattered. Tyler stood, shoving his chair across our tile floor.

"Why did Dad have to die anyway? Didn't he think about me, and my life?"

With an oath, he grabbed our back door knob, hurled it open and slammed it on his way outside.

Tyler hadn't displayed much emotion in past weeks. I must let him go. I was glad we'd arisen early. He needed time to process, or at least try. I edged one of my curtains ever so slightly.

Tyler sat on a parched portion of grass, crying. Rags, our Golden Retriever, tried to comfort him with his swinging tail and a tongue-licking. Our dog didn't know his back yard home was no more, as well.

I took inventory of our lawn: basketball hoop at the top of our driveway, lacrosse goal in the back, jungle gym Santa'd brought his third Christmas hugged ground only feet away. I'd miss this. I felt like pieces of me were being shed with each moment, disappearing to a place I could not go to retrieve, like wind-blown autumn leaves.

We'd bring our dog, his house, basketball-hoop, and lacrosse goal—in hopes of a future. Nothing of Tyler's would be sold. My son was not responsible for problems compounded by loss of his father. Only my possessions would be liquidated. It didn't matter anymore. It hurt to feel. I just wanted it over as quickly as possible.

A truck motor sounded in our driveway; a U-haul Tyler's friends agreed to pack. They bargained to help in exchange for lunch, dinner, videos and snacks this evening. I failed to tell these strapping young men they'd also have to return Gloria's furniture to St. Edmonds, to make room for ours. I'd mention this tidbit after lunch. Timing is everything.

As I opened our front door to welcome them, I saw our auctioneer and his lecherous assistant exiting their car. The Realtor's car parked behind.

"Show time," I said to myself, trying valiantly to raise my shoulders, hold my head high and display a welcoming smile.

Ruth

Dollar Store. I used my pencil stub to add this to my errand list. Sam, Jr. needed school supplies.

I'd wanted him to join me for an outing. No way. He was completely smitten with this house-reconstruction.

Mr. Wilson had been so patient, showing him how to hold a hammer, drive a nail, measure with a tape and read a level. When I'd last checked on him, Sam Jr. was busy sanding with a sand-paper-wrapped block.

This move had turned into such a wonderful learning experience. For this time in my life, literal home-schooling provided entertaining attention for Sam, Jr. which I was simply unable to give. He was happy, and so, I was too.

He was so excited about a high school lacrosse player moving in. He'd met Tyler when he visited earlier this week. Mr. Wilson encouraged them both to help paint Tyler's new room.

That room hadn't looked fit for anyone when I first ventured into that basement. However, when you have no place to live, it'd look fine, I suppose. Now, that dank, dark hole was being transformed into a young man's room. It was OK. Actually, it was better than OK—it was cool.

Sam, Jr. and I shared a tiny room upstairs. My bed filled most of our room. My linens and favorite pillow made it like home. It's odd how familiar covers and an old pillow can bring comfort.

Sam, Junior's Spiderman sleeping bag lay near the foot of my bed. He loved it probably for the same reason I did my pillow—a little piece of home. Since it was a sleeping bag, this whole experience became an adventure. Our suitcases lay opened on remaining floor space. A small closet held my skirts and dresses and Sam's pants and blazer, nothing else.

In my childhood, we often took in a cat with kittens or a dog with puppies. I grieved to keep them in a box in a dark laundry room by themselves. I thought they'd be happier to run free. Daddy'd explained a mother animal with her babies feels more secure in a small, confined place. They feel less vulnerable to the outside world.

Strangely, that's how I felt in this small room with Sam. In the dark, with walls closely around us, surrounded by our few belongings, I felt protected from danger. We were secure. No one could hurt us. Sam needed to feel safe, and I needed it more.

Onward to Dollar Store.

I yelled goodbye through the basement door, and grabbed my coat.

The shopping center parking lot was packed. I eased into the first vacant place. As I walked toward stores, I noticed cameramen. From a TV station, I guess, hunting some big story or celebrity. I'd noticed their vans behind me while driving. I could hardly imagine anything newsworthy at this strip mall.

Bright colors from all manner of sundries lured me through isles once I was inside. I was glad for the distraction these displays could bring. I wondered about purchasing something for Gloria—as a thank you. Nothing in this store could measure up to my gratitude, but I didn't have much cash. As I chose pencils, I noticed a journal—rather attractive, really, for its price. I'd add a bright-colored ink pen, and a coordinating gift bag.

Exiting the store with my purchases, I was suddenly blinded by camera lights. Unknown voices hurled questions like poison darts:

"How do you feel about your husband's leaving you for a male prostitute?"

Another reporter leered, "Have you met his gay partner yet?"

Another voice echoed this intrusion, "Who's going to fill your gay husband's place at your church?"

I was dumbstruck. *How did these people know me? How could they be so heartless?*

Forgetting my purchases, I pushed through the growing crowd, and escaped to my car. I slammed my foot against the accelerator. I sped, unseeing.

When would this end? Would this nightmare ever be over?

How I got home is anybody's guess—my home, not the place where my husband and I'd resided. That place no longer existed in any sense. I wanted my room, my place of peace; my box with my young, safe from onslaughts from the world.

I felt as if I was walking through water to enter the house and climb stairs. No one was there except workmen in the basement. I assumed Sam, Jr. was with them.

I could not think about him now. I opened my bedroom door, and fully-clothed, crawled under my covers, pulled my comforter nearly over my head, and hugged my pillow to my aching chest.

"Have mercy on us, Lord, have mercy on us, for we have endured no end of contempt. We have endured much ridicule from the proud, much contempt from the arrogant. "
Psalm 123:3-4 (Bible, NIV)

Sunday

Katie

It's almost 4:00. We should've gone to church.

Sundays are always difficult.

Our daily routine changed on Sunday. If Don was going to be out of sorts, it'd be Sunday.

He never joined the boys and me at church, so that would give us a little time away; a shorter day, a relief. A leg-up on Monday, when our routine would usually go back to normal—when he'd return to his office and the boys and I would proceed through our weekly activity schedule.

On Sundays, if we went to church, we could stay for afterglow, when children could play and eat snacks. I often volunteered at their nursery, which could easily keep us occupied—physically and mentally—until nearly 2:00 p.m. I might even stretch it to 2:30 with clean-up.

Timmy had awakened with a runny nose, this morning. I didn't feel comfortable about his being around other children. Germs were a big issue in that nursery, so I wouldn't risk exposing anyone else's child. Not a way to keep friendships with other moms, that's for sure. So, reluctantly, I'd decided to stay home. Mistake.

Sunday was too long a day to spend at home. Few things could distract Timmy. He had no fever, and he was bored: probably just allergies.

We needed to get out of here, but where could we go for diversion?

I ran through my list of possibilities. Most places were closed on Sundays. The YMCA closed by 5:00, Saturday. Walmart stayed open late. Maybe after dinner I'd take Timmy there while Jeremy busied himself with homework. Don would be gone—hopefully soon—to his office, to prepare for his week (whatever that meant).

Only a short time before dinner is over–our only landmark for today. As I thought about it, much of our lives were scheduled around avoiding Don. It was an ever-changing puzzle figuring just what might set him off— a sequence I never quite got right.

He always said I was the cause of his problems—all of them. I'd tried everything, over eighteen long years, to change aspects of my personality or habits I thought might upset him. Nothing ever worked, though. I didn't even know who I was, anymore.

I was so tired of this way of living. Walking on eggshells was my constant preoccupation. I was weary of it now, after trying madly to please an un-pleasable person, all these years.

I had to ride this out, somehow. Mark said, just six more weeks. I had no other choice. It seemed like an unreachable goal. I'd try, but tension was heavy, especially today.

Quiet was not a prerequisite for hearing Don's pacing upstairs. It had intensified steadily since this morning. I'd started fixing dinner early, as a result. I didn't want any problems.

I found myself moving quickly, now, almost to the rhythm of this background pounding of footsteps. Bump, bump, bump.

Although it was clearly too early for dinner, I just had to end this day.

Pounding sounds of Don's steps on hardwood grew louder and more pronounced. Bump, bump, bump, bump. Today, he seemed exceedingly anxious. Had he ever been quite like this before? Same play, same act; different scene, I concluded.

The children sensed it, too—like calm before a storm, when animals go and seek shelter. We'd been through this before. Without words, we knew things were out of kilter. A storm was approaching.

Jeremy was positioned at our table, staring into space, tapping his pencil to the beat of background percussion. Timmy curled in a corner with his blanket, his thumb planted in his mouth. As I darted around with food containers, I questioned this craziness, but I couldn't think about that. Not now. I must concentrate on just getting dinner over.

His pacing quickened.

Oddly enough, it was punctuated with distant thunder. A thunderstorm at this time of year was unusual. I hugged my kitchen sink, while gazing at dark, threatening clouds.

I'd peel potatoes. Yes, that was next. Water in the pot was now at a rolling boil. Steam poured overhead. Slivers of potato skins collected helter-skelter around white porcelain.

I peeled a carrot and gave it to Timmy. I peeled another and handed it toward Jeremy. He pushed it away.

The pacing quickened. Footsteps sounded heavier, louder. Bump, bump, bump.

Why not just load the kids into the car and go to MacDonald's?

They needed a decent meal, though. It was Sunday, for heaven's sake. We had more than our share of fast food. *But would one more night make any difference?*

I was tempted to switch off the stove and leave. Seeing Timmy in only a diaper and t-shirt, made me stop. I'd have to go upstairs to get his clothes. That move would necessitate passing Don in the hallway. No, I'd continue with this meal, rather than risk anything.

My heart thundered. I felt light-headed with its quickening beats, which countered in a syncopated rhythm with Don's footsteps. I didn't want to recognize my fear, which was such a prevailing part of my life.

I released the refrigerator door handle and stared inside—at nothing, really. My hand trembled, markedly. *Oh God, I prayed silently, "How much longer do I have to endure this prison."*

I was shocked by my thoughts.

My marriage was not a relationship of love, but control. I was a prisoner in my own house. True, but it hurt too much to ponder this truth. It would do no good.

Keep moving, I told myself.

All of a sudden, I heard bellowing from upstairs, "Kate."

Oh, God. He only used the name Kate when things were bad. Timmy started to whimper. Jeremy sat still, but kicked his feet on his chair legs, rhythmically, eyes widening.

I turned back to the sink to pretend to be involved in peeling carrots. It sounded again.

"Kate!"

Words electrified, with more emotion than his last call. His heavy steps sounded on each of the hardwood steps, as he kept repeating my name. It would be seconds until he was in our kitchen. I thrust my peeler blade faster.

"Where's dinner?" he screamed.

I turned to answer, and felt his fingers gripping my arm, followed by a blow to the side of my face. The peeler bounced off a counter as I careened across the floor.

Once I caught my balance, Don danced around me as if guarding someone in basketball. Oddly I saw his eyes focused on something way above my head. *What could he be looking at?* Hallucination, no doubt.

Timmy cried, "Mama."

Oh, Gosh, Oh, Gosh. Timmy, how can I get to Timmy? Don could hurt Jeremy, too. He could hurt us all. He could kill us all.

My hands felt like I was holding ice. My throat constricted. I feared if I had to scream I wouldn't be able to emit any sound, like those horrible dreams when you can't run and you can't scream.

I had to do something, but what? I couldn't think—life was sequencing in disconnected slides now—fast forward speed.

I noticed a small window of opportunity to bypass his swing. I'd try to dive passed him and get our cordless phone. Before I could move, he reeled around and struck me again.

I sprawled to the floor. I could hear nothing but ringing. Everything's fuzzy. I tasted blood on my lip, but I could not rise. The baby was crying somewhere, way in the distance.

Clouds bobbed at the ceiling. My mother and father floated past. What were they doing in my kitchen? I needed to get up . . .

Darkness.

"Have mercy on me, Oh, God, have mercy! I look to you for protection. I will hide beneath the shadow of your wings until this violent storm is past"
Psalm 57-1 (Bible)

Chapter 17

...And Again

Sunday Evening

Glory

It's been like heaven, itself—beyond words. But, today, Sunday, stark reality has exchanged itself for my four-day dream with Bill at the Cross Roads Inn.

I already missed his touch. My longings were almost painful. I'd definitely crossed over the chasm between calling him friend and redefining him as much more.

I shook my head to force myself back to the situation at hand.

More reality as Ruth heaved a huge bag of this week's mail for me to sort. Mostly bills, I notice, along with the newspaper. I must cancel this. No one in this house needed to see anything in this paper, except grocery coupons.

News, almost always bad, was certainly something we could do without. There was enough pain and suffering in this one household to fill volumes of papers. Ruth might read some one-sided take on her problems, and it would likely increase all our suffering. We didn't need any of that.

Bills. I took a deep breath and gulped my tepid tea. I'd have to take care of these this week.

I needed to contact my brother, George, about power of attorney. With Mother's doctors and hospital bills starting to pour in, plus expenses of both houses, I certainly could use some help. My limited savings were dwindling.

Funds were set aside for Mother's care and the upkeep of our rental properties, but, they were all in her name. My siblings and I'd discussed this problem, but legal steps hadn't been taken. They'd talked of formalizing it, but they were busy, and probably forgot. I understood, but things were getting tight.

A token salary had been earmarked from this Tuesday night program, but those scant funds would not come for another week. They'd hardly make a dent. I'd call him first thing tomorrow morning.

I settled with a section of newspaper before I tossed it. I shook my head as I skimmed one of its articles.

News centered on an Amish farmer in Pennsylvania whose farm was raided. He was taken into custody. An informer told police he was supplying raw milk to his friends. Six police cars arrived, arrested this farmer and took him to jail.

This was silly. It'd be one thing if he was selling illegal drugs, but raw milk? What would happen if they caught farm hands guzzling raw milk. . . addiction, or some violent behavior against society? Pleeze—

I imagined drug dealers selling raw milk along with their marijuana or cocaine. I imagined truck loads of milk containers hidden in dark alleys and unsavory places. I laughed at pictures in my mind. "Much ado about nothing," I quoted Shakespeare.

Another article, positioned further down the page, reported someone impersonating a police officer. Something about a dismissed cop, with inside connections to police communication, continuing unauthorized activity in Baltimore city and surrounding area. The public was urged to call police regarding any suspicious activity. I skimmed words, bored with information unrelated to me.

Snow/ rain mix expected this weekend summarized a weather block.

Construction plans for I695 scheduled to begin tomorrow. One lane open, east bound, alerted commuters for tomorrow morning's delay.

Blah, blah, blah.

Uh-oh, not good: at the bottom of this front page was a large picture of Ruth's husband,—his new look and his new beau. There was an accompanying article which I wouldn't read. Gossip, that's all it was. I quickly tossed the whole thing in the trash and asked Sarah to dispose it soon. Ruth didn't need to see this.

Sarah was putting finishing touches on dinner. Her cooking was amazing. I could only guess what it would be tonight, with smells of Garlic, tomato, basil and oregano wafting into my little space. Ymmm. If I didn't watch it, instead of my wheelchair, I'd need to be rolled out of bed each day with a crane, or something.

Rebecca was setting the table and the tray that would bridge my wheelchair arms. Ruth was occupied upstairs.

Tyler and Sam, Jr. had taken their food downstairs to enjoy a football game in the 'male' room, not minding poor reception. Tyler's bed, pool table, and possessions had been delivered earlier this week. Although a bit prematurely in view of renovations, it was close enough and the boys relished a place of their own.

I was told pictures of sports idols were already on walls, and stereo equipment and speakers set up, ready to play music (Did they even call that stuff 'stereo' anymore? I'm dating myself again).

Mr. Wilson insisted on additional ceiling insulation, so Tyler could play his music and have his space, without disturbing us ladies. Fine with me. I could hardly wait to be off these crutches, to see its progress. Amazing what could be done with a dilapidated house in a relatively short time. Kudo's to Mr. Wilson and his team.

Mari curled in one of her peach brocade chairs, studying a brochure describing Real Estate classes. The course was relatively short, and with her decorating gifts and her love of houses, I encouraged her to pursue it. The displaced homemakers program would help fund a portion of its cost.

Dark circles underscored her eyes. She was exhausted from her move yesterday, but hope filled her tired eyes. Maybe this class would keep her mind off finances and Tyler's schooling. One thing at a time.

With Sarah's beckoning, Rebecca, Ruth and Mari pulled stools around our new island. I wheeled close to the door, balancing my tray on my wheelchair. Close enough to be a part of the conversation but not in the way.

I was enjoying the symphony of rattling china, glasses and silverware, as well as animated conversation, when I thought I heard a soft knock at my door. I glanced out a window; maybe a branch. Wind gusts had picked up, but nothing was in view.

"Did anyone hear a knock at our door?" I asked.

Everyone quieted, but shrugged, indicating they had not.

There it was again.

"Didn't anyone hear that? I know I heard something," I countered. It was too vivid to be my imagination. I'm sure I heard footsteps, Was it a child's cry? Sometimes a cat's cry could sound like a crying child.

Ruth arose, still chewing, and wiping her hands on a napkin, "I'll check"

Upon opening the door, at once paled and wide-eyed, she screamed, "Katie. Oh, no, oh no, come in."

We gasped.

Katie stood, balancing Timmy on her hip, dressed in only a thin t-shirt. Her right eye was swollen and her eyelids shaded with red and purple. Blood oozed from her nostrils, and her lips. Her arm was visibly bruising, with red finger marks above her elbow. Welts reddened her cheek and neck.

"Honey, honey. . ." we chorused.

Timmy wailed.

Sarah ran for ice. Ruth retrieved a wet cloth and proceeded to gently wipe her face. I transferred to the couch and encouraged her to sit.

"Who did this to you?'

None of us needed an answer. Silence was chorded by Timmy's sobs. Ruth, eager to distract him, grabbed his hand and walked him toward our basement door.

"Timmy, let's visit the big boys. Tyler and Sam would love for you to see their new room."

Timmy reluctantly accompanied Ruth, thumb firmly wedged in his mouth.

"You need to go to a hospital." I said.

Katie retorted, "No, no, I'm all right. I don't want anyone to see me like this."

"Honey," I coaxed, "you need to be checked to make sure you're all right."

How could I persuade her to seek help? When I gazed at her bloody face, and welts on her neck and arms, I realize how close any of us are to this and worse. Any relationship could turn nasty. Never say never. So many women and children were victimized; many had, and no doubt, would continue to be maimed or killed, sadly by those they loved.

Katie demanded, "No, no, I'll be fine. I just need to rest."

I'd witnessed this before as a social worker, far too many times. It was humiliating for a battered woman to seek help.

I softly embraced her, allowing her to cry.

"Sweetie, I'm really glad you came here. You can stay as long as you need to. You're safe here."

"No" she countered. "If he finds me and Timmy here, all of you will be in danger. I can't risk that. I may have been followed."

In my experience, I doubted it, at this point, anyway. If her husband was like many abusers, he'd be tired from his released tension in the conflict. But he'd be fearful, and tomorrow, well, he could be angry she'd escaped his control.

"Katie," I reiterated, "just visit a hospital to confirm you don't have a head injury. If that goes untreated, something could happen. Then who'd care for Timmy?"

A look of horror crossed her face. "Oh, no. Oh, no."

"Honey, Mari can drive you, and Ruth will go with you to take care of Timmy. I'll call my best friend, Julia, since I can't go. She'll know what to do. She's the best person in the world. She'll be with you, I promise."

I hated for Rebecca to see this. She'd eaten nothing for dinner, and she was now huddled in a corner, crying. Sarah's arms encircled her.

I signaled for Sarah to make a plate for Timmy. She cut a banana for his plate, and I asked Rebecca to deliver it to Timmy.

Sarah proceeded to put another banana, honey, flax oil, milk and some vitamin powder in the blender for a smoothie, in case Katie could not chew. She brought her nutrient-dense, smoothie plus straw to Katie.

"Sarah, sit with Katie, while I call Julia. Mari, please warm your car. Take some blankets out with you. Plenty are in my hall closet. Ruth, dress Timmy warmly and drive Katie's car with Timmy in his car seat. Katie will need her car later."

They silently nodded.

I wheeled my way toward my phone. I dialed Julia's number, and anxiously waited for her to answer. When she did, I spoke in hushed tones.

"Glory, what's the matter?" she asked, alarmed by my tone.

"Jules, Katie has come here, badly battered by her husband."

"Oh my word."

"Call House of Ruth and any others who might help, and meet Katie over at Midtown in thirty minutes or so. No, she doesn't want treatment, but she'll go for the sake of her child. How could someone do this to his own wife, in the presence of their sons? My cast keeps me from coming, but I'm sending Mari and Ruth to the hospital to meet you. Yes, Katie and the baby will need a safe place to stay for tonight, and probably the next couple of days, at least. They'll both need counseling, also. House of Ruth can provide both."

"I'll make some calls and report back." The phone clicked.

"God, please protect Katie and Timmy. Please put your angels in charge. In Jesus' name, Amen." I crossed myself.

Katie had done some planning. Their coats were in her car, as well as overnight bags. Smart girl. Many women were not educated in having a plan for safety. *How had she found this house, though?*

Ruth dressed Timmy in his coat, and Mari draped a coat around Katie. We didn't want to cause undue movement with unknown and unattended injuries.

They advanced to their cars, protected by darkness.

"He will send help from heaven to rescue me {from} those who hound me."
Psalm 57-3 (Bible, NLT)

Sunday Night

10:20 p.m.

My phone rang. It was Julia.

"Glory, Katie's going to be all right. Concussion and broken nose, but her teeth and jaw appear fine—at least superficially. I've called House of Ruth, and Mari and Ruth will drive them to their shelter, as soon as we get out of here," Julia recounted.

Intercom voices and noisy buzzers of a busy hospital sounded in the background.

"The hospital called police. It's ugly. She won't press charges—their reputations, you know. She has agreed to a protective order—little safeguarding there. Too many women and children are hurt every day, despite orders. Pictures were taken for police records. Useful evidence to support her grounds for divorce and custody of the baby. There's no guarantee, of course. A judge could do anything.

"She and Timmy will be safe tonight and can remain as long as needed at the shelter. The center will help her find work, safe housing, and day care. Not a perfect answer, but it's not a perfect situation, or a perfect world, as you well know."

"I know, all too well."

I was thankful for what House of Ruth had done for me, and for many of my clients over the years. Many women from the college were victims of violence from casual dates or boyfriends. It was an ugly world, indeed. I shuddered.

"Oh, Glory, I nearly forgot. I'll need to cancel your class Tuesday night. I'll post a sign tomorrow."

"Oh, no you won't; especially after this. It's imperative we have it. Who knows what other women will come this week needing us." I was resolved.

"How are you going to do that? You can't even walk or get dressed." Julia added and laughed.

"The girls will help me. Somehow we'll get it together."

My lack of clothes and ability to walk were certainly something I did need to consider. I'd have to come up with something quickly.

We must avert another possible tragedy. Who knew what poor soul might come tomorrow, needing help.

'Glory, you're too much. OK. I know I can't stop you, but I'll be there to unlock the door and set things up, at least. Now take care of yourself and pray. She's not out of the woods yet."

Chapter 18

First Light

Monday Dawn

Katie

First light. My grandmother used that term to describe time just before the sun actually rises. She'd recall it as darkest right before dawn.

This has got to be the darkest point of my life.

Hot tears pool my eyes, and my throat feels like it's closing, making each breath a conscious effort. Once, who remembers when, it was unconscious and uncontrolled, and even unthought-of. My heartbeat is in my head, lips and my nose. Each time my arm slides across my covers I'm ever aware I'm unwell.

Well. What did it mean, anyway? I used to take it for granted. Nothing was well.

What actually had happened last night? How on earth had I even gotten here? I know Mari, Ruth, and Julia drove me from the hospital. Timmy cried himself to sleep hours before we arrived, I think; fogged recollection.

I now lay in a soft, clean bed at a women's shelter. Could I have ever imagined in my deepest despair I'd ever be in a shelter? After all, I was raised in a middle-class family. I had a Bachelor's degree from a prestigious university. I had dreams, and I had opportunities.

I used to think shelters were for the homeless, the indigent, and the unemployed, those without hope. I guess I am all of those things right now. I have come to the very bottom of what life can be.

As I'd run from my home, Jeremy yelled that he hated me and I wasn't his mother. Those words stung even worse than physical pain. I knew I was intellectualizing adolescent emotion, but his words stabbed my heart.

The escape meant leaving all I had behind, including my older son. I had to run for safety from my own family. *Was I such an awful wife and mother that this is now my lot, after eighteen years of marriage?*

All I had to show for the last eighteen years were two overnight bags, one for me and one for Timmy, diapers, robe and nightgown, $20, and a broken nose, cut lip and concussion? Tears burned my swollen eyes and nose as they continued to drop and roll into my bandages. I could sink no lower.

I could not go home to North Carolina. No legal custody arrangement, yet. I could not take Timmy across state lines, maybe not even out of Baltimore. Besides, Don would think of that, which might endanger my parents' and sister's safety, as well.

I could not tell them. Would they even believe me, anyway? Would anybody ever believe me?

Don was too well known in this community. He would most certainly lie about my disappearance. He had to, in order to justify himself and to discredit me. He'd told me when separation papers were delivered, if I went through with divorce, he'd kill me.

I believed him, then, and still do, now, but no one else would. He could be so charming: a Dr. Jekyll and Mr. Hyde, or, in this case, Dr. Ward and Mr. Hyde.

Jeremy is so confused. I love him, but I can't trust him. I'd have to let him go. I could not risk his anger and his father's abuse for the sake of the baby or for me, any more.

I had no friends to call. This was hardly something you could share with Junior League. It would be instant fodder for gossip and the end of my life, that's for sure.

I did have Gloria, Mari, Ruth, and Sarah. Even Julia, whom I'd never met until last night. They were my true friends and the only ones I had. Until now, had I ever really had friends who would've helped me like those women last night? If it had not been for them, there would be no one—no one at all. This experience has given new definition to friend, that's for sure.

Today was Monday, I knew that much. Last night, a kind lady said there'd be breakfast, but I can't remember when. Timmy would be cared for in their day care facilities while I was occupied in a support group and counseling sessions. How could I talk about any of this to anyone—a counselor or a group?

Darkness just darkness, that's all. My humiliation was all encompassing, and failure. Utter failure.

I must go to our Tuesday night meeting. I just have to. If there is one other woman who from seeing me and hearing me, would seek safety, I had to go. Maybe my bandaged nose, bruises, or cut lip could avert another tragedy. It was the only good thing that might come from this horror.

Tears coasted through my hair onto my damp pillowcase.

"Please, God, Lord Jesus, please help me, help me please." I repeated until sleep returned its escape.

"I was overcome by distress and sorrow.
Then I called on the name of the Lord.
"Lord save me!" . . . When I was in great need,
he saved me."
Psalm 116: 3-6 (Bible, NIV)

Chapter 19

New Digs

Monday

Glory

"Girls, you must help me plan for tomorrow night."

Weariness was prevailing this morning. Drained women with glassy eyes stared as if asked to run another marathon, having just finished the Boston. Only their children had slept.

Ruth ventured, her voice strained, "Gloria, you know we'll do what we can. What do you need, exactly?"

"Well, Jules is preparing our meeting room, so we're fine there. However, there's one essential thing we're overlooking."

Eyebrows lifted with caution, and coffee cups hung in wilted hands, as if suspended mid-air.

Undaunted, I continued.

"Look at me. Where can I go in a nightgown with no underwear?"

Silence, as their eyes scanned my head to my feet and back again. Uproarious laughter followed: a gift sorely needed.

"I can't even hike panties over my cast, let alone jeans."

More uproarious laughter erupted.

"Someone has to shop for me. Nothing fancy, as there's little cash for clothes. Look for a thrift store bargain."

Sarah and Mari stepped forward to complete this mission, pronto.

More laughter.

"Have mercy on me, girls. I must wear your choices, but remember, you have to accompany me. My outfit will reflect you, as well."

More giggles and hilarity, "We know, we know."

They disappeared on their quest.

I must call my attorney brother. Finances needed to be put in place, post haste.

"Hello, Joyce? This is George's sister, Gloria. Yes, fine, and I hope you are. Is George in? Rather urgent. No, no—Mother and I are fine, but I must speak with him. Five minutes, tops, I promise."

"Glory, what's up? You and Mom all right?" He sounded distracted.

"Georgie, stop whatever you're doing and listen—just five minutes."

"Yes, Mom," he teased.

"I need power of attorney for Mother's funds. I've got bills coming from everywhere and I can't use any more of my savings. Things are tight."

"Sure, Glory, not a problem. Your name is on her medical power of attorney already. I'll draw up papers. The rest of us will be pleased you're in charge, formally. No one could do a better job."

I mumbled under my breath, *"No one wants the job, either."*

I'd heard from exactly no one in my family since our fateful meeting, months ago—my all but unanimous appointment to in-charge position. I still harbored anger.

I know resentment will eat me alive if I don't give it to God to handle. I thought I'd done that. That's my problem: I'm always taking back issues I've given God, as if He needs my help. Pathetic.

"Have you gotten anyone to help Mom when she comes home?" George inquired.

"I can't do a lot with my cast, but I've scheduled phone interviews. Nothing promising yet, but more should apply this week, I hope."

"Glory, must go. I'll notify the banks. You'll have access to money in a couple of days."

"Just a minute, George: another favor."

"Shoot—I've only got a few—"

"A friend's husband is the minister in the homosexual affair; the hot media news. She and her son have nothing. Would you meet with her— just once— to review her rights? No, I don't expect you to take her case. Just a few minutes. I know you're busy, but after all I'm doing, you owe me, Bubba. Thanks, I love you, too."

It's about time he did something for me. To quote Mr. Wilson, "A lot of people owe me. It's time I call it in." I nodded my head in affirmation.

That's the answer. I'm going to start asking—when I think about it.

Tuesday

Mari and Sarah retuned with wardrobe enhancements: an ankle-length, gypsy-type skirt, tie-dyed in rusts and green, sashed at the waist. It concealed everything but my massive foot. Sarah donated her olive leotard top to coordinate, as it snapped at the crotch, eliminating the need to step into it; important criteria for clothing these days.

A leather cord strung with various shapes of wooden beads was a necklace bargain from a clearance table. Chew marks, from a child or dog embellished some of its beads. Sarah confirmed these dents added interesting texture.

Uh-huh. I saw Sarah elbow Mari, (which prompted Mari to nod in agreement).

Hardly my style, but was a rather intriguing ensemble, none-the less. The gauzy texture of the skirt was reminiscent of the 70's era. A little Bohemian for a middle-aged woman, but certainly had to be better than a nightgown. Beggars can't be choosers, after all.

The underwear was the real hoot.

I stretched to pull the boy's extra large, scotch-plaid boxers over my immense plaster foot. Boxers, Mari decided, were the only imaginable option to fit over my huge cast.

Certainly, I'd agree.

Three selections were packaged together. I thanked her for shrewd shopping—three for one. Black with yellow smiley faces and navy blue with American Flags were the others. How nice.

A tough choice, as you can imagine.

They turned out to be quite comfy, actually. If I lost weight, though, they'd probably settle around my ankles, no doubt adding additional interest to my skirt's lower ruffle.

My bare leg, sans panty hose, was paler than pale, goose-bumped and red-streaked from cold. We decided my beige flat was that foot's safest and most attractive choice.

The pumpkin orange cape, a true find, in every sense of the word, covered me from neck to knee. At least my color scheme, except for the boxers, was in seasonal fashion.

I was set, but grateful I was unable to check my appearance in a mirror.

Mari's large car's fully-extendable seat was the only one able to accommodate my plaster, extended leg. That became my obvious choice for transportation. The only other option was lying flat, in the rear of Sarah's station wagon. Left to, no doubt, bounce from side to side like a ball in an active game of racquetball; tethered only by the weight of my casted left appendage.

I held on for dear life to the hanging loop above the passenger door while cruising in a reclined position. Mari finally slowed, steering her car onto grass. She parked as closely to the door as possible to decrease the distance I'd have to manage crutches.

I was grateful.

Our room was on the main level, so except for a few steps below the stoop, I was home free. I pondered my dilemma of these few steps.

I licked my lips, preparing for my next hurdle.

I'd sit on the first one and scoot up remaining risers on my bottom. I hoped my skirt would not tear, or loosen, and reveal my undergarments.

Reaching the top step, already exhausted from my effort, I notice my skirt had pulled partially loose and slid to below my hips. My sash lay on the bottom step.

My scotch plaid boxers skirting the edges of my green leotard top, were now visible for all the world to see. The cape, which I hoped would mask my entire ensemble, failed to meet my lowest expectations.

I shook my head in utter dismay.

"What in the world?" Jules howled as she opened the door.

We laughed until it hurt.

She hoisted me from my armpits. Then, she helped me balance against the wall until I could arrange my clothes and crutches. Just one small threshold elevation and I was there.

From the other end of the hall, I could hear the familiar chugging of the coffee urn.

"Does that machine carry on like this every week?" Jules asked and giggled, as I nodded.

"It nearly jumped from the stand after I plugged it in. Listen, I must go. Do you need anything before I leave?" She howled as she assessed my outfit once more.

Mari called out, "We're fine."

We were all becoming family. A few weeks ago, we were total strangers, isolated in our own worlds. I needed to journal about this. God was here.

I wonder what Mother Superior would think. I like to think she'd be smiling.

Within minutes, visitors' footsteps could be heard from the hallway. The girls were excited to see who'd come.

Mari whispered, "It reminds me of sorority rush in college, wondering who'd join. In this case, who can we help?"

Within ten minutes, nine women sat in our circle; some with name tags, some not.

The door opened again.

"Katie." We exclaimed.

We embraced the young woman with blackened eyes, swollen, sutured lips and bandaged nose. Puzzled expressions abounded.

As was the tradition, I explained resource lists. I invited them to get coffee.

"We are not a sterile group, but a group for support and camaraderie." I recited.

I glanced from face to face: women still hugging themselves, like an identifying badge for the broken-hearted.

"If anyone needs to share, I'll reassure you. I'm a professional social worker, under a professional oath of confidentiality. I encourage everyone to respect that. If any information were to leave this room, many people could be hurt—innocent ones."

I glanced toward Katie, who sat looking humiliated, with her head bowed. With my words 'innocent and hurt', she held her head high, so all could better see her bandages. Her medals of having survived more than a threat—a threat she should've taken seriously.

"I'd like to add, if anyone is in a foreboding situation—for yourself or your children—please see me after our meeting. Help is available. Don't be embarrassed. You are not alone."

The girls had arranged me in two chairs outside our circle: one for me to sit and the other for my seat-sized foot. They took their cue, sensing needs and leading our group, realizing my limitations.

Ruth, Mari and Sarah openly shared about their husbands, financial fears and no jobs. They hoped, with their confessions, others would feel safe to share their concerns.

Katie, with eyes closed, admitted to being taken to safety by her friends. She and her little boy were now in a shelter. Her eyes betrayed her embarrassment, but she was encouraged. Her confession might prevent another tragedy.

I chose to remain silent during the course of our meeting. Again, I'd see how things would unfold. Mari, Ruth, Sarah, and Katie surprised me tonight. They reached out to others, far beyond their abilities to give—giving out of their need.

One newcomer ventured a hand, but raised it only as far as her arm would allow, without removing her elbow from her desk top. As if her desk extension was giving her the only support she had, physically and emotionally.

She began, "Three weeks ago, my husband informed me of his being transferred to Chicago. He didn't intend to take me or our children, but his secretary. He offered me our house."

She choked. "I have four little ones less than six years of age. Two are still nursing. I have no parents to help. I have no money for child care. My major was history in college, and I have no job skills. How can I exist and take care of my children?"

She wept. "My lawyer expects a six month-wait before our case is docketed, and heard by a judge. How can I live until then?" She lowered her head in her hands.

Another woman lifted her hand. Her husband had been unjustly accused of fraud, and although innocent, after four hearings, was sentenced to three years. In the meantime, along with mounting court costs and other legal fees, the other side had taken their house, their cars, their furniture and all of her jewelry including her wedding rings and an inexpensive watch, her only timepiece. She'd be without his income for the next three years, and, at present, she could only secure a minimum-wage position at a department store. How could she survive? She had nothing, with two teenagers to feed and clothe.

Each week, their stories were more heart-wrenching. I slowly shook my head. Hearing these agonizing accounts was wearing on me. So much pain.

To my astonishment, Sarah arose.

"Gloria, it's time we prayed for these women."

She pushed my chair to our circle's center. I could hardly believe it. Sarah, who didn't give credence to God was asking to have prayer?

I joined a circle made up of Katie, Mari, Ruth, Sarah, and most of the group's other women; holding hands around these two women who sat distraught and without hope.

I finished and added, "God promises to hear all our prayers. When you return to your homes, tell God your need for his help. Ask these things in the precious name of his little boy, Jesus."

"We were under great pressure, far beyond our ability to endure so that we despaired of life itself. . . But this happened that we might not rely on ourselves but on God . . . who will continue to deliver us. . ."
2Corinthians 1:9-10 (Bible, NIV)

Chapter 20

New Directions?

Wednesday Morning

Katie

I replayed last night's confession. I'm humiliated, even now, at having spilled so much to so many strangers. I felt like a news anchor describing some inner city violence.

After my words tumbled out, though, I felt unchained, somehow; relieved of a huge burden I've been carrying, all by myself. Maybe someone benefited from hearing my sordid tale.

I sure hope something good came out of it. Someone, although I don't remember who, said secrets keep you alone . . .something like that. To add to it, I'd found secrets keep you vulnerable, and in fear, as well.

I'm glad I went last night. I needed to be involved in daily routine, again. A schedule gives me some sense of security. As if I have a little control in my totally out-of-control life.

I'm slouched in an arm chair in this shelter's commons area now. Timmy's playing happily with other toddlers in their day care center. I'm relieved for that. With so much on my mind, it's important his safety is of no concern.

What about his emotional health, and Jeremy's?

I can't go there. It's a level too high to reach right now. I can only concentrate on basic needs: food, shelter and safety—yes, most importantly, safety. Anything else is a luxury—a dream I simply can't grasp onto.

My counselor asked if I'd thought about a job and a permanent place to live.

What? I felt like I'd been shaken and dropped out, like dust balls from a vacuum cleaner bag, landing in a lump in an empty trash dumpster.

Job? Place to live? My head hurt even trying to think. What happened to me in these last three days, anyway? My doctor warned my concussion could bring some confusion. My thinking was murky.

I still felt like I'd awakened from a hideous nightmare. I seemed unsteady, not being able to trust reality. What was reality and what was fantasy?

For the past eighteen years, I'd operated on the premise I had an average marriage—maybe a little below average lately; not great, but whose was, anyway? I assumed my husband loved me and my children loved me. After all, I loved them.

I'd grow old with my husband. We'd live happily ever after—until we were old and gray, with grandchildren and great-grand's—white picket fence and all that: something like *Father Knows Best* or *Leave it to Beaver*. Yes, definitely the Cleavers—with sons like Beaver and Wally, and me in a white apron, baking cookies.

Instead, the reality was my husband hated me enough to kill me. Perhaps my older son hated me, too. My marriage was over and had been for months, maybe years. Maybe it was over before it began. There may even be another woman (God bless her.) I am homeless, without money, and a young child to raise singularly, without help or hope. I'm having trouble crossing that chasm—too much reality, too quickly.

Sometimes I imagined, if I just went home, we could start over. I could restart the life to which I'd grown accustomed. I was happy as a mother. I was happy in my house. My life was familiar. The same type of deluded thinking as when I was nine cm dilated in labor: I'd imagined if I could just go home, my pain would stop, and I could return to my non-laboring state.

When I focused on my throbbing nose and my swollen eyes and lips, I realized that life could never be again. It was mind-boggling and sad, exceedingly sad.

In a few minutes, I'd have another counseling appointment with someone. I didn't know with whom, really.

I'm embarrassed. I can only imagine how I must look. Thankfully there are few mirrors, here. So disgusting, dressed in the same sweat suit I've worn four days straight—all I'd packed, besides PJ's and a robe. I guess I hadn't planned so well.

I had one other pair of panties I'd alternated, hand-washing my used ones in the sink and hanging them over the headboard to dry at night. At least I had clean panties after my daily shower. I'm thankful for a shower.

The people were nice here. The other women, though different from me in many ways—lifestyle, education, experience level—seemed to be able to cope better than I was coping. Maybe it's because they were exposed to this type of experience before and had some understanding I didn't. Maybe they could just handle life better than I could. Maybe they were just able to hide their confusion better than me.

How long would I persist in this funk? Tears dripped from my swollen eyes and slid into bandages on my nose.

"Katie?"

I glanced up and moved toward the woman who called my name. I could do that much.

> "Day and night, I have only tears for food.
> My heart is breaking
> as I remember how it used to be."
> Psalm 42:3-4 (Bible, NLT)

Wednesday Afternoon

The afternoon counseling session is over. It helped clear my head a little, but I'm exhausted. She's given me a stack of papers to read, similar to ones I received on my first visit.

I guess she knew I hadn't read those first ones. They described the abusive personality and keeping safe. My bruises and bandages were clear indication I hadn't done my homework, I guess.. . pretty obvious.

She'd talked about my making a new life. *A new life?*

I still had a life as a mother, and wife, didn't I?

She said I needed to find a new home? I could not return to my own house. I'd need protection to return to my own home. Somehow, home and protection did not belong in the same sentence.

Oxymoron: home was safe, wasn't it? Home was personal. Home held a certain amount of identity. Home was secure.

All gone.

I needed to think about getting a job. An agency could help locate a dental hygiene position for me. I still held licenses to practice in Maryland and North Carolina, where I'd attended school. I hadn't practiced in a long time, though.

It's scary, thinking about practicing, and thinking of leaving my job as wife and mother. Failure there, I guess, with no second chance.

She said they'd help locate day care. Poor Timmy.

I'd stayed home with Jeremy. Timmy deserved to have a mama who was at home with him. Course, look at Jeremy. He was no model of a perfect child —despite my efforts. Could it be, because of them? That hurt too much to consider.

I just had to do what I had to do, I guess. First, I had to call my lawyer. I may as well do it now. Then maybe I could take a nap before dinner. My head was splitting, and my nose and lips were throbbing.

I approached the pay phone, which was secure, whatever that meant. I searched for my lawyer's card. It was in my change purse, with just enough change to make one call. All I needed.

Twenty-five cents dinged through circular slots at the top of this pay phone, while I pushed buttons for numbers embossed on his card. Dial tone, dial tone; yes, ring.

"Yes, this is Katie. There was a bit of a mishap this weekend. Timmy and I are at House of Ruth shelter. Well, it's not that bad. It's better than being with my husband, I guess. May I speak with Mark? He just walked in? I'll wait."

I tried to sound as cheerful and nonchalant as possible. Dignity is what I needed—fake dignity, but dignity, nonetheless.

"Mark, this is Katie."

Tears started again. I didn't want to cry. It burned my eyes, made my bandages wet, and stopped up my throbbing nose.

"Don went berserk on Sunday, and I ended up at the hospital. Timmy and I are staying at the shelter now. Yes, broken nose and concussion. Yes, pictures taken. No, I didn't press charges; protective order. I tried to stay like you told me, but I had to leave."

Mark interjected. "No, Katie, you did right. The jerk, I can't believe he really hurt you. Such a coward to hit his own wife — and in front of his sons, no less—gees.

"We need to schedule an emergency hearing as soon as possible. You need to get clothes for yourself and the baby. You need to find a safe place to live."

Wait a minute. He's going too fast; too much information. I need to plan to return, retrieve our clothes and find a place to live? How could I do all that? I could hardly think as it was. How could I possibly find the energy and the wherewithal to do more?

"You have a credit card? Find an apartment and charge your first month's rent and security deposit. Is it in your name? Don't use a joint one, because your location will be on the bill. In fact, get cash on your card. He won't be able to trace it."

I tried to take in words he rattled off. Maybe I should write this down. I don't trust myself to remember all or any of it.

"You know his schedule. If you're careful, you can return and retrieve at least some of your belongings while he's at work and Jeremy's at school. Take someone with you and be prepared to run if you have to."

Retrieve and run. I think I can remember.

"He may have changed your locks or may decide to, if he hasn't already. You must act quickly. Remember, don't go alone and don't take the baby with you. If he discovered you, he could take him. Make a plan. I know it's hard to think right now, but you must act and you must act quickly. I'm hanging up to file an emergency petition before 5:00 p.m. Call me on a secure line when you've made a plan. I'll do my part. Now, stay safe."

I returned the receiver to its hook. *How could I do all that?* I sighed deeply, rubbing my temples. I must think. *Come on, Katie, try to concentrate.*

I know. I'll go to Gloria's. Maybe the girls can help me plan. I'd have to wait until dark, in case someone recognizes my car. 'After dark' was not long. Days were short, and street lights usually brightened by 4:00 p.m.

Wait a minute. Sarah's planning to rent rooms in her house. Maybe Timmy and I could live with her.

"When you go through deep waters and great trouble, I will be with you. When you go through rivers of difficulty, you will not drown. . . .Do not be afraid, for I am with you."
Isaiah 43: 2-4 (Bible, NIV)

Chapter 21

Final Exams

Sarah

"Where is Rebecca?"

I re-checked my watch. Almost 3:15. We have a pediatrician's appointment in fifteen minutes. We can't be late for this physical. She needed it for sports. I needed it for encouragement. Rebecca didn't look well.

Through my passenger window I see her soccer team approaching. Most walked in tandem, laughing and stumbling as teen-aged girls were known to do. Rebecca lingered, alone.

Hmmm, she'd always been so popular. Troubling. Well, fifteen was a tumultuous age. I recalled my own adolescence.

I checked my rear-view mirror, eyeing the lengthening car-pool line. Good, Shelly's behind me. She'll open a space. I waved and called her name, signaling my urgency. Without a friend in line, getting to the main access road could take forever.

After a 10-minute drive, Rebecca questioned, "Where are we going, Mother? This is NOT the way home."

"Time for your check-up— for sports, you know." I said cheerfully. A joy-killer, I knew, and I braced myself for her retort.

"Mom-m-m, why?" Rebecca whined. 'I'm getting sick of people asking about my health—my teachers, the nurse, and now you. Can't everybody mind their own business?"

So, others had noticed. I'd call her school nurse in the morning.

I patted her leg. I was astonished to feel bones protruding beneath baggy shorts.

Gorgeous dimples had once been her signature. Her face was now gaunt, and her cheek bones protruded sharply.

I stroked her hair. Gone were her shiny, auburn curls. Thin, lack-luster wisps were their replacement.

Pulling onto the graveled lot, I coaxed, "Come on, Honey. The faster we get in, the quicker we leave."

Rebecca sat stoically silent. Her mouth set in a line. Her ankles crossed and arms hugged her chest.

"Let's get this over, Ok?" I continued.

"I hate this" she yelled, her eyes flashing. "Can't I just wait in the car?"

"Becky, you know the procedure."

Rebecca exited, slamming her door, punctuating her irritation. "And stop calling me that baby name."

Minutes lapsed in the waiting room. Finally, a familiar nurse called, "Rebecca, time to get weighed and measured." She glanced at me, "My, she's getting tall, isn't she?"

I smiled and nodded. At fifteen, I was no longer entitled to join her in the examining room. She was grown up, right? But she was still my baby.

I looked beyond my Parents magazine to a couple of toddlers playing with some *Playskool* and *Sesame Street* toys. I remember that. It wasn't so long ago when Joel joined me for checkups and we watched Rebecca enjoying those toys. Rebecca's progress bonded us. I sighed deeply.

After twenty minutes or so, the nurse signaled. Her doctor needed to discuss her exam. I tagged along to his office. We strolled the hall I'd walked thousands of times: passed the vision screening room, and potty chairs for toddlers needing urine samples.

Dr. Rosenstein glanced up, stone-faced. He pushed a chair toward me.

"Good to see you, Sarah. Sorry to hear about you and Joel. Everything all right?"

I hated that question. Everyone knew things were not all right. No answer was appropriate or sadly, wanted. I nodded.

Dr. Rosenstein methodically polished his glass lens, stalling.

"Sarah, I'm concerned about Rebecca."

"Oh my gosh, is she all right?" I stumbled, my words tumbling out like dice from a Yahtzee game cup.

He leaned forward. "She's showing signs of acute anorexia nervosa. Are you familiar with that term?"

He pulled a lined chart from Rebecca's file.

"According to her height, I'd like to see her weight falling somewhere in this range." He pointed to a black line.

"Uh-huh."

I'd never seen a chart like this. It took me a few seconds to even register what any of the lines were. It looked like a piece torn off from one of the old road maps, buried in my car trunk.

"Her weight has dropped 20% since last year's visit." His pen traced a red line. "Her menstrual periods have ceased. It's significant."

I stared at red and black lines. Still puzzled, I was trying to grasp the meaning of these lines, so obvious to him, without appearing entirely clueless.

"I'm suggesting a specialist. Follow her recommendations to the letter."

My mind was still back on those lines. I just heard part of his last statement—something about a specialist.

I ventured, wanting to downplay my rising fear, but wanting to seem in touch,

"Doctor Rosenstein, don't you think it's just stress? Maybe it'll get better if we don't make too much of it?"

"Sarah, if there's any drop in weight when I check her in three weeks, I'll recommend residential care."

He extended his hand, signaling an end to our conversation.

I stumbled into their restroom, numb by information overload, with rising terror battling denial. I used a miniature sink next to miniature toilets to splash water on my face.

A toddler, whose mother was fastening her jumper straps, spoke, "Where's your little girl?"

I smiled, "I don't know."

How I wished I knew where she was, what her thoughts were, where her head was.

Exiting, I hear her say to her mommy, "Is her little girl lost? She must be sad."

Yes, all of the above. I gulped.

She's lost, I'm lost and her father's lost—very lost. Our family is a lost cause. I grimaced with this unintentional play on words.

Friday morning

A Pikesville lawyer agreed to see me at 10:00.

Joel actually sent him money for his retainer fee: generous of him. Our uncontested divorce promised to be quick and easy. I did not say cheap.

"According to his letter, you'll get your house, its contents, the car, and the retirement fund." my lawyer read.

That would also include the bills, I thought.

He continued, "Any work lined up? Two minimum-wage jobs aren't going to go far with private school and a mortgage, you know."

I wanted to counter sarcastically, but didn't.

"I could legally twist your husband's arm for alimony. Certainly, Rebecca needs child support. but, . . ."

he opened his hands, palms up, "the truth of the matter is, he's somewhere in Israel."

Don't you think I know that? I wanted to respond, but bit my tongue instead.

"He's given you the assets, but also the liabilities. Assets can actually be a liability. You cannot withdraw money from retirement funds because of your age: high penalty. You already know about expenses associated with a house and car."

I sighed.

"I don't want to exert too much muscle against Joel. If he gets angry, he'll be unable to see Rebecca's needs. I'd suggest we just go for child support, if I can even locate him. We can hire an investigator, if necessary."

That's an idea, I thought.

"Perhaps Joel's kept contact with Hopkins. In that case, his location should be fairly easy to ascertain. Maybe he'll agree to pay health insurance. That'd be something: dollars and cents add up, over time."

Yeah, right. I thought.

"Check his benefit package. He may still be on payroll as a consultant or something."

"Maybe" I mumbled.

He leaned across his desk toward me, raising his eyebrows.

"Of course, my extra work needs to be compensated by someone."

His expression indicated a response. What could I say?

"Think about what you want to do. Let me know how you'll pay for it. Then we'll start."

Friday Afternoon

2:17 p.m. The store was empty. Just enough time to call that specialist before our usual after-school crowd descended.

I flipped yellow pages as I cradled the phone on my left shoulder. The edge of the heavy volume jabbed against my right thigh, partially supported by a tiny portion of cluttered counter.

"Yes, this is Sarah Morganstern. I need to make an appointment. Yes, I'll wait."

I was placed on hold while she checked her schedule. "Odious elevator music," I mumbled, clenching my teeth.

"Thursday, Oct. 4, 10:15. Thank you. Do you accept insurance from Johns Hopkins? $200.00 co-pay, paid in cash our first visit? I see. Yes, we'll arrive early for paperwork."

How could I afford this? Rebecca needed it so I'd take her, without question.

I must find Joel. I might not be able to pay my lawyer to search, but I could do my own investigation.

I'd call Hopkins. Certainly, they had an address for sending checks we weren't receiving. I'd check benefits, too. I was his wife, after all. I knew his social security number. We had not divorced, so I had every right to his information.

The front door bell dinged.

"Can I help you?" I shoved the yellow pages beneath the counter.

Chapter 22

More Tests

Five Days Later

Glory

"Morning," I called, hearing the back door open. 6:30 a.m. Sarah scurried in with yawning Rebecca in tow. She stationed herself at my stove to fix breakfast; first for Tyler, and whoever else had a schedule, and for Rebecca, who generally only wanted a smoothie and banana.

I noticed she rarely finished her smoothie, and most of her banana was left in its skin. She consumed little most mornings, before waiting in their car to be taken to school.

She was so thin. I knew her weight was a concern for Sarah, so I never spoke of it. No one did. Red flags, certainly, but my thoughts would remain unspoken for now.

Since her school was closed for teachers' meetings, today's schedule changed. Sarah had taken the day off to spend sorely needed together time.

Mari took advantage of this chance for extra help, to bribe them to help clean her house. She'd pay Rebecca since she could've been having fun with friends. It wasn't much, but enough to buy a lipstick or cheap earrings, maybe. She reasoned Sarah and Rebecca could share quality time at her house. Two birds with one stone.

Since her house was devoid of furnishings, cleaning would involve filling garbage bags with leftovers, accumulating in closet corners and under beds. Stuff no one wanted or wanted to move, either. That, plus polishing kitchen and bathrooms wasn't too much, she reasoned. The three would leave after breakfast.

I fumbled with my crutches. I was determined to reach that island without help.

I was finally getting the hang of these things, but it was far more difficult than it looked, when I'd watched others. I'd always thought their rubber top rested under your armpits and the user swung like on a monkey bar.

Not quite, and not quite so easily, I'd found.

First of all, those foam-covered ends looked more comfy than they actually were. Secondly, crutches did not support my weight under my pits. Both sides hit about four inches below, immediately behind my breasts.

This bruised portion of my body had little meat on the bones. To avoid pressure there, I balanced more of my weight on my palms. Although they'd become calloused over past days, my hands hurt. The process was arduous. To add insult to injury, my upper back and neck stiffened most days, from less-than-ideal posture.

Then there was my cast to consider.

Although our weather was cold, my leg perspired under that heavy plaster. I couldn't wash my leg, of course, so a particular odor of perspiration and Iodine permeated—becoming less attractive as days went on.

My ankle itched and no help for it. That itching could've easily sent me over the edge some nights. Ruth suggested extending a coat hanger, but I couldn't bypass my knee, to reach its narrow ankle bend in this cast. I'd have to devise something, as it was becoming an obsession.

Maybe there was an anesthetic one could spray. Which end would I spray, though? Certainly the toe area was not open enough to reach my ankle. The top of the cast was almost mid-thigh. No access there, either. I'd have to try a coat hanger again, I guess—maybe two joined together, or something. Pleeze.

In the midst of enormous, life-threatening problems in this household, why did a miniscule thing like itching, seem to cause the most intense anxiety?

I loped into my kitchen, moaning with each step. The pounding sound of cast and crutches sent Purrfect scurrying.

"Are you all right? You sound awful." Sarah asked.

"Oh, fine, really. Pay no attention to me. I'll get through this, somehow."

She put her spatula down. "At least I can help you onto this stool."

She wiped her hands on her natural colored apron with bright green letters, reading "Greens Are Green." She steadied my stool, while I wiggled on.

"Sarah," I began, "Mother's being released in a few days, and she and Lucille need help with meals at St. Edmonds. Would you consider being their cook? It'd be a salaried position. Although it's not much, it might allow you to drop one of your present jobs."

Sarah held her spatula mid-air and looked intently.

"I know you have your house to consider, but there's plenty of room to even stay at night to ease your schedule. In fact, you could use their kitchen to prepare food for all of us. It's huge."

Sarah pondered this, while seeming to stare through walls.

"That's an interesting idea. Can I think it through today, and get back to you? I need to put it on paper. My mind's like scrambled eggs now. Can I let you know tomorrow?"

Sarah

The sky blanched with an almost pink cast, like it did just before snow.

That forecaster reported only an outside chance of precipitation. It's early for snow, but this cold is penetrating. *When had a weather forecast been accurate, anyway?*

The three of us squeezed among cleaning supplies in my car. I was thankful for warmth generated by our closeness.

Rebecca looked unusually pale. She rubbed her head.

"Are you all right, Honey?" I asked gently.

"A little headache."

I replied, softly, as not to draw Mari's attention, "Tylenol's in my purse."

Rebecca shook her head, denying any help from me, not even a hug.

I recalled her untouched banana at breakfast. She consumed only a fraction of her smoothie over the last few days . . . maybe the last few weeks. I couldn't remember, exactly.

I'd discreetly included a baggie of oatmeal cookies and a container of milk with our trash bags. Just in case she was hungry later. How long had it been since Rebecca said she was hungry, or approached a refrigerator for food, though?

I was looking forward to her specialist's appointment tomorrow, eager for answers. On the other hand, I dreaded the verdict. I hated to admit it, but she looked even thinner than before, if that were possible.

I couldn't go there. She'd get better. She had to. I purposely started thinking about our chores, as a distraction.

I chose bathrooms while Mari took her kitchen. Rebecca was given the job of dusting window sills and bookcases, and light vacuuming.

After working steadily for two hours, I needed a break. I rose from my knees and straightened my back. Then arched it, lifting my arms high in a yoga position guaranteed to relieve muscle tension, or so I'd been told.

Cleaning bathtubs was brutal, and there seemed to be dozens in this house. Certainly, I was not cut out for housecleaning on a regular basis.

I'd offer cookies and milk to Mari and Rebecca. Surely, Rebecca had to be hungry. I hoped she'd be hungry.

A crash from downstairs jolted me. I jumped at Mari's urgent call.

"Sarah, it's Rebecca."

Racing down the curved staircase, I see Becky sprawled on the living room floor, rigid. Uncontrollable jerking commenced, as her eyes rolled back.

"What's happening?" I shrieked.

Mari knelt beside Becky, tilting her head and rolling her body to the left.

"I think it's a seizure" Mari said, softly and calmly.

I'd never witnessed anyone having a seizure. It looked so scary. Fear smothered me. I could only whisper.

I wanted to do something to help, but all I could do was stare in horror. I felt totally paralyzed. Whatever first aid training I'd ever received dissipated in proverbial thin air when my training manikin turned into my daughter.

"Rebecca, Honey, Mama's here."

As her jerking subsided, Rebecca drifted into sleep.

I cried, "What else, what else?" My mind blurred, paralyzed with the reality of inconceivable circumstances.

Mari spoke softly.

"Sarah, has she ever had a seizure?"

I shook my head. "No"

"I think your pediatrician needs to be alerted."

"Of course," I answered, not even able to think that far.

She sounded so far away. I tried to counter dizziness. Mari noticed,

"Tell me Rebecca's doctor's name. You rest. I'll call."

Mari arose, hesitated and knelt again.

"If Gloria were here, she'd be praying. I know you're not a believer. I was raised in a very conservative Episcopalian home. We did not pray in public."

I stared, clinging intently to each of her words.

"I've done things in past days, I would never have imagined. These are desperate times. Would you mind if I prayed? I don't even know how or what to say. I'll start with the Apostle's Creed, and ask for God's help for Rebecca, OK?"

Mari ended with crossing herself.

"Fear and trembling overwhelm me.
I can't stop shaking. . .
But I will call on God and the
Lord will rescue me. . ."
Psalm 55:5, 16 (Bible, NLT)

Glory

"When do you want to leave?" I called exiting my half-bathroom.

Ruth, who'd been staring at nothing, now jerked, wide-eyed.

"Oh, Gloria, you scared me. What did you say?'

"Sorry." I laughed, "Just wondering about our schedule. I need to visit the Dollar Store."

"What do you need?"

"Undies. I'm down to my last pair of boxer shorts."

Ruth giggled and said. "OK. We'll put that at the top of our list today. Now. what's your idea for a job for me? I'm down to my last few dollars and my last pair of undies, too. I'm at my end."

I was quiet until she completely finished what she needed to say. Then I shared my plan.

"So, I've been advertising for weeks. There's no one worth their weight in salt for day time, although I may have someone for the night shift. You've taken such good care of me over past weeks. I can't imagine a better person to help Mother and Lucille."

Ruth continued to stare, but her expression was brightening.

"I'm willing to pay you every bit as much as I'd planned to pay a nursing assistant. Plus, your room and meals will be included. That house is so spacious; you and Sam, Jr. could just stay there, if you want. How's that sound?"

Ruth closed her eyes and lifted her hand for me to stop.

"Let me get this straight: I'd care for your mother and Lucille, look after their house, and get a paycheck with free room and board?"

"Uh-huh." I confirmed.

She grabbed my hands, "You're not teasing me, are you? This is for real, right?"

"Do you need time to think?"

"I don't have to. Are you sure it won't bother them if Sam's with me?"

Ruth was bouncing now.

"You don't know Lucille. She loves children. Mother doesn't see her own grandchildren at all. There are lots of children in that neighborhood to play with. The workmen will soon be finished here; no entertainment after that. Besides, he doesn't need to be here, dealing with us ailing women, right?"

"When do I start?"

"Let's drive by St. Edmonds after the Dollar Store. We'll see the house and meet Lucille. Then we can visit Mother."

Sarah

Thank goodness Midtown Memorial's waiting room was relatively empty. Rebecca would be embarrassed at having too many people watch her while she dozed.

At fifteen, you imagine the whole world's watching you. Only as you become a worried mother do you realize everyone's so wrapped up in themselves, most could care less about anyone else—even someone in need, sadly.

Paperwork had been signed, health insurance card copied, and a mountain of administrative details completed. I hoped, anyway. Those women at the desk stared at me as if I were a criminal. The utter lack of consideration of some people amazes me. *This is a hospital, for goodness sake. Was there no compassion in a hospital?*

I returned to orange, bus-station style chairs lining the wall. Eight chairs plus end tables were hooked together with an iron bar. I guess they didn't want these chairs disappearing. As if anyone wanted dirty chairs?

I could do nothing but wait. I hated waiting. I hated not knowing. It seemed all I'd done in past weeks. Wait, work and worry. Nothing was secure; nothing could be taken for granted—nothing on which to build hope.

Dr. Rosenstein hurried through mechanized doors, removing his overcoat, and jostling a white lab coat over his 6' plus frame.

"Sarah," he extended his hand. "I need solid data. Tests may take some time."

I nodded.

He addressed the burgundy-haired lady at the desk. She used our paperwork to point down a hallway. She scowled at me, again. (*What had I done, for heaven's sake?*)

Dr. Rosenstein signaled with a tilt of his head, "Follow me."

Mari, Rebecca and I stumbled toward an examining room. Mari supported Rebecca from one side, while I bolstered her from the other.

Three hours later, tests were complete. Our doctor attended Rebecca.

"Sarah, let's allow Rebecca to rest here. You and I can talk elsewhere."

I glanced at Mari, who signaled she'd return to the waiting room.

Dr. Rosenstein guided me to a small consult room. He motioned me to sit.

"Sarah, I'll get right to the point: Rebecca is a sick girl. Her weight has dropped significantly since our last visit just days ago. Her thyroid and other hormone levels are abnormal. Her blood sugar and blood pressure are deviant. Her electrolytes are aberrant. We can't allow this to continue."

"Doctor Rosenstein, I've been trying to encourage her to eat. I fix healthy foods. She hardly puts anything in her mouth. We have an appointment with her specialist tomorrow. I don't know what more I can do." I pled, remorsefully.

He placed both hands on the table, palms down.

"Sarah, there's nothing you or I can do at this point. She's fighting her body. This downward spiral can only be turned around by Rebecca, herself. I'm admitting her into a hospital where she'll receive the best care."

He paused, and then continued, "Frankly, I know little about anorexia, except increasing numbers suffer. By releasing her to a specialist, she'll be in better hands. I'll evaluate her progress regularly, and notify you of changes. Rebecca will be transported by ambulance, momentarily. Let's get her settled before you join her."

He extended his hand.

"I'm sorry I can't do more to help. Has Joel been contacted?"

"I don't know where he is." I suddenly sobbed.

I was embarrassed at not knowing the location of my own husband. Shouldn't that be a given, something every wife ought to know? I was trying so hard to just find out that small, but crucial fact. If he only knew how I searched in my thoughts and actions, day and night, to answer the question of where Joel was. No one understood my helplessness.

"I understand," he said, leaving me alone with my tears.

Yeah, right. HE, all knowing Dr. Rosenstein understands. Suddenly, I couldn't stand his all-knowing, line-reading, arrogance. How dare he say he understood?

I dropped my head and let myself sob. I'd try to pray. God must know where Joel is and He must know how to help Becky.

"Please God, if you're there; please help me and my little girl. I can't handle this by myself any more. I'm out of answers and out of hope."

I could see orderlies wheeling Rebecca through automatic doors, loading her into an ambulance. I wanted to go to her, but could not.

I turned back, sadly, to see Gloria, Ruth and Mari rushing to join me.

"Come unto me, all you who are weary and are burdened, and I will give you rest. . . . You shall find rest for your souls. . ."
Matthew 11: 28-29 (Bible, NIV)

Later that afternoon

I'm so glad Mari was with me this morning. What if Becky's seizure happened when she was alone, or at school? What if I'd been at work? I shuddered. Any of those scenarios would've been much more difficult to manage.

Wanting to dismiss this morning, I concentrated on driving to this new hospital. Not completely successful, I focused my wandering thoughts on my to-do list: call Hopkins about Joel; contact Jack; call Country Day about a six-week absence from school.

What about Country Day? If Rebecca was out for six weeks, she'd return after Thanksgiving. She'd be in no condition for final exams, having missed so many classes. Then what? *With no money for second semester, what was the point?*

First things first: I must find Joel.

The hospital receptionist signaled to me. More paperwork; *wouldn't you think hospitals could share at least some of this stuff?*

She said Rebecca rested in a dormitory behind the main building. She needed to adjust without parental intervention. Visitation was an hour on Sundays, 3-4 p.m.

She'd need clothes and toiletries; no medications. Favorite stuffed animals or security blanket were acceptable.

In a few minutes, Rebecca's doctor would speak with me. I could take a seat, while waiting.

I noticed a pay phone in the corner. I'd use my time to make calls.

"This is Sarah Morganstern. Yes, I did call yesterday. There's been an emergency. Dr. Morganstern's daughter has been hospitalized. It's urgent he be notified immediately. No, as I said yesterday, I have no information on his whereabouts. This is urgent. I'll be at this pay phone for only fifteen minutes. If you find anything, please call 555-4567. After that, leave a message on my answering machine. Could you inquire at the American Embassy? I see. It's not in your jurisdiction; confidentiality. Thanks."

I placed the handset on its carriage just long enough to get a dial tone. Dropping coins into circular slots atop the phone, I proceeded to dial Jack.

"Yes, Barbara. This is Sarah Morganstern. Can you ask Jack to call, please? My daughter's been hospitalized. I need his help. I'll be in the hospital waiting room for fifteen minutes. In another hour or so, I'll be on my way home. Thank you, Barbara."

There, I've contacted everyone who can help me. *Could Joel have contacted his parents?* Perhaps, but I didn't want them to know about Becky.

Maybe I should call tonight, though, in case he left a number. I could be brief. Perhaps they did need to know, as did my parents. *What could I tell them?*

Why had this happened? Why, except stress? Wasn't everything related to some kind of stress? But not giving your body food? It's bizarre. What normal person doesn't want to eat?

I loved to eat. I'd always had lots of food around our house. Rebecca and I'd enjoyed cooking and eating together—once.

Even when she'd gone through a pudgy stage around eleven, I'd always encouraged her to eat. I'm so against dieting for children. She's growing, after all.

Maybe this doctor had answers. I sighed.

The phone rang. I grabbed its receiver at the sound of the ring as automatically as a bell once caused Pavlov's dogs to salivate.

"Yes, this is Sarah Morganstern. What can you tell me? Uh-huh. No phone or actual address, at all? Surely, you have ways of finding your faculty members while they're on sabbatical. Please continue to try all avenues. I'll be here for another. ." I looked at my watch, "eight minutes. Thank you."

As soon as I hung the receiver, it rang again. I grabbed it.

"Yes, this is Sarah. Thank you for returning my call, Jack. I called Hopkins. All they have is a post office box. They're continuing to hunt. Yes, he still has insurance coverage. According to their records, he still holds faculty status. Yes, I'd appreciate any ideas. Thanks, Jack."

I swiped tears from under my lashes, but I didn't care who saw them.

Only a mail box to go on. Bummer.

"Ms. Morganstern? I'm Doctor Grimwalt, pediatric psychiatrist on staff.

That Night

Glory

What time is it?

A lightening flash and vibrations of crashing thunder awakened me. Gee, this storm's really bad. Sheets of water poured down glass panes.

I must make sure everybody's all right.

No power, though. I flicked lifeless switches. The darkness was only lessened by intermittent flashes, momentarily illuminating my space.

I searched for my robe. Where is it? I felt my way around my room—the chair, the doorknob. No robe. Well, it didn't matter.

I called for Ruth and Mari. No answer. I shouted again, more loudly, more urgently—still, no answer.

My heartbeat thundered. Where were they? I called again, frantic.

Gingerly stepping down stairs and clinging to the side rail, I called again. No response. I groped for my back door knob.

Outside I could see flood waters. Oh my. The girls and children were struggling in deep water. Rivers of black, murky water rushed across the yard. Bobbing further down the block were women from displaced homemakers.

I ran back to my hall closet and grabbed rope. I threw all the rope I had. I couldn't help anymore because I was out of rope. I could hear them screaming. I could do nothing.

"Oh," I jerked awake, wet with perspiration. Another dream. *When would these dreams end? What could they mean?*

2:22 a.m. My heart beat wildly.

Chapter 23

A Little Bit Of Light

Thursday

Mari

I circled the block of old brick buildings, reportedly having received a facelift. Baltimore's urban renewal restoration hoped to bring business downtown.

Dome-shaped awnings sheltered windows and doors. High gloss black paint polished its main entrance. Gleaming brass hardware adorned paneled wood, and shiny engraved plaques listed professional offices housed within.

Evaluating this part of their project, I concluded it was still a tired building in a bad part of town. *Façade: that's all it was—kind of like my life had been. Stunned by that sudden revelation, I wondered from where that thought had come.*

This accountant had known my husband well—the good and the not so good. We'd met a few times at parties, but never conversed. He was Pete's friend and colleague, but I knew nothing more about him than that.

I dreaded this appointment. I didn't want the multi-dimensional, multi-color picture, or even the parameters. My thumbnail sketch of my financial picture was detail enough.

I couldn't run anymore, though. I had to see exactly what I had or didn't have so I could plan accordingly. No more dodging.

"I have a 10:00 appointment with Mr. Dawson, please, Ma'am." I addressed a receptionist.

"And you are?" the woman behind the desk asked curtly.

"Mrs. McGuire, Mrs. Peter McGuire."

I opened my bag, and found a calling card. I passed it to her.

Sometimes, I wondered whether people had difficulty understanding my accent, given rude responses I'd receive; hence, my calling cards.

My mother always said a correspondence wardrobe is as essential as a professional clothing wardrobe. I wondered whether I'd ever use these things, or my monogrammed, informal notes. I'd used those notes a lot, actually, for sympathy, get-wells or thank- you's. In Baltimore, where I remained a foreigner, I used my calling cards, too. Today was prime example.

She glanced at it, then at me and pushed my hand away. "Got it."

She tilted her head, signaling me to retreat to leather chairs, along the back wall. I sat, as directed.

An end table held a large amber glass ashtray. No cigarette butts, but smeared ashes clung to its bottom; a reminder of another's pain.

Within minutes, Carl approached, smiling and extending his hand in my direction.

"Mari Carroll, how good to see you."

He sounded genuine with his greeting. I smiled in response, extending mine.

Back in his private office, he pointed to a chair where I might sit, as he settled into his. He clasped his interlaced fingers.

Leaning forward, he gently spoke "I was so shocked to hear about Pete. Are you and Tyler all right?"

A courteous introduction people offered to bridge an unpleasant occurrence.

"We're fine." I nod, having learned my widow's lines well.

Although he was a lot kinder than our lawyer had been, I felt frustrated with his words. *There were times when I just wanted to say, flat out, "No, we are not fine, we haven't been fine for some time now, nor do I expect to be fine anytime soon, either."*

I remembered Mother's warning of being poised, so I smiled instead.

"I guess we're meeting today to discuss numbers."

"I guess so," I felt like saying sarcastically, but didn't.

He leaned over his desk, adjusting his tortoise-shell-framed glasses and opened our thick file. I noticed stationery with names I'd heard, but knew nothing about: Fidelity, Exxon, Oppenheimer, Enron. . . Carl removed a long spread sheet, folded it in half and proceeded.

"Mari, I wish I had better news for you. You've spoken to Pete's lawyer, correct? He reviewed the situation?"

I nodded.

"I've received invoices from your Realtor, and auctioneer. Unfortunately, your house did not bring what Pete hoped when he decided to sell. It cleared its First Bank mortgage, which is good news. The profit margin was small, however."

I squeezed my eyes closed like I did when my dentist tells me "just a little pinch."

As with my dentist, if it were going to be a little pinch, he probably wouldn't mention it at all. Anyone knew it really meant: prepare for more. Similarly, I knew I must brace myself for news, yet forthcoming.

"Pete had some stocks, but the market has been on a down turn. The sale of these funds would not change your financial picture. I'd advise leaving them alone."

"I see."

In other words, no help there.

"The liabilities are extensive. We can pay your mortgage, certainly, and that's important. We can pay your Realtor and auctioneer."

"That's good."

Nothing to stand up and cheer about, but something positive.

"However, you have loans for three vehicles and a boat, a contract with Hilton Academy, $50,000 outstanding in credit cards, and your biggee is $100,000 outstanding to the Internal Revenue Service."

Silence.

In your asset column, you'll have about $15,000 if we cover it all but the IRS. His life insurance policy was borrowed against years ago. The few thousand remaining will cover funeral expenses—nothing more. Do you have a place to live?"

I nod.

"What's its cost?"

I explained our barter arrangement.

"She sounds like a real friend. That's good."

"She really is."

"I'd recommend selling at least two of your cars for liquidity. Any antiques or jewelry to sell? In a distress market, they probably won't bring close to their value, I'm sorry to say.

"I'm researching private sales for some things."

"Good. Have you looked for a job?"

"I'm taking a course to become a Realtor. Hopefully, it will bring in something soon."

"That's a start. I must say, however, until the IRS lien is paid off, you won't be able to obtain credit. That can pose a problem for future houses or college. However, the government will sometimes lower their interest rate if they see you're in earnest. Sometimes, they'll even make a deal if they see something is better than nothing. Since you're a widow, I might be able to talk with the feds and decrease it a little."

"Really?"

I had to admit, that was encouraging.

"I'll do what I can. What are your priorities?"

"Survival. Honestly, I'm baffled. Pete talked about investments. I assumed we had a solid portfolio."

Carl nodded. "I knew him well. His portfolio was solid, at one time. He got into a high risk end of the market, because of some short-term success years ago. The more he lost, the more he kept playing. He thought his ship would come in—like a gambler. If I may be blunt, his drinking got the best of his perspective. He made a lot of mistakes. That's all I can say—a lot of crazy mistakes."

"Well, sir, apparently he did, but that doesn't help me now. What can I do about his poor judgment now?"

Carl shrugged.

I continued, "The most important thing for me is Tyler's graduation. He's as stunned as I am, with the loss of his father and his home. His life is falling apart right now. Since I'm under contract anyway, he'll finish at Hilton. I'm hoping they'll consider a tuition adjustment."

He nodded. "Worth a try."

"We can certainly sell Pete's car and boat. I can trade mine for a more economical model, to pay down that loan, but I'd like to let Tyler decide about his car."

Carl nodded encouragingly, 'See what you can come up with. I'll see the mortgage, auctioneer, Realtor, funeral director and most of your credit cards are covered. I'll try to work out something with the feds. I can't promise anything but I'll try. Approach the school, go car shopping and see about reducing your loans. Sell what you don't need. Let me know what happens. I'll keep in touch."

He stood and extended his hand. "Take care of yourself, and give our best to Tyler. Shirley sends her love."

I extended my hand and smiled my most confidant smile. I blinked away tears.

I drove slowly through downtown streets, joining the maze of cars heading for 183 ramp toward the county. Beethoven's Fifth Symphony roared through my speakers: a fitting backdrop for my storm-driven emotions.

I'd try to pull myself together for this afternoon meeting at Hilton Academy. Hopefully lunch would lift my blood sugar so I could be in control this afternoon. I felt shaky.

Try as I might to resist it, anger, stuffed beneath my poise, surged through me, feeling like the same forceful pressure as water suddenly spouting from a fire hydrant.

"How could Pete have left things like this? Why did he have to drink so much? Didn't he know his family needed him?"

I slapped my palm against my steering wheel.

What a fool I'd been to have married him. Didn't I see any signs? Why didn't I listen to Daddy? What a loser. Now I'm left to pick up pieces of a wasted life.

I pulled over. I don't ever remember being this out-of-control. The more I tried to stop my sobs, the more they dominated.

"God," I screamed. *"What on earth am I going to do? Help me."*

I must think rationally. It was doing no good to blame Pete. He was gone. Only his funeral expenses remained. I would not look back.

I'd sold our house and could sell most of its furnishings. I'd talk with Hilton. Carl would try to make a deal with the IRS.

Think positively. I have a place to live, rent and utility free. Tyler would finish at Hilton. I had enough food to eat, simply for sharing my furniture, paint and supplies from my basement.

Look at the other girls. Ruth had no money, unpaid bills, and a little boy, too. She'd lost her reputation and was facing public ridicule, as well.

Look at Katie. At least I didn't have a husband trying to kill me. She had nothing, either, really, and she had a 3-year-old to care for, by herself. She was also victimized by rumors. She suffered now, alone, in a woman's shelter, of all places.

Look at Sarah; whose husband had left her in financial ruin. Her little girl was in a psychiatric hospital.

No, I would not complain. *What made me think I was immune to tragedy? Why not me?* I would not allow myself to remain in self-pity, although, in some sick way, it felt good to say poor me.

Feeling guilty was futile, though. I'd allow myself to cry, if need be. I wasn't living in Mississippi anymore, where I had to hold my head high. I didn't have to act any more. I was a destitute woman. I must survive and survive I would. . .with God's help. He was all I had. Perhaps, He was all I needed.

I recalled stories from my mother and grandmothers of how women held their homes together when their men died in wars, and the South smoldered in ruins. I'd call on the hope of my ancestors. When I'd read historical accounts and actual letters, these people depended on God... and God was real to them. He took care of them. He'd take care of me and Tyler, too. I knew it. I felt inspired. I continued my drive home.

After lunch, I drove to Hilton Academy. I approached their familiar driveway and turned into their visitor parking area, within sight of his lacrosse field. I could see Tyler in his #7 jersey.

I'd forgotten. College scouts were watching—a big day for Tyler. I needed to pray for God to open doors for my boy.

I love him so much. I want him to have the best. *Didn't every mother want that for her child?*

I wanted to watch him play. I glanced at my watch. No, I had to hurry.

I'd met with this same counselor when Tyler first entered high school. I remember thinking she genuinely cared about her students.

Mrs. Emerson graciously welcomed me into her small office.

"Mrs. McGuire, I'm so glad to see you. It's been a few years since our last visit. Please let me extend my sympathy to you on the recent loss of your husband."

I nodded without response.

"Well, we have much to discuss. I'm thrilled to say Tyler's grades are top-notch and that's important in terms of college acceptance next year. Scouts are here from a number of schools. Tyler may be chosen for a lacrosse team position. You're blessed to have such a gifted son. I know you're proud of him."

She continued, "I sense he's taken his father's death extremely hard, though. Some of his teachers have commented he's distracted and not himself. Of course, that's to be expected. I understand you've moved recently?"

OK. Here goes.

Because of financial issues, I explained, we were forced to sell our house quickly. We'd moved in with friends for the interim.

Why lie about it? Rumors were all over school, anyway. It was a tight community, with few secrets. I'd need financial aid, so I may as well get it out in the open. (I tried to disguise my desperation).

The counselor hesitated, and then spoke. "I assume, from what you've just said, college may be a struggle? Tyler has his sights on Princeton, and Yale as a second choice, because of his lacrosse interests."

Mrs. Emerson lowered her head and turned her pen back and forth. She looked up again.

"I hate to say this, but the chances that Tyler would be eligible for financial aid are limited at the Ivy's. Although he's an excellent student and an athlete, it's highly competitive, as you might imagine. The fact he's male and not a minority. . .well, there's little chance for assistance. Some excellent state universities would welcome him, and might extend him a lucrative scholarship —first, because of his academic standing. Plus, his lacrosse would be an asset, as well. Your being a widow might help. Some universities give a significant break if a parent returns to school with a student. There are loans."

She opened her file and displayed several brochures for my perusal.

"You graduated from college, did you not? Do you think, as an alumna, you'd be able to help him gain entrance to your alma mater?"

"I graduated from UNC-Chapel Hill."

"I think Tyler might qualify if he continues to do well this year. Their standards for acceptance are high, but many of our past students have attended and excelled there. He might even secure a lacrosse scholarship, as well. That campus would be a nice fit for his personality and his gifts. University of Virginia is also an option for lacrosse. Although Tyler would be out-of-state, your cost would still be considerably less than most private universities."

"Mrs. Emerson," I began, "I'd appreciate your confidentiality with regard to my finances—especially with Tyler. He has enough on his mind with SAT's and lacrosse. He's just lost his father and his home. I hate to destroy his dreams. After Christmas, I'll discuss constraints with him."

"Of course."

"It's going to be difficult enough to keep him at this academy for his last semester."

"I understand, Mrs. McGuire. You and Tyler have been with us from the beginning. He's a fine young man, although struggling now with grief and just being seventeen, frankly. We'll do all we can to help. Here at Hilton, we try to assist our families. However," she continued, "we're limited in what we can actually give for his last semester. I'll take it to our board. In view of the unfortunate circumstances and his being a graduating senior, perhaps they'd help. I can't promise anything, though."

"I understand."

"As you requested, I'll certainly continue to encourage Tyler, and you can be assured of my confidentiality in the matter of finances. You have my word."

She extended her hand across her desk.

"Thank you, Mrs. Emerson. Please keep me abreast on SAT's and any college news."

She nodded and smiled.

"In you our ancestors put their trust . . . they trusted and you delivered them. They cried to you and were saved. In you they trusted and were not disappointed."
Psalm 22:4-5 (Bible)

Katie

We'd agreed on $500 per month, which included utilities and use of her laundry and other appliances. The decision was right. It was safe. It was good.

I'd probably have to share it with someone else. One other boarder was needed to make it work. Wasn't I sharing space with strangers at this shelter? No big deal.

Her backyard was fenced for Timmy. Day care was two blocks away. Perhaps I could find work in nearby Liberty and Reisterstown Road areas.

Work was yet another issue.

My face needed to heal before I interviewed. I looked scary. Bruises were fading, but gravity pulled colors down. Yellow replaced purple above my eyes, and the purple fell beneath them. Bruises which had circled them now pooled on my cheekbones. Rainbow hues edged frayed bandages.

Sarah saw bruise-concealing makeup in a Pikesville pharmacy. When my bandages come off, I'd go there. I'd definitely need a makeover before being received by the public.

Next week, I'd have sutures removed. My face would heal, my doctor reassured me. Emotional scars from my husband's actions would probably remain forever. He told me I didn't ever have to tolerate abuse. (Although I'd revealed nothing, I was fooling no one. The cause of my bruises was obvious to everyone but me).

I couldn't describe the humiliation that revelation dredged up—much too painful. I could drown in that if I allowed myself. I closed my eyes at the thought.

I must concentrate on future plans. Focus, Katie, focus, I coached; kind of like "breathe, Katie, breathe," I mouthed during final stages of labor.

I needed uniforms for work. I was not the size person who could walk into a store, choose a size 10 and wear it out. I wore an extra small. Even that would need to be hemmed two inches at their leg bottoms. Since I've lost weight, a couple of inches off the sides and the waist may be required, too.

Mari had seen scrubs at *Goodwill* yesterday. Even that was a stretch for my budget, for sure. I'd have to find that store to scour for small sizes. Then, if I was lucky enough to find some, they could be altered. That would take about a week. Just in time for my soiled bandages to come off. I was more hopeful, already.

I may have failed to do my reading homework, but I'd made decisions.

A first step, wasn't it? It certainly was.

For the first time in maybe years, I had hope.

Thursday evening

Sarah

Backing out now would not be easy. Last week, I'd asked to join them at this evening prayer service. *What could I have been thinking?* It's not like they forced me to come. *They hadn't even extended an invitation. I'd asked.*

Now I was nervous. I hadn't been in a church since I was fourteen years old.

I took my time buttoning my coat. My fingers trembled. I lingered as the last one out the door. *Was it too late to just not go?*

Even if I changed my mind, they wouldn't think less of me. It didn't matter what I believed, or if I believed, they still cared.

Well, I'm ready. I may as well go.

It's so cold and dark tonight, but glowing lanterns flanking this modest church's entrance pierced the darkness; welcoming us out of the cold like a lighthouse signaling lost ships.

I was last to squeeze through its door, still holding back. I glanced around cautiously. I don't know what I'd expected.

I guess I anticipated a huge crowd of people laughing and talking, like my hometown community church; neighbors who'd known each others' families for decades.

Anticipating coming into an established group had been disturbing. I'm a stranger. I didn't want to be center of attention. I didn't want to be so obviously on the outside, either. I just wanted to ease into this experience, slowly; test the waters. If I decided not to return, it'd be no big deal. No one would miss me. If I was introduced to a lot of people, I'd feel obligated, or something.

I was coming to find God, or hoped to, anyway. I was searching for insight into the creator of the universe...my universe, whom I'd recently begun seeking. *Would others be able to tell I had questions about God, do you think?*

Surprisingly, it appeared nothing like I'd imagined. Candles and diffused lighting illumined the small sanctuary. Hymns played on a muted organ. Men and women of varying ages and social-standing noiselessly huddled in short pews. Obvious health challenges distinguished those with physical needs; pained expressions communicated needs for hope. No talking. This unexpected calm comforted me.

The priest quietly welcomed congregants. No formal sermon tonight but Holy Communion at the close, for those desiring it. This service is for prayer and meditation only; scripture can be found in the *Book of Common Prayer* and the bulletin. All requesting individual prayer are welcome to come to the front.

"In the name of the Father, the Son, and the Holy Spirit, we ask your blessing of peace on all who are present this evening. Come. Receive God's blessings. I will begin reading from St. Paul's Second epistle to the Corinthians, verses 3-4, 8-10: Please follow in your bulletin."

"Praise be to the God and Father of our Lord Jesus Christ, the father of compassion and the God of all comfort, who comforts us in all our troubles so that we can comfort those in any trouble, that we ourselves have received from God... We were crushed and overwhelmed beyond our ability to endure and we thought we would never live through it... But as a result, we stopped relying on ourselves and learned to rely on God..."

"The word of God for the people of God. Praise be to God. Amen."

He finished with the recitation of the Lord's Prayer. The organ continued to play softly—almost beyond perception.

After the reading, Mari and Gloria chose to kneel on kneelers to pray. Ruth and Katie remained seated, as was their custom from their backgrounds.

What should I do? I'd already felt so different. Should I sit, as I'd done, growing up? Perhaps I'd be less conspicuous if I knelt. Could others tell by looking at me I was different?

I decided I'd feel less obvious kneeling. I'd never knelt in a church, though. *Was there a special way to do it?* I shifted my eyes to the right, carefully avoiding turning my head, so I wouldn't be noticed.

I couldn't see. Glancing to my left, Ruth and Katie sat with eyes closed and heads bowed. *What if someone sees me looking around? What would they think? But, those who've been here before and aren't like me, should have their eyes closed already, right? They won't know I can't make up my mind.*

I leaned over and pulled out the worn velveteen-covered kneeler and rested my knees. I clasped my hands and leaned my head onto my hands.

Huh. Kneeling helped focus my thoughts, away from distractions, onto God—the whole reason I'd come

Dear Father in heaven, I prayed silently, *you know why I've come. I don't know you, though. I think I want to. No, I need to. I need to, desperately. You're the only one who can help me. I know it's been a long time since I've come to you. There's a lot of things I've been doing I'm not proud of. In fact, a lot of things I'm ashamed of. Please don't leave me in this awful place of indecision. I don't know how I could've thought I was too smart. Look at the mess I've made of my life, and those I care about. I'm not smart enough to do anything. And Lord, can you care about Becky, especially?*

One tear fell, and then another. I needed to know God loved me and my little girl. *Did he care about my broken marriage, my sick child and my lack of money to live?*

I gave up trying to stop tears I could not suppress. I gave up trying to control the life I could not control.

I felt Ruth's and Gloria's hands on my shoulders. I didn't care anymore what others thought of me. I needed supernatural help, and I didn't care who knew it.

Mari walked down the aisle. Mari, who never showed emotion, was shedding tears. Gloria whispered she'd join me if I wanted to go to the front for prayer.

Why not? I looked up and noticed at least six others at the altar rail. I wanted all God could give me.

My knees shook, and tears blurred my sight. I was depending on Gloria's help to get there.

As I stood beside the rail, I realized Gloria couldn't help anyone. She was back in the pew, trying to manipulate her crutches. *Who'd helped me down that isle? Who knew?*

I could hear Mari requesting prayer for her finances and her son. I prayed silently for them. Someone asked for healing from a disease. I prayed silently for this unknown woman. Katie asked for protection. Ruth asked for forgiveness and the power to forgive. (*Of what did Ruth need to be forgiven —she was an angel. I was the one who needed forgiveness.*)

Within minutes, fingers touched my forehead and made the sign of the cross. My weeping started again.

"God has heard your prayers. He wants you to know He loves you so much. You are his daughter. You are forgiven."

I felt as if a huge weight lifted from my shoulders. I'd been given a fresh start. I wasn't alone, anymore.

Someone loved me. Someone really loved me.

Alone in my room, as I prepared to sleep, I unfolded the bulletin from my purse. Grabbing my reading glasses from my bed-side stand, I re-read those verses printed on the insert again:

Psalm 6:6-9: I am worn out from sobbing. Every night tears drench my bed. My pillow is wet from weeping. My vision is blurred by grief. . . The Lord has heard my plea. The Lord will answer my prayer.

Psalm 5:2, 8: Listen to my cry for help, my King and my God. . . Lead me in the right path, O Lord. . Tell me clearly what to do and show me which way to turn.

Psalm 55:1-2, 16-17: Please listen and answer me, for I am overwhelmed by my troubles. . . I will call on God, and the Lord will rescue me. Morning, noon, and night I cry out in my distress and the Lord hears my voice.

Psalm 22:24: He has not ignored the suffering of the needy. He has not turned his back on them. He has listened to their cries for help.

Psalm 25:16-17: Turn to me and have mercy on me, for I am alone and in deep distress. My problems go from bad to worse. Oh, save me from them all.

As I lay under my goose down comforter and my organic cotton sheets, and felt the cold emptiness from the other side of our bed, I grasped my covers close around me. I read through these words once more. I didn't feel so alone tonight.

I vowed to carry this paper with me and read their words every day. They would be my lifeline out of a dark, dark hole.

I would not let them go.

"How often we look upon God as our last and feeblest resource!
We go to Him because we have nowhere else to go, and then we learn that the storms of life have driven us, not upon the rocks, but into the desired haven."
George MacDonald

Chapter 24

I Once Was Lost But Now Am Found

Friday

Sarah

"Just a minute, don't hang up." I spoke to the air.
"Yes" I answered the fourth ring, out of breath.
"Yes, Jack. You don't mean it. You found him? I can't believe it. You didn't exactly talk with him. You left a message. You said 'emergency', right? Thanks so much, Jack. Bye."

I whooped. Maybe Joel will call.

Later

The phone.

I squinted at my clock. 12:30 a.m. Who, what. . .? "Emergency" flashed in my mind. Rebecca.

I grabbed the receiver, croaking, "Hello?"

"Sarah, it's Joel."

"Joel, why haven't you called? I know you obviously need to do 'your thing' in Israel. It always was your first love, but you left me holding the bag. I can't make it, Joel, and now Rebecca's in the hospital—"

"Rebecca's in the hospital? Is she all right?"

I spouted a synopsis of past months, in less than 10 seconds. I was unloading, but I had to tell it quickly, before he disappeared—again. I ended with "And Joel, if it doesn't work, she could die."

I moaned, feeling the weight of it all.

"Dear God in heaven."

Since he hadn't hung up, I felt I could elaborate. The bases were covered, so I dumped some more.

"Sarah, I thought since you had the house and retainer money, that'd be all you'd need."

"Joel, did you consider your daughter? Our parents can't help," I asked.

"I wish you hadn't told them. Why did you do that?"

"Because Rebecca and I can't live, that's why." I snapped.

A heavy sigh drifted from the other end.

"She adores you, Joel, and from her strange perspective now, I think she believes you've left because of something she's done. She doesn't understand your love for Israel. You need to come home to see her, at least."

"I don't know when I can get away." Joel stalled.

"Joel, consider your priorities." I reasoned.

"OK, OK," he replied.

"Can you at least give me a phone number or an address where I can reach you? Hopkins didn't even know."

"Yeah, yeah, this is a pay phone—no phone on my compound. I'll wire my address. I'll see about getting back, but my girl friend won't like it."

There it was.

I paused, considering this last statement. I wanted to scream, but stopped.

Although the possibility of someone else was always there—way back in my subconscious mind, mostly—I'd always cancelled it out as a product of my overactive imagination. After all, I wouldn't cheat on him. I wouldn't risk destroying my marriage with some fling. *How could he?*

Now he's spoken it. His words gave credence to my worst possible scenario. I had to wonder if all his phone calls and trips to Israel were ever about his zeal . . . ever. Perhaps it had been another woman all along—or other women, as the case might be. I couldn't stomach that realization. Even if it was true, and obviously it could very well be, it was just too painful to fully consider.

"Joel," I said, with as much control as I could muster. I would only address his actual words, not my thoughts. "This woman needs to know you have responsibilities. With or without me, Rebecca is your flesh and blood. She deserves life. I need to be able to care for her."

No answer.

Was he on drugs or something? Where had his mind gone?

I would wait for his answer. The least he could do was respond to my plea.

Silence. He said nothing.

I felt as if someone had thrust my brain's gear shift from 5th to reverse, without even slowing down. Cold panic replaced tears. This was a man I'd depended upon. I swallowed hard.

I didn't want to consider the thought which seeped into a crevice in my conscious mind: *Is it possible he could be exactly as he'd always been? Maybe I'd imagined his being caring, and responsible. Had he ever cared about us? Had all the caring been mine?*

I had to get off this phone. My receiver felt as heavy as a 50-pound barbell.

"Joel, mail me your address, please." I muttered.

I tried to sound patient, as though communicating to an emotionally-deranged individual who needed to be directed to reality—gently.

"Thank you for calling."

I replaced my handset. I must notify Jack tomorrow morning. This could be the last time I'd hear from him.

I stared at my ceiling. A long night ahead and sleep was not coming.

"As a friend of mine, he betrayed me.
He broke his promises.
His words were as smooth as cream
but in his heart is war. . ."
Psalm 55:20 (Bible, TLB)

Saturday morning

Clock hands jumped to 10:45. My hospital appointment was 11:15.

I jerked my hat, and scarf from my wall rack and fished my gloves, keys and several paper to-do lists from my pockets. I depended on these paper segments.

Some would label them as a pretty sorry excuse for organizing life. It worked for me, though. As soon as a list was complete, I'd toss it, exhilarated with my accomplishment. What joy to discard one, ceremoniously into a circular file: progress, on a tiny scale, but progress, nonetheless.

If forced to study a long list, scrawled in a notebook, or heaven forbid, a day planner, the size of a library reference book, I might misplace it and risk losing my entire life. Too much to consider; I could only grasp pieces, not the whole.

I recited my litany, approaching my car: breakfast was over; check-mark; food in the fridge for lunch and dinner; check-mark; tote for Rebecca; check-mark.

Cuddled beside me, as if a pet, sat Rebecca's bag; packed with, but not limited to, several days' worth of outfits, jewelry, cosmetics, nail kit and polish, electric toothbrush, floss, shampoo, conditioner, spray, hair dryer and curling iron, perfume, and vitamins. Tape player and tapes were padded between layers of clothing. A large manila envelope wedged into its side pocket cradled get well cards from friends and teachers.

I suspected vitamins were contraband. Under the circumstances, that staff had to agree they'd help maintain some degree of nourishment, surely.

I reviewed one of my paper fragments. Yes, I have it all. I'd included lawyer's and pediatrician's numbers, and Gloria's phone number.

You'd think I would've memorized these, by now, wouldn't you? My brain just couldn't handle more details. *Did I unplug my iron?*

I cruised residential streets to avoid Northern Parkway. Shoppers would be out. I did not want a hold-up this morning. I was so anxious for news. She'd only been there a few days.

I'm surprised they wanted to see me so soon. Maybe they had time to evaluate and have decided this residential program is not needed after all. She needed to be home and back at school; return to normal life, as it had been—once.

When, exactly, had that been? Normal, that is? It seemed so long ago when life was normal. Had our lives ever been normal? What did that mean, exactly?

I coasted into the hospital parking lot. It looked dreary, almost foreboding this morning. Tree branches were iced—even individual blades of grass. Unbroken clouds were streaked with gray lines, like craze lines on an ice-covered pond—warning caution.

Suddenly, I wanted this meeting over. I just wanted Becky home.

I moved warily, feeling salt crunch beneath my feet, burnishing worn marble steps. I wiggled through heavy doors, concerned about their closing on me, if I didn't cross their threshold quickly.

This main room seemed darker than I recalled. Dark leather seating and dark mahogany end tables, lighted by small table lamps, no more than 10 or 15 watts. *Do they even make 10 watt bulbs?* Probably custom-ordered, designed to provide quiet and calm for anxious mothers, like me. Today. . . no calm.

I was reminded of rooms arranged this way in black and white horror movies from the 1930's or 40's. I half expected Boris Karloff to emerge from somewhere.

I walked toward the reception desk, taking a relaxing breath and a purposeful stride. I bounded, nearly leaping as I tripped over a rolled edge of carpet.

"I'm Sarah Morganstern," I blurted out, trying to act more dignified than I obviously looked, grasping the desk's edge; trembling, realizing I could've sailed through the air.

The receptionist lowered her chin and raised her eyebrows, to focus over her reading glasses.

"Yes, Mrs. Morganstern. Please take a seat. I'll notify the doctor."

A settee was nearby. Yes, that looked comfy. 11:08. I had some time.

With pocketbook and tote perched on my lap, I glanced around. I drummed my fingers on my bags. A bad habit, I knew, but I couldn't control it lately.

I hated to wait. Waiting meant bad news. At least it seemed that way lately.

Startled to hear my name called so soon, I called, "Yes, I'm Sarah Morganstern."

I balanced my bags and strode quickly in the direction of the voice, being particularly careful to avoid rolled carpet edges.

The ancient elevator's metal–grated, screened doorway seemed reminiscent of vintage elevators from childhood. *Were they actual elevators, or were they the same horror movies I was reminded of minutes ago?* I shrugged and its doors closed.

The tiny carriage moaned its ascent. Finally, bouncing a few times, doors creaked open, and its metal grid scraped along the floor.

I trailed a few steps behind my guide, silent. Whirring electric typewriters and humming office machines droned in monotonous percussion,

She stopped at a tiny consultation room. I assumed the chair opposite a desk was meant for me.

"The doctor will be with you shortly. Would you care for water?"

I shook my head "No thank you."

The leather chair felt hard and unyielding, like sitting on a stack of newspapers. I shifted my weight to get comfortable. I checked my watch.

No reading material except that printed tag, hanging from beneath this seat cushion. I'd read that.

It occurred to me I'd never read one of these tags, except my bed pillow. I didn't really intend to rip it off, as it warned. *Were there pillow police somewhere? Geeze.*

Bored, I started counting brass upholstery tacks. Growing more fidgety, I drummed my fingers on both chair arms, and kicked my right foot which crossed my left leg. *I know I'm drumming, again but I can't help it. I can't.*

I wondered about other people who had sat in this seat. *Were they waiting for news of their loved ones, too? Did they feel as uncomfortable as I felt?*

Could there be a two-way glass mirror like on TV? You know, where others observed a criminal without their knowing they were being watched? *What might they ask me, anyway?*

Maybe they'd interrogate me about whether I'd nursed or bottle-fed Rebecca, whether I'd used disposable or cloth diapers, or how I potty-trained her. I tried to recall, did I use the book "No more diapers" or "Potty success"? I couldn't remember.

Was I a negligent mother because I didn't remember?

Maybe they've concluded I'd done something to make Rebecca the way she was. Perhaps they'd concluded I was an appalling mother, as my lack of answers about potty training or diapers indicated my being unfit.

Obviously Joel thought so. Maybe they'd say I was the one who needed residential treatment.

I pondered that. Perhaps a several-week stay wouldn't be so bad; a nice vacation from my problems. That vacation would certainly cost me more than I could ever afford. Surely, they wouldn't suggest that.

My thoughts were interrupted by a soft voice from a small-statured woman, clad in a lab coat. She looked kind enough, I guess.

I needed to act in control as best as I knew how. *What would that mean to a psychiatrist? Would she know I was trying to act sane as opposed to being naturally sane, without trying?*

She extended her hand to me, and slid into her desk chair. She smiled, gently.

"Mrs. Morganstern, it's nice to meet you. Rebecca has told me what a great mom you are."

Surprised at her unexpected kindness, I wailed, "I hope so. I love her so much."

She passed tissues from a lower desk drawer. "I know you do. You must be worried."

I nodded. "Yes."

I dabbed my eyes and blew my nose. I couldn't speak. I'd wanted to act in control.

Was this the best I could do?

"I wanted to meet with you as soon as possible to discuss Rebecca."

I nodded, "Thank you." I tried to look appreciative.

"I'm sure Dr. Rosenstein has described the complexity of issues surrounding this illness. Little evidence exists for successful treatment options."

She hesitated, looking to me for confirmation.

I nodded.

"I understand you're a single mother, and you, alone, are responsible for Rebecca's care."

"Yes," I nodded.

I grabbed another tissue. *I hoped she didn't quote articles about children from broken homes. I'd read them. I wasn't born yesterday.*

"First of all, I want to encourage you. We know how difficult this is for you."

Do you really? I wanted to say, feeling anger at her even assuming she knew how I felt. *My daughter's in this hospital, ill, with no known cure, and my 50-year-old husband has left me for the Israeli army. I've had to deal with all of this alone, and without resources.*

I didn't say it, but I yearned to.

If she knew my thoughts, what would she think of me? Maybe these doctors could surmise thought, too, based on behavior or body language or something unbeknownst to me.

The doctor continued, "I'll be honest Mrs. Morganstern, since Rebecca's been here, she has not responded to any therapeutic approach. Her condition continues to decline. She's exceedingly fragile."

I sucked a deep breath.

She paused, "We're aware of your insurance limitations—only thirty days for mental health issues."

I countered, darkly, "But look at her. This is physical. Her body is dreadfully sick. She's malnourished. She looks like a concentration camp survivor. How can you call it mental?"

She held up a palm, to stop me.

"You're absolutely right. It is certainly a physical problem. Some even think it's triggered by chemical or hormonal imbalance. However, insurance companies view it as a mental health issue."

She shrugged.

"We're doubtful Rebecca will respond significantly within a 30-day window. We simply don't have the resources. However, I've researched, and found a center in Durham, North Carolina with some promising treatment results."

I perked up, "You have? Really?"

"A multifaceted-approach addressing physical, emotional and spiritual aspects. From what I've read, great strides have been made within a month's time frame. Of course, not all are success stories, but some are."

"Huh."

Hope. Something positive.

"This is what I'd like to propose: We could transport Rebecca to North Carolina today, if you're in agreement. She could begin their program tomorrow."

She reached in a folder and displayed a colorful brochure. She slid it across her desk.

I saw pictures of a contemporary-styled campus, exercise facilities and smiling staff. It looked like a happy place; one Rebecca might enjoy, maybe.

"Mrs. Morganstern, if you agree, there's a chance, in thirty days, you could see some progress. However, if you decide to leave her here, I cannot promise anything. The decision is entirely yours."

She stood.

"Study this brochure. See if this is what you'd like to choose. I must emphasize, you're working against time. If we wait, today's space may be filled. If you want her to begin as soon as possible, transportation arrangements will have to be made quickly. I'll give you ten minutes."

Only ten minutes? I imagined I could hear a giant clock tick, like on game shows. I imagined clock music would be piped into this room, pressuring alternate doors to open.

Tick, tick, tick.

I picked up the brochure. Too stressed to comprehend wording, I focused on pictures and deciphered brief by-lines; opening my eyes wide, trying desperately to concentrate. My heart beat like an imagined ticking of a clock. Tick, thump, tick, thump, tick thump. . .

I didn't want to send her to North Carolina. It was a day's drive, for heaven's sake.

Was I being selfish? Yes, I guess I was.

If it meant the difference between life and death, and those were the actual stakes, how could I deny her? After all she was fifteen, almost sixteen. In less than two years, she'd be off to college. If I chose to keep her home, she might not get to college at all. She might not get through high school. She might not live.

"*God,*" I mumbled, "*I know I've been a miserable person, and I have no right to come to you now. I need to ask you what to do, not for me, but for Becky. She's my baby girl. I don't want her to die. It'd be so hard to send her to North Carolina. What if that's not right either? Help me with this.*"

A light knock startled me as if it were a TV show buzzer, I half expected to hear. The doctor looked at me, eyebrows raised and eyes questioning, asking my decision, without words.

I nodded my head, reluctantly.

"Would you do this if it were your little girl?" I asked.

The doctor did not return behind her desk this time. She rested a hand on my shoulder.

"Mrs. Morganstern, I would. I know you're thinking, 'How could she know how I feel? It's not her daughter we're discussing. She doesn't have to send her only child to North Carolina. She has no idea. Am I right?"

I looked at the top of my shoes; my silence confirmed her words.

"Mrs. Morganstern, I do know how you feel. You see, I lost my daughter to anorexia nervosa. At that time, nothing was known about the disease that killed her. That's why I chose to specialize in this area of medicine. That's why I chose to speak with you, myself. I would've tried any program, anywhere in this world. There was nothing. No one could help her. I'd do anything to have one more minute of life. I did not have that privilege. You do."

Hers was not an expression of judgmental criticism, for mistakes I might have made. It was a face of kindness—for my child, and compassion for me.

"I so appreciate your sharing this opportunity with me." I whispered.

"I believe you've made the best decision. The quicker she's admitted, the quicker you'll have your daughter back."

"I'm leaving, now, to confirm travel arrangements and secure a place at this facility. Rebecca is in our commons room upstairs. I'll authorize a nurse to direct you, for goodbyes."

The door clicked.

"The Lord, your Redeemer, the Holy one of Israel says I am the Lord, your God who teaches you what is good
and leads you along the path you should follow."
Isaiah 48:17 (Bible, NIV)

I sprinted to the elevator, and waited interminable minutes to get to their top floor. As its grated screen opened, I ran to the end of the hall.

Through a glass door pane, I could see Rebecca sitting alone on a sofa. She looked far worse than I'd remembered just a couple of days ago. *Had I been so preoccupied, I hadn't seen how dreadful she looked?*

"Rebecca, Honey?"

I embraced her frail body, no more than a mere skeleton.

"Oh, Honey. I've missed you so much. Let me just hold you."

I stroked her head, fingering wisps of hair. Sadness engulfed me. *What was happening to my child?*

Rebecca sat contented, with her head on my shoulder, silent.

Rebecca never sat contented. Even as a preschooler, anxious to run and busy herself exploring life, the only time she'd let me hold her like this was when she was fevered with tonsillitis or an ear infection.

What could I do? I know. I'll sing.

As a sick toddler, I'd rock her. We'd sing along with a plastic record player's lavender and green plastic records. *Fisher Price*, I think *So long ago, what songs did I sing?* As I cuddled her, I remembered one of my *Sesame Street* favorites:

"Sing, sing a song, make it simple to last your whole life long. Don't worry that it's not good enough for anyone else to hear, just sing, sing a song. DA,DA,DA,DA,DA."

After a few rounds, Rebecca began to giggle; a breathtaking sound I hadn't heard in ages.

"It is funny, isn't it? Do you remember that song, Rebecca? Do you remember how we used to sing with people on *Sesame Street*? Was it Maria, or Big Bird?"

She laughed again. "Oh, Mom, that's silly."

"No, you're the one who's silly. Don't you see how profound those words are?"

I laughed with her.

A nurse approached and whispered out of Rebecca's earshot.

"Mrs. Morganstern, I just received a message from our front desk. Dr. Morganstern is here to visit. Is it all right if he joins you?"

I looked at her in amazement, "Of course."

"Guess what, Honey? Daddy's coming up—he's come home to see you."

Her eyes were round.

As the door opened, we caught our breath, astonished. Nurses, who safeguarded the entrance, glanced at this person, entering; then quickly averted, standing immobile as palace guards at Buckingham palace.

Joel entered in all his glory. His graying hair had grown to his shoulders, and was topped with a cap. He'd grown a full gray beard, flowing half-way down his chest, and dressed in full fatigues, top to bottom. Leather army boots completed his ensemble. He looked a cross between Fidel Castro and Santa Claus. If he had not been announced, I wouldn't have recognized him.

Shock and sadness caused his face to redden as he saw Rebecca.

Rebecca embraced him.

That was my cue.

I gathered my coat and pocketbook, and signaled to her nurses I was going. I blew a kiss to Rebecca.

Closing the door gently, I realized this was the last time I'd see Becky for six weeks. Certainly I'd miss her, but I was confidant.

It'd be like sending her to summer camp. I could do this. After seeing her this last time, I knew I had no other choice.

I'm glad Joel could witness this. He had no idea how sick she was. Certainly, now, he'd feel an obligation to help.

Surely.

"Their appetites were gone and death was near. . ."Lord help" they cried, in their trouble. {The Lord} spoke and they were snatched from the door of death."
Psalm 107:18-20 (Bible)

That Night

I'm not sleepy; my mind's running high-speed, alert with my day's memories.

I tried turning up my thermostat. Feeling guilty about added expense, I got up and turned it back down. I microwaved a glass of soy milk, in hopes that would relax me.

Phone rings startled me. I grabbed my receiver before its ringing stopped.

"Hello?"

"Mrs. Morganstern, this is Dr. Bloom, Rebecca's doctor."

"Yes, Dr. Bloom, is Rebecca all right?" I asked, trying to mask alarm in my voice.

"Yes, of course. I'm sorry to have called so late. I hope I didn't awaken you."

"No, of course not."

"I wanted to reassure you. Rebecca arrived safely at the facility. She's getting settled. You've given Rebecca a chance at life."

"I hope so. I'm so worried."

'You have reason to be. You've made a difficult decision, but under the circumstances, the best one, I believe. I've contacted Dr. Rosenstein and Rebecca's psychiatrist, and reviewed our plans. They're hopeful. I'll keep you abreast of any progress."

"Thank you, Doctor. I need to look forward to a regular update."

"Indeed you do. I'll keep in touch. Do you have any questions?"

"A million, but no, not really"

"Understandable. Take care."

"Thank you"

Phone rings.

Who could it be now?

I clumsily grabbed the phone beside my bed, "Hello?"

"It's Joel."

"Joel, do you have any idea what time it is? It's 2:00 a.m."

"I know. I have jet lag, and can't sleep."

"But I have to get up early for work."

"Yes, but I need to talk about Rebecca. Didn't you feed her? She looks like she barely survived Auschwitz. I left her in your care. How could you?"

"How could I? How can you even ask me that? You go across the world, with no word, no help, and you ask me what I did?'

"I gave you the house and the car. Isn't that enough?"

"Enough? Enough? I can't believe you said that. We had a marriage, Joel. We have a dying daughter, Joel. What did you think would happen when her Daddy leaves and doesn't come back, her school career is over, a major chapter of her life suddenly ends and she has no idea why?"

"This has nothing to do with Rebecca. I simply don't love you anymore. I've found my dream in Israel, and my girlfriend shares my passion."

"Your girlfriend? What kind of woman is she, anyway?"

"See, there you go. You're always whining about something. You don't understand me like she does. She's my soul-mate. She'd never behave like you. It's you who has the problem."

I thought when Joel saw Rebecca, he'd see his need to be a responsible father. *What was this?*

Joel interrupted my thoughts. "I don't owe you anything. You'll hear from my lawyer before I go back. This confirms I never loved you. I should never have left Israel." Click.

Chapter 25

Saturday Night - Alive

Saturday morning

Glory

I stirred honey in my tea, and glanced at Ruth, pouring milk in hers.

"What are you doing today?"

"No real plans; just relax and go with the flow" Ruth sighed.

"Well, Jules is dropping me at my hairdresser's to revive my locks and paws. So, your patient will be someone else's responsibility for a few hours."

"Wow, a day off. Before I consider that, I must tell you: I met with your brother yesterday."

"Was he helpful? I hope he was well-behaved. He's second from the baby. He can be mischievous—at least he was in elementary school."

Ruth giggled.

"Driving downtown was quite an experience. For someone raised amidst corn fields, it was something else, I can tell you, but I'm proud of my courage. I needed a confidence builder. I must admit, though, my knees were shaking after parallel parking on Charles Street. I actually got it on my first try, even with honking horns and yelling drivers."

"You actually parked on Charles Street during rush hour?" I stared, horrified, but duly impressed.

No one I knew had ever attempted parallel parking, downtown, at rush hour, no less—ever. Amazing.

"You can close your mouth now. Yes and I'm here today as proof. I don't know whether I'll try it again. A parking garage would be easier. But if I have to, I know I can."

"Wow, what spunk. You're going to do just fine."

"The meeting was not as confidence building. I'd rather not face my life's fall-out; not a pretty picture."

"Whose is?" I added.

I braced myself for news which could not be good, I feared.

"I opened up at gut level. He'd read the papers, so he wasn't entirely ignorant. He might be able to help."

"That's good."

What else could I say, after all? I felt obligated to be affirming.

"George said, although Sam's left his church, he may still have benefits, legally mine because of our seventeen-year marriage: health insurance, life insurance, retirement funds, social security and maybe other things relating to Sam, Jr.'s care. At some point, he'll have to find employment."

She helped him write his dissertation, so she knew he could teach at a college. A university wouldn't care about his sexual orientation. He could do research, or any number of things.

"There are problems, though."

"Like what?" I asked, thinking it was all a nightmare.

"If he moves, it'd be difficult to enforce his responsibilities. There'd be scheduled visitation to consider."

I hadn't really thought about that. Goodness.

"I haven't heard from him in over three months and he's shown no interest in Sam, Jr. I don't want little Sam visiting with a male prostitute present."

I shut my eyes. My imagination was creating dreadful pictures of what little Sam might be exposed to. If this concerned Tad, I would've been frantic. I would've considered moving to Tasmania, or at least New Zealand. Ruth seemed a lot calmer than I would've been in her situation.

Ruth suddenly paled. "It might be easier to do nothing. If I can make it on my own, maybe he won't be interested in Sam, Jr. No support, but safety."

I had to agree. Extremely hard financially, but it seemed like the best course of action overall.

"I'm so grateful for George's help. I do need a lawyer, I see now. It seems more complicated than before

I knew such things. They don't teach legal aspects of divorce in church, you know."

"I do know."

"Could you subtract George's fees from my salary? That's the only way I can pay him." Ruth said, as an afterthought.

"We'll work something out, Ruth. Don't worry."

Sounds of footsteps interrupted our conversation and caused us to look toward the staircase. Mari skipped into the kitchen, dressed in jeans and Tyler's sweatshirt (A far cry from her usual Neiman Marcus outfit).

"Morning."

"Where're you headed today?" I asked.

"Clean and close up my house, for good. Today may be my last free day, as next week, I'll be taking my licensing exam. If I pass, I'll be on my way."

She grinned and sang "Da-da", throwing her arms outward, in a deep curtsy; a diva seeking applause.

We answered her curtain call with claps and hoots.

"Should you go, all by yourself? I've been reading about crime around that area, lately. Remember our rule about the buddy system?" I warned.

She waved her hand to dismiss my words.

"Sometimes incidents occur, but that's true all over this city. A private security force circles regularly and, our alarm system's on. I'll be all right for a few hours."

"I'd feel better if someone joined you." I said, shaking my head.

Ruth interrupted, "Mari, I don't have anything scheduled. Let me come. I'll be close to Midtown Memorial, so afterward, I can visit Gloria's mother."

"OK, then. I'd love company and your help."

Later

"Glory, I'll help you into the salon. Then I'll leave, do some errands, and pick you up, later." Jules instructed.

I struggled with my cape and crutches, while Jules strained to steady me at the curb. After I balanced, she accompanied me to Sylvia's desk.

Sylvia, with eyebrows lifted, gazed at my cape, and unkempt hair, two weeks overdue for color and trim. Her eyes slowly dropped from my head, my gypsy skirt, to my feet and then zeroed in on my face. Without missing a beat, she hissed, "Do you have an appointment?"

Jules stifled a laugh and looked away. No doubt she was trying to calm herself, having realized the gravity of protocol here. Memories flashed back from when we reported to the principal's office for passing notes in class: déjà vu.

"Yes, at 10:00."

I checked their clock for confirmation. Remembering the five-minute rule, I glanced in direction of 'the door'. I knew a detention room was stationed somewhere beyond.

At that moment, someone wrapped only in a towel and turban, cotton balls stuffed between each of her polished toes, peered from the opening. She whispered, sheepishly, "Excuse me, where's the ladies' room, please?"

Sylvia glowered, fiercely.

We shifted our now wide eyes from Sylvia to this poor be-toweled body.

After extended silence, this poor soul, almost dancing an Irish jig, whispered, "That's fine. I didn't mean to bother you. I'll just look around." She backed away and gently eased the door closed.

Jules, wide-eyed, remained silent.

I mumbled, "The detention room is down that hall."

Jules nodded her head, "Ah-h."

Suddenly realizing what I'd said, she burst into laughter. Trying unsuccessfully to stop, she retreated to the opposite side of the room.

I could hear her snorting. As always, she left me alone to face the consequences.

Sylvia, narrowing her eyes, jerked her head, signaling me to the reception area. Struggling to navigate my crutches, I obeyed. I joined Jules on the sofa among four ladies who abruptly scowled, then returned to studying dated copies of Town and Country.

"Now, why do you come here, again?" Jules whispered.

"It beats me. Maybe just so I can laugh." We giggled.

Pierre skipped into the room, singing, "Miss Gloria, Miss Gloria, your stylist awaits."

Jules smiled and whispered, "I'll return in two hours."

Mari

We sat cross-legged on my bare kitchen floor, moaning after three hours of heavy labor. Ravenously, we tore through cellophane-wrapped goodies Sarah'd packed; neither speaking until satiating bites were sufficiently chewed, swallowed and washed down with sweet tea.

"I'm glad you came, Ruth. This house once held such special memories. After Rebecca's seizure and Pete's death, I don't recognize this place I used to love. It seems so cold and empty now—kind of eerie."

Ruth sensed it too, but should she confirm that? What does one say when there's nothing comforting to say?

"It's got to be hard for you." reaching for tea, and stalling until words came. "I didn't clean our manse. Maybe I should've. It would've been the responsible thing. I just didn't want any more to do with it. Someone's probably cleaning for the next pastor, calling me all kinds of names because I left such a mess. They're calling me names, anyway, so. . ." she shrugged and smiled half-heartedly. "I admire your sticking with this. You're a lot stronger than I am."

I stared and my mouth dropped open. "Stronger than you are? Ruth, how can you say that? I wish I could be as strong as you. Neither of us has anything, we're both raising sons alone, and you've even faced public humiliation. I don't know how you handle invasion of privacy with such grace. You're always smiling."

Ruth glanced at her half-eaten sandwich, and sighed deeply.

"I don't always feel gracious. You don't know how many times I've cried myself to sleep, fearing what could happen to me and Sam, Jr."

I was silent for a moment, pondering her answer.

I had no idea Ruth didn't always feel as accommodating as she seemed. I felt so confined with my pain and so inept at handling things, I never realized others felt those same bungling feelings about how to get through life.

"I'm sorry, I didn't know you cried about your little boy like I do mine. Even though you have a strong faith in God, you still cry."

Ruth met my gaze and added, "You always look like you're so together. That's something I admire about you. We're pretty good actresses, aren't we?"

I smiled, "At times, I guess. As life plays out, I'm losing my ability to act."

I immediately recalled millions of times I hid behind 'poise', only to have realized I was hiding nothing: emperor's new clothes.

Ruth answered, "It's painful to be honest, but it's painful not to be. Let's finish, shall we? This house is giving me the creeps, too, and it's not even my house. We need to get out. You aren't coming back, are you?"

I replied, "I couldn't make myself. I can't wait to lock its doors for the last time."

We stuffed our remaining lunch in our mouths and checked each room. In thirty minutes, we were loading cleaning supplies, vacuum, brooms, rags, and garbage collected from this home's carcass.

Ruth buttoned her skirt, pulled a sweater over her head, and called, "I'm going. You won't be much longer, will you? I hate leaving you alone, even for a few minutes. Please hurry."

Stretching a sweater over my own head, "I'll be fine. Thanks for your help."

The front door lock clicked. Within a minute or so, I heard her car door slam and her car motor turn over.

I absently stepped into my skirt, exchanged my sneakers for heels and ran my fingers through my hair.

I'd check the lights in each room. Closing each door would close my past, for good.

I glazed my fingers across wallpapers I'd chosen, as if stroking a cold cheek of a departed loved one. My house carried my signature, unique as a fingerprint, but faded, somehow. It was like my child—my dead child, now.

I checked the nursery, having been Tyler's brother's room for only three days. I gently re-closed the door to a room carrying an airless odor of a space unhappily sealed for too long.

My fingers glossed lightly over carved wall moldings and intricate weave of silk draperies. My fingers repulsed with the contrasting roughness of Pete's den's grass-cloth wall-covering.

Errant tears escaped. *Stop.* I scolded myself, as I quickly fingered remaining switches.

A car motor groaned. Odd, given visitors rarely drove to this end of my street. Maybe Ruth had forgotten something.

I parted window blind slats. Nothing, I could see. Probably a repairman parked behind massive holly bushes, blocking my view.

Maybe I should check our garage before I go. I jimmied the kitchen door lock which had always stuck, and strode across our yard. Only trash cans lined its dank space. I should drag them to the end of our alley for garbage pickup, Tuesday.

I struggled to my driveway's end, panting with my effort. I would not return for these cans. Let new occupants take them. I could care less. I trudged back up our hill and re-opened my back door, securing its lock behind me.

Refrigerator plug pulled; stove unplugged. Thermostat to 55, or maybe it should be 50. I don't know. 50 it would be.

I opened the basement door and checked that light and water heater switches were pushed off. I re-bolted it. I circled downstairs bathrooms. No water running.

OK, all done, I think. Pete had always taken care of these things in other moves. *Why couldn't he have left something to help me—some instructions. . . anything?* I sighed.

Storm clouds draped our front windows—so dark outside. I shivered. I suddenly felt hate for this place; dread replaced sadness. It represented nothing but death now.

I listened for the lock-click, as I pulled the front door closed, one last time. My fingers searched deep within my coat pocket for my key for securing its double lock.

What's that noise?

The wind howled. It had to be holly branches scratching against the side of my house.

Hair strands plastered my eyes and mouth. I pushed them back unsuccessfully, while I fiddled with the key—simultaneously, balancing a storm door with my left shoulder.

There it was again; an unmistakable sound of twigs moving and breaking. Another product of my imagination, coupled with renewed dread for this place.

Stop it, I scolded myself.

I'm not going to let imaginary noises distract me. I had to get home. I set my focus on trying to get this door to lock.

I just couldn't seem to get my key to trigger this double lock. With my hair continuing to blow across my eyes, it was impossible to see and use my left hand to synchronize the required door handle-pulling with the key turn. I bit my lip with frustration, trying to get it right.

Suddenly, a gloved hand slapped across my mouth. My impulse to scream was thwarted by its pressure. No sound.

What's happening? Dear God. Panic coursed through me like an electric shock as I tried to break free.

A raspy male voice hissed, "Scream and I'll kill you."

I thrust my arm toward the door frame. Years ago, my husband had installed a silent alarm which traversed the entire molding. If I could just touch it, I might be able to activate it. My finger glazed its wire. Maybe Pete had left something to help me.

Hands grabbed me more forcefully. *Had our alarm system been de-activated with the auction? Oh, God, please, let it not be so.* I reached for the wire, again, but his grip tightened.

I whispered a response from the prayer book, *"Lord, have mercy, Christ have mercy, God have mercy."*

His push landed me against roots and branches, and hard, unforgiving ground. I whimpered as ice-covered leaves pricked my face and my legs. I tried to wriggle from his grasp, but the more I struggled, the more forceful his hold. One hand gripped my throat. The other hand clawed my clothes.

God, am I going to die? Will I be left here to be murdered? I pled, silently.

All I could distinguish was his dark ski mask in the shadows. I smelled the vile stench of violence. *Who was this person? Why did he want to hurt me?*

He removed his gloves and lifted his hand, I spotted his large ring. I knew that ring—but from where?

Incapacitated, I prayed without words. *God save me. Send angels to help. If I must die, please take care of Tyler. Please God. Take care of Tyler.*

With fading hope, I heard a distant siren; then another. Reflections of blue lights mirrored against my glass storm door. *Had our silent alarm worked?*

When sirens grew louder, my attacker cursed, "Did you do that?"

That voice. I knew that raspy voice. My mind blanked its connecting memory.

He struck me with a closed fist. The ring's prongs grazed my face and neck. He kicked me, shouting "New Orleans slut," and escaped through foliage.

I whimpered, my limbs trembling uncontrollably. I was afraid to make noise. He might return.

Minutes passed. I heard footsteps approaching. I squeezed my eyelids shut.

"Oh, God, is he coming back to kill me?"

"No, No!" I screamed. My voice sounded like someone else's; unrecognizable as my own.

"Police."

I continued to scream even after they found me. My outburst was unstoppable. My body was not my own, but behaved as if under some alien control.

Two officers hovered. Crackling words sounded from walkie-talkies.

"Ma'am? An ambulance should arrive momentarily."

So cold. Sick. . . .

Unrecognizable people belted me onto a sheeted surface.

So cold.

Escalating voices of strangers shouted to one another, oblivious to my terror.

Medicinal odors; flashing lights.

Darkness, again.

Smelling salts.

I could feel roughness of gravel under wheels as I rolled somewhere. So many people surrounded me, yelling.

My arm hurt. I tasted blood, slowly oozing from my lips and nose.

A blanket—someone was wrapping me in a blanket, securing my shaking limbs.

So cold.

A doctor and a nurse entered while others left. The room quieted.

"Where am I? What's happened?"

She replied only that I was in a hospital. I had been assaulted.

Fogged memories of my attack rushed through my consciousness as quickly as the speed of a lacrosse ball in one of Tyler's games. I could only scream. I didn't want to scream, but it was beyond my ability to stop.

Medicine was authorized. I smelled rubbing alcohol. Glaring memories interrupted my vision.

"I don't want anything. I want to leave. I don't want to be here. I need to go home to my son."

I scrambled to roll off the table, but she gently pushed me down.

"You need rest. You've been through quite an ordeal. This medicine will calm you."

My arm repulsed with injected cold liquid. I whimpered. It burned.

Fuzzy. My tongue was thick.

I was forgetting to scream.

"The Lord watches over those who fear him. . .He rescues them from death and keeps them alive. . . Only he can help us, protecting us like a shield."
Psalm 33:18-20 (Bible, NLT)

Saturday lunch

Glory

I felt so much better after my hair was highlighted and my nails polished. I'd been scolded by my manicurist about the sad state of my hands. I pointed to my crutches and she said no more.

I'd chosen 'blush' this time. 'Urban rose' clashed with my orange cape: tacky.

Jules had driven me to the restaurant's entrance, convinced as slowly as I labored with crutches, I'd be smashed flat as an Osage orange if I attempted crossing Roland Avenue. She delivered me as close to the front door as possible, and then returned to park at the end of the next block—again

I thought this was Sarah's last weekend to work, but I remembered her early hospital appointment.

Jules tore into a package of crackers and tossed two in her mouth.

"Well, Glory, this morning was quite entertaining, but I must say, they did a great job."

"Thanks, Da-ling." I answered, shook my hair dramatically and giggled.

She laughed and said, "So update me: I've only gotten momentary glimpses of you since our last lunch. How's your leg?'

"In ten days, I'll be rid of this thing. I can hardly wait. It's kept me down. As you know, I'm not a patient woman.'

"Amen, to that."

Our server approached and relayed Sarah's message to consider today's special.

"The flounder's scrumptious—stuffed with crabmeat. Split pea soup is served with sour cream and chervil. If you like, I can place your orders now so they'll be hot." He said with a cheerful grin and a dramatic wave of his hand.

We nodded. He called back, "Earl Grey?"

"Earl Grey" we answered in unison.

"I miss Sarah. It's not the same without her."

"Bless her heart. Things are so tough for her; for all the girls. Just when I think I couldn't hear anything worse, something else happens. I ache for them."

Julia sighed, "I don't live with them like you do, but when I've been there, it's been excruciating. How's Katie?"

"It's going to be a long, hard road for her, I think. She's begun to focus on a new life, which should encourage her from returning to her old one. She has enough life skills to make it, and her profession will give her a start. She's hopeful, now, I think."

I'd witnessed Katie go from fear, before her battering incident, to despair, while she recuperated at the shelter. Moving in with Sarah and starting a job has given her a positive goal to work toward. I wouldn't say she's enthusiastic yet, but she's definitely on her way up, for sure. I just hope nothing else happens to interrupt her passage.

"Please pray for her safety. He has the money and the power to make her miserable after he starts losing more control. Not something I enjoy thinking about."

Julia spoke, "Of course. How's your mother?"

"Oh, Jules, I haven't told you. Ruth's agreed to be Mother's companion. What she lacks in training she more than makes up for with kindness and dedication. In addition, Sarah's agreed to provide their meals."

"What an answer." Julia proclaimed. "It'll help everyone. How's Mari?"

"She says little. I'm beginning to see her wear down, though." I slowly shook my head, recalling past days.

Poor girl's had so many concerns about finances and losing her home; plus grieving her husband's death and being a mother to Tyler, who carries his own anger and grief. She tries to hide it, but she's lost weight. Dark circles below too-puffy eyes are clues she's not sleeping well. I worry.

"She's always maintained such a strong persona, giving the impression that everything's under control." I add.

"Like Scarlett O'Hara?" Jules guesses.

"Exactly. She's trying so hard to tread water on her own, and maintain her poise. I'm not sure how she'll fare if life gets more difficult. It's so painful to come to the end of your ability and feel so utterly helpless, isn't it, Jules? God will be waiting with open arms to take control of it all, of course. To finally choose to turn the driving over to Him is such a relief."

Jules nodded, while munching crackers.

"I've hit rock bottom any number of times, when I've thought things couldn't have gotten worse. All I could do was surrender, and God took over. He sent you, Jules, to be my friend on that rocky road."

I shake my head, recalling some of the tough times.

"And you to me, Glory, and you to me." Jules commented softly.

Our server brought our soup and assured us our main course was forthcoming.

Julia recited our traditional blessing, and added a request for God to give His protection.

Certainly, we all needed protection.

The pea soup disappeared from our cups as quickly as if we'd starved ourselves for weeks on a desert island. This comfort food was welcome on this bitterly cold day. Winter was coming in as a lion in 'Balmer'.

Our fish arrived, moist and delicate, over-flowing with crabmeat, flanked with julienne carrots and squash, and a fresh salad, dressed in simple vinaigrette. We forked bites at record speed, laughing as we recounted today's beauty shop experience.

"I must say, your hair looks ma-velous, Glory. That shop is certainly filled with local color."

"Except my being afraid of arriving five minutes late and risking whatever punishment might be doled out, I enjoy it. It provides pampering I seem to crave. I enter another world there—an escape from reality, I guess."

I giggle thinking again about Pierre, Sylvia, the streaked-haired manicurist and the imagined detention room. It's such fun.

Julia laughed, and asked, "What about dessert? I can't believe I'm still hungry. I wonder what's yummy? Sometime we'll have to go to Hausnerr's. I haven't been there in years: scrumptious desserts are on that menu. Let's go some weekend, OK?"

Our young waiter returned, asking about dessert.

"Sarah said the black forest cake's a winner." He whispered as if passing on a secret.

"She was right about our entrée, so how about it Jules? Shall we share one?"

"Yes, let's, with Earl Grey refills."

"Earl Grey." I affirmed, and we giggled.

I hesitated, while pondering a resurfacing idea. "Jules, what's the college offer in terms of education for displaced homemakers? You once mentioned some education help. Sarah and Ruth finished two years, but married before they finished degrees."

They're so bright. I'd love for them to have an opportunity to graduate.

"I was making reference to GED and job training. I don't know about college. There's nothing at our school, but benefactors might be approached about scholarships. I'll look into it. It's an idea, needing to be pursued, not only for these women but others later. Hmmm."

Jules reached into her bag for a pen and notepad.

"Oh, I almost forgot. I've got something for you." She added, as an afterthought.

Julia retrieved an envelope, scribbled with my name. She handed it across our table with great pomp.

"Mail, your highness."

Inside I found folded pieces of paper, roughly three inches square. No names attached. Most read, "pray for me", or "help me."

I squinted at Jules. "Where did you get these?"

"Mailbox. You haven't been by since you broke your leg."

"What a puzzle. No signature; just a plea for help."

I can't think whose they could be— someone in our group, maybe. No one has asked whether I've received their notes, though. It's odd.

Julia shrugged and sipped from her cup.

Our server approached with a cordless phone, his boyish grin had been replaced with an alarmed expression.

"Are you Gloria Harris?"

"Yes, I'm Gloria," I answered puzzled. "Who would call me here?"

"Someone named Ruth. Emergency."

Early Sunday morning

Mari

Red clouds smear a dawn sky. No sun.

I'm sitting atop a stool next to a pay phone at the end of this dormitory hall. It's early enough I won't be disturbed. In the distance, I hear a lone toilet flush, but nothing else. Quiet.

Katie lent me her robe last night. I tried to pull it snug. It was barely large enough to wrap around me, but its sash kept it closed and cozy.

I'd borrowed change from her, at some point. Cold metal brushed my cut finger tips as I checked its pocket. Yesterday sequenced a blur.

Clink, clink, clink, dial tone. I pushed "0"

"Operator he-re. Number, ple-ase."

"Yes, operator, I'd like to call (639) 555-8236."

'Deposit one doll-ar in co-ins, ple-ase,' resonated a sing-song voice.

"Clink, clink, clink, clink. Your call is be-ing connected. Ple-ase stand by."

I tapped my trembling fingers on the side of this wall. I noticed my hand was deeply scratched, too. Holly bush, I guess.

"Hello?"

The operator chimed in, "Your par-ty is on the li-ne. You may begin."

"Hello. . . Mama?"

A long silence followed.

"Mari? C'est Marie? Mon Dieu, Mon Dieu, merci beaucoup, merci. Ma cherie, ma cherie, ma petite jeune fille."

"My God, thank you. It's my dear little girl."

"Mama je t'aime!" I love you, Mama. Help me, please, s'il vous plait. Je suis tres desole, tres triste.

Chapter 26

The Hearings

Three weeks later

Katie

"Hear my prayer, O Lord... Don't bring your servant to trial! Compared to you, no one is perfect. My enemy has chased me. He has knocked me to the ground... I am losing all hope; I am paralyzed with fear... come quickly, Lord and answer me."

At some point last night, I'd opened my Bible and happened on Psalm 143.

My grandmother read her Bible daily. Curiously, as a child, I'd asked her why she read it over and over.

She answered, "It's new every morning. God provides special direction for me, custom-designed for each day."

I never asked again, but her words burned into my heart.

Now, in my time of need, I realized God's help was what I had not sought in my life. I'd made decisions based on book-knowledge, when my own knowledge fell short. A professor once said, "You don't have to know everything. You just need to know where to look it up."

Books fell way short, I'd sadly found. Books never helped when Jeremy had year-long colic. It seemed no one had ever been in my position—ever. If they had, they were too tired to write about what worked, or maybe they just gave up. Maybe they just died.

I'd once thought wisdom could be found in great medical institutions. After years of experience with pediatricians and other medical and dental specialists, my husband being one, I discovered they surely didn't know all there was to know.

What was so disturbing was the arrogance many portrayed as they sat behind their desks. An attitude which conveyed to a patient, she was every bit as ignorant as she felt. While the experts, played God. Yeah. Probably guilt at not living up to what they represented made so many want to escape with drugs.

I had an uneasy feeling the law profession was the same. They weave a good tale. . .for a price, a hefty price. Had Sarah's or Mari's lawyer done any more than add to their sense of hopelessness? Couple that foreboding with a big retainer bill—a down payment of promised help. No guarantees, of course, for more and more time, and more and more money spent. What a joke.

How had I become so cynical? I'd been around. I'd heard stories from women in displaced homemakers and at the shelter. It was not an isolated problem. These women had suffered under hands of so-called professionals, only to end up in a more desperate and destitute position now and forever.

My lawyer promised a good settlement plus custody of my boys. . .or, at least Timmy, at today's separation hearing. I could count on child support and alimony to help begin a new life. *Did I even dare hope in that?*

I'd taken both sons to a psychologist for evaluation, prior to leaving home. No good news there either. The difference was he gave me no hopeful promise for the future, regardless of money spent. At least he was honest about it.

Both sons suffered from a lack of a relationship with their father, or any positive male figure, he surmised. No surprise. His painful conclusion was that Jeremy's intense anger was directed toward me because I'd been a lousy father. Although I'd been a loving, self-sacrificing mother and had done more than most mothers would've done.

His words hit me like a bucket of ice water thrown in my face; kicked while I was down. I'd spent every waking minute trying to be the best parent I could be.

"What?" I screamed.

He said boys need their fathers as well as a mother.
I agree with that. I waited for further explanation.

Since I was never designed to be a father, even my best efforts at trying to fill that gap created anger from my son.

But why anger against me?

Memories flashed, bringing to mind my trying to teach Jeremy to hold a bat and throw a ball so he could join T-ball at five. Baseball was certainly not my forte, but wasn't a little knowledge better than none at all? His father was always at his office, or too tired or disinterested in helping his son with skills—for sports or life.

When his father finally saw him play, he cursed me. I'd taught his son to throw like a girl, he said. It was not my intention, certainly, but as I sat in that psychologist's office, it hit me: I was a girl, or a woman, as it were. I would not be anything other than who I was. Maybe I hadn't done it right, but what I did was out of love.

To add insult to injury, the psychologist condemned my staying in this abusive situation. As a result, Jeremy was marked for life to be abusive like his father. Even Timmy, only three, had seen enough to subconsciously encode behavior for use in his future relationships.

My heart's desire was a perfect family for my boys. As hard as I tried to achieve that, I'd failed, miserably. Now my sons suffered and would continue to suffer, for the rest of their lives. I was condemned to suffer from my mistakes for a life-time, as well, through my sons.

Counselors were like other professionals—opinionated to be sure. Encouraging? Hardly.

Last year, I shared my concerns with my church minister, hoping he could advise me. Give hope.

He remained silent as I shared a condensed account of my marriage. At first he looked at me, incredulously, as though I was inventing it. Then he finally deemed I must stay married even at the risk of my death, because Jesus died for those he loved. He quoted a scripture about a wife's being submissive to her husband and God hated divorce.

I could agree God hated divorce. How could a loving God witness the excruciating pain my sons and I were experiencing and approve of that?

Certainly, Christ died for those he loved, but his death was redemptive—the ultimate sacrifice of love for all people he loved. What would be the purpose of my death?

I'd read that often quoted Bible clause about submission, most men are so eager to stand behind—regarding a woman's role. St. Paul's other part of that statement says a husband must love his wife as Jesus loved his church (which, in fact, was enough to suffer and die for it). A husband ought to love his wife as his own body, describing a loving, mutually-giving and protective relationship as an example. Don's and my marriage was anything but caring or giving, and certainly not protective.

What encouragement had he given me? Our meeting simply added more confusion and guilt, on top of what I already carried. He hadn't even prayed with me. Isn't that what a minister's supposed to do? I left feeling dejected and rejected.

Even veterinarians could not be counted on. I recently heard of a family taking their cat to a vet for yearly shots and their cat was euthanized, by mistake. Then they were given the other mangy, sick cat to take home with them. No doubt as a consolation prize or something. Perhaps they were told they could rid themselves of grief by helping a hopeless, sick animal have a nice home for his remaining days. Maybe even that they were considered selfish and uncaring to want their own cat instead of this poor substitution. After all, they could be happy, knowing their beloved Fluffy was in a better place. Hmpf.

And dentists? I won't even go there. I'd lived with one for eighteen years.

Politicians? No comment at all.

My face warmed with recollection of my dreadful experiences. Surely there had to be some helpful, encouraging professionals somewhere, but they'd been sadly lacking in my life. No help I could depend upon—ever.

Shaking my head vigorously to flee from these memories, I looked back at my Bible I'd closed. Was it too late for God to help me? He was my last and only resource.

I was sick, thinking I'd inadvertently caused my sons to suffer. Suddenly, I was more regretful for leaving God out of my life; leaving Him as my last possible recourse, having tried everything and everybody else, marred by human limitations, for help first.

In the still dark morning, I knelt by my bed. My Bible fell open to Isaiah 54:

"And I will be a father to her sons. . . ."
Was that my answer? Could I count on that?

"It is better to trust the Lord than to put confidence in people. . ."
Psalm 118:8-9 (Bible, NLT)

This day already started sadly. I kissed Timmy goodbye in the midst of screams for me to stay. Separation anxiety had become a regular part of our morning routine, much to my dismay; more guilt, more heartache.

Gloria agreed to drive me to Towson court house. She'd be there for moral support and a ride home. I really didn't want anyone there, actually. I was ashamed. I wanted it as private as possible. It should only be our two lawyers, a judge, me and my husband, right?

I needed Gloria there, though. She'd been through this. She also seemed a lot stronger than I felt. I was frightened beyond words. I felt like the psalmist when he described himself as being paralyzed with fear.

I'd arrived at Roland Avenue now. Sarah waved for me to come in for breakfast.

The last thing I wanted was food. If I didn't eat, I'd feel shaky. I might pass out during questioning. What would happen then? I'd force myself to eat.

Glory

I was barely able to grip the ignition key with my trembling hands. I reassured Katie I was cold; a small part of the truth. Petrified, is what I was. I did not want to go to this thing. Too many memories were buried which I didn't want exhumed.

Why was I even doing this? I did it because I cared. It was the right thing to do. I could imagine Jules chiding me about always doing a task no one else would do. Jules was the same, though.

Surely, she had other things she could be doing other than help students, or volunteer at the shelter. She didn't have to stay at the hospital with Katie, Mari and countless others. She didn't have to help me so many times, either.

No, Jules and I, along with countless others, had learned to lean into the wind, despite an emotional tug to do nothing. Shoulder the storm. We knew peace was on the other side.

I settled uneasily on a rear courtroom pew. Katie had spoken with her attorney, who looked rattled. Apparently he'd seen the opposing lawyer slip behind chamber doors and speak directly with the judge, minutes before. Clearly, this was illegal, but apparently there were no other witnesses. He could do nothing. No doubt, a surprise awaited. He encouraged her, though, saying the law was on her side.

I remember being in her position so long ago. I, too, had survived an abusive marriage, and not only was I trying to separate from my husband, I was going up against a good-ole-boy system with all its power, coupled with his money. Things had not looked hopeful, although my lawyer tried to encourage me. After all, his fee payment depended upon its success.

At her lawyer's beckoning, Katie walked to the front. I looked to my right. I saw her husband, and presumably their older son, Jeremy.

Although Katie described Jeremy as wearing almost orange shoulder-length hair and multiple piercings, he sat visibly transformed; no doubt primped for this occasion. His neatly trimmed hair was now a natural chestnut brown. No pierced jewelry was noticeable. He wore a tailored blazer with a prep school seal on his pocket, a starched white shirt, and a regimental- striped tie. He looked like an all-American prep student. His lawyer had set this stage convincingly.

I looked to my left and saw Katie's mother-in-law, sister-in-law, and numerous cousins filling seats. They were invited to increase Katie's stress and embarrassment, I knew. This lawyer had planned well.

My eyes drifted to her husband's lawyer. As he turned and looked toward the back, shock nearly stopped my heart.

Could it be? My former husband was Katie's husband's lawyer.

I hardly recognized him. He was heavier. His once dark hair had grayed. It hung as if uncombed, badly in need of a trim. His blazer was crumpled in back, looking as if it'd been slept in. He'd never have looked so disheveled while married to me.

The many years of heavy drinking had taken their toll. His face was splotchy and puffy. His nose was bulbous, lined with enlarged veins, indicative of long-term alcoholism. His eyes landed on me, squinting. His scowl changed suddenly to a cocky grin.

His teeth revealed gross neglect. You'd think his client, a dentist, would have bartered for treatment. Perhaps that would come when his bill was presented at the end.

My shock and momentary fear made me want to look away. I even considered leaving. Instead of being averted, I stared back at him, trying to appear undaunted.

What should I do? What could I do? I tried to make sure my expression didn't reveal my fear. I felt like I was on trial, not Katie. Perhaps I was.

I coaxed myself, silently. *I will not be afraid.*

Katie was called to the stand, ignorant of what lay ahead.

Charles began, "Your Honor, if I may approach the bench. I have information which may have bearing on this case."

After the judge replied, "Approach the bench", Charles hiked his trousers, buttoned his jacket, and strode toward the judge. His client beamed, confidently.

The judge opened his folder, perused its contents, and turned to Katie. "Repeat your name and address for the court."

Katie spoke her name, but what looked like terror crossed her face. Her eyes widened, and she looked at her hands.

"Your Honor, I'm living away from my home, presently, in a safe place. I don't know its exact street address."

The judge prodded and sneered, "You are living in a place, separate from your husband and older son, but you do not know its address? How can you receive mail?"

Katie hesitated, "Your Honor, I have a post office box."

The judge asked again, "What about mail addressed to you and your husband?"

Katie answered, "I must visit my—or our—house regularly to check mail. I check to see important bills are paid. I also check for any mail addressed to me.

The judge paused and said, "Your grounds for this separation are based on physical abuse and desertion."

At this, Katie's attorney stood and added, "Your Honor, we have copies of her hospital records and pictures of her face. May I approach the bench with these exhibits?"

The judge held up a palm, to stop him. "Mrs. Ward, has your husband ever struck you in prior years of your marriage?"

Katie answered, "Yes, Sir, your Honor, a number of times."

This was documented by an affidavit received by Don's lawyer. No surprise.

He queried again, "Why did you stay before? Why did you decide to leave now?"

I could see where this line of reasoning was going. I knew from years of hearing my husband's cases, this would not fare well.

Katie didn't answer.

The judge asked again, "Mrs. Ward, were you intimate in the months after his other hurtful episodes? (An old law remained on the books, pronouncing if intimacy occurred after abuse, even weeks or months or years, the victim condoned the behavior by consenting to this act.)

Katie slowly answered, "Sir, he said things would change. He said it wouldn't happen again. I had children to consider. . ." Her voice cracked badly under pressure.

"Mrs. Ward, do you have a job to support yourself, since you claim to be on your own?"

"I'm a dental hygienist. I'm signed with a temporary staffing agency."

"By your own admission, it is only temporary. Is that what you're saying? How long have you been working for this agency?"

I hung my head and cringed. I could not look at Katie. This was too painful.

"Your Honor, I worked two days last week."

"Two days? Is that what you call a job? Do you plan to return to that office? Has that dentist offered you a permanent position?"

Silence.

The judge paused, dramatically. "In my opinion, this is a viable marriage. No child support or alimony indicated."

Don grinned broadly, happy to not have to support her or Timmy for a while.

Katie's attorney protested, "But, Your Honor, I have pictures. . ."

The judge glowered, gavel positioned to strike.

"Son, unless you want to be charged with contempt, I suggest you remain seated."

His gavel sounded.

"Case dismissed."

Katie's muffled sobs interrupted our wordless ride home. I drove slowly through residential streets toward Charles Street. I was trying to sort my thoughts, and tamper my seething anger.

This day had been worse than I could've imagined. I was bombarded with feelings I could no longer ignore.

My court hearings for separation and divorce had been no less tragic than today's. Since it'd been fifteen years, memories were numbed. I thought I'd forgotten my pain. I thought I'd forgotten my ex-husband. I'd moved on.

Yes, I dreaded reliving this horror of my own life, today, but I thought I'd forgiven and forgotten. *On the contrary, I felt fear when I saw him and what else?* Rage and hate. I closed my eyes wanting to close out that truth.

Not only was I hurting incredibly for Katie, I realized my anger was as much toward that man who hurt me as for Katie's distress. The purpose of my going was to offer comfort and support. It was apparent I needed to address stuffed emotions threatening to poison my own life.

How could I have been so arrogant to think I could offer anything to help anyone else, when I hadn't dealt with my own issues? I raked my fingers through my damp, perspiring hair.

It was all too much. I didn't want to think about this. *Hadn't I gone through enough? God, how much more must I face?*

In a flash, I realized I was angry at God, too. What kind of person had I become? I'd been acting so self-righteously. Thinking I could actually offer someone else help when I was in as dark a place as anyone. *Had I been playing with God, too?*

At dinner, we sat in silence, mindlessly moving our peas, potatoes and meat circuitously around our plates. Katie opened, with a word for Sarah.

"I'm sorry I won't be able to help you with your house."

Sarah swallowed her last bite, and grabbed her water glass to drink, allowing the pause to prepare words. She blotted her lips with her napkin.

"Frankly, it doesn't matter. My lawyer called. Joel wants our house on the market immediately. So, my loss is his loss, too. But, Katie, I've loved having you and Timmy stay this week. It's really helped distract me from Rebecca's absence. My house is so big. It'd be much too quiet without you. If you'd just stay until it sells or until Rebecca returns, it'd mean a lot."

Katie replied, "Thank you. My lawyer promised to file an emergency plea for support; within six weeks, hopefully. Maybe I can pay then what I can't now."

Sarah nodded. "It's OK."

I paused for a moment. "I feel like I've had the wind knocked out of me. I've got to get out of here—even if it's only for a few days. Anyone want to join me for a Thanksgiving break in North Carolina?"

Wide eyes. Silence.

Mari was first to respond. "Gloria, would you be making a stop at Chapel Hill? Tyler could visit that campus. Maybe I could help a little with gas."

Sarah blurted, "Could I come along? Durham is close to Chapel Hill. I'd love to see Rebecca, even if it's only for a few minutes."

Katie, with a little hope expressed in her sad eyes, added, "Gloria, my family is only minutes from Raleigh. I'd love to go. Oh, for a little comfort. . .Southern Comfort."

We laughed, gently, sorely needing humor.

I answered, "If we split the gas and take our own food, we could probably do it reasonably. Maybe we could switch cars with Jules, and take her SUV. It has tons of room, so we could stretch a little bit."

Looking at expectant faces, I was reminded of my son's expression, waiting for Santa.

I mused, "Bill could meet me in Chapel Hill, and the three of you could take the car to your respective places. We could meet Sunday afternoon, how about it?"

"We are hard pressed on every side, but not crushed; perplexed but not in despair, persecuted but not abandoned, struck down but not destroyed."
2 Corinthians 4:8 (Bible, NIV)

Chapter 27

Heard It Through The Grapevine

Mari

I reached the end of myself with my attack. Maybe I needed one final blow to open my eyes to a new beginning.

I've always considered myself strong. I could tackle anything with a little hard work, a little charm, good planning and a lot of poise. Sounds like Superman—able to jump the highest building in a single bound. My perspective had been as preposterous as that cartoon hero.

Trying to keep all my balls juggling, while maintaining a set of standards that proper people seemed to know how to meet, simply required too much energy.

My juggling balls have dropped and rolled somewhere I can't find.

My husband's passing signaled a death to castles in my sky. I'd blamed his drinking and gambling. Now I see I was as much a part of creating our artificial life as he'd been. Maybe I'd even pressured him into making disastrous decisions, in some unconscious way; pressured him, into needing to escape.

At my counseling session, I recognized my life as a theatre set: nothing more than a painted face propped against a piece of wood. No depth, no dimension. No stability. I remembered downtown's urban renewal, and nodded its similarity to my life.

My make-believe marriage was anything but model. My perfect house, decorated in the best money could buy, had been sold at public auction. I'd owned an exquisite house, luxury cars, and designer clothes. *Had I owned them? No, I'd leased them. They owned me.*

The wonderful mother I portrayed myself as being had caused me to deceive my only son into thinking money and its trappings were what constituted success. Pie-in-the-sky brought happiness.

Except for my new friends, my life was a sorry, sorry mess. Calling Mama and asking forgiveness was the first right thing I've done in years, after surrendering to God. I felt unshackled in having failed. Anticipation and fear of failure was far worse than accepting it. In fact, I've never felt as blithe.

I could do nothing to redeem my past, but maybe I could affect my son's future. I must tell him the truth. That would be the most difficult.

I'd already been honest with Hilton Academy. That candor had not killed me. Although disappointed, I even survived when they refused aid for Tyler's final semester. I'd prepared myself for a worst scenario, and their refusal was part of it. I could accept it. I'd been truthful and had no regrets. I was free from one more thing to worry about. In fact, afterwards I'd felt unshackled, having released a heavy load I'd struggled to carry far too long.

The loss of my home, husband and security, including my identity (pseudo, as it was) had signaled the first level of honest surrendering. My attack had taken away any shred of false dignity I'd managed to hold onto. I was down to bare-bones Mari, naked with no props to support my wretched act—and it was OK.

I focused on the back and forth swing of windshield wipers, clearing dirt from the glass. I could see Tyler clap his stick high against a friend's stick, signaling, "See you later". I listened to crunching sound of cleats digging holes in frozen earth.

"Mom, need time to shower, OK?"

"Take your time. We're going out to dinner—not five-star, but we're celebrating, nonetheless."

"Huh?" he answered, squinting.

"I passed my exam" I grinned.

"Way to go, Mom." He raised my arm, giving my palm a high five.

MacDonald's was crowded and noisy, as usual. Tyler found an isolated table, empty only because it was farthest from their play area.

I studied his face. His angular jaw, his dark beard shadowing his chin, heavy brows, and broad shoulders made me see, for perhaps the first time, Tyler was not a little boy, anymore.

Little ones darted to and fro with catsup-covered cheeks. Some displayed tempers because their frenzied Mothers enforced they drink milk before playing. I gulped as I realized I'd never be in their position again.

My baby was a man. It was time I treated him as one; truth time.

"So, how does it feel to be a real-life, professional Realtor, Mom?" Tyler grinned as he gulped a fist-full of fries, swallowing before he'd barely chewed.

"I think I'm proud." I giggled and said.

"Only a week 'til Thanksgiving— any plans, Mom?"

Here goes. I swallowed and cleared my voice.

"That's what I want to discuss with you, Ty. We've been invited to join Ms. Gloria on a trip to North Carolina. It'd be fun to check out lacrosse programs at UVA and UNC, don't you think?"

Heavy pause, and more silence. I closed my eyes, waiting for the less-than-enthusiastic response which would surely follow.

He sighed, impatiently, "My heart's set on Princeton, Mom. I've wanted to go since Chad visited. You know that."

I looked down and focused on my shredded napkin. *What can I really say? Princeton is out of the question. Do I tell him now, or wait until after Christmas?*

Why wait? I recalled removing countless band-aids from Tyler's limbs when he was a child. I explained it hurt for a shorter time if I ripped it off quickly than if I pulled it slowly; less time for pain. More time for healing tears.

Yes. That was my answer. I must tell him everything, now...and yes, tears could be healing.

"You were barely ten when he visited. We haven't heard from him in years. It may not be what you've imagined. You've never even seen Princeton. Besides, I thought you were impressed with the Carolina and Virginia coaches."

"Yeah, they were cool."

"Both universities are reputed as some of the finest state universities. Both are especially good for lacrosse."

I joined him in stuffing a few fries in my mouth—chewing mine before swallowing.

"Why are we doing this, Mom?" He stopped eating and stared.

"OK, Tyler. There's no way around it, so I'll just say it. I spoke with Dad's accountant. We have no money—not for Princeton or any other private college. No money for anything."

His mouth dropped.

"What happened to the money from selling our stuff?"

I covered my face. Tears flowed. I refused to run to the restroom as I would've only days ago.

"Mom, I've never seen you cry. How bad is it?" He paled and straightened.

"Bad."

"Is that why we're living in that house?"

I nodded.

"Is that why we never eat by ourselves anymore, but always in that group of yours?" Sarcasm oozed in his tone.

I breathed deeply and started again.

"That group, you so loosely call it, are my dearest friends, who have given us a place to live and free food so you can graduate, Son."

"Exactly how much do we have to live on?" He glared.

"That's my concern, not yours. I took this Real Estate course to keep afloat. We may not be living in the manner in which we're accustomed, but I need to address that, too. We were living a lie, Tyler. We were dressing, driving cars, and living in a house we could not afford."

Purposely, he pushed his half-eaten Big Mac aside.

"We've lost material things, but we have each other. In our loss, we've been given a gift of a second chance, to see that friends and family are most valuable. I've also met the living God who loves us. I'm trusting Him to provide for us."

"God? Neither you nor Dad ever told me anything about God. Did God do this to us? Did God take Dad? Did God make us poor?"

He slammed the table's Formica surface.

"What about me? You and Dad went through all our money, but at least you had college. What's left for me?"

His face reddened. He tried to hold back tears, as I'd modeled for years.

"You'll get college. Your choices may need to be made from a different sample of schools, that's all. From what Mrs. Emerson said, you're a model student and star athlete. Scholarship opportunities abound."

OK. I've dropped the bomb. Now time to clean up after the fall-out. I'll ease in with the positive. *There had to be a positive, right?* Think, Mari, think.

"My school knows about our problems, too?" he snapped.

Uh-oh. I grimaced. Another bomb I didn't mean to drop. Diplomacy and tact would have to smooth over this.

"As a widow, they know our needs are greater than before, that's all."

"Let's go." He stood abruptly, scraping his chair against the floor.

He lobbed his trash and slammed the door, banging a wall on his way out.

I slowly stood. I encouraged myself, I'd done this thing. I'd been honest. Tyler had faced a huge disappointment tonight. This outburst was predictable and normal.

It didn't mean my heart was not breaking though. I was through with appearances. I allowed tears to flow, unhindered.

I let our car motor idle as its temperature warmed. Rubbing my hands together, I said, "After we visit North Carolina, you and I are flying to Mississippi."

He looked at me as if I'd lost my mind. "Mississippi? What for? You told me we have no money and now you say we're going to Mississippi, of all places? Is there a school—there— you want me to visit, too? I don't even think they play lacrosse down there."

He glowered, his face pressed against the passenger window. He kicked his shoe into the side of his door.

"No. There's something else I haven't told you, though."

"Are you kidding me? You dump all this on me, and then you say there's more?" He yelled.

"When I was feeling low, I made a phone call."

"Yeah, to whom, God?" He mocked.

"I called your grandmother. She's sending plane tickets for us to visit. She wants to meet you."

Katie

My stomach tightened in anticipation of my third day of work; employment outside-my-home-work, that is.

I hadn't needed an alarm. My out-of-control life kept my mind entertained all night. My on-going video, replaying past months—and years—usually started its play cycle about 3:30 a.m. My returning to sleep proved futile. Reacting emotions would inevitably strike a raw place, like an ulcer in my mind; creating more debridement of my wounded heart. Burning tears seeped as if rinsing this new sore—again.

It's a relief to get up and do something. Do anything, rather than continue to crave sleep's escape which will not surface.

I listen for sounds from Timmy, as I ease my body away from his. As I mentioned before, he's only been able to sleep with his head resting on my shoulder and his thumb in his mouth.

More guilt, as if I didn't have enough?

My pediatrician warned me about allowing my child to sleep in my bed. *So, what?* Our life was dreadful for me, an adult, but the fear and uncertainty it must create for a 3-year-old was more than I could imagine. If he felt secure to sleep with his head on his mother's shoulder, so be it. At least one of us would sleep.

What did pediatricians know about children's sleep, anyway? Where were most of them when their own children were pre-schoolers? Probably in medical school, internship or residency, while wives—or mothers—or nannies—took care of their children. They knew about sickness and drugs, but how much did they know of love and nurture?

Ditto with potty training and pacifier. How important were they, anyway, in the whole scheme of things?

It totally escaped my control. I could only ride this mule. At some point, I'd reach an end.

The end: what thoughts did that conjure up? I couldn't even imagine. *Would there ever be an actual end of worrying about my boys, fearing Don's antagonism, or obsessing about basics of food, shelter, and safety for one more day?*

I tiptoed to our bathroom. I closed its door before switching on a light, so Timmy would not stir. After using the toilet, without a flush, I tiptoed to Sarah's laundry room to iron my scrubs. I'd have everything ready before I showered and awakened Timmy.

I never knew how much time I'd need for this process. I never seemed to time it right. Was it my life, now, or lack of organizational skills which would forever be the bane of my existence?

I plugged the iron and set up the board. The dryer load was a huge mound, this morning: glued with static. Snaps crackled as I separated uniform pieces from the ball.

Footsteps. My heart stopped. They moved closer to this room. I took in a great breath, preparing to scream.

Sarah peeked through the doorway.

"You scared me something awful." I spoke with muffled tones. I put a finger to my lips, signaling her to speak softly.

"Sorry," Sarah grinned. "I couldn't sleep, either. I thought I'd chat before we start today's race."

"Do you have a memory video, too?"

"It's dreadful, isn't it? I want to sleep—just one night of uninterrupted sleep. After a few hours of sleeping from sheer exhaustion, my mind says, "Intermission over—time for the next showing.""

I wondered how many showings were required before my movie left town and moved onto a dusty shelf somewhere, like forgotten classic Hollywood films. I longed to put mine to rest on a forgotten shelf in my subconscious, never to be viewed again. Would there ever be such a time? I was holding out for a new movie: a comedy, next time. I'm through with drama and horror.

I laughed quietly. Pathetic. Somehow, commiserating made it seem less so.

"Talk to me while I iron," I said.

Sarah sighed, "Did you ever dream you'd be in this situation? I wanted to be a devoted, stay-at-home Mom, with a perfect marriage, perfect home, perfect child. . . Well, my life's a far cry from that."

"My dreams are long gone, too. I think my life was mostly dream and only a little reality, anyway. I wonder what was authentic in my life. When did I start creating and believing my make-believe was real?"

"Same for me. I thought Joel loved me. I thought we were happy. That fairy tale's ended. It's scary to think it may have been my imagination all along."

"I know about that."

Did I ever. Sharing these secret thoughts with a caring friend encouraged me. I knew she was sane, honest and was trying to live life the best she knew how, as I was. As we all were. I was comforted realizing my reactions were not aberrant, but probably normal for the circumstances we women were finding ourselves.

I needed to feel normal. I needed to feel someone else trusted me enough to share her dashed dreams.

Perhaps I was not as guilty of doing everything wrong as so-called professionals led me to believe. Maybe somewhere deep inside me, I had a compass that was leading me in the right direction.

"On the other side of the coin, what I thought was make-believe is true. I refused to believe in God for years. I called Him make-believe. I exchanged the truth about God for the deception of my dreams. My broken dream is much too hard to bear without hope. God must be the answer to surviving disappointments." Sarah added.

She paused, realizing she had uncovered a profound truth. Something she'd need to reflect upon. *What other reality had she exchanged for a fantasy?*

"Even though I've always believed in God, I put Him in a Sunday morning compartment. He had no part in my day-to-day life. I didn't know who He was and I didn't care. I can't handle even one day without trusting Him to help me. Life's too hard." I concurred.

As I spoke these words, I was struck with the fact that it took losing everything, to come face to face with myself and my need for God. The thought began to dawn in my conscious mind: perhaps good could come out of all this. *When I come to the light at the end of this tunnel—which I certainly hope will be soon—might I be grateful for all this? I can't imagine.*

"I've finished ironing, so I must shower quickly and wake Timmy. Thanks for talking." I held up the iron, "To another day."

Sarah returned our toast with a box of *Cheer*.

After showering, I buttoned my robe, and re-entered my bedroom. Urine odor permeated the air: another wet diaper.

I'd need more time to strip sheets and run the washer before I left for work. How much more could I squeeze into an already packed morning schedule.

"Timmy, Honey, we need to get up for school." I kissed his head.

I positioned him over my shoulder. He was getting big for my 5' frame. Even with his thumb firmly planted in his mouth, he wailed, "No, No."

I hobbled to our bathroom as quickly as possible. "No's" grew more intense. His feet bounced on my thighs and his fist on my shoulder. Stepping onto a bathroom rug, I let him slide onto the floor, still howling. I began filling his tub.

"NO BATH. NO BATH." he yowled.

I glanced at the clock. I hated to rush him, but I had no choice. I placed him, straight-legged and crying, into the warm water. I tossed in his favorite rubber ducky and wind-up turtle.

He batted them away, and kicked his legs. This was so hard. I understood. I longed to go back to sleep, just like he did. Both of us were exhausted.

A knock at the door welcomed distraction. Sarah emerged holding a mammoth cookie.

"Timmy, guess who just visited?"

His tear-filled eyes were diverted.

"Cookie Monster knows you can't have cookies before breakfast, but this cookie's special. Gobble this one right away."

He withdrew his moisture-wrinkled thumb, giggled and reached for it.

"Thank you." I mouthed to Sarah. I rapidly wiped him with a soapy washcloth as he stood.

A fresh load of guilt dumped, after dropping him at Day Care. I could hear his wails all the way to my car. I wanted to comfort him, but I could not.

I released a breath, slowly. *Was this what life would be like from now on? Goodness. How would I make it?*

I shoved my gear shift into reverse, turned to check my descent from the driveway, and entered an approach lane to I83. The sun was just rising, but traffic was like 5:00 p.m.

Directions were confusing. I'd never been to Aberdeen, so finding this office would be an adventure. I scoped the passenger seat to make sure I'd brought necessities: Fluid-resistant lab-coat, non-latex gloves, face-masks, protective glasses, license, lunch and a thermos of Sarah's coffee.

A sign flashed: "Expect delays—accident ahead."

Oh, no, stopped cars. I had at least an hour and a half drive. There was no hurrying this. I joined the queue.

I needed to relax, but warm air beckoned too much relaxation. Poor timing. If only I'd felt this relaxed five hours ago. I was hyper, but I was bone tired, as my grandmother often described.

Too cold to crack my window. I'd try coffee, and search for an oldies station. Yes—Beatles songs—double play: "It's been a hard day's night and I've been working like a dog. . ." and "Here comes the sun. ." I sing my morning inspiration.

A gigantic tooth-shaped sign hung precariously above the office door supported by heavy chains. "M. Sawyer, DDS. We cater to cowards."

No comment. I shook my head.

I grabbed my supplies and pocketbook, and raced through their front door. A packed waiting room greeted me. *Uh-oh.* I winced. Eight minutes late. *How could it be?* I tried so hard.

The receptionist glared as I approached her desk. She pointed at their clock.

'I'm sorry. An accident. . ."

"Traffic is no excuse. Your patient's seated in room 3." She pointed down a dark hall.

"DIANE." she bellowed to the air.

A stocky, spectacled woman suddenly appeared, smiling with lower teeth only.

"You're late." she growled.

I tagged close behind her down a long hallway. Diane tossed the chart onto a counter and exited. My first patient sat, goggling <u>Sports</u> <u>Illustrated</u> swim suit issue.

"Good morning," I said cheerfully.

The man glared, pointing to his watch. "You're late."

He sized me up with the lewd expression, he'd been using while studying magazine super-models.

I sighed deeply, and mumbled an apology. *"Dirty old man"* I muttered to myself.

I dumped my belongings, including my coat, on a small corner chair, not knowing where else to put them. I pushed my arms through lab-coat sleeves, trying to untangle static-cling bunching both sleeves and hem. I pushed glasses over my nose and gloves over my fingers.

The man pointed to the floor.

A pair of undetected panties, glued to my lab-coat with static, had chosen this minute to loosen their grip. The undergarment was now delicately poised on the floor beside his chair.

Would I ever live through this humiliation?

I kicked my panties away from view, hoping out-of-sight, out-of-mind. My face burned. I longed to start this day over, and it was only 8:10 a.m.

"Thank you, sir. I'll address them after I finish your teeth."

I positioned the chair to see into his mouth, my cheeks still flaming.

"I can't lie down. I get claustrophobic." He glowered.

What did lying down have to do with claustrophobia? Fear of enclosed places shouldn't affect his reclining. *How did this man sleep if he didn't lie down? How could I work in his mouth if I could not see?*

I straightened the chair to appease him. I'd try standing.

My back strained with leaning. I winced as I shifted my stance to see. The light was in a fixed position for a reclining patient.

I fumbled with instruments, unseeing.

My morning dragged at a snail's pace; ditto with my afternoon. My eyes drifted to the clock every five minutes—interminable.

Three screaming children arrived after lunch. Their appointments were followed by a woman who spoke only Japanese.

Her daughter remarked, "She's just arrived from Japan. She speaks no English,"

She left the room with no further instructions. She mumbled something about picking up her children and returning later.

I knew no Japanese. I smiled and mimed questions like, "Are you in pain? Teeth? Floss? Gums bleed?"

Finally, an average-looking woman presented as my last patient. She seemed pleasant. Maybe my day would end well.

I draped a lavender napkin around her neck, and asked if she was from this area; indifferent casual conversation—nothing more.

She'd always lived here. She worked from home. She taught her two children from home—a home-body.

I rotated my mirror around her mouth and used my instrument around her incisors, moving toward her molars on the right side. She interrupted me with a juicy sneeze. I retrieved tissue from the counter.

As I stepped toward her, she noticed my name badge, "Ward, Ward, where have I heard that name?" She wiped her dripping nose.

I shrugged and settled into my work again.

Suddenly, she turned in the chair. "Are you from Towson?"

"Yes, I am."

She gasped and pointed her finger, "You're the one who's married to a dentist?"

I stared in amazement.

"Yours is the divorce just everyone's talking about around here—around everywhere, I guess. It's the worst I've ever heard about, except maybe those in movie magazines."

"By the way, you won't believe this," she grinned and lowered her voice as if sharing a juicy piece of gossip," but I actually live right next door to the woman he's been seeing." She giggled and added, "Isn't that a coincidence?"

Then her expression grew serious, like a reporter interviewing a witness on TV news, "Is it true you're shacking up with a younger man?"

I half expected she'd pull out a microphone from her hip pocket for an account from her star witness.

She acted as if this was the most exciting set of circumstances she'd ever stumbled upon. I expected her to begin salivating like a carnivore gazing at its prey, planning its predatory attack.

I stared, unable to close my mouth.

After my initial shock, not really knowing how I could respond (how would Amy Vanderbilt address this in her etiquette book, volume 2, 1990 edition), I signaled for her to sit so I could finish. I moved my instrument through her mouth at record speed. Tears clouded my vision.

I raised the chair, grabbed my belongings and scooted from the room. I heard her call out, "Am I done?"

I raced through the front door. My arm knocked their "we cater to cowards" sign, leaving it swinging wildly—nearly knocking it from its heavy chains.

The utter humiliation of this entire day was incredible. *How could she have been so cruel? But, how could she have known? Did she have any idea how upsetting it would be for me to know scandalous rumors had reached gossip circles an hour and a half away?*

Plus, PLUS, this woman, by her own admission, never left her house. I knew no one here. *Was there no common courtesy, anywhere? Was there nowhere I could go to escape my utter shame?*

How much worse could this get? I imagined I'd end up fighting paparazzi. I could just see my picture emblazoned on the front page of supermarket tabloids, right next to the picture of that three-headed baby.

I laughed through tears. I could almost picture a wild-eyed, wild-haired me on its front page: giant headlines, revealing the shame of the Towson divorcee. They might even claim that the three-headed baby was mine.

I smiled, wiped my tears and began my long trip home.

Home. Baltimore was not my home, nor would it ever be.

"{Lord} Rescue me from the oppression of evil people."
Psalm 119: 134 (Bible)

Sarah

"Hello?"

No answer. I barely heard Ruth's voice from the study.

I'll start breakfast.

Blue flames burst from gas jets. Sizzling butter congealed eggs in the cast-iron pan. I spooned Ruth's homemade strawberry preserves. All ready.

I tip-toed toward the sound of Ruth's voice. Through a cracked door, I see Lucille, Nana and Sam, Jr., sitting mesmerized. Ruth had a regular classroom. She's so animated, I could listen for hours.

I knocked gently. Sam, Jr. jumped up in a flash. He was a growing boy, and always hungry. I remembered my wasting Rebecca, who was never hungry. I sighed, regretfully.

After the other three finished, Ruth and I enjoyed an indulgent second piece toast, loaded with butter and preserves.

"Ruth, I hope you didn't mind my listening earlier. You're a marvelous teacher."

"Oh no," Ruth reddened. "I'd like to be, but I'm really not."

"I wouldn't say it if it wasn't so. You know me better than that." I laughed, looking away, escaping into my own thoughts.

"Sarah, what is it?" Ruth noticed my faraway gaze.

"I still don't know what to do about Rebecca's schooling. She's ahead in her work. That's good news. Considering her health, I don't know what to do when she returns."

Ruth paused, and then answered. "Sarah, I have an idea."

"Any ideas are welcome. Please."

"If you'd trust me, I could help teach Rebecca for the rest of this year. She'd be here and this is a wonderful place. Lucille could teach her things in this kitchen. You'd be here to teach her every morning. She could have her reading assignments while I work with Sam, Jr. Mari has agreed to teach us basic French. Tyler's a math whiz. He could help her with that. She might take an SAT review class or English from the community college. Just ideas, of course; you asked, right?" Ruth shrugged, her face reddened.

How could I have been so lucky? God had brought these wonderful women into my life, handed me a job, helped my sick daughter and now this woman has just volunteered to help with her education? What had happened? I was stunned.

Ruth looked into her cup, uncomfortable with Sarah's long hesitation. Did Sarah think her ideas were unsuitable, and couldn't figure out how to say no, tactfully? After all, she was used to exclusive private-schooling. Her cheeks burned.

Ruth studied Sarah's space-gazing.

She suddenly felt so stupid. Why did she even say what she did? Why did she think she was good enough or smart enough to teach someone else's child—an academically-gifted teenager, no less? This girl was used to all the best when it came to education—teachers and opportunities. Just living with a Harvard graduate-father is far more than she could ever provide; she, a country bumpkin, raised in a corn field with only two years of college as teaching credentials.

Now she was afraid Sarah was struggling to say no tactfully. *Not only were her words cockeyed and ill-timed, but this embarrassment would probably affect their relationship forever. Every time we talk, Sarah will think of her ridiculous suggestion.*

"Have I offended you, Sarah? Don't worry about hurting my feelings, please." Ruth offered, still gazing into her cup, to hide her embarrassment.

Ruth's words righted me to the present. I stared at dear, loving Ruth who looked as if she might burst into tears any minute.

I felt guilt at my rudeness—going off in my own thought-world had always been a bad habit. Teachers and my parents had always criticized me for daydreaming. Until now, I hadn't thought it could hurt someone. I hadn't thought about anything except my own feelings.

I suddenly realized how self-centered I was—had always been. Not only had I acted ungratefully, I had been impolite and uncouth. That stung. My cheeks suddenly flamed.

I reached across the table and squeezed her arm. "Ruth, nothing could be further from the truth. I'm so sorry to have given that impression. I was actually thinking about how God had sent you as an angel to help my little girl. You are part of His miracle for me and Becky."

Ruth felt her whole body relax with relief. She couldn't help but grin.

Sarah considered her part of God's plan. Maybe she could do something for Sarah, Rebecca and for God, too. Maybe God was showing her another path where she could be useful—outside church walls, apart from her husband—by caring for Nana and Lucille, and now helping a friend solve a seemingly impossible problem. Maybe she was able to do something important. Maybe she was part of a much larger plan.

God had not deserted her after all.

"My concern is that I couldn't pay you, Ruth. You need to be compensated. There'd be expenses. All I could do is cook for you—that's all. If you really mean it, I'd be eternally grateful for any help you can give my little girl."

Ruth waved her hand dismissing her concerns.

"Used high school curricula cost next to nothing. Someone might loan us books. Gloria might have testing materials. Libraries have resources. Thrift stores often carry donated texts. No problem.

"Huge networks of home-schooling parents connect in this Baltimore-Washington-Annapolis area. Trust me. These parents are eager to share their successes as well as challenges with newcomers, so beginners won't have to reinvent the wheel. There are even conventions, with seminars and exhibits for text books and anything else a parent might need."

"Huh."

I knew nothing about home-schooling. I'd researched all private schools in this Baltimore/Washington area—both day and boarding. I knew their stats on student-teacher ratios, teacher qualifications and college admittance. It now occurred to me, there was another option for education—a whole realm about which I knew nothing at all; an entire network of mothers and resources I never knew existed.

Mothers, who were helping each other and helping their children, at the same time.

I felt an excitement similar to that when I first traveled to Israel so many years ago. I was eager to be a part of a new country, a new world. I realized I was now in another new world; A sub-culture, composed of caring women who'd found alternative ways for meeting their goals—even in trying circumstances. Excitement made my heart beat faster.

"She could live here. She could heal, gradually, and not be under stress of yet another school." Ruth went on.

"How perfect," I replied.

I wanted to jump and shout. Here was my answer, as plain as day.

"We can work out details later. One thing about home-schooling: you make your own schedule. Find out her graduation requirements. She may even be able to finish early."

I marveled. Things were going to be fine.

"Trust the past to God's mercy, the present to God's love, and the future to God's providence."
St. Augustine

Chapter 28

Spa Day

Glory

I can't wait.
 Jules has given me a 'spa day' birthday gift. I've become dependent on our sharing laughs. Our friendship remains a lighthouse in a sea of darkness, that's for sure.

Chilled, I hurried through its now familiar entrance. Turning from hanging my coat, I stare straight into Sylvia's eyes, appearing in her usual no-nonsense mood.

I grinned and almost giggled. It wouldn't have been nearly as fun if Sylvia were anything other than who she was.

I approached her desk with all the respect as one approaching the bench in a courtroom. Being groomed at this salon was an exceedingly serious matter. I almost curtsied as I stepped a little closer to Sylvia, who glared over her rhinestone-studded half- glasses. I studied her red hair and her scowl. I'm reminded of Alice approaching the queen of hearts in <u>Alice in Wonderland.</u>

"Yes?" she mouthed, her lips closed in a straight line.

How did she do that? I tried to set my own lips in a straight line. Then, embarrassed she might guess I was copying her, I smiled. "I'm here for our spa appointment." I glanced at their clock, happy I'd arrived twelve minutes early.

I'm proud of my punctuality.

She glanced at her book, then at me, with boredom or irritability. I couldn't distinguish which—perhaps both. "Is your friend with you?"

"I expect her any minute" I answer.

I didn't want Jules to get in trouble.

"Take a seat," she muttered and called for Pierre. He was in back with early birds getting perms, I suppose; judging from scattered paper–covered pink and green curlers, and permeating ammonia vapors.

"Yes, ma'am," I quickly turned toward cushy arm chairs in the next room. Ah, new magazine issues. Good. *I was tired of re-reading spring and summer editions.* I snatched October's issue of <u>Baltimore</u> <u>Magazine</u>. Reading material was at a premium. Some women were willing to fight for new issues, I'd heard. I almost expected to hear hisses, like Purrfect protecting a meal—perilous territory, this beauty salon.

I had at least ten minutes to peruse this volume. I paged from its last page to its front cover. That suddenly seemed odd. I'd always read a magazine from back to front, letting pages drop one by one from my left hand. *Why am I suddenly conscious of this?* Maybe other readers read differently. I glanced from right to left. Others seemed to be reading from front to back; maybe today, I'd reverse.

A large jeweler ad displayed diamonds on black velvet on the inside cover. I passed the credits page and ads for Dooney and Burke bags, Elizabeth Arden lipsticks, Macy's and Ralph Lauren designs. Holiday foods spanned its middle.

As I was about to turn page twenty-nine, I noticed a full-page fund-raising ad for a holiday recipe contest, sponsored by <u>Baltimore Magazine</u> and Junior League. $10,000 and an appearance on *Good Morning, Baltimore* television show were the grand prize. Submissions were due by November 15.

Sarah flashed to mind. She was, by far, the best cook I knew. She could win this. I must alert her, as Tuesday was their deadline.

I scurried to the desk. "Sylvia, may I please use your phone? Urgent."

She narrowed her eyes, and scowled, making me wish I hadn't asked. I held firm, and did not cower. Eye-contact was important. Reluctantly, she passed her phone.

Pushing buttons of my long-ago memorized number, I waited for a pick-up.

"Ruth, it's Gloria."

"Hi. What's up?" Ruth sounded distracted.

"Is Sarah still there?"

"She's right here, actually—perfect timing. Hold on."

The handset clattered to the floor. It was a busy time at St. Edmonds. No doubt, Ruth was trying to do something with her right hand and shoulder the receiver in the crook of her neck.

Movement in the background, chairs shuffling, clanging dishes, muffled conversation.

"Hello?"

Sarah also sounded sidetracked.

"Sarah, it's Glory. Get a pen and paper, fast."

———-

I felt increasingly pleased at discovering this contest notice, and catching an excited Sarah. I smiled hugely. Suddenly, I was jolted from my thoughts with the front door blowing open, and a red-faced, wind-blown Jules standing at its entrance.

I addressed Sylvia, "My friend has arrived."

Sylvia rolled her chair backwards, pressed her hands to her knees, and heaved herself to full standing. She proceeded to the back room, calling for Pierre.

She wasn't nearly as tall as I'd imagined, although large in girth. I was surprised. I expected her to be much larger—maybe the size of a Colts linebacker. I glanced at Jules and giggled, feeling like a girl again.

Music sounded with a trumpet fanfare. Pierre appeared from behind the wall, dressed in a tuxedo. He did love drama.

"Ladies, if you'll come with me?" He approached 'the door,' and bowed.

The door. The door had been an enticement from the time I'd first come into this salon. *What would we find back there? Where would it lead?* We looked at each other, images of the unknown dancing around our imaginations. We followed hesitantly, at first, but Pierre signaled to hurry.

"Your spa day is beginning." he encouraged.

The door creaked open, and we entered a dark, narrow hallway. Shadows from scented candles on tall candle-sticks, lining our narrow space, flickered onto walls and ceiling—a little scary. It actually reminded me of an Edgar Allen Poe tale, enacted on a vintage black and white screen, circa 1940.

Jules shoved my shoulder and forced me go first. Her eyes were wide. I smiled. I envisioned Vincent Price or Peter Lorre walking down just such a dark space—a catacombs, of sorts.

The hallway snaked around a few turns and bends. We passed at least ten doorways, and descended a darkened staircase. Pierre, sensing our excitement, turned and whispered, "Your special room awaits."

The stairs ended and we halted, stunned with what was ahead. A glass-enclosed alcove stood before us. Glass doors and walls perspired with moisture from a heated room on the other side. Plants covered its perimeter, which resembled the Aquarium rain forest, downtown. Screeching sounds of parrots and birds were obviously piped over hidden speakers, but were effective, none-the-less, in setting this stage.

He bowed, slightly, opening the door, "Ladies, your room for today."

At 85 degrees, healthy plants hugged walls and windows. Aqua-tiled, heated chaises holding individually rolled towels and robes graced the center of this room. Opposing these chaises was an expansive window wall, showcasing a courtyard garden, where ornamental shrubbery shimmered with clear-colored Christmas tree lights. Breathtaking.

Pierre demonstrated a sound system control; several choices included classical, elevator music, country— he made a face as if this choice was in the worst of tastes— or simply a delicate sound of wind chimes and water flowing—his personal favorite.

We could enjoy herb tea, detoxifying water with cucumber and lemon slices, or cranberry juice. Pineapple and mango slices were in the next room for our enjoyment. Along the back wall were a sauna, a shower resembling a waterfall, and a Jacuzzi, filled with lavender-infused water. He informed us lavender cleansed the mind and spirit.

"Ah-h," we chorused.

Sylvia promised to snap photos, throughout our day, to remind us of our special experience. Our day would end with a shampoo, and style, and a foot and hand massage.

Having ended his orientation, he bowed with a flourish, saying, "Enjoy, ladies." With a twirl, he disappeared through the portico.

We squealed with delight. "Do you believe this?"

Chapter 29

Morning News Edition

Glory

"Umph," we chorused, straining with effort. We wiggled into our swimsuits; more moaning as we tugged. Our spandex one-pieces had obviously shrunk in storage.

A sauna was first, we'd decided. Jules was hoping detox water and hot air might shed pounds she'd added last summer. She was determined to spend the day with just that purpose in mind. She planned to squeeze into something dazzling for the holidays.

"Speaking of holidays, Jules, what are you planning for Thanksgiving?"

"I've been so busy, I've scarcely thought about holidays."

"Well, I have a proposition for you. After all, you owe me one, remember?"

"Uh-oh, I sense it's pay-up time. Of course, you get me in this 5x5 sauna, where I can't easily escape, to bring this up. Nothing like feeling cornered."

"No, it's not bad—just a favor between friends." I laughed.

"Uh-oh. That sounds even more ominous, Glory. Spill it out."

"We've all had a miserable autumn."

No one could disagree with that.

"Amen to that." Jules eagerly agreed.

"I asked the girls to join me on a long weekend in North Carolina. I need a fresh perspective."

"I don't think I can get away, but thanks anyway."

As much as she'd like to get away, she had far too much work to do here.

"No, I wasn't going to invite you. I wanted to use your SUV."

'Thanks a lot. Nothing like using someone," she countered.

"Oh, hush. Your car would be a more spacious ride, that's all. However, I do have something to offer, in exchange."

"Really? What consolation prize?"

She couldn't wait to hear what that might be.

"First of all you get to use my car. I know, that's not what you had in mind." hearing a moan.

What did she expect? Pleeze.

"Ruth wants to have a real Thanksgiving celebration at St. Edmonds. She's planning her school activities around this theme. She insists you come and bring a date."

I'd love to see Jules find someone. She's so beautiful—a gorgeous figure—much more graciously endowed than mine: ravishing eyes, face, long legs, small waist, curves where curves were important; unlike my own which were lost in childbearing. . .(at least I think that was the last time I saw all those things, or cared either, frankly). More importantly, she was so beautiful inside. She'd make a wonderful wife and mother.

There were few choices, though; I knew from my own fifteen years of being single. Slim pickin's' for those of us over thirty-five, as a friend from Alabama used to say.

"A date? Goodness. I'd really have to think about that, but yes, I'd love to come— sounds wonderful." Jules replied.

It'd been years since she'd been out on a real date. When a woman reached a certain age, the available sample reached diminutive proportions. She'd certainly been asked out enough times, only to discover half-way through the evening, that a wife would be keeping his bed warm when he returned home; or, a wife at home, who just didn't understand him the way she did; or, another wife was not really what he had in mind. Then there were the widowed or divorced guys who looked like starved, stray dogs, needy in every respect. No, work had kept her mind off what might have been. Her biological clock was ticking its last tick, and a husband was as illusive as a dream.

"Mari's so disappointed Ruth's not going, she's retrieving stored Christmas decorations, and plans on decorating. She wants it extra special for them all, but especially Ruth and little Sam. Lucille's polishing silver and dusting heirloom china. She and Sarah are planning a traditional—and not too traditional—meal. You know, nothing's traditional about Sarah, who insists on cooking all but yeast rolls, which are, of course, Lucille's specialty; she's freezing the rest.

Tuesday afternoon we'll push off, to beat holiday traffic. It's always horrendous the day before Thanksgiving." I continued.

The last time I'd traveled holiday interstates, I swore I'd never do it again. I was stuck on I495 for hours. I remembered my full bladder. Nope. That bladder had become less reliable in recent years. I can't take that chance.

"You only want me to enjoy an elegant Thanksgiving meal and switch cars with you for the weekend?" Jules reiterated.

She usually spent holidays at home, grabbing a couple of classic movies from the library to pass the hours. Yes. It'd be a treat to celebrate Thanksgiving, for a change.

"That's it—except you need to find a date." I giggled.

"Oh please. That's about the easiest favor you've ever asked, Glory. But, let's leave this sauna. I'm about cooked. I don't know whether it's this heat or a hot flash, but I need air." Julia waved her arms furiously.

We grabbed our towels and headed toward the Jacuzzi. We continued our conversation, lounging in fragrance-infused bubbling water. Jules started,

"Now, I need to hear everything about everything. Out with it all, and don't dare leave anything unmentioned."

As I said before, no one enjoyed hearing a good story more than Jules. I usually disappointed her by making my descriptions far less intriguing than she liked.

"I'll try and do my best to please you, if only for your car." I giggled.

"Maybe I'll withhold my car, depending upon how juicy you make your story. Wait. Let me get comfortable."

She rolled her towel behind her neck and extended her long legs and wiggling toes in the water.

"This water smells heavenly, doesn't it? Glory, did you know Lavender was good for cleansing before Pierre told us?"

"Actually, no, but I do remember Mother Superior collected it and encouraged us to rinse our linens and hair in a lavender rinse. I never asked why. I figured it probably had some religious significance everyone knew but me; something I should've heard in class but was distracted, giggling and passing notes with you, instead.

"Oh, before I forget, can you and Ruth monitor the displaced homemakers class Tuesday night before Thanksgiving?"

"Glory, I don't know if I can do it like you. Leave a list of what to cover. I'll try."

Goodness. What could she do for those women, looking to her for help and consolation? Then again, she'd suffered through widowhood. Pain was pain, after all.

"Ruth will know what to do. Just pray, and it'll come together. Each class sort of evolves, depending on who comes and what needs arise. You can handle it, I'm sure."

"Are there any new situations at our class?" Jules asked more pointedly now, given she'd be leading this group.

If she'd be subbing, she needed a head's up on any situation which might merit attention.

"Not really. The mystery girl's still a puzzle." I added.

"Do you think there's a connection between her and the notes?" Jules asked thoughtfully.

This mystery girl was an enigma. She had to admit to being intrigued with this woman since Glory mentioned her. A real puzzle she could sink her teeth into. She'd get to the bottom of this. This woman would be a mystery no more. She'd find out what's what.

"I never considered that. Now that you mention it, though, it could be. For whatever reason, she doesn't feel comfortable staying more than a minute. That's not as surprising to me as the fact so many do feel comfortable opening up. You know what I mean?" I answered.

"I do. It's hard to bear your soul, particularly when there's shame or embarrassment." Jules responded.

She had things in her own life of which she'd been ashamed, certainly. Things she'd even kept from Glory.

"I think that's a big part of the problem. The women's low self-esteem prevents them from sharing their pain. Most feel like failures, wondering how they've failed so miserably. They're alone and trust no one, but at the same time, they want to trust someone so much." I added.

"And speaking of hurt, how's Mari doing after her attack?" Julia asked, gently.

"Counseling has helped. She's kept so busy, as if nothing's happened; denial, I think. She's dealing with it on a subconscious level, though. Since I've moved back to my room upstairs, and she's down the hall, her crying outbursts in her sleep awaken me. When I've questioned her in the morning, she has no recollection."

Jules added, "Poor girl. Considering her attack and Katie's violent experience, I'd consider nightmares normal for all of you."

"Speaking of bad experiences, I need your help."

I ventured cautiously, not sure I really wanted to share.

Jules sat up and looked straight at me. "Glory, you're not in any trouble, are you?"

"No, of course not, I just didn't tell you about Katie's separation hearing."

"Was it bad?" Jules winced.

"Awful, and it didn't end in Katie's favor." I announced.

"Heartbreaking, huh?" Julia flinched.

"For me, as well as Katie" I added, wondering whether I wanted to say more. Too late now; I'd already said too much.

I paused, as we climbed from the Jacuzzi and headed toward heated chaises.

Julia admonished, "Well, Honey, you've always been empathetic to a fault, you know."

Settling on the warm towel-covered surface, I closed my eyes, steepling my nose and mouth with my fingers.

I really didn't want to relive those gory details. I must share them with Jules, though, to gain objective insight.

She's the only person who'd understand; the only person close enough and yet unbiased enough to lead me toward constructive thinking and a right course of action, if one was required.

Jules had known Charles. She'd been with me through all my past suffering. She'd helped me when my raw emotions prevented rational decision-making. Even as close as we were, baring my soul was still humbling.

I gulped, trying to sort ideas. I took a deep breath, released my fingers and uncovered my mouth, and turned on my chaise in her direction.

"No, Jules, this was different. Charles is Katie's husband's lawyer."

Chapter 30

Yellow Press

Glory

My words spit out as if each one was rancid. Just thinking about Charles made me feel nauseous.

Julia gasped, her eyes grew large and her hands jerked to cover her mouth. "You've got to be kidding."

"I wish I were. Jules, I was completely taken aback. I'd never asked about her husband's lawyer. It never occurred to me. What are the chances it'd be Charles?"

Julia looked incredulous. "Did he see you?"

"Unfortunately, he did." I described the whole scene as I remembered it.

"I can't believe it. He really looked bad?" Jules grimaced.

"His alcoholism is obviously as bad as ever. His face, teeth and general appearance attest to that," I confirmed.

"What did you do?" Jules grasped the edge of her seat.

"What could I do? His legal tactics were as calculated and nasty as ever. Throughout the hour, I remembered my own loathsome hearings. The really troubling thing was the rage arising from some dark place within me. I thought I was rid of that, Jules. Whatever made me think I could help others when I haven't overcome my own issues? I feel awful because I even feel angry at God."

I hung my head with my disclosure.

Julia was quiet for a few moments, "Glory, you've told me you've forgiven Charles."

I nodded. My cheeks burned.

"God has given us ability to remember bad things more than good, much of the time. He heals our hurts if we allow him, but scars remain. Memories can awaken old emotions which He doesn't always lessen right away."

She paused, trying to grapple for purposeful wording.

"Uncomfortable memories bring compassion for comforting others with theirs. It's your past suffering that makes you uniquely qualified for directing displaced homemakers. They sense your past heartache, and know your compassion's real."

"Thank you for that, Jules."

Jules could always bring fresh perspective.

"Frankly, Glory, I think a lot of what you carry, comes from being an adult child of an alcoholic, and the first-born—being driven to do things perfectly in order to be approved. God loves you, Honey, in spite of your imperfections. You know that. The only way He can help us is when we approach Him with our weaknesses—in this case rage—and depend upon His strength to forgive ourselves, others and even Himself."

I remember someone saying God never wants us to waste suffering. Hmmm, that's something to think about, for sure.

"Jules, you've given me an idea. Maybe these women are suffering from faulty thinking from their childhood experiences, too. I may plan some sessions on forgiveness with adult children of alcoholics and survivors of abuse in coming months."

"There you go. Remember, forgiveness must be practiced daily, I've found. If not, it becomes too easy to slip into bitterness. Like in 12-step programs: one day at a time, like conquering alcohol, drug or any other addiction. "

She patted my arm, encouraging.

I'd never really considered unforgiveness an addiction before, but it was, of course. It can become an ugly habit. I wonder if it wasn't un-forgiveness that had driven my mother to alcohol; one addiction in a vain attempt to cover another addiction—an interesting consideration.

"Jules, you know me better than I know myself, most times. What would I do without you?"

"Please, enough. Now, tell me the rest of your news." Jules waved her hands dismissing my comments. She moved to the floor to do crunches.

"Ruth is doing beautifully at St. Edmonds. Mother and Lucille just love her and Sam, Jr. He provides lightness only a little boy can to a house filled with only adults, far too long. She's a Julie Andrews in the <u>Sound of Music</u>. She sings and plays, and their house has been transformed. She's even offered to help Sarah teach Rebecca when she returns. Sarah's thrilled."

"What a perfect solution, Glory." Jules grinned.

She smiled as she pictured Ruth singing and dancing through Swiss Alps in a mountain dress and laced weskit.

"Mari's busy with Real Estate. Tyler joins her when his schedule allows. She feels safer going to houses with someone, and Tyler seems to enjoy it."

Jules returned from the Alps and righted herself back in the spa. "What was Tyler's reaction to the attack?"

"I don't think she ever intends to tell him. It's private for her. She's trying to get over it without undue concern for Tyler." I replied.

"I agree with that decision." Jules nodded to validate. "How about Katie?"

"She received no support; a travesty. Her emergency hearing is Christmas Eve." I added.

"Scheduled Christmas Eve?" Jules stared, mouth gaping, incredulous.

"Can you imagine? No doubt it's Charles's plan to capitalize on her holiday distraction. She's visiting her family for Thanksgiving. Apparently, they know nothing about the pending divorce and certainly nothing about Don's abuse. I wish she had the freedom to stay with them. Her husband would never let her out of his control, though." I continued.

"Control is the key word, of course. When I think of what you went through, Glory, when you were married. You mistook control for love. You weren't aware of a difference. You were so giving and yielding; you didn't know his control was not his kind of love. You were oblivious of the danger with which you lived. I couldn't tell you. No one could. You had to see it for yourself." Jules recollected.

She hated to remember what fear made up every day of Glory's life, then. She couldn't have stood it, that's for sure. Glory has always been so compliant and self-sacrificing, though—aiming to please others, often at her own expense.

I replayed her words, recalling those lost years.

I so wanted to love and be loved by someone. Jules was taking me to the crux of the issue.

It hurt, but I needed truth.

A tear crept to the edge of my lids. Must be the cleansing action of Lavender, Pierre told us about.

"Boy, are you getting into my head, today, Jules." I frowned at her, feeling a little vulnerable.

Julia laughed. "You know I don't mean to upset you, Glory, you know that, don't you?"

She knew her friend so well. In an effort to help, she could be too direct, sometimes. She was always thankful for Glory's honesty with her, but she had to be careful with Glory, whose feelings were so tender, so sensitive. She wanted to encourage, not wound. Truth without kindness could be more hurtful than an insult. She wouldn't hurt Glory for the world.

"Of course, and your comments don't go unnoticed, either. They give insight, whether I want it or not. Thank you very much." I said, grinning.

I laughed, starting to feel my muscles relax.

Jules smiled. "Thank God. There's the glorious giggle from the Glory I know and love."

At that moment, Pierre approached us with his forearm draped in a linen towel. He carried two champagne glasses, and hand-printed, calligraphy menus. We "oo'd" and "ah'd".

"Oh, Pierre, this is wonderful. Thank you," we gushed.

Pierre twirled around. "For your pleasure, ladies, and I shall return."

"Isn't it neat to be treated like this, Jules?" I reclined on my heated chaise which felt like a heating pad. I closed my eyes and imagined I was lying on hot sand at Ocean City or Dewey Beach.

"Hey, Jules, I've got an idea. Pierre could be your date for Thanksgiving dinner. I bet he'd come."

I needed to direct our conversation away from the hard discussion before Pierre's arrival.

Julia sighed. "I'm afraid he'd turn me down. I'm too old. Speaking of which, how's Bill?"

"Oh, Jules, I miss him bunches. I can't wait to spend time with him again. I'm so in love." I sighed, audibly, faking a swoon.

Jules almost spilled her champagne, sitting bolt upright.

"Wait a minute. You didn't tell me you were in love. You've never said anything like that. When did this happen?"

"Absence makes the heart grow fonder, as they say. Since our time at the Cross Roads Inn, I've begun to think of him . . . differently, that's all."

My mind was running wild with thought meanderings about being on a deserted beach —imagining Bill's sharing a blanket with me—only me, seagulls, slapping waves and Bill. Ah.

"Does he know this?"

"I don't know." I answered dreamily.

"You don't know? You haven't told him?" Her voice was rising, trying to figure out her obviously clueless friend.

I'd definitely gotten the rise I wanted. I'd play this for all it was worth.

"Well, not exactly, but I think he knows. I'm pretty sure he does." I answered, flippantly.

"If you haven't told him, how's he supposed to know? Glory, you're hopeless."

Jules announced in her schoolmarm voice and waved her hand at my apparent ineptitude.

Purposely ignoring her display, I strolled to the counter for a mango slice. "Want some, Jules?"

"Glory, you haven't answered my questions. Get back here, and yes, bring me two slices on your way."

"Earl Grey?"

"What do you think—of course, Earl Grey."

"God does not comfort us to make us comfortable, but to make us comforters."

Dr. Jowett (as quoted from Mrs. Charles Cowen, 1925).

Chapter 31

We've Got A Ticket To Ride

Saturday Night

Glory

I crawled between flannel sheets and plumped my pillows. As soon as I'm warm and comfy, I'll call Bill. I'd looked forward to this particular call for days. I reached for my phone and dialed.

After three rings, he answered, "Bill here."

"Hi, Honey. Did I call at a bad time?"

"You know there's never a bad time for you to call. Everything all right?"

"No, because you're not here with me."

"And, where are you, exactly?"

"Well, I've been at the spa all day, and now I'm curled up under the covers and have no one to show off to."

I decided to tease him, just a little.

"Hold onto that thought. I'll be there in . . . how long would it take me?"

We laugh.

"I miss you lots." I purred.

Realizing I'd be seeing him in a matter of days, I gave myself permission to enjoy romantic imaginings.

"Oh Glory, you don't know how I love hearing those words."

"Well, would you like to hear me say them in person?"

Now, for my surprise.

"How do you figure?"

"Want to pick me up at the Carolina Inn, Tuesday before Thanksgiving?"

"You kidding me?"

"No. I'm coming home for Thanksgiving." I squealed.

"You're not joshing, are you?"

"It's for real. I can't wait. Can you spare a seat at your Thanksgiving table?"

"Oh, Glory. You know I don't go anywhere for holidays. With Catherine in Oregon, you're the closest thing to family for me—and the most loveable. How long can you stay?"

"I'll be traveling with the girls, but once in Chapel Hill, they'll be going their own ways. Tad hinted at spending his vacation with his girlfriend at Appalachian State. So, I'm yours for the long weekend."

I wanted my words to dangle a carrot in his imagination. I was feeling playful, and wanted to hint about romantic opportunities. I wrapped myself tighter in my comforter, imagining his embrace.

"You mean for four days, I'll have you all to myself?"

His grin expanded from ear to ear. Her feelings had not changed over past weeks since his visit, as he'd feared, since she was back amidst all her stress.

His memories eased back to the softness of her curves when he held her—leg cast and all—in his arms. He felt youthful expectancy as he thought of next week.

"You got it. Try to plan a nice welcome for me, OK?"

I giggled, a little seductively. *Who says 40-somethings can't feel amorous?*

"What did you have in mind, Dear?"

He loved it when she teased. He was savoring her every word.

"I'll just leave that to you." I added with an alluring lilt to my words, before saying goodbye.

Tuesday

Our trip day! I whooped. I must call Jules before 7:30, for our car switch. We'd pack and then get out of here.

I stumbled to my kitchen, as quickly as I could manipulate my gimp leg. Earl Grey was needed, definitely. I heard Mari shuffling about. No doubt, she'd want tea, too.

As I opened the refrigerator door for milk for my cup and Purrfect's bowl, I heard footsteps coming from our basement.

"Tyler? Is that you? Up already?"

"Yes, Ma'am."

As I could see, his lacrosse equipment coupled his luggage.

I glanced at his pile. "That's funny. I don't see any school books. Did you forget?"

We both laughed.

"No, Ma'am. Not on my vacation."

He seemed excited about this trip. What Tyler had fussed over, was obviously now giving him excitement.

"Sarah's packing snacks and sandwiches, and there's room for a cooler if you want sodas. Eight hours driving, at least. Do you have a book?"

"I do. I've also got my game boy, a tape player, tapes, and my earphones. I'll try not to disturb anyone—promise."

"Oh, we won't be bothered. Tad's got me enjoying Dave Matthews and Tim Reynolds."

"Cool." Tyler grinned.

"Tad's looking forward to showing you around. His coach is on campus until Wednesday night, and some of his fraternity brothers will be staying around during the entire break. He plans to introduce you."

Tyler's expression set.

I hesitated when I noticed

"Honey, it's all right. Tad isn't pressuring you. He just wants you to feel welcome. I know college is not the best topic for you right now, but it might be nice to visit some, and get a feel for what's beyond high school. It's exciting."

"Yes Ma'am." Tyler exited, thundering down basement steps to his 'male room'.

Mari descended the stairs "I just caught the end of that conversation. What did he say?"

"Not much. He's all packed" I pointed to the pile. "When I told him about Tad's plans, he clammed up."

Mari nodded, "He still dreams of Princeton, even though it's impossible."

"It's hard to change directions of dreams." I replied.

It seemed changing dreams was what life's been about lately, for everyone.

Grabbing my tea, I headed for the first floor phone.

"I'm calling Jules about her car."

Dial tone, button tones, finally, pick up.

"Morning, Ready for our car exchange?"

"The question is, are you ready to learn to drive an SUV? It's a lot bigger than your little thing."

"I guess I have to, right? It's too late to turn back now. "

I sang words from that old song. ". . .it's too late to turn back now. . . I believe, I believe, I believe I'm falling in love. . . ." I hummed the rest and twirled around—picturing myself, back sometime in the '60's.

"Meet you at the parking lot at 7:55?" Julia laughed. "You're crazy, you know?"

I glanced at my clock. "It'll be a rush, but yes. Ready for class tonight?"

"All set. We're aiming to arrive early to set up. It's a go, and, Glory?"

"Yes?"

"I've decided to take guests for Thanksgiving dinner."

"Tell me what handsome date you've found in Bal'mer," I teased.

"Pierre and Sylvia."

"You're kidding."

I was thankful to be close to a solid chair.

"Well, they're such lonely people. Ruth said 'The more the merrier.' I think it'll be a blast."

"Jules, you're something else. I can't wait to hear how it goes."

"I'm off. See you in a few."

Jules was waving her arms, signaling her personal parking place. It bore a new sign, printed with her name.

"You never told me you had your own space, with your own signature sign. When did that happen?"

"Just one of the perks that come with the job," she said and laughed.

"Glory, you need to know how to drive this thing, so let's put a move on. I have a meeting in ten minutes."

"Yes reserved-parking-space-sign-owner, Ma'am." I saluted.

Jules giggled, "You're such a nut. There's no trick to any of this. This lever is for cruise control—an absolute necessity. It'll save you big bucks when you pass through speed traps. Trust me."

"Jules, you know I do not speed."

"Well, I remember several times and you remember, too, Glory, we both saw blue lights. I'm not talking about K-mart blue light specials."

We laughed.

"All right, cruise control."

"Now here's the control for the radio-tape player. If Tyler brings his tapes, you can play them on this . . . if you dare."

"A make-up mirror sits on the reverse side of the visors—important for the girls. Here are controls for heat, air conditioning, and rear-window defrost—for icy mornings. Registration, road service card and insurance cards are in the glove compartment. Under the back carpet is a panel opening for tire stuff."

She pointed to a second key.

"This key unlocks tire lugs, or whatever they're called. I've never used it, so your guess is as good as mine as to how it works. Prayer is your best course of action if you get a flat. Road service is good, but help can take forever. Any questions?"

"Windshield wipers?"

Jules looked at me as if I didn't have any sense. "Glory, they're right here on the steering column. Should I be allowing you to drive my car?"

We laughed.

I adjusted the mirror, belted the seat belt, and put the gear shift in reverse, and waved.

Chapter 32

Destination: Past, Present And Future

Tuesday afternoon – late

Mari

"Mom, do we have to do this?"
Tyler was hesitant about meeting Tad. I don't know why, exactly, but I didn't pursue. Maybe it was because he didn't know Tad. Maybe connecting with someone who was a part of this school, made him feel obligated, somehow. Maybe he was afraid he might enjoy it and think twice about Princeton. Any or all of these could add confusion to his already overwhelmed perspective.

I considered how I would've handled this situation at seventeen. Maybe he wanted to make his final choice independently, and he wasn't sure he wanted it to be his mother's and father's school. This was tough—socially and emotionally. I would've felt anxious, too, having thought about it. Hadn't I married because I wanted to make my own decision about my life? He needed space.

Tyler was alert to details as we strolled from Franklin Street through the quad, passing classrooms and dorms, toward sports fields. "It's huge," he gulped.

Compared to his small school, it was, undoubtedly. Despite being Thanksgiving break, a sizeable number of students remained on campus. Tyler eyed each one.

Although I tried to direct his attention to architectural features of campus buildings, he was focused on people-watching, or, more specifically, girl-watching. Several turned his head. I smiled. A real change from his all-male prep school in Baltimore, that's for sure.

Tad jogged to welcome us as we approached the field. Balancing his stick and helmet in his hand, he introduced himself, and clapped his hand onto Tyler's upper arm.

"Hey, McGuire, I hear you're quite a lax player." he grinned.

He turned toward three others who were practicing their stick skills. "Yo, guys. Up here."

Addressing Tyler again, "Coach told us about your record—Very cool."

Tad introduced the others. "Bring your stick. There's an extra helmet. Let's throw some balls."

Tyler jogged onto the field, not looking back. Twenty minutes later, he eagerly joined them at their fraternity house. He looked . . . almost happy.

Alone in my hotel room, I called for an early wake-up call, to allow time for our 11:00 flight to Memphis. Tomorrow would mark Tyler's first visit to Mississippi, and his first time meeting his grandmother. I felt both excitement and shame.

My face burned. How could I have waited all these years to share my son with his grandmother? "*God, forgive me,*" I whispered.

Tyler conversed eagerly on the plane trip—unusual, for him. He spoke of team members he'd met, and dinner at the 'Rat' (Rathskeller) restaurant, with pitchers of sweet tea (the mainstay of the South), and greasy garlic bread, like nothing he'd ever eaten.

I remembered eating in that same place with Pete, so long ago—same bread, same tea, same grease.

I smiled, but did not reply—no pressure, advertently or inadvertently. This was his experience, not mine. I purposed to surrender any desire to control— my life, his, or anyone's.

As he gazed out the window, he commented on the mountains as we crossed into Tennessee, and then the flat land as we descended near Memphis. I informed him this was the birth place of Elvis Presley.

Tyler looked at me quizzically, "Who?"

"Sorry, wrong time," I laughed.

"How much longer?" Tyler asked.

"We've got almost two hours of driving, south of Memphis. You excited?"

"Yeah, I think I am. I didn't think I had any grandparents. Tell me why you never told me before?"

"Well. . ." I swallowed and reconstructed the past from my recollections.

Glory

Katie and Sarah, eager to get to their destinations, dropped me and my bags at the Inn parking lot.

I called, "Meet back here 9:00 Sunday. Have a super holiday."

I watched them speed away, neither looking back.

Bill wasn't due to arrive for another thirty minutes or so, which gave me a few minutes to freshen-up. I took a minute to take in the surroundings.

The uplifting colors of yellow, rose and green on printed chintz and silk in this lobby made me imagine walking into a spring garden. Warm sunshine filtered through large windows, and made it seem like summer. Although November by the calendar, the piedmont often had Indian summer days. Temperatures were mild, and this sunshine warming my arms and face felt heavenly.

Exiting the ladies room, I decided to explore. I studied vintage pictures mounted throughout the hallway, dating back to the 50's and 60's—a different time and place.

I was jolted by a touch at my elbow.

"Madam, may I take your bag?"

"Bill!" Tears suddenly puddled my lids.

With an arm around me and a soft kiss on my cheek, he said, "Let's go home."

Tuesday night

"Honey, you want to wake up?"

I'd dozed most of the four-hour trip, and now felt gravel crunch beneath his wheels.

"My house," I cried.

Candles lit my windows. The brightness of the interior lights and a Thanksgiving arrangement of gourds on the door stoop welcomed us.

After disengaging the ignition, Bill pulled me close and whispered, "Welcome home. It's been a long time."

Snuggling with him, back home, was what I'd dreamed about, for so many months.

Ruth

"I miss Sarah today," I mused.

Lucille made rolls early this morning, and prepared breakfast since Sarah was away. Sarah promised all meals were labeled and in the freezer—enough for the week, including our Thanksgiving feast. No one had to cook anything. Just heat and serve, or defrost, heat and serve, as was the case now.

Lucille leaned over, taking warm biscuits from the oven. Bacon and eggs sizzled in the seasoned cast-iron skillet.

"Come on in, Honey. Breakfast nearly ready" smiled Lucille.

"Lucille, you weren't supposed to be working while Sarah's gone. You promised." I protested.

"Honey, what Miz Sarah don' know, won't hurt none. I jes itchin' t' make some breakfast agin! Where's our darlin' boy?"

"Oh, he'll be down in a minute, I'm sure, when he smells bacon cooking. He's never eaten as much as he has since we've been here."

"Honey, he be growin'. He need some meat on 'em bones. Make me happy wen a boy like t' eat."

Pulling up a chair, Ruth recalled, "Wasn't it fun yesterday? I don't know when I've had such fun decorating for Christmas. Mari's decorations have transformed this house. Sam, Jr. loved helping, especially since he could join Tyler and Mr. Wilson."

"It be good for 'em. He be thinkin' about bein' a big man. That's good for a boy, Honey."

"Yes, it really is. Since Sam doesn't have a brother, and at the present time, doesn't have an attentive father, these relationships have been wonderful for him."

Lucille had seen last week's paper, but didn't let on she knew about Ruth's husband. She merely forked eggs and muttered, "Yes 'm."

"It was like a Christmas party yesterday, Lucille: all of us running around making everything bright and Christmas-y. Nana loved it, too. She thought we were having a party, especially when Sarah served hot cider with cinnamon sticks and your home-made gingerbread. Shrubbery lights have made it so dreamlike—almost like a movie set. I'll switch them on this morning to keep the spirit."

"I'm going to miss the girls, Lucille, but I'm looking forward to a wonderful Thanksgiving. Sam, Junior's so excited. We'll all polish silver serving-pieces today. That will be our school activity. We'll play Christmas carols as we work. I'll leave it to you to remove food from the freezer and prepare our turkey."

"How many there gonna be here, anyway?"

Lucille allowed herself to be excited. She hadn't been to a party since her fam'ly reunion fifteen years ago, and never in this house. She helped Miz Holland plan parties lots 'a times in years gone by. She'd never been a part of 'em. It be her job, and she be thankful for it.

But now, she'd be part a' th' celebration. She'd gotten a new dress and would have her hair dun. She be fam'ly now. She'd always felt like fam'ly, course, raisin' all the youngins'. She luv 'em all.

'Til now, it be my work. Now I be part 'o th' family. She repeated that again to herself, and couldn't help let her grin spread 'cross her whole face.

"Well, only you, Nana, Sam and me, plus Julia and her two guests."

"Who're her guests?"

I laughed a little trying to imagine who Jules would bring. She was such fun. I loved being in her company. No one could make all of us laugh like a visit from Jules.

"I don't know. She said they're people from the beauty salon, who don't have anywhere to celebrate Thanksgiving."

Lucille laughed her warm laugh.

"That be jes like 'er. Ev'n when she was a young'n, she take care o' folks. She always take care o' folks."

After breakfast, Lucille and Nana took their coffee to the sunroom as had become their custom, while Sam and Ruth started their studies. Not without lighting inside and outside lights first, though. A glistening air of excitement prevailed.

At 10:00, Ruth answered their phone.

"Yes, this is the Holland residence. May I help you? Oh, I'm sorry. Sarah is out of town for the holiday. I can take a message for her. I expect her to call this evening and retrieve her messages. Yes, of course. Let me get a pencil."

"All right, now whom shall I say is calling? <u>Baltimore Magazine</u>. Yes, she did enter the cooking contest. Oh, yes, I know she'll be excited about this news. Can I take a name and a number so she can return your call at her earliest convenience? You can give her details. Good bye and thank you for calling."

I squealed, placing the receiver on its carriage. Running to the sunroom, I shouted, "You're not going to believe this. That was <u>Baltimore Magazine</u>. Sarah's a finalist in the cooking contest."

Saturday Night

Glory

"Oh, Bill. I don't want to go back to Baltimore—away from you and home."

"I'm glad you put me first on that list."

He held me in his arms. "Come on. We can finish packing in the morning. I just want to hold you and never let you go."

I allowed him to carry me to the sofa, and we lost ourselves in the crackling backdrop of the fire.

By 9:30, he excused himself, saying he needed to get something. He hobbled toward the kitchen, and I teased about his foot being asleep.

Moving into the warm spot on the sofa he'd vacated, I teased "You've been gone too long. Your spot has been forfeited."

At this, he dropped to one knee, "Well, I guess I'll just have to stay here, at least for now."

I giggled and pulled his arm to join me. Raising his hand, still on one knee, he placed a black velvet box on my palm.

"Glory, I love you more than words can say. Marry me, please."

His seriousness startled me.

Oh my gosh. I felt myself stiffen. My mind jumped from playful desire to dreaded responsibility and fear.

He pulled me into his arms. "How about it?"

"Bill, you know I love you. There's no better person for me in the whole world. You also know I'm afraid."

"I know you've been afraid in the past. From what you've told me, you've had every reason to be. Glory, I'm not your ex-husband. I'd never think of betraying you. Please take this ring. I want you for my wife."

I opened the small box. Within it sparkled a solitaire-cut diamond. It was exactly what I'd always wanted. One we'd seen strolling by that jeweler's so many times.

I gasped, "Bill, this is so gorgeous. It's the one I've always admired." I circled my arms about his neck.

This was the moment I'd secretly dreamed about, but dreaded at the same time. I couldn't skirt the issue anymore; I must decide one way or another.

"When can we get married? Just name the date." He whispered as he nuzzled my neck.

My memories sequenced back to when Charles proposed to me. It was an odd evening. We'd been out for hamburgers at a local dive. I don't even know why I decided to go out with him.

I'd stopped dating him a month or so before because our relationship, if that's what you could call it, was just not going anywhere. The eagerness seemed all mine. His cold, self-centeredness had not warmed over time. Of course, I hadn't recognized it as such. I interpreted it as quiet self-confidence.

When he'd heard one of his classmates had taken me out and was quite interested, his curiosity perked. I became more of a challenge, I suppose. Unlike now, with no tender offerings, not even holding my hand, he announced, "I think it's time we get married. It'd be important for my law career to have a wife, and sons. I must consider that. What do you think?"

When I recall it, he said nothing about loving me, or wanting me to share his life. In fact, there was nothing about me. It was all about his career and his image. I'd refused that night.

He arrived on my porch the next day, demanding I rethink. He was amazed I'd refused him. He must marry me.

I don't really know why I reconsidered, but in a weak moment I'd done just that. How could I have not seen his selfishness then? I was flattered, I guess, since the word was out, no woman ever refused him anything.

I felt a coldness run through me with that memory. I felt myself stiffen. What if there's something I was overlooking now? I certainly did not want to make another mistake like that.

"Bill, I've still got Mother to care for. It's not fair to you."

I used this time-honored excuse neither he nor I could argue over, to buy time. This was too crucial a decision to make without time, right?

"Glory, I've waited this long. Please don't use an excuse. I'll give you all the time you need. Just wear this ring and remember how much I love you. Then come back to me, promise?"

"Even if it takes months?" I mouthed weakly.

I looked into his kind and loving eyes. I felt his arms close in around me, causing my muscles to melt, in response.

What was I thinking? When I'd looked into Charles's face last week, I saw nothing but self-centered, self-destructive animosity for everyone—perhaps even for his own life, also; an empty shell of a man, consumed by his addiction and perhaps his vain attempt to run from whatever demons had been chasing him all these years.

I compare that image with the loving kindness of this dear man who now embraced me; the one who'd been by my side all these years, to help me and support me when there was no one else.

This was not a tough question on a test. This was someone who loved me, would protect me and who wanted to be with me for the rest of his life. Yes, someone I'd come to trust, and could trust. Someone to receive the love I was so reluctant to show, but desired so desperately to give. I had to admit that truth.

"Just remember this night, O.K.?" His lips touched mine, and his arms eased me down into the cushions. Yes, I knew I'd marry him.

The fire crackled and a log fell, breaking the silence.

Chapter 33

A 'Weak' Of Sundays

Sunday night

Katie

Well, I'm back in Baltimore. It seems like mere minutes since I was with family, enjoying a break. I felt suddenly thrust back to reality, like that transporter used on Star Trek Enterprise. Here one minute, some other realm, the next, unaware of dangers yet to be encountered. *Maybe I'd just dreamed going away, and I'd never actually left. How depressing.*

I shuddered at the renewed realization of dangers that lay ahead. Our Christmas Eve separation hearing loomed like a black cloud ready to burst. I dreaded it.

This next one had to go better than the last one, just with the law of averages.

I was now driving to Don's office to retrieve Timmy. I couldn't wait to see my boy. I smiled thinking about his angelic face with his thumb stuck in his mouth.

I chose to go there or to a public place when retrieving him from a visit with his father. I didn't want Don knowing where I lived. Unfortunately, because of public records, he probably already knew. He probably knew whatever I did, for that matter. I'd heard similar reports from women in the shelter.

I called Don from a pay phone–untraceable with caller ID. He sounded rattled and irritated. The old tension, once a chronic tightness in my stomach in response to his moods, instantly re-emerged, having been dormant for a week. Fear, again.

I'd meet him next to his office building. I would not go in. He'd bring Timmy out. I suddenly wished I'd brought one of the girls along.

I whispered a quick prayer, *"God please protect me. You're all I've got. I was stupid to come alone, but since I'm here, please send an angel."*

As my tires eased onto the corner street beside his office, I saw Don exit his door, dragging wailing Timmy by the arm. Bags of clothes, toys and Timmy's other belongings were piled, curbside. My heart sank.

"Timmy, Honey, Mommy's here," I called in a happy tone.

Don growled, "You didn't tell me you'd be so late. Don't you know I have things to do? I've already taken care of him for four days, what do you expect of me? It's just like you—never thinking of anybody's time but your own. You're so irresponsible."

Shaking, I jumped from my car and scooped Timmy in my arms. I held tight, trying to draw renewed strength from his touch.

"Timmy, let's get in the car. Don, do you have his car seat?"

He cursed, marched to his car, unhooked the seat and threw it in my direction. It bounced onto the sidewalk. Without looking, I heard the slam of his car door and the peeling of rubber as he left.

"OK. Let's get buckled in and go home for a cookie and bedtime story." My voice quavered.

After loading the stuff, I tried to calm myself, repeating, "It's over". It was over. He was gone.

What was wrong with him tonight? Then, I remembered: it was Sunday. I closed my eyes, imagining what could have happened.

Silently I prayed, "*Thank you, God, for protecting us.*"

I gripped my steering wheel tightly to stop my trembling hands. Maybe I should never have left Timmy and gone to North Carolina at all…but wait. . . .

I smiled. The fact that Don had such a tough time taking care of Timmy, might work in my favor. It's hard to manage a toddler, a rebellious teenager, a girlfriend, a business, and an addiction. Don would probably not want to watch him for more than a few hours again. He certainly would not want full custody.

Yes, this could be what I needed to raise my child.

Sarah

"Night, everybody, see you tomorrow morning"

After unloading and re-loading stuff at Gloria's house, I began my trek across Northern Parkway. It seemed longer tonight than usual. The stretch across the bridge into Mt. Washington seemed dark. Wind whistled through branches. Street lights flickered. Thanksgiving seemed years ago.

North Carolina had been sunny, and maybe not warm, but seemed brighter, somehow, than Baltimore did now. Maybe it was because I'd seen Rebecca.

Bittersweet.

I liked the residential program from the start. The campus offered so many things for young women to enjoy—games, sports, exercise facilities and a beauty salon; no mirrors, only windows—interesting. Part of their rehabilitation, I guess.

Visitation was limited to thirty minutes each day. Not much, but it was something. Rebecca was getting stronger, I could tell. The bad news was she must stay at least into December. They didn't want her to risk losing what progress she'd gained by leaving too soon.

Rebecca looked so much better: more good news. Although not completely back to normal, she looked a whole lot better than she had a month and a half ago. She was eating. That was good.

She wasn't able to eat normally, though. Her diet was hardly more than baby food. Her body had been starving, and nourishment had to be taken in small amounts, frequently, throughout the day and evening.

Girls were rewarded for eating anything, their doctor said.

Although she looked better, (the good news), her hormone levels were not where her doctors wanted to see them (the bad news). She still had a fine hair covering on her cheeks, and sparse hair on her head still looked both lifeless and brittle.

She participated in a mild exercise program, designed to aid in relieving anger, depression and anxiety, and increasing desire for food. The young women were encouraged to express their emotions through music and journaling. Rebecca was enjoying her violin, which she hadn't played for years. A natural way of treating an unnatural disorder, I concluded.

It seemed like a happy place. Rebecca seemed content. Good news. I'd have to postpone her return until Christmas; bad news.

I'd made it this far, though. I could make it to the end. God would help me. He had so far.

I entered my dark house and proceeded to light rooms. Before I left, I remembered I'd turned our thermostat to 55 degrees to conserve fuel. *Goodness, it was cold.* I shivered.

Forget that. I jacked the metal regulator to 75. I needed some warmth, and I rationalized Katie and Timmy'd want it cozy tonight, too. I couldn't let little Timmy be cold.

I'd make a quick batch of cookies, for him to enjoy with milk before bed. I hope there's milk left — sadly, only powdered occupied an almost empty space on a pantry shelf. Not as good, but I could blend it with frozen fruit and honey, and he could enjoy a snack before bed.

I was thankful Katie and Timmy were staying here; someone to love on, when I missed my little girl so much.

Chapter 34

Monday, Monday

Monday morning

Glory

"Hey, Jules, we're back safe and sound." I waved out the window.

She bounced up and down as I parked. "Oh, my baby, my baby." she shrieked.

"Are you crazy? Since when have you called me your baby?"

"For heaven's sake, I was addressing my car." She smoothed nearly every reachable inch, checking for dings and scratches.

"This is a great car, by the way. Thanks so much for switching."

As I lifted my hand to wipe an errant hair from my eye, astonishment crossed her face.

"Glory!"

"What?"

"Your hand? What is it?" She grabbed my left hand.

I had longed, yes dreamed, of this particular moment: to see Julia's full-blown reaction to this surprise. I want to record this whole thing—every detail—in my memory to tease her in coming years.

I must act nonchalant and ho-hum, I coached myself. It was so hard to do that with this huge grin inside just dying to escape.

"Oh, it's just this thing at the end of my wrist with extensions called fingers; a recent acquisition," I answered flippantly.

"Oh, hush. Is that what I think it is?" Jules was breathless.

"It is," I grinned. I bounced up and down like an excited little girl.

She hugged my neck. "I'm thrilled, Glory. I've got to run, though, but if you don't call tonight with details, I'll die, just die."

"How was your weekend?" I was eager to get a preview of events before she bounded off.

"Super, but obviously not as good as yours" she sniffed and scooted up the hill, waving, "Saturday for Earl Grey?"

"Earl Grey." I called back gleefully.

Monday night

Jules

"Glory, why won't you call?"

She knows I need details. My life's force demanded them. How could she keep me waiting like this? I glanced at my watch. If that phone doesn't ring in five minutes, I'll call.

Engaged? I just can't believe it.

Glory's not as open as I am, which is why waiting is so frustrating. If it were me, she'd be alerted every step of the way. . . at least about good stuff.

I had my own secrets, of course, suddenly stung with memories—things I'd told no one. I couldn't dwell on those. I'd learned the hard way: that was a downward spiral leading to a pit of depressive darkness.

Painful recollections motivated me to action—to help others. Wasn't that life's goal anyway? Well, maybe not for everyone. Trying to use my suffering positively was how I chose to process life. Of course, some days were easier than others. Sometimes it was a daily uphill battle.

I was thrilled she'd even considered remarriage. Perceived failures had left huge scars. Self-protection comes with betrayal—licking one's wounds, so to speak. Glory had handled this well, choosing forgiveness and God's protection. Would her past allow her to be completely open to a husband?

I didn't know.

I'd always hoped to remarry—planned to. God has not sent anyone, yet. I've held onto the passage in

Isaiah 54 –'He'd be my husband.' I haven't been lonely, although alone, but I often wonder if I'll share the rest of my life with someone.

Enough. I'd call this minute. I'd hide my curiosity behind discussing last week's displaced homemakers meeting. I just hoped raw emotions of tomorrow's meeting won't give her cold feet about her own future.

Yes. It'd been a full five minutes.

Gloria answered the first ring.

"That was fast. I know. You've been waiting for my call with baited breath." I laughed.

"Actually, no, I've just crawled between the sheets. My phone's beside me." She didn't hide her yawn.

"Don't fall asleep yet. We have important business to discuss: not only Bill, but last week's displaced homemaker meeting."

"Oh, yeah, I almost forgot about tomorrow night."

She hadn't even thought about tomorrow night's session. She needed to get up early tomorrow and start working on that. She'd set her alarm.

"Come out of the clouds, girl. That rock on your hand blinding you?"

Glory laughed, "All right. I know you, Jules. You're just dying for details"

"Spill it all. If you leave out anything, you know I'll worm it out somehow." I teased.

"Same for me, Jules; I want to hear about Pierre, Sylvia and Thanksgiving. Whatever possessed you to take my comment seriously about asking Pierre?"

"Your words stuck in my brain. So I asked. Sylvia mumbled about no family. She'd never been invited anywhere for Thanksgiving. Pierre looked eager, but sad. His family was gone. He had no plans, either."

I recalled their reactions, and smiled. It's such fun to give a surprise.

"You always amaze me. So how'd it go?"

"We had a ball. Pierre, with his dramatic flair, took full advantage of the audience and insisted on acting as head waiter. He wore a tux with tails, and brought spectacular hors d'oeuvres. Your mother didn't know who they were, or me either, for that matter, but she's always enjoyed a party. Lucille, who never gets out, didn't want our evening to end."

"And, what about Sylvia?" Glory giggled, eagerly awaiting more details.

No one could tell a story like Jules.

"Sylvia wore an emerald velvet gown— stunning with her green eyes and red hair. She brought delectable imported chocolates. I saw another side of her, that night. She really has a great sense of humor. It'd been years since I've had such fun."

"How wonderful—I think we should invite them for Christmas, too."

"They'd be disappointed not to be invited. They're family now. Who else is coming to Christmas dinner?"

"As you might expect, my brothers and sisters have other plans. So far, the list includes, Mari, Tyler and her mother, Ruth and little Sam, Katie and Timmy, Sarah and Rebecca, Tad and his girlfriend, Bill, and perhaps his daughter. "

"Now the good stuff. What about your new sparkler? Now Glory, don't just give me headlines, OK?"

Glory related as many of the details of her trip as she could remember and ended with his proposal.

"I'm amazed you even accepted that ring. I thought you'd never consider remarriage."

"I promised I'd think about it. With Mother, Lucille, the houses and all, it's a lot to contemplate. He said he'd wait."

"Glory, you're a mess. Don't you know there will always be responsibilities and difficulties? Could they be convenient excuses to avoid hurt?"

She thought for a minute. "Do you think so?"

"Glory, we're back to the crux of the issue. If you trust God to lead you in the right path, you've prayed about it, and if you know He only wants the best for you, what do you have to fear? Pain's inevitable. I was reading something the other day: Did you know if you remove a butterfly from its cocoon too soon, it won't be able to fly? The struggle to free itself gives strength to fly."

"I've struggled so much all of my life, Jules, I just want rest from it."

She again pondered the decision she was contemplating—more issues to struggle with on top of what she already had.

"You've had fifteen years. It's time to step out. We both know marriage is not easy, but neither is living alone, frankly. I'm excited for you. Moving on, though, I need to tell you about last week's class."

"I almost forgot. Did it go smoothly? No problems, I hope."

"We did fine. I don't know whether it went as you would've wanted, but we made it. Mystery girl joined us."

"Really?" Glory's breath stopped with this news.

"Yes. She stayed when she saw it was only Ruth and Me."

"You mean, I caused her to leave?"

Goodness, she hoped she hadn't done anything to offend her. But how could she? All the woman did was take one look at her and run.

Still, she felt badly. What could she have done to persuade her to stay? She recalled the last time she'd witnessed her entrance and exit. It occurred to her then, something was distinctly familiar about that girl—her stance, her persona, something. Some memory was trying to emerge, but she couldn't grab it.

"No. Apparently, your paths have crossed. She knows you, or has known you, or knows of you or something. She needs help, but she's embarrassed to face you. She shared nothing else. I'm agreeing to meet her privately and find out how we can help. I guess this one's for me."

"Huh." Gloria muttered softly.

She was still thinking about how she could've caused those evenings to have been more welcoming for this person, who apparently she'd known—although how and from where, she still could not guess.

"Anyway, it requires no action—or guilt, I might add—on your part, Glory. Promise me you won't feel guilty about what could have been, like you always do. I'll keep you posted, within constraints of her privacy, of course. I just thought you'd want to know. I think she authored those notes, too."

"The plot thickens." Glory answered, still amazed at how Julia has always been able to read her mind—a conundrum, for sure.

Later That Night

Gloria

Who's calling "Gloria" and "Help"? A faint cry was obviously coming from some distant location.

I had to investigate.

Finding my flashlight buried under dishtowels, I checked its batteries. When had I last used it? Who knows?

Belting my coat, I cautiously ventured into murky darkness.

From my porch stoop, I contemplated my next move. Was it coming from my garage? Not likely—who'd even want to venture into that place? I'll start there, anyway.

I dreaded entering that old building alone in this dark. Who knew what might scamper across my feet, or worse, land on my head. Now, within inches of its door, I realized this voice was coming from the direction of that alley. Following it wasn't any more appealing than entering my garage.

Crunching gravel with my scuffs (why hadn't I grabbed shoes, for goodness sake), I waved my light, right to left. I shuddered, considering animals lurking or some social deviant out at this hour, planning some hideously grisly action. I stopped and listened (remembering a long ago warning given by some unrecalled person: stop, look and listen).

I alerted to that wooded area at the end of this block. Odd, that I could hear someone all the way over here—getting louder and more distinct by the moment. I quickened my pace, erratically waving my light.

Someone was struggling in what resembled mud or quick-sand. (Was there actually quicksand here? I recalled movie scenes from jungle swamps in that old movie African Queen.) I focused my beam.

Could it be? Yes—mystery woman, complete with sunglasses, hat and scarf. What in the world?

I extended a large branch for her to grasp onto. In her panic, she yanked forcefully. Unprepared for her strength, I tumbled in.

We struggled. She tugged, while I tried to repel her.

I screamed, "Stop! I can't help you if you keep pulling me down."

My screams awakened me.

2:22 a.m.

I was bathed in sweat.

I grabbed my covers, chilled from moisture. I breathed deeply to slow my heart rate.

I hoped sleep would return quickly.

Chapter 35

Nowhere To Run, Nowhere To Hide

Wednesday Afternoon

Jules

"Goodness, it's 4:30. I've got tons to do."

I gulp a mouthful of cold coffee, causing me to smack my lips and shudder at its bitterness. Yuk. Medicinal value, I reminded myself.

Paper piles—numerous and multi-sized. I could certainly use a bigger desk.

Who was I kidding? If I had a larger work surface, I'd fill that up, too, and wonder how I ever managed with this one, all these years.

I shook my head. How had I jumped onto a track where life was run by most urgent rather than most important? Hmmm, I'd have to contemplate that, but not tonight; Too many deadlines, and not enough time.

I stretched.

OK. Hunker down, nose to the grindstone, and all that folderol.

A soft knock vibrated the glass door panel. *Who could it be at this hour?*

I could never see who was on the other side of that glass. It was maddening. Fluorescent glare forced me to actually go to the door and squint, like Mr. Magoo, remembering that nearly blind cartoon character from childhood.

It's probably best I couldn't see. If I didn't want to entertain the person, what could I do? I couldn't hide. Where would I hide anyway? Whoever's on the other side, seeing perfectly, would howl watching me conceal myself under my desk's knee hole.

Reluctantly approaching my door, I see an especially distraught Mari.

"Come in. What 's wrong?"

I'd never seen Mari other than reserved and unruffled.

"Sit down, Honey."

I pulled my chair close.

Mari threw a folded Baltimore Sun onto my lap.

"What's this?" I scanned it cautiously, trying to understand Mari's reaction. A handcuffed man's picture centered its front page.

Mari shouted, "It's my attacker. I haven't been able to recall anything until I glanced at this picture, and recognized his ring. The moment I saw it, the whole sordid thing flashed before my eyes."

I rubbed my eyes. I tried to squeeze this crisis amidst my own cluttered thoughts.

"What should I do?" Mari cried.

I hesitated. Given my background, I knew exactly what she was feeling. What could I say?

"Mari, I don't pretend to be a psychiatrist or lawyer. I can tell you, I share your pain, though—more than you know. You see, I was a rape victim as a teenager. I've blocked most details from my memory, too. I understand the violation you're feeling. I can't tell you how to deal with it, though."

Mari's eyes widened with my revelation. Her pacing quickened.

"You need to seek professional counsel that House of Ruth can offer. They'll help you handle this in the healthiest way. Given everything you've had to face this year, you need their support more than ever now."

"Should I call police? Other women who experienced his violence should know he attacked me, too" Mari shouted.

"Well, that's an idea."

"He needs to be punished." Mari barked. She threw a wadded Kleenex toward a trash can and missed.

"Of course, and the police have taken him into custody. Consider something, though. When he is punished, will that take away your pain? Will it change anything? I'd talk with House of Ruth before you call anybody."

"Shouldn't I do something else?" Mari yelled.

"Think what your actions might set into motion. If the police are contacted, it'll become public. You may have to testify openly. You haven't told Tyler, have you?"

"No" she quietly acknowledged.

"Can you be absolutely certain this is who attacked you?"

`"Yes, I recognize his ring. I noticed that ring on that lecherous clerk's hand when I visited the auctioneer."

"Knowing your eye for details; I don't dare suggest you could be mistaken. But the man, Honey, does his face resemble your attacker?"

She lifted the paper again, and stared at its grainy, black and white photo, which showed one side of his face, at a distance.

"I can't tell. Actually, my attacker wore a ski mask."

"Exactly. This man may have stolen that ring. It could be someone entirely different. Can you be absolutely certain from this picture, forgetting his ring?"

"No" Mari let the paper drop to her lap.

"I'm not saying it couldn't be. I'm just saying, before you do anything, you need to consider how this will affect you, Tyler, and a potentially innocent man, at least in your attack. I would guess police took DNA evidence from beneath your fingernails at the hospital. That information is on file. I suspect if anything comes up, they'll contact you first. They may not want your discussing this with anyone while they do their investigation, either. At least that's what I've seen on TV."

We smiled.

"Let's visit the counseling center and find out what their lawyer advises. We'll get dinner, first—we can grab a quick bite at that small café on Cold Spring–my treat."

"Sounds good," Mari consented.

"Mari, before we leave, why don't we pray for God's wisdom in this. He'll lead you in the right direction, and most of all, he'll calm your fear."

I bowed my head and began to pray, *"Father God. . . ."*

Katie

My house has sold. Now I must move Timmy's and my things before settlement, Friday–bittersweet news.

Don't get me wrong. I'm delighted it's over. Since our house was first listed, Don had been intent on doing everything he could to impede any party's interest.

Since he and Jeremy were still residing there, my court-appointed Realtor would alert me before a showing, so I could make it presentable. Each time, I'd have to notify Mark to schedule a safe time to enter.

Presentable was yet to be defined. Most times, I'd been greeted by a sink full of unwashed dishes, overflowing garbage in waste baskets, newspapers scattered across floors, mail piled on every imaginable surface, and food-laden dishes in front of the TV.

Upstairs was worse. Piles of dirty underwear littered both bathrooms. Scattered clothing, both clean and dirty led a path to both rooms.

Rumor reported Don's girlfriend had moved in the day I left. *Couldn't she have done at least a little bit of cleaning? What kind of woman was she?* I'd never been a perfect housekeeper, but this was unimaginable.

Mark smirked with my account, saying it probably wasn't that she was a slob as much as their shared goal for of sabotaging a sale; thus increasing my misery. Probably right, but I had to clean it—how else would it ever be sold, otherwise?

I needed at least my portion of profit from its sale. The longer this house sat without being sold, with the two—now three—of them living there, the more it might appear I had deserted. Then squatters' rights, I suppose. I couldn't consider that scenario.

Most times, a week's worth of work had to be completed in a two-hour period, assigned by Mark and Charles, Don's lawyer. Forget scrubbing and vacuuming. I usually tore through three floors of living area; scooping and carrying all manner of items to replace in drawers, closets, cabinets, washing machine and garbage.

It's been exhausting. I'm more than relieved to be done with it all.

My poor cat was behaving as if she hadn't been fed for days. Perhaps she hadn't. If I had a permanent place to live, I'd take her with me. Timmy missed *Kitty* and so did I. On the run, I could barely care for him and myself. *What could I do with a cat*? It was best she stay here until other arrangements could be made.

Now I'm faced with packing boxes, and moving Timmy's and my personal belongings in an exceedingly short time. I'd needed to have most things hauled to a storage unit several days ago, as I could only carry items which could be crammed in my compact car. Since Sarah's house was furnished, nearly everything had to be stashed.

Now, with big stuff squirreled away, I was down to what no one wanted to move or claim. I'd brought garbage bags to sort between *Goodwill* and trash.

I breathed deeply just looking at this cluttered space. I had no energy to do any of it, today. I could hardly force myself to face it—too many memories, too much junk, too much fatigue.

I'd decided to take an early lunch break after working steadily all morning. I assumed I'd be alone most of the day. After nourishment and caffeine, I could complete it by 1:00, give or take. Then Don could take his stuff, without my being there: a workable plan.

Mark warned Don would arrive around 5:00. That gave me a margin if I worked past 1:00. I could only think in terms of 1:00, however. The thought of dragging this process any longer was something I couldn't fathom. 1:00 was my deadline.

After going to St. Edmonds to join Ruth for lunch, I traveled back to complete this thing. As I cruised slowly down the winding road, and approached my yard, my mouth dropped open.

A woman, Don's girlfriend, I presume, was stacking my boxes into her truck. She was now dragging my grandmother's mirror toward her destination. All the while, Don directed with verbal commands, but was not actually doing the packing, himself.

Throwing any good sense out the window, I ran within ten feet of her. "Wait a minute. That's mine. Those things are mine." I shouted, protectively.

Don glanced toward me and then her. Realizing he'd been authorizing her taking what was not hers—(i.e. stealing)—he called to her, "Karen, check those boxes again."

Then turning to me, he bellowed, "You always make trouble wherever you go, don't you? What are you doing here, anyway? Things would've gone smoothly if you'd just stayed away."

Hearing commotion, Jeremy ran from our house, and headed towards this woman, comforting her. She draped her arm around his shoulders, ignoring me, and headed up porch-steps and into my house...MY house.

I was dumbfounded. *What was happening here?*

Suddenly I didn't care about boxes or mirrors, or anything else. No words could describe my feelings. *Was this a dream? How could any of this be happening?* It was beyond reason.

I drove, wanting to escape the surreal scene. All I could do was stare into nowhere, mystified.

What was an appropriate way of behaving in this situation? What would Abigail Van Buren, of Dear Abbey fame, have to say? Stunned, unable to think, I wanted to call my mother. She always knew how to respond in a socially difficult situation.

This woman had taken my husband, my son, my belongings. *What could I do?*

Nothing—absolutely nothing at all.

Thursday afternoon

Mari

"Julia, this is Mari. I'm so sorry to bother you."
"It's fine. I was just wrapping up paper work."

Julia shuffled papers as she spoke.

She was hunting for that paper clip. It was her last one. She scolded herself under her breath for not stocking up last week when she knew that box was empty.

"The police called about DNA from my nails, and they need to question me. I'm afraid."

"I'll go with you." Jules syllabled, dropping papers and forgoing her search for her missing clip.

"I'd appreciate it. I don't have strength to drive. Would you mind?"

Mari's words breathed, barely above a whisper.

"See you in thirty minutes." Click.

"Dear Father in heaven, it's Mari again. I need your help. I'm so afraid. Help me do what's best, for me and Tyler...."

Chapter 36

Under Lock And Key

Friday morning

Mari

The main office phone rang. My extension button lit red.

"Hello?"

"Officer Cook, here, Mrs. McGuire, please."

"This is Mrs. McGuire. How can I help you?"

"Ma'am, your accused attacker has escaped custody. I'm coming by your office to escort you home."

I whimpered, "Am I in danger?"

"The accused knows nothing about your statement. However, I'd consider him dangerous. We'd feel more comfortable if you were in a safe place until we can restore him to the holding facility. Are you free to leave now?"

"I can be ready in minutes."

A gentle male voice asked the receptionist to see me. She directed him to my door. From a distance, he appeared about fifty, and well-dressed. My phone button lit red, again.

"Can I help you?" I steadied myself by clutching an end table beside the opening.

He graciously extended his hand, "Mrs. McGuire?"

"Won't you come in? Are you interested in selling or purchasing a residential property?"

He chose a chair, reserved for clients. I gently closed the door, and returned to my place behind my desk.

His manners were polished, I observed. His smile was boyish. He leaned forward, pulling an identification badge from an inside pocket of his fashionable sport jacket. Handsome.

"Mrs. McGuire, I'm a plainclothes officer with Baltimore City police department. I've been sent to escort you to your home and ensure your safety until this escapee is secured.

"Since this involves your privacy, you can pretend I'm a potential client, looking for a piece of property. When we leave, just pretend you're going to show a house. I'll escort you in an unmarked car to your home. No one will think anything out of the ordinary. Your protection and your privacy are of utmost importance to me." He smiled. "I hope you're not frightened."

"Sir, I would not be truthful if I said I wasn't. This situation is terrifying. I appreciate you're considering my anonymity. My closest friends know about my attack, but my teenage son does not. It's imperative he not find out. He's just seventeen. He's recently suffered his father's death and the loss of his home. I don't want to add to his angst. I hope you understand."

"Mrs. McGuire, I do. I have a son, about the same age. This may all be wrapped up momentarily. I hope so, but for whatever length of time it takes to find this man, I'll make sure your residence is protected. You can contact me if anything—I mean anything—suspicious occurs. You'll be protected. However, it'll be as inconspicuously as possible."

He reached into his pocket. "Here's a beeper to wear. If you have a concern, you may signal me with this. If I hear any news, I'll signal you with an unlisted number to call me. Does your home have a security system?"

"Yes, sir, I'm renting rooms from a woman who owns the house. She and my son are the only other residents, except our dog and cat. We have daily visitors, though. Will that cause a problem?"

"Not at all, just tell me their names so I'll know who to expect. Please go about your normal routine. Be assured, my aim is to protect you and your son."

"Thank you." I released a breath.

I was feeling better already. This kind man would be watching our house, with the authority of the Baltimore City police force behind him. He'd protect me, Tyler and my friends until this attacker was found and locked up.

I never realized police could be so helpful to people who'd been victimized. I felt relieved there actually were government workers who cared. I felt better about paying years of back taxes my husband had evaded. Although strapped with incredible debt, at least I could feel relieved my money would go to pay salaries for kind, responsible people like Officer Cook.

"Shall we go?" He stood.

Exiting my office, I addressed my receptionist, "Alice, I'll be showing my client several properties this morning. This afternoon I'll be working from home. Please forward any calls. Thanks, Alice."

Officer Cook escorted me to our house and assisted opening my door, with little fanfare, lest neighbors be alerted. What a gentleman.

"Now lock your door and set the security system. Don't be afraid. You have your beeper, right."

I nodded, confirming I understood his instructions.

"Keep your cordless phone with you. If I receive any news, I'll call. I'll beep you first, though, as not to alarm. Remember, you won't know exactly where I'll be. Be assured I will protect you, all right?"

I searched his soft eyes, and found his voice strangely comforting.

"I'll leave your car in your driveway. Your key will be under the driver side mat."

"You're Ok?"

"I'm all right, thank you."

"By the way: I'll need to know when one of your friends visits. You can signal me with the beeper. When

I call, you can just give me their names. Addresses and phone numbers would be helpful, too, for documentation purposes, only. Police department policy, you understand."

I nodded, closed and double-locked the door, and depressed security buttons beside our light switch.

Rags rested in his dog house. Purrfect, having been asleep, looked up, mewed, stretched, and went back to sleep. Tyler was at school. Gloria was out. Our house was tranquil.

I mounted the steps wearily, one at a time. I draped my coat over a chair, and sat on my bed. I couldn't be afraid any more. Fear took more energy than I could continue to muster.

I reached for my prayer book on my bedside table. A folded paper, lodged between pages fell to my lap.

What is this?

The numerous creases took awhile to separate. Individual words bounded from the paper "Peter Andrew McGuire, 1945 -1991." It was his funeral bulletin.

I slowly turned its cover. Several scriptures adorned the pages. *Funny, I don't remember any of this.*

I recalled that day as a series of blurred slides with no continuity or associated narrative, color or music. Now printed words bolded from this paper jarring my awareness:

"Peace I give you, not as the world gives, give I to you."
"Do not be afraid, for I am with you always, even unto the end of the age."
"I will never leave you or forsake you."

I read these words several times. They were balm, just for me, for such a time as this.

The 23rd Psalm centered its back cover:

"The Lord is my shepherd I shall not want. He makes me to lie down in green pastures. He leads me beside still waters. He restores my soul. . . .Yea, though I walk through the valley of the shadow of death, I will fear no evil for you are with me. . Surely goodness and mercy shall follow me all the days of my life..."

I closed and re-folded this bulletin and gently placed it inside the book's front cover. Pete had left me a treasure, after all, in midst of ruin. These words, recalling his death, represented life—a new life.

I clutched the book to my chest. I would not be afraid, for He is with me. I would trust.

Chapter 37

Holiday Joy

Friday Evening

"Are those cookies done yet?"

"This first batch is ready, but they're hot. Be careful." Sarah proudly placed cookies on a special red, heart-shaped platter—one we reserved for celebrating good news—and made it our evening's centerpiece.

Our kitchen island had become our Friday night gathering place. Sarah was preparing smoothies to go with these whole-grain-fruit cookies. Tonight's smoothies contained frozen strawberries, bananas, flax seed oil, honey, vanilla yogurt and some green powder of questionable identity. If it came from Sarah's kitchen, it'd be therapeutic, and yummy.

Jules started. "You know, girls, I've been getting my information second-hand from Glory. I don't feel satisfied with basics anymore. I want real facts I can sink my teeth into. I will not leave tonight, without it all."

She punctuated her declaration with popping a warm cookie into her mouth.

We giggled. A newsy gossip session with Julia was always such fun.

She added, "Can you believe Glory's gorgeous rock?"

Mari added, "It was old news when I got back. When I commented about it, she answered, "What, this old thing?"

Julia chided, "Glory, you didn't."

Gloria laughed, enjoying having created a little drama.

"What's news tonight?" Julia continued.

All eyes turned to Sarah, who was arranging the next batch of warm cookies.

Julia exclaimed, "Ah-ha. What's with you, girly?"

Sarah grinned, "I won the cooking contest."

She screamed and jumped. Hoots and cheers resonated from the rest of us.

"And," she continued, "I'll be on *Good Morning, Baltimore*, Monday. Mari, you've got to help me with clothes. I've never even seen that show, so what will work?"

Mari grinned. "They'll probably give you an apron, since you cook. Didn't they say?"

Sarah shook her head. "I can't believe I'm going to be on TV. I've got to figure out how to tape it and show Rebecca. She won't believe her old mom."

Mari strode to the basement door, "Tyler, do you know how to tape a TV show?"

"Piece 'a cake."

"There's your answer: my son, the resident tech genius."

Mari quipped, "I have another surprise for you, Sarah. An out-of-town couple wants to see your house ASAP. They love Mt. Washington, and are impressed with your square footage, and the size of your kitchen. We'll have to spruce it—fast. I can decorate and make it look extra special . . . but only if you want me to, of course."

Mari suddenly reddened; embarrassed for presuming Sarah's house needed decorating.

We cheered.

Sarah's countenance fell, as she slumped on a stool. "Where will Rebecca and I go? What about Katie and Timmy?"

Gloria interjected, "There's room for everyone at St. Edmonds. Sarah, you wouldn't have to drive every day, and Rebecca could be available to our master professor, Ruth."

Ruth reddened, "Oh, you all. I'm not really a teacher."

Gloria patted her arm. 'You're an excellent teacher. Look what you've done with little Sam, Mother, and Lucille."

Katie asked, hesitantly, "Mari, will closing be soon, if it's a go?"

Mari recognized her concern and answered, "We're flexible. We won't forget about you."

Katie addressed Gloria, "Thank you for inviting us, but it'd be unwise. With Don's unpredictable behavior, it could be dangerous. I'll look for a safe place, a distance away from y'all."

Mari answered, "Trust me. I'll find the perfect place."
Katie nodded and mouthed. "Thank you."

How much longer would she have to run and hide—cat and mouse?

Ruth changed the subject, "Mari, I've got a surprise: our house won first prize in the Christmas decorating contest. It'll be pictured on the front page of our community newsletter. But there's more: the photo was picked up by a Baltimore Sun reporter. Our house will be featured in its special holiday issue."

Ruth fished a piece of paper from her pocket, and handed it across the island.

"Call Monday for an interview. She also wants permission to reveal your agency name, for holiday decorating tips."

Mari hesitated, "I'm certainly flattered, but I don't feel comfortable having people call and visiting unknown homes, though. How would I handle that?"

If her attack happened at her own house, what could happen at strange houses?

Jules swirled her glass, "You might take one of us along on your visits, and leave your real estate card; creative advertising."

Mari's eyebrows rose. Reconsidering, she added, "Tyler might go. He's enjoyed visiting houses."

Julia added, "Tomorrow morning, visit that business supply store in Towson and design business cards. Advertise your services as a decorateur d'interieurs, specializing in holiday events. Although, you might also consider adding re-decorating listed houses, to maximize their potential."

Mari looked excited. "Do you really think I could pull it off?"

It could be fun, at that; lucrative, too, maybe.

"Absolutely," we crowed.

Sarah smiled, "I have more good news. Rebecca's coming home for Christmas—to stay."

"Really?" we chorused.

"Of course, she'll need continued counseling. She may even have to re-visit Durham at set intervals, to ensure healing progress."

Her homecoming would be the only Christmas present she'd ever need again.

"Wonderful. It's almost over." Ruth encouraged.

Gloria quietly added, "Ruth, George sent a letter outlining Sam's legal responsibilities before he attempts to leave Baltimore. I don't know what it said. I just wanted you to know he's handling it."

Ruth nodded, "I'm glad."

"Oh, I have news: I spoke with some administrators of our college, about DH's being allowed to register for college classes. We're trying to drum up funding from private benefactors." Julia reported.

"You mean we might be able to finish our degrees? I'd love that." Ruth looked hopeful.

"Me, too" agreed Sarah.

Ruth nodded, "It'd take two years or more for me. It's a mouth-full, but certainly hope of a new direction."

Julia yawned and stretched, "Well, I've gotta' go. Early morning dental appointment; routine check-up but I still must rise early." She turned to Gloria "Are we on for lunch tomorrow?"

Gloria added, "Just wait—I have more news. Jules has been awarded teacher of the year."

Hoots and cheers abounded from our group.

Julia waved her hand, dismissing it. "On that note, I do have to run."

Gloria confirmed, "11:30 for Earl Grey."

"Earl Grey," Julia quipped.

"If we had no winter, the spring would not be so pleasant; if we did not sometimes taste
of adversity, prosperity would not be so welcome."
Anne Bradstreet

Chapter 38

Folks Wrapped Up Like Eskimos

Monday Evening

Mari

"Mari, Tyler, here's dinner; I must run." Sarah announced, entering and leaving in one fluid movement as in a choreographed ballet.

Although Christmas anticipatory joy tried to reign, Tyler's Princeton rejection marked yet another emotional low watermark.

I'd known Princeton was out of the question. Even with a full athletic scholarship, I couldn't uphold a student's expenditures, particularly influenced by affluent friends. Even with this acknowledgement, that letter came as a shock. His application was rejected on academic merit. No confidence bolster, that's for sure.

I called from the basement door, "Tyler, dinner."

"Not hungry," he spoke to the air.

I knocked and hesitated, "OK if I come down? Decent?"

Hearing no reply, I slowly and purposely descended, allowing him time to arrange himself.

"Gee, Ty, great decorating."

"Thanks," he absently replied, eying a lacrosse ball, rise and fall between his hands and the ceiling.

"Mind if I sit? Want to look at a house, Saturday?"

"I dunno, Mom. I might hang out with th' guys—throw some balls and stuff."

"That's fine. I'll ask another Realtor to join me."

"Well, I guess I could go. I kinda' like seeing different places."

The lacrosse ball rose and fell, again and again.

"Maybe Real Estate is a business I could get into. Mr. Wilson's taught me a lot about building and fixing things, and schooling isn't long or expensive."

I hesitated. "Ty, you're bright and talented. Whatever you choose, you'll succeed, I'm sure. You could do well at Real Estate, but you might also excel with building contracting, or architecture, or many other things, for that matter. Choose something you want to do, not because it costs less. Don't discard college yet."

My eyes wander to a waste-basket full of tossed college catalogs in the corner, poor kid.

"Yeah, but I can't go to Princeton." His tone decreased in force and volume, as if saying it again would bring more pain.

Tyler hated thinking about college. It seemed like his life ended these past couple of months. He didn't have a home anymore, he didn't have a dad, and now his dream of Princeton– his only dream—was gone, too. Every test and paper, every lacrosse game and practice, every play, every ache and pain, he'd kept his eye on his goal of playing for Princeton.

He hadn't known his cousin, Chad, well; not at all, really. He'd wanted to model himself after that cool college guy who'd spent time with him, that vacation. Chad had taught him to throw a lacrosse ball—heck, he'd even taken him to a couple of games at St. Andrew's School, where he'd played when he attended high school. Tyler wanted to have a life just like Chad's. *Who else did he have to look up to?* Dad hadn't spent any time with him—he was either gone most of the time or drunk.

He hated it when Dad was drunk. He always worried about having friends visit, for fear of their seeing his father slurring his speech, falling into walls, being sloppy. Chad's cool image had given him something to hold up and be like. Now—because of his Dad's stupid car accident, they were too poor to go. 'Course, he was the one who failed to make the cut at Princeton. It was his fault, too. He felt tears brim his eyes. He turned his head from his mother not wanting her to see him cry—like some stupid baby.

"That's a disappointment, for sure." I answered softly.

I could see Tyler's face and neck redden as he said the name, Princeton. My heart broke to see him suffer so much over past months. And yet, I knew I could do nothing. He needed to deal with this disappointment on his own.

I ached wishing things had been different. I wanted to cuddle him like I had when he was a little boy who'd skinned his knee or faced some disappointment.

There had never been setbacks as compounded as the ones he'd faced this year, though. I'd never faced disappointments as compounded as the ones I'd faced this year, either. I swallowed down a sob which was poised to erupt. My eyes burned with fresh tears.

"I'm not ready to consider another school. Any other place will always be second choice." He stated this truth an octave lower and quieter than his other sentences.

I pondered. "Ty, a second choice, can be a second chance, and perhaps the very best choice of all."

Wasn't that what I was learning so late in my life? I had no other words of wisdom to give him. I was just learning myself, and I was floundering, at that.

He spoke again, "Maybe I'll spend the summer with Grand'Mere. A lot of things need fixing in her house, and she can't do it. She's so lonely, living by herself."

"Ty, how kind—she'd be thrilled to show off her handsome grandson."

There. He was trying to find a new way, a new path; Hope.

Tyler blushed, "What if I took a year off? Not go to college right away?"

I could hear a tremor in his voice, as if he wasn't sure how to find a new start in life.

"Let's wait before making any big decisions. There's no rush. A few months is not going to make a lot of difference."

"OK" Tyler mumbled, his eyes fixed on the ball he tossed, less forcefully now.

"Excited about Christmas break?" I ventured to change the subject.

"Kind 'a. I just want to sleep."

"Well, you can sleep some. I need you to help Mr. Wilson hang more lights and greenery for <u>Baltimore Magazine</u> and <u>Baltimore Sun</u> photographers."

"You kiddin' me? No more lights. I'm sick of light-hanging."

I tousled his hair. "Come upstairs. Sarah made lasagna."

Tyler's head rose from the pillow and the ball dropped. "Garlic bread, too?"

"Garlic bread, too."

The Wilsons

"Harry, Harry. Do you hear me?"

Doris hunched under attic eaves, and mumbled out loud.

"Don't ask me why we keep storin' things up here ev'ry year. I can hardly see for nothin' and th' light's nearly burned out."

She drew her hand across her brow to shift hair from her eyes.

"Where were they anyway? Every year I tell myself, Doris, you need to go under those eaves and clear out all that stuff you've been storin' since God created this earth."

She sneezed three times. She stood and waited. Whenever she sneezed it was always four times, never just three.

"Ah -ah-ah choo."

There it was. She wiped her hand across her nose to wipe away the dust.

Now back to her search. She squinted toward the other side of the unfinished section. No real floor's up here—just a few boards laid 'cross rafters and insulation.

She glanced at her feet.

Mercy, what if I stepped th' wrong way and fell down through.

She stopped and contemplated just how far she'd go.

Certainly no further than th' second floor. Course, she'd put on weight over th' years. That, plus momentum, might land her in th' basement. Oh law. Wouldn't that be a heck-of-a way t' go, and bein' nearly Christmas.

She mused about who'd find her. She guessed Harry would, but Lord knows, he could fall asleep watchin' th' news and never miss her 'til th' next morning when he got hungry for breakfast. I hope he'd remembered about my plans for th' final, ya' know, th' end? She couldn't even think the words, let alone say them.

She'd never set any written plans for what she wanted—at th' end, ya' know. She wondered who'd come to th' funeral. Most all her family was gone, 'cept her sons. She had her friends from church, and card club. Since she'd been workin', though, she'd all but given up playin' Canasta and bridge. *What 'bout music? I hope they didn't play the droning kind everyone seemed to have at funerals.*

Goodness, what if she didn't die when she fell, but just injured herself real bad? Oh, law, she hoped they wouldn't hook her up t' those machines, you see on television stories. All those tubes and what all, coming from every part of a body . . . *Why was she thinking 'bout this stuff?*

"Harry, Harry? Where are you?"

Doris heard footsteps, maybe coming up from th' basement.

"That you, Hon? Doris, where are you, anyway?"

"I'm up in th' eaves." she bellowed out the opening.

More footsteps rising.

"Doris, what in th' world you up there fer?"

"Harry, I'm trying t' find Christmas lights and ornaments. I've gone through any number a' boxes and I can't seem to find a one."

"Hon, don't you remember? You told me las' year, "Harry, I don't want t' have t' go back up in th' eaves agin. I'm afraid I'll fall through th' ceiling." Don't you remember? So, I put all th' boxes in th' basement."

Doris let out a deep breath and sighed. She blew upward to dislodge the hair which returned over her eyes.

"Well, can you at least give me a hand so I kin git out a' here without fallin'? Lands, Harry." Whew, it's musty up there. Remind me never t'go back in there again."

"Doris, Hon, ev'ry year I say, 'Doris, don't go back up there. Just tell me. I'll go up fer you', but you ne'er ast me. Ne'er once."

"Humph. Well, what were you doin' in th' basement when I first called?"

"Gettin' Christmas decorations."

Harry howled, whisked a dust ball out of his wife's hair and stole a kiss while he was at it.

"Go 'way," she grumbled, and then allowed herself to laugh.

"Where're they anyway?"

"Don't come down, yet, Hon. I got a s'prise."

Harry galloped down to their living room: rustling paper, boxes pushed across hardwoods.

"Now close yer eyes, Hon."

"Oh, all right, but hurry. I don't have all day."

She heard shuffling footsteps slowly climbing creaking steps.

"OK, Hon, open yer eyes."

She slowly released her tightly closed lids. Sputtering with laughter, she studied her husband. He was dressed in an over-sized, moth-eaten Santa suit. His head was topped with a worn red-velvet hat. The fur ball on the end had definitely seen better days.

"What d'ya think?"

"Harry, are you thinking a' dressing up for th' boys? Oh, what fun? I haven't seen that 'ole suit since Dickie was a toddler. Oh, th' boys'll just love that. I'll find more fake fur at th' Center Street notions store, and fix th' hat. Maybe I'll sew some on th' jacket. Turn 'round. Let me see th' back. I know. There's a store down there that sells all that foam rubber; you know th' one. We'll make you into th' best Santa there ever was. Let me give you a kiss."

"Maybe I should wear 'is ev'ryday—with mistletoe. Would ya' give me more kisses?"

Doris flicked her hand across his back side.

"Come on, Santa. We need t' plan th' best Christmas lil' Sam and Tyler ever had."

"Hon, kin we have some 'a that good gingerbread you used t' make, and fix a turkey wit' all th' trimmin's? I'll git some ole'fashioned candy canes from down th' yard. I might git out th' ole train set and set it up in th' basement. I'll bet th' boys'd git a kick out a' that. We'll set up th' lil' village with houses and animals, an' all, jes like when th' boys were lil'"

"Oh, an' I'll get some a' ole Mr. Schwartz's homemade Moravian ginger cookies. He's still alive, isn't he? I'll have t' check. He's gettin' on up in age, as I recall."

"Remember th' Christmas board game we used t' play with th' boys? We used t' keep it next t' Candy Land in Steve's room. I'll fill stockin's, and we'll have t' get a tree. Oh, Harry, I don't know when I've been so excited."

Doris and Harry embraced. Then, raced to find their Sears, Montgomery Ward, and JC Penney Christmas catalogs, too.

Tyler and Sam, Jr. would make this the very best Christmas they'd had in years.

Chapter 39

Tightly Wrapped Gifts

Mari

Two weeks. That's how long Tony'd remained at large. His hearing had been postponed until after the holidays. Officer Cook had protectively scoped our residence, without break.

Morning and night, I calmed myself by reading verses in Pete's funeral bulletin. Odd, how peace emerged from a funeral bulletin. Even when Tony escaped custody, I knew I couldn't continue to be afraid. After all, didn't God protect me during my attack? I had not been raped or maimed. Hadn't police arrived just in time? Wasn't my life spared?

Although I'm certainly relieved Tony's behind bars, my emotions have changed little with that news.

Strangely, I've been rather indifferent as to where he was. Tyler and I were safe. That was what mattered.

I recalled all the times my life had been spared—that boating accident as a teenager, my car wreck at sixteen, being a front seat-passenger countless times while my husband drove drunk... God had spared my life. *Why? Who knew?* I know now, beyond a doubt, I will not leave this world until it's God's time.

The Lord is my shepherd. I could count on His promise to take care of me.

"I trust in God so why should I be afraid. What can mere mortals do to me?"
Psalm 56:4 (Bible, TLB)

Saturday morning

Katie

"Hello."

6:00, by my bedside clock.

"Katie, this is Susan, from the agency. Could you work this morning? Sorry it's last minute. I know you don't want Cockeysville, but their hygienist's child is sick. No one else can work."

I understood about a sick child. Timmy certainly had sick days. Cockeysville, though. I cringed. As long as it wasn't Don's office, how bad could it be? It was only 'til noon, after all.

"I'll call my sitter."

"Great. Call back." Click.

My drowsy day care provider extended a conditional yes; only for morning. She needed to prepare for her holidays, too.

By 7:00, I'd deposited a pajama-clad Timmy and proceeded to I83. Early Saturday morning traffic was not usually problematic, but one never knew. Since it's the Saturday before Christmas, *Toys R Us* and every mall store would be opening before 6:00 a.m. Holiday traffic was unpredictable.

Well, I could only do my best. After all, what could they do if I were late? Fire me? I think not. I was doing them a big favor.

The morning patient schedule proceeded routinely. In another hour, I'd be out of here, with holiday pocket change. The signal light blinked, alerting me to my patient's arrival.

"Jules, what a surprise."

I promised a quick check-up. We laughed, reciting our last minute errands.

"Any problems with your teeth?"

"Lots of Earl Grey stain, I'm afraid—my downfall."

I laughed. "A sparkling smile will be my Christmas gift to you, Jules. Any plans for this afternoon?

"Actually, I'm picking up Mari to shop for some last minute items at that adorable gift shop at Kenilworth Bazaar. She's leaving her car to make it look like she's home today."

"How come?" I removed my mouth mirror and instrument so I could understand her answer.

Why would Mari want to leave her car? Perhaps to save gas; doubling up for shopping trips was a good idea.

I should've thought of that. We all had to monitor expenses, especially with rising gas prices.

"Apparently, Officer Cook thinks it's safer for her—for all of us, he said. He's still watching Glory's house."

"Wait a minute. I thought Mari's attacker was back in custody?" I was puzzled.

"Yes, that's true, but Officer Cook seems to think it'd be wise to continue surveillance for a while, just in case someone else might be involved; not only for Mari's protection but for all of us who go to her house. Mari says he has all of our names for documentation."

"Gee, that's really nice of him. Do you think he might be smitten with Mari?"

"I think." Julia added and giggled.

"Wow. It's only 11:35, Jules. Maybe we'll both be out of here by noon."

I glanced at a tooth-shaped clock, eager to do a few quick errands before I retrieved Timmy from his sitter.

"Good. You know I'm not a patient woman." She laughed.

I flossed her teeth and rinsed her mouth a final time. After removing her damp napkin from its neck chain, I reached in a drawer behind her chair.

"Here's a Christmas red toothbrush for you, Jules. See you Christmas day."

Sarah

Good grief. Her shuttle should've arrived by now. I figured nine hours, give or take.

Why hasn't anyone called? I paced anxiously in front of our phone.

Rebecca's coming home. It's seemed like ages, since that fateful departure day.

So much has happened. I'd won that contest, our house has a buyer and I've been on television. Who would've ever imagined? Now, we'll be moving into St. Edmonds, and I might even return to college. I couldn't wait to share this with Rebecca.

How could I have ever thought there was no God?

The phone rang.

"Her shuttle's arrived? I'm leaving now. Goodbye."

I cheered.

I sprinted to our driveway, allowing the screen door to slam behind me. I revved the motor, and my old Volvo headed east.

Oh I just can't believe it. There's the shuttle and my beautiful daughter.

"Rebecca? Is that my girl?" I called out.

I jumped from my car, barely taking time to remove my ignition key.

"Yes, Mommy, I'm back."

She was still thin, but embracing her, I felt flesh padding her shoulders. Her face had filled. Not quite dimples yet, but. . . . Somehow, I'd buy her new clothes to replace these taut ones she'd obviously outgrown. She deserved it.

"How do you feel, Honey? Glad to be home?" I held her close.

So much I wanted to say and so much I wanted to hear. Right now, I just wanted to take her home and start a new road to a new normal. I grinned just seeing her smile. It had been so long since I'd seen her smile.

"Yes, but I'm going to miss it. I left a lot of good friends behind. Oh, and Mom, I've been practicing my violin. I can't wait for you to hear me play."

All I could do was gaze at her bright eyes and smile.

"Mom?"

"Yes, Dear?"

A really nice nurse visited most weekends. She read us Bible stories, and told us about God. Mom, do you know Jesus?"

I smiled, "Tell me who He is to you, Honey?"

Gloria

It's 9:00 p.m. I still have time to visit Ruth.

"Anybody home?" I called softly, not wanting to wake the household.

Ruth arose from a chintz overstuffed chair,

"Glory, I was just thinking about you."

"Sorry it's late."

"I'll fix tea." Ruth said.

"Thanks. Please make mine decaf. I want to sleep tonight."

I glanced around, "Isn't this gorgeous? This house has been transformed."

Ruth nodded, "A Christmas wonderland."

"Want to join me at the Christmas Eve service?"

"Gee, I could use some peaceful reflection."

"Far from the madding crowd," I quoted Thomas Hardy's title.

"I hope relief will come with this New Year. I'm in a slump."

Ruth felt as if all the pain and anguish she'd felt throughout these past eight months were peaking this evening. Life seemed so overwhelming. She'd tried to blame it on PMS. Certainly that was part of it—what woman didn't struggle month to month, but this tension felt on-going, with no let up.

"I sensed that. Holidays aren't always happy, you know." I added.

Contrary to what TV ads were quick to try to persuade everyone, holidays were not always full of cheer. Buying stuff and entertaining did not automatically bring joy, unfortunately. Usually most of us felt loss of loved ones and relationships at Christmas; exhausted with stress of shopping and running at a maddening pace, all with spending much more than we knew we should. Songs of cheer just seemed to underscore loss for those of us whose lives were less than picture-perfect.

"Is it that obvious? I've been trying to be upbeat." Ruth didn't even attempt to smile.

"Ruth, you're the most joyful person I know, but I'm cognizant enough to realize when things are off."

She didn't answer immediately. How could she describe her feelings?

"My anger is what I find so vexing. It feels so enormous, it scares me. My family never modeled how to handle angry feelings. As a child, I retreated to my room, shed a few tears, and topped it off with a smile and a shrug, repeating, "Get over it." Years of pent up emotion makes me feel like a pressure cooker, ready to explode with the slightest provocation."

Gloria measured, "You've lost dreams, trust, home, everything. Anger is part of grieving, Honey. Besides, what's happened to you and Sam, Jr. is wrong—legitimate anger there, too. I've struggled with that same type of anger toward my ex-husband. Dealing with anger constructively wasn't modeled for me, either. My mother escaped to alcohol, and my father escaped to his work and who knows what else."

"So what do you do?" Ruth glanced at me, questioning, while twisting fringe on a sofa pillow.

"I have to surrender it one day at a time, like a recovering alcoholic, I have to ask God to take it. It's like when my kitchen-sink leaks. I call a plumber, instead of wasting time, trying to do something I'm not able to do. I must constantly remind myself vengeance is God's job, not mine. I might add, plenty of women have tried to take things into their own hands and reside in our prisons, today."

Ruth mused, "Sometimes I dream of returning to my old life, before all this happened—when my son and I did not hurt. That's silly, I know. Maybe it wasn't even what I remember its being. Maybe there were signs all along, I just didn't want to recognize. Maybe I chose to ignore what was right in front of my eyes, as clear as day. Now I play another charade."

I raised my eyebrows, questioning.

"In front of others, I pretend it's OK. I'm over it. In reality, when I consider how Sam's selfishness has dragged us through the mud, I find myself seething. Poor little Sam often cries himself to sleep, but he never complains. He just accepts. I could just scream. Sam has not even called him. I don't know whether he'll even remember Sam, Jr. Christmas day."

"It's awful, I know."

Poor girl, I knew exactly how she felt. I studied the painted design on my teacup, trying to think of some kind of encouragement I could give.

"There's coming a time, I'll have to face him, either in court or some other place. I'm afraid of losing control—of rage and of hate." Ruth continued.

The pillow in her lap sailed to the other end of the sofa, punctuating her outrage.

I turned my gaze to the spoon in my cup. I'd be furious, too. My similar anger toward Charles was not as honestly labeled as Ruth's.

Rage and hate . . . pure and simple.

I'd concealed mine, sugar-coating it as my feeling hurt. *But weren't these feelings justified? How was one supposed to act when someone causes your world to fall apart, and leaves you to pick up the pieces?*

I added, "I'm not implying if you meet with Sam, you shouldn't reveal your pain from his selfishness, certainly. That day may never come, though. Like me, you're probably already rehearsing your script for that imaginary day, over and over, refining your phrasing and fueling your anger; a futile exercise, I've discovered. Someone, I don't know who, once commented about that: it's preparing poison to give another, and then drinking it yourself every day—all day."

"You've got that right," Ruth said through clenched teeth.

I continued, "A friend once suggested a method for jumping off that merry-go-round and finding temporary closure: Her advice to me was to compose a letter—not necessarily to be mailed. Pen all your feelings. Leave nothing out. Remind him of how he has hurt you and Sam, Jr. After you're certain nothing has been left out, hide it under your bed. After a set time, burn it. Then visualize locking this letter and your anger in a suitcase. Hand it to God, and watch Him throw it onto a garbage heap; irretrievable. End this with thanking Him for taking out the garbage."

Ruth stared eyebrows raised; tilting her head, looking but unseeing.

"This exercise has helped me when my anger seemed more than I could handle. Repeat this when direct confrontation is impossible—with anyone—even God. Tangible proof you've released it. Finished"

Ruth nodded slightly, looking through a distant window into darkness.

"Overly simplistic, perhaps, but it's indispensable for me—safe when confrontation is not." I added, not entirely sure she was listening.

Silence, as she turned from a window to gaze at the tops of her fingernails.

"Ruth, may I offer another suggestion? Some quiet time, encourage Sam, Jr. to talk about his daddy, and any sadness over moving, loss of friends and his old life. He needs to know it's safe to share with you; OK to cry, and express angry feelings, appropriate for his age and maturity. He needs to be assured he's not somehow responsible for Sam's leaving or for your sadness."

Ruth turned her face away.

"Children's views differ from adults and his feelings may surprise you. Sam, Jr. will have to eventually deal with his father on his own terms. You have no control over that. Help him know you're approachable. I didn't communicate that to Tad, and it has not played out well. I accept much of the blame for many of his problems. Ultimately, he'll find his own way, too, though, just as you and I will."

Ruth had begun to sob, quietly.

I ended, "Think about that footsteps poem. I can't remember it exactly, but it goes something like this;

"Someone was looking over his life and saw a pattern of two sets of footprints, walking. During life's hard times, he noticed only one set of prints. He asked the Lord, "You walked with me all my life, except the hardest times. Why did you leave me all alone when I needed you so desperately?"

The Lord answered, 'I didn't leave you, my child—that's when I carried you.'"

"Every evening I turn my troubles over to God—
He's going to be up all night anyway."
Donald J. Morgan

Chapter 40

God Rest Ye Merry Gentlemen, Let Nothing You Dismay

Katie

"Timmy, Honey, time to get up. It's Christmas." I grinned hugely and sang "Jingle Bells".

Yesterday's separation hearing left me tightly wound. Unable to sleep, I'd awakened Timmy at dawn. Unlike other sunrises, I wanted to start this day. It promised surprises—good ones, happy ones. My little guy needed to look forward to something. Fun had been sadly lacking in his short life.

Sarah's Monster cookie was routine bath bait now—whatever worked. Climbing from the tub, Timmy jerked from my hold and raced to hanging, trinket-filled stockings.

I loved having an excuse for dressing him in special clothes. With meager earnings, I'd chosen navy, short suspendered-pants, a collarless matching Eton jacket, and a white shirt, collared with Christmas red piping. Securing him on my lap, I slipped new white knee socks and black and white saddle shoes on his wiggling feet.

I stole a kiss and smiled. He looked like a picture. No one could guess the troubled life this child had experienced.

Nothing new for myself, of course; what mother has? My old clothes hung like unfinished fabric thrown atop a bent metal hanger. It was all right. Who was I trying to impress?

I'd brighten my face with blush and lip gloss and circle my neck with Grandmother's pearls. At least I'd pass for pictures. Mother often advised, "If you have nothing else, good pearls will make the day," nodding her head with finality.

Pearls were the mainstay of a southern lady. *Grits*, I thought and laughed; a code-word no one in the North understood. It stood for 'girls raised in the south', but meant so much more.

My nails were appalling. Torn cuticles, broken nail tips peeked from all ten fingers. Too late to do anything except brush a quick coat of clear polish and buff rough edges.

I'd bitten some at yesterday's brutal hearing. Thankfully, it was wrapped up in an hour. Relief, I'd gotten full custody of Timmy. My child support award lacked what was needed, as Don was granted custody of Jeremy. Once my part of child support was subtracted for Jeremy, the total fell short of meeting my basic expenses.

Mark assured me I could appeal. I refused. It was over. No more.

Don would not be a happy camper today. Yesterday, he'd angrily stormed from the courtroom because of his designated child support; no doubt because it wasn't tax-deductible.

I shook my head, amazed. My troubles were far from over, I knew that. They might just be beginning, but at least, for today, they were on hold for Christmas.

Preparations were long underway, when I arrived at St. Edmonds. <u>The Baltimore Sun</u> and <u>Baltimore Magazine</u> had already interviewed Mari. Photographers were still snapping pictures of house and table.

I gasped with the magnificence of that ten-foot tree, glazed from top to bottom with treasures from Mari's and Nana's collections. Sparkling lights flickered reflections in glass ornaments.

Packages peeked from beneath this tree, carded with Timmy's name. The girls had pitched in. *What would I have done without them this year?* I unpacked my Santa Claus packages for Timmy and mingled them among the others. Jules had hung bulging stockings from a nearby mantel. Timmy's Christmas would surpass his dreams.

I silently thanked God. "His name shall be called Immanuel. . .God with us." That was true.

I sadly recalled past Christmas's when Jeremy and I'd decorate a much smaller tree. I always wanted a small one so my boys could help hang ornaments. Cardboard cut-outs of *Sesame Street* characters, a big purple Barney, and Sponge-Bob jiggled on branch tips. Handmade knick-knacks, plastic candy canes and scotch plaid ribbon bows mingled the grouping. Popcorn chains were erratically woven among bric-a-brac. A rustic nativity scene nestled under that tree's canopy, resting on a red and white gingham tree skirt draping a stand; homey, rustic, and personal.

I gulped a tear.

Shaking my head to rid memories, I focused on this tree. I much preferred gazing at it, now; thinking it belonged in <u>Architectural Digest</u> or at least, <u>Southern Living</u>. No memories.

It was an 'exodus' tree for all of us: leaving the old with promise of new—new years, new Christmas's, new directions, new dreams.

Ruth

I'd arisen before dawn this morning. I'd awakened to hearing Mari scurrying around our first floor. *Had she slept, at all?* With her consultations this week and her anticipated interviews from <u>Baltimore Magazine</u> and <u>Baltimore Sun</u>, she looked frenzied but jubilant.

Yesterday, she welcomed a surprise delivery of flowers. The card read "Merry Christmas, from your friend, Officer Cook." We giggled as she read it, as we'd rarely seen Mari blush.

Mari was overjoyed with her mother's arrival. Sam, Jr. had joined Tyler on the airport trip to meet her yesterday. The first time Tyler had driven this distance alone. Yesterday, they'd stood taller, sobered with this adult responsibility.

I shared in her happiness, of course, but I realized how I missed my own mother, desperately. Perhaps Mom and Dad would surprise me with a phone call today.

My parents lived in a remote province of China, with the nearest phone miles away. They were unaware of my heartbreak. Should I bare my soul over the phone and dampen their Christmas?

No. I'd wait for another time.

I planned on entertaining Nana and Sam, Jr. upstairs, this morning. The excitement might create distress. Nana wandered aimlessly and anxiously these past weeks, with little knowledge of her whereabouts. It was best to keep her distracted with Sam, Jr., whom she adored. Sarah would serve breakfast in our upstairs playroom, while the three of us played simple games, and minimized confusion for the mistress of this house.

Commotion from downstairs invaded upstairs, of course, as our morning progressed. Unable to contain, I helped Nana bathe, spritzing her with *Arpege* perfume, her favorite. I fastened her new party dress, and she looked beautifully festive. I hoped she could enjoy today, somehow.

After readying Nana, I was faced with my own dilemma: I had precious little that was suitable for an elegant Christmas party. I remembered my amethyst pendant and matching earrings, my treasured wedding gift.

I teared a little.

My cream-colored knit dress would have to do. I winced remembering my weight gain since its last wearing. Time to retrieve that girdle, as Mother always called it. She recalled them as a huge improvement over laced corsets from her mother's era. Now they were called body shapers. A rose by any other name is still a rose, or in this case, a thorn by any other name is still a thorn.

Girdle, corset or body-shaper, they were still horribly uncomfortable. I hated it, but sadly, it was my only recourse. It would limit my eating. There was only so much room and no margin for expansion in that thing; so much for holiday comfort food.

Sam, Jr. had been darting downstairs, counting his packages, and being the official food tester in Lucille's and Sarah's kitchen. He announced he'd help clean by finding bowls he could lick.

I'd dressed him in an almost new Ralph Lauren sweater I'd found at a thrift shop. I coupled that with beautifully tailored plaid pants, looking as if they'd never been worn.

Adorable.

Countless lights sparkled. Sarah and Lucille completed final touches for food, and chords from Handel's "Messiah" sailed through our rooms. Pine scents mixed with cinnamon, nutmeg and ginger wafted through the expanse. The stage was set.

I smiled in my mirror, fluffed my hair, and replaced scuffs with black patent pumps.

Chapter 41

Storms On The New Year Horizon

Katie

"What time is it?" I rolled over. 2:00. Again. I grabbed my ringing phone quickly, not wanting to disturb Sarah or Timmy.

"Hello?" I croaked.

"Kate. If this legal process continues, you won't live to see the end." Click.

"What? Hello, Hello?"

My entire body trembled, causing my receiver to weigh heavily in my grasp. I huddled away from my bed.

"God, what can I do? How did he get this number?" I sobbed.

"I'm scared—for me and Timmy. Rebecca doesn't need this stress. PLEASE HELP ME" I shouted, not meaning to.

Sarah knocked and softly called.

"Katie, are you all right?"

I hugged my knees and cried.

"No, No I'm not all right."

Sarah embraced me.

"Sh, Sh. Tell me about your call."

Fear kept me from re-capturing sleep, but I tried to put his threats behind me. This had been one of several, awakening me in just days. I must make another plan. Plan B–or was it C or D—would have to come together on my morning commute, I guess.

I ventured to start my car a few minutes early, so its heater would vent warmer air than ice cold. A red thermometer gauge registered 22 degrees.

As I approached my car, I looked. Not believing, I looked again, squinting to focus.

"Dear God. . . what now?"

All tires were flat. Rubber curled from gashes like gaping surgical wounds.

Racing back through our house, I pounded Sarah's door.

"Someone slashed my tires." I yelled.

"Katie, call police."

"I guess I must. Can you drop Timmy at his sitter, please? I don't want him frightened."

I must keep Timmy safe. . . and now, that means being away from me.

"Of course, I'll do anything, you know that. Please move in with us at St. Edmonds. There's safety in numbers. He wouldn't dare do anything if we're around."

"That could place everyone in danger. I'd never forgive myself if anything happened to y' all. I've got to figure this out myself, somehow."

"We're a team, Katie. You're not alone, you know that."

Yes, we were a team, but I felt all alone in my fear now.

"I so wish I could get out of here."

"As in this house or Baltimore?"

"Baltimore."

Anywhere but Baltimore; I wanted to forget everything about my life here. I wished all past memories and future worries would just disappear.

"Where would you go?"

"Beats me."

Where could I go? I longed to 'fly away as on wings of an eagle'. That was a line from a Psalm I'd just read this morning. Boy, did those words ring true—more now than ever. It's amazing how its words could come to mind just when I needed them—just like my grandmother's words described: dynamic and new every morning.

"If you didn't know anyone, how safe would you be? You'd be like a lamb left to wolves. Besides that, legally, where could you go?"

"Just my dream; I have no money to leave. But some day, I'll be out of this insufferable place, once and for all."

"All right, get Timmy ready so we can take him. Promise me you'll call police."

"I intend to, along with canceling my work. I may call House of Ruth, too. They might be able to advise me. Maybe, I should even stay at their shelter for a while, to throw off the scent."

"That's an idea."

I placed Timmy in Rebecca's arms with his cookie, I locked and double-locked the door, hooked its chain, and made sure our security system was set.

I closed my eyes and repeated a Psalm I'd read during the night:

"Oh how I wish I had wings like a dove—then I would fly away to the quiet of the wilderness. . . How quickly I would escape—far away from this wild storm of hatred."

I dialed (919)-555-2555.

"Mommy, it's Katie."

"Rescue me because you are so faithful and good,
for I am poor and needy and my heart is full of pain."
Psalm 109:21-22 (Bible, TLB)

Chapter 42

Just Looking Around

Julia

Goodness, 9:30 already. I must speed up—too many things on my 'to do' list for a Saturday morning. I mumbled my litany: pick up stamps for thank-you notes and return gift disappointments; Dry cleaners *(I certainly hope they removed that egg-nog stain. Laughing splattered it onto my silk blouse. How embarrassing.)*

Doctor's office was next—for my annual flu shot. *Thankfully, the receptionist reassured a brief appointment.* Lastly, relax over lunch with Glory. *I'll concentrate on smelling those crab cakes—ymmm.*

Realizing another five minutes had passed with my staring into space, I disposed of my tepid coffee. I grabbed my coat, slid into boots and bolted my side door.

Yes. Spot out of my blouse. The doctor's parking lot overflowed. I'd grab a space near the post office. Two birds with one stone.

Parking on a neighboring side street, I checked there'd be enough room for the rear car to get out. I wanted no one to have an excuse to ding my baby. I soothingly wiped my hand along its back fender.

I fished in my pocketbook for change to feed the meter. I glanced at the building beside which I stood. I noticed a professional sign announcing: Don Ward, DDS.

Huh. Now I know where Katie's husband's office is. I'm glad I don't have to park here often.

Coughing mothers and runny-nosed children mingled in the small space within this medical facility: Flu season. *Why on earth did I make an appointment for today of all days, and expose myself to this?*

Finding no unclaimed seat, I waited near the front desk. A toddler hugged my calf, crying "Mama." Then, gazing way up and realizing he clutched the wrong leg, wailed, and, toddled to his mother's waiting arms. I smiled. He reminded me of Tad, so long ago.

I glanced out a window beside the desk, to pass time.

Hmmm, there's someone studying my car. It looks like Mari's Officer Cook. No, it couldn't be. I squinted.

Why is he in Cockeysville? I thought he was a Baltimore City officer. Odd. Perhaps I'm mistaken. I'd only seen him that Friday everyone was at Glory's house.

I looked again. *He disappeared into Ward's office. Dental appointment, I guess.*

"Julia," a nurse bellowed, impatiently. I pushed through the door behind her.

I sighed deeply, relieved by only a brief delay.

Glory

11:50. Where's Jules? It was certainly like her to be ten minutes late, but twenty minutes late, without calling?

Maybe it's this watch again; always needing new batteries. What was so wrong with the old fashioned kind, you just wound every day? One never knew when these batteries would quit. They were known to expire at inopportune times, necessitating fitting an unplanned errand at an inconvenient store, in your already packed day.

I recalled the last time I needed one. I'd visited any number of stores, each justifying their particular reason for not carrying my particular watch's battery. I have no recollection which store finally had the fit. I'd no doubt have to re-address that entire group, and hear all manner of explanations. Perhaps they were right—it might be cheaper to just purchase a new watch. Some kind of racket to sell more watches, I suspected. I was not born yesterday.

Surely, she'd be here soon. She did mention errands this morning. This was holiday season, after all. Traffic and long lines were part and parcel of the holidays. I, of all people, could relate to waiting in unmoving lines and snarled traffic.

I flicked my watch with my finger. *Nothing*. I'd try banging it with that knife next.

To pass time, I'd browse through that orphaned newspaper, a few feet away. I burrowed through my pocketbook for glasses. I kept two pairs. The stronger was needed for this tiny print. *Why don't newspaper publishers use letters people can read?* If print were larger and maybe bolder, there'd be a larger subscription base. If people couldn't distinguish words, why would they buy a paper? Definitely worth a letter to the editor.

Why am I concerned? I don't order that paper anyway, I remembered. *Oh, well.*

I paged through after-Christmas sale ads, onto their Society section. I studied displayed pictures, among more ads—Hutzler's and Stewart's—50% off sale. *Must visit this week*, I made a mental note.

Of all things, I gasped. Colored photos featured my house on St. Edmonds, aglow with all its exterior and interior lights: magnificent.

Oh, and look. There we are, at our table. There's the roast, flanked by a companion vegetarian entrée—displaying Sarah's winning contest entry, no doubt.

Oh, pleeze. Horrendous picture; I look like I'm posing for a mug shot taken for a criminal file. No, DMV photos were always the worst. More like that.

I must have this paper. I'd request it from the maitre'd, if no one claims it. The girls must see these—such fun. I giggled.

I paged further, past legal announcements, and ads for estate auctions. Uh-oh, Ruth's husband's image was showcased in its Religion section. Apparently, he granted an interview, informing press of accepting a clergy position with the newly formed Intra-Urban Church.

"The San Francisco parish is one of the largest in this denomination." he informed. When queried about its beliefs, he answered, "We minister to the urban community. We welcome all, but concentrate on unique needs of the culturally and sexually diverse." When questioned further, he said, "Most of our membership represents the Gay and Lesbian communities, of which I am proud to be an active part, having publicly 'come out' in recent months."

The reporter pointedly asked about his former church and his wife and son. He abruptly countered, "No Comment", on advice of his lawyer.

I must call George. Sam had a job.

"Dental implants" in bold print, advertised Katie's husband's practice. His toothy smile and smoothly combed dark hair portrayed a con-artist, if I ever saw one.

"Dentistry for Cowards."

Right. He should certainly know something about cowardice; well said.

Oh, there's Sarah, trying to balance an enormous replica of a $10,000 check. The by-lines quoted: "This check will go toward my daughter's needs."

This prize money would barely cover Rebecca's program's initial six weeks—nothing more. It was a beginning, and certainly a huge help.

Paging again, "There's Mari. Oh, she looks lovely, posing in our hallway, pretending to arrange lights on greenery. This was well-needed publicity for much-needed business. Tyler's school expenses and college application fees were compounding.

"Glory."

Finally, Jules arrived. "Sorry I'm late, Glory. Errands. Let's order. I'm starved."

I leaned back. "OK, how about our usual oyster stew? It's still an "R" month. I don't know about their specials." I signaled to our same waiter from last time.

"Broiled cod with lemon sauce, and broiled salmon with mustard sauce—both are served with julienne vegetables and rice." he recited.

Jules added, "Both—with Earl Grey. Don't forget Earl Grey."

The waiter disappeared.

"Jules, wasn't Christmas ma-vel-us!" I overexaggerated my words in hopes of getting a rise. I do hope you had fun. Bill was so glad to finally meet my life-long, best friend."

"Oh, Glory, he's a wonderful man. I couldn't have chosen a better match for you, if I'd discovered him myself. Of course, if I'd discovered him myself, I'd kept him for myself."

She giggled.

"I don't know about that, Jules. Paws off, he found me."

She laughed. "He sure did, and don't let anything come between you. He's so much more than Charles ever was. I'm sure you realize that, after your courtroom scene."

"Speaking of which, I didn't tell you: Katie did all right at her Christmas Eve hearing.

Jules leaned forward, eager with the enticement of news.

"Don wasn't interested in scheduled visitation. It tied him down, he said. He didn't challenge her having freedom to visit North Carolina, either. He wanted to appear generous, I suppose. That's the good news."

"Uh-oh, I sense there's another shoe to drop." Jules eyes narrowed, expecting the worst.

'He's so angry; he's begun to harass her with middle-of-the-night phone calls. She put blocks on his numbers through the phone company. Seven is their limit. He went so far as to put one extra line beyond what could be blocked, so he could continue to get through.

"You mean he has EIGHT phone lines now?" she repeated incredulous with his extreme strategy.

"You got it. Of course, they're all listed as business lines."

"Of course."

The man's actions were bizarre by any standard—even in view of a tax deduction.

"News from a tenant, from one of their rental properties, warned Katie of an episode last week. Apparently, Don ordered one of his staff members to break into her home, thinking Katie was there. He will stop at nothing."

"Unreal."

"You've got that right. On a happier note, Timmy had a wonderful Christmas. Santa's stocking you filled was a hit. Didn't you love Pierre's electric train set-up?"

"Wasn't that fun? Pierre was full of himself, with tux and tails. He especially enjoyed dancing around in front of those cameras. Hilarious." Julia grinned.

"Oh, by the way, look at this section of the Sunday paper. You've got to see this."

Julia lifted her glasses to her nose, which now hung on a hot pink rope, of sorts. Hot pink, she declared, was her signature color.

I had to admit, it was a striking accent with her dark hair and eyes. It made wearing glasses around her neck less frumpy, she'd explained. So Jules-like.

Seeing Sam's picture, she raised one eyebrow and tightened her lips.

"Does he think he's fooling God? I'd think even he would see the hypocrisy of leaving his wife and son, his church, and taking another pastorate. On top of which, it's nearly 3000 miles away from a wife and son, to whom he's legally committed, and who need his support to exist. Well, culturally diverse, or not, I would not support a church with a minister who came with that kind of curriculum vitae."

"Go, Jules." I thrust my fist in the air.

"Now, what else?"

"Look: an ad for Katie's husband's practice."

Julia's eyebrow lifted again. "Cowards, huh? Well. Speaking of which, Glory, I parked beside her husband's office this morning. I'd never known exactly where in Cockeysville it was located. Now I'll know to stay away."

I shrugged and zeroed back to the newspaper. "Now, for happier news, keep turning. There."

Julia slowly studied pictures, clearly enjoying each one.

"Our Christmas party: what fun. Oh, look at me. I look enormous. . . and my hair. . Glory, how could you have let me be photographed that way?" Julia looked aghast.

"Oh, Jules, you look wonderful, but if you really want a laugh, look at me," I giggled and said.

A smile crept across her face, and she stifled a laugh.

"Told you, didn't I?"

"Well, these pictures should give Mari some healthy publicity, and Sarah, too. I wonder where that will take her?" Julia continued studying details of her photo.

"I don't think she's thought beyond bills." I responded.

She'd just shown me the huge pile she's collected, with more coming each day.

She nodded. "Rebecca certainly looked better than she did in October."

"Obviously, she's not completely well yet, but she's recovering. That wig was beautiful, wasn't it?" I confirmed

"That was a wig?"

Jules was shocked. It appeared so natural. If Sarah had not told me differently, I wouldn't have known, either. The color and style looked anything but artificial. Amazing what can be done these days and worth every penny of what must have been quite costly.

"Her anorexia caused her hair to fall out. This wig is to help her recovery." I added.

"I'd think so. You know how self-conscious teen-age girls are about their hair and appearance."

"How I remember. What happened to us?" I giggled.

"Too many things to keep up with, besides we wouldn't be able to see ourselves without our glasses, remember?" Jules laughed and leaned back in her chair.

She continued, "Are you ready to start a new year?"

"A lot's going on; class starts next week. Mari and Sarah have prepared her house for a final showing. They're hoping for a quick sale."

Maybe a quick sale would relieve Sarah's money worries. Certainly, a sale would help Mari's finances, too—in addition to building her confidence as a Realtor: two for one, there.

Jules added, "Oh, by the way, I forgot to tell you: funding for D.H. college education options may be available as soon as this coming semester. Apparently, our private donor left a trust fund."

"Fantastic. The girls will be thrilled. Ruth's also spoken to me about testing Rebecca. She's incredibly bright, and although short of credits to graduate, Ruth's wondering about possible dual-enrollment at college. Maybe she could start with a course or two, while attending with her mother."

Julia traced her finger around the tea cup, considering my words.

"I don't know. I've heard about other colleges taking dual-enrollment students. Perhaps since she's Sarah's daughter, she'd be eligible for aid. I'll have to look into that."

Julia purposely answered Glory with little emotion. She didn't want to raise anyone's hopes. This was not her decision and Glory knew her limitations. This would have to be brought before the board, and approved by who knows what committee. This type of option spelled long-term in every way. Realistically, a decision might be considered, but doubtfully in time for Rebecca's case.

Well, she'd pray. God was in control of the impossible, no one else. *I've survived day to day remembering past miracles which seemed totally inconceivable. Recalling these marvels gives hope.*

Jules snatched a slip of paper from her pocket and scribbled some notes.

Julia interrupted her writing, looked up and said, "Glory, while I was at my doctor's office getting a flu shot, I think I noticed Officer Cook examining my car. Odd."

"Really?"

That was interesting. I'd never seen him, myself. I'd only heard about him from Mari. Apparently Jules had run into him guarding my house one Friday evening we'd all gotten together.

"Other than the fact that he was looking closely at my car, I don't know why I even noticed—except this time he wore a Baltimore City police uniform. Why would he be in Baltimore County, when his uniform indicated he was working? What do I know, though? He could live in Cockeysville, for that matter." Julia answered, with a pensive pause.

"Are you sure it was him? Why was he looking at your car?" I asked.

Julia shrugged. "I'm not even sure it was him. Afterwards, he disappeared into Ward's office; dental appointment, perhaps.

"Huh. Did you see those flowers he sent Mari at Christmas? I think he's interested, what do you think?" I giggled.

"Absolutely . . . and another thing, Glory?" Julia said.

"What?"

"Have you forgotten? My birthday's next week. I'm looking forward to a spa day."

"How could I forget? The sooner, the better."

Chapter 43

Late Breaking News

Monday evening

Glory

"Hi, Glory."

"Jules, are you still awake?" I yawned.

"Everything OK with you and the girls?" Julia started, nonchalantly.

"Same, but, as you know, things could change at any time."

She laughed, "Glory, your melancholy is showing again. Don't create worries, please."

I yawned again, not trying to hide it, and added. "It's realistic, don't you think?"

"Yes, but look at the miracles."

"You're right, of course, but, Jules, I know you didn't call at this hour to chit-chat."

"Well, there is something else. . ."

"Let's have it."

I sat up to better concentrate. I knew Jules. I might agree to one of her fast ones, if I wasn't careful, and alert.

"It's time you met our mystery girl. She's not thrilled about it, but I've done as much as I can. She's yours, now. When would be convenient to meet? I'll see she's there."

"Why do I feel ominous about this, Jules?"

I couldn't control my frown.

"Your concern about this one is not just your worry-wart tendencies. This isn't easy or happy. She must see you—the sooner, the better."

If Glory only knew what this troubled woman had told me; well, she would, soon enough. Her confession would not be welcome–no, not at all. It had to be done and done quickly, for sure.

"I'm free Wednesday. Name a time." I answered, too fatigued to fully consider added significance.

"4:30, my office. It's sound proof, and at that time of day, an interruption is unlikely."

"What can you tell me before going into this?"

I expected some humor from Jules. Her grave tone sobered me. I rose from my bed and headed to my front window—my favorite nighttime thinking spot.

"Make sure you're 'prayed up'."

"What?" I laughed, but not to express humor. Discomfort was more like it. Jules was not teasing.

"Pray more than ever, Glory." Julia whispered.

"Jules, you're making me nervous."

"No, you're making you nervous. Just view it as an ordinary counseling appointment. Call me afterwards. In fact, come to my house for Earl Grey and dinner." Jules added, trying to sound upbeat.

"I guess." I answered, hearing my voice quaver.

Fully awake now and I was feeling less and less tranquil.

What could be so vital about this meeting? What did it have to do with me?

Wednesday

"Why am I so anxious?" I scolded.

I dreaded this meeting. Not only was this woman an enigma, Jules was behaving mysteriously, as well. Of course, this woman's privacy must be protected. I understood that.

Jules had never kept important details from me. *Or had she?* Even best friends erected shields, not to be secretive, but for protection. At least until they felt safe enough to share, or considered how sharing information could affect future outcomes; ripples on a pond.

Promptly, at 4:28, I walked the shadowy hallway devoid of voices or office noises. Up ahead, light from Jules's florescent fixture sliced a wedge out of darkness.

I quietly measured my steps. *Why? I didn't know.* To avoid upsetting this person, I guess; like approaching a stray cat—slowly, to decrease fear and establish trust. *Why was that so important?* I remained frowning.

I've counseled hundreds of women as a social worker. *Why am I sensing this is different?* I peered through her office window.

Jules's desk was piled with paper stacks. I smiled. Jules's system of organization was unique—overwhelming to me, but she knew where every scrap of paper was. No one dare touch it, or else.

I smiled, picturing Jules with her pointy finger warning some well-meaning soul, who only wanted to help straighten.

Mystery woman sat, fidgeting with brown scarf fringe, which covered her chin and mouth. A knit cap enveloped her head, hair and ears. Huge sunglasses covered whatever was left. I thought of Afghanistan women covering their faces with burqas.

Why did she need cover? The temperature was at least 70 degrees. She must be broiling. I almost laughed.

All right, here goes. I knocked gently to warn her of my entering. She jerked, and lowered her head, avoiding my eyes.

"Hello." I greeted cheerfully, as I headed behind Jules's desk.

"Can I offer you coffee? I know Julia keeps plenty. I can't vouch for its quality, but—"

I shrugged with a half-hearted smile, trying to break tension with a feeble attempt at humor.

She remained unyielding.

I waited. Nothing.

I glanced at a clock. Minutes passed. I was becoming impatient. *Let's get on with this, already,* I felt like saying, but didn't. I drummed my fingers on the paper-covered surface.

Suddenly, the woman ripped off her cap, unwrapped her heavy scarf, and shaking her hair, dropped her sunglasses.

"Karen," I said, dumb-founded. "What's this about? Why the get-up?"

She'd been my neighbor when I was married. We'd interacted more times than I could count—community and church events, fund raisers, and neighborhood get-togethers. I recalled her personality as distant and cold; she'd acted strangely toward me then, but I'd chalked it up to my imagination.

As if gathering courage, she straightened her back, and stared directly into my eyes. No words, though.

I leaned toward her. "Are you in some kind of trouble or something?" I asked guardedly.

She spoke flatly; softly, at first, and then increased volume.

"Gloria, I need to ask for your forgiveness."

Her lips lifted in contempt, after emptying her words.

Karen questioned herself, why she'd ever agreed to this. Julia had persuaded her it was the right thing to do. She'd convinced her that getting it off her chest was what was needed. Now that she was here, she felt like she was strapped in an electric chair, awaiting execution. She could feel sweat slide down the middle of my back and coast between her breasts.

"Whatever for?"

I was dumbfounded. We'd never had any relationship—certainly none to merit forgiveness—or anything at all. Never friends; passing acquaintances—no more, no less—and it'd been years since that, even.

"I may as well just say it. My affair with your husband ended your marriage. I also helped devise dirty legal tricks used against you. It was mean, I know. Looking back, I don't know how I could've allowed myself to be a part of any of it." Karen confessed, without emotion—something like reading unrehearsed words.

My jaw dropped. I heard my own sharp intake of breath.

"You're probably wondering why I'm confessing this now. Well, Charles and I are no longer together, but I can't rest." She spoke with head down, fingering fringe again.

It was out now, finally; done. Perhaps she could leave soon, Karen hoped, still wondering how she could have been talked into doing this.

I was stunned. My blood seemed to stop flowing, as if frozen in its course. I gripped my chair arms to steady my trembling hands. Time suddenly stood still.

Floodgates of my worst locked memories suddenly burst, resurrecting my horror video. I wanted to push delete, or at least stop or pause buttons. The betrayal, the rejection from family and friends, unfounded condemnation contributing to loss of my reputation, and my total helplessness; it all began with this woman and her lies.

Karen rose to leave.

I raised my palm. I tried to swallow against my constricting throat. I squeaked a "No, wait."

She tentatively backed into her chair; eyes wide, like a guilty child facing a severe teacher—with nowhere to run or hide.

I started, "Do you have any idea. . ."

I stopped. A frightening surge of adrenaline exploded somewhere behind my eyes, kidnapping body parts as it coursed downward: rage.

I shook my head forcefully, hoping to turn back an onslaught of emotions, to which I desperately wanted to yield. Conversely, I willed to find a tiny shred of rationality, to grasp and hold onto—tightly. My thinking mind was fallout now.

"God, save me from me. . . I can't do this," I demanded, silently, clenching my teeth. It was not a prayer, but a desperate plea.

Silence. I felt extremes of chills and heat, alternating from one to the other.

I could not face her. I turned my wheeled chair to stare—*at what? What was I hoping to find? Anything to divert; it didn't matter what.*

I enunciated, "Did you spread those false rumors around our neighborhood, and our church?"

I heard a firm yes.

I squeezed my eyes. My anger was blinding.

"Do you have any idea of the pain my son and I've suffered because of your insensitivity and your lies?" I blurted out.

She hesitated, and spoke, still with little emotion. "I'm beginning to, I think, but I guess I'll never know." She twirled a piece of hair.

"Can you just tell me why you thought what you did was justifiable? I just need to try to understand your motivation in this sordid thing."

Karen was hoping her confession was all that would be required. She hadn't banked on giving a reason. *What reason? She'd have to dig deep.* Somehow reasons never affected decisions she'd made over the years. Her decisions were made from love for a man—or maybe lust was more like it. *Once bound, intimately, then it was probably loyalty, she guessed.* Then, once she was trapped in an unimaginable situation, she guessed it was fear of what would happen if she didn't go through with. . . whatever. *Everything seemed to be controlled by some man.* It was irrational, she knew, but once she'd gotten involved, it seemed impossible to turn around.

How had she allowed herself to be persuaded to be honest today—with Gloria and suddenly with herself? She felt slight twinges of shame, but she couldn't go there. She must justify her actions and avoid incrimination.

"I used to see you at church and around town. You always looked so beautiful. You seemed so happy. I looked at your husband, who seemed so much more handsome than mine, and his being a lawyer seemed so important, somehow. The more I compared my husband, and considered my disappointment from my unfulfilled dreams, the more I fantasized about having yours for myself. Married to your husband seemed like a dream come true." She hissed and narrowed her eyes. Her lips curled with disgust.

She'd always hated the fact that this woman, sitting across from her, had her life so easy.

"Ha." I interjected with bitter sarcasm, unable to control my outburst.

Hardly a professional response I quickly added. "Go on."

"I didn't start out planning to do any of it. I'd run into your husband at neighborhood events, and we'd talked; flirted, really. We sometimes saw each other around town, and exchanged pleasantries. I fantasized he could be mine, dreaming my life could be happy, like yours. Of course, now I know differently."

Her tone was loud and accusing now. I observed her staring off in space with her recollection, as if watching a memorized scene from a too often-watched movie.

"Really? What pray tell, have you figured out?" My pointed words shot like poison darts.

Karen's eyebrows lifted as she considered her words. She traced grooves in the wooden chair arms as she started to speak. The question was one she hadn't considered until now.

"Well, now that we are, or were married, I realize what a miserable existence you had. His drinking is out-of-control, and his violent temper. . . Well, you of all people know about that." Her hissing had been replaced with a more contemplative tone.

I didn't respond.

"As a lawyer, he's arranged things so I have nothing after our divorce. No point in even trying to fight against his good 'ole boy network. If I get out of this with my life and a nickel, I'll be lucky." Karen spoke to air, as if I wasn't there; her tone, caustic.

At least she's feeling pain, now; feeling justified at hearing Karen's words.

It was all too much, though. I felt stabbed multiple times, and was now being left to die. Even that scenario would be less painful than what I endured now. I dared not speak.

I tried to think. *If this were an unknown client with someone else's story, how would I handle it?* I must pretend; step outside this emotional tornado in which I'm spinning. But, no, I could not put myself in another position to even try to understand.

I hesitated a long time, trying desperately to gain control.

All right, had I lived a perfect life? Hardly; *that was a fact on which I could build a frame of reference.*

Arising in my mind, like a sunrise, gradually focusing on a dark horizon was a forgotten picture of six-year-old Gloria, shopping with Mother. Tired, and hungry, I wanted to go home. She'd been impatient with my complaints. Ignoring me, she continued looking through clothes. As I sat, bored, under a circular rack, I noticed a bowl of candy on a nearby counter. It was probably for customers to sample, recalling now, but at the time, I didn't know that. I suddenly wanted that candy. I had to have that candy.

My pressing desire replaced my longing to leave. If I had just one piece, I'd feel so much better. I knew it was wrong. It wasn't mine. I just had to have that candy, though.

When no one was looking, I saw my chance to take a piece. At first, I was ecstatic. I had what I'd longed for. I got what I wanted—and needed.

That night, my conscience plagued me. The memory replay made me nauseous. The peppermint had not even tasted good. I'd always preferred chocolate over mints. I threw up in my bathroom.

Lucille, having been alarmed with my heaving, asked if something I'd eaten had upset me. I cried "yes", confessing the miserable thing; sobbing with uncontrollable spasms.

How had she responded?

I tapped a pencil lightly on the desk. I'd been holding it so tightly just seconds ago, it'd almost snapped in half. *I replayed my memory. She'd encouraged me to tell God I was sorry.*

As I obeyed, I felt freed. God removed my gut-wrenching guilt. Lucille reassured me that God forgets all about transgressions, when we ask Him to forgive us and ask Him to show us a new way—a better way.

She promised never to speak of it. Her mercy was the best gift she could've given me—the best gift God could give me; anyone could give anyone.

I released my breath slowly. My thundering heart slowed. I felt my skin cooling. *The question was, am I, anyone?*

That episode in my young life had taught me invaluable lessons. In fact, grace may have changed the direction of my life. Would mercy change this woman's life?

I spun my chair further around. An embroidered copy of The Lord's Prayer hung on the back wall. It read: "Forgive us our trespasses as we forgive those who trespass against us" stood out boldly.

I closed my eyes. My heart thundered again.

But this woman hurt me—terribly. She'd stolen my husband, and destroyed my reputation.. . .my hopes. . . my dreams. I hated what she'd done to me.

I was now vacillating between two difficult options: clemency or retaliation.

If I kept replaying this, again and again, yielding to hate, would I be hurting her or myself? A valid question: who would actually hurt?

She'd asked for forgiveness.

Had I ever been forgiven? That answer, of course, was yes. Had I deserved it?

That answer, of course, was no.

I slowly turned to face this woman, who looked as if she would bolt any second.

In my imagination over past years, I would've loved seeing her suffer. In some sick way, I wanted her to. I wanted to see her squirm and hurt and feel pain like I had.

But there was no pleasure in it. Not now.

This realization surprised me. I took a deep breath, or maybe a couple.

I leaned forward and picked up Julia's metal stress balls, designed to diminish stress if rolled between fingers, I presumed. I tried to twirl them around, and, confounded, finally, set them aside. I couldn't make them work

I remember their being advertised in a high-end catalog. *How could Jules have spent her hard-earned money on these things? Perhaps she knew something I didn't.*

I was suddenly aware of the ticking of a clock, completely unnoticed seconds ago.

I looked back at Karen and decided to speak. I wasn't ready to say anything—especially anything good. I'd have to trust God to do this through me.

"I want to thank you for the truth, risking my anger and not knowing how I'd respond. It took courage. I can't say it makes me happy, but you knew that when you came. In reference to your request for forgiveness, I do—not because I want to but because I need to. I can't say I excuse your actions or your reasons," I licked my lips before finishing, "but I'm willing to give it up."

I swung my chair around slowly, and pointed to embroidered linen.

She looked up, colored, and looked away again, pushing some hair behind her ear.

"Thank you for disclosing this unknown piece of the puzzle, so I can find closure. This whole episode needs to be put behind us, for good—never to be brought up again. For me as well as for you, OK?"

She bounded from the room. She did not look back, nor acknowledge a good-bye.

It didn't matter. Enough: enough for tonight, and enough for a lifetime.

I glanced at Jules's clock. 6:30. I could not leave yet. My legs wouldn't hold me. I lay my head on the desk, still trembling, uncontrollably; like I'd experienced with a near-miss of a car accident. A tear fell onto Jules's papers.

I heard a gentle knock. I closed my eyes. *Please, no more with this woman. I'm spent. God, please, I can't bear anymore.*

A blurred Julia opened the door.

"I knew you'd be tired so I decided to bring dinner to you: Chinese, with Earl Grey."

"Earl Grey," I weakly mouthed.

"Forgiveness does not change the past but it does enlarge the future."
Paul Boese

Chapter 44

Open Door, Again

Saturday

The alarm buzzed. I lay there, letting it ring out, not wanting to relinquish my warm covers just yet. Purrfect, alarmed because the buzz continued, delicately stepped onto my chest and mewed in a cat dialect she'd once used with kittens. I smiled, keeping my eyes shut.

Realizing the nice approach was failing to arouse her mistress, Purrfect began to use more persuasive methods. First, she dragged her Persian plume tail across my face. Getting no results, she resorted to kneading my head—claws out, no less.

"OK, OK." I yelled. To which she responded by tearing down stairs, assuming I'd follow her for *Gourmet Kitty*.

I stretched, pleased it was Saturday. Jules and I were celebrating her birthday at the spa. When I reserved our day, I reminded Sylvia about Julia's birthday.

Sylvia answered, "Yes-s-s, I think we can handle that. 10:00, and leave details to us."

"Got it" I answered, and surrendered the plan to experts.

After this emotionally churning week, I could use a day of rest and pampering. Goodness, I never want to go through another week like this, thank you very much.

Wednesday's meeting took the starch out of me, as Lucille used to say. I was still limp, taking that analogy a bit further. Maybe a little wrinkled, too, as I passed by my mirror on the dresser. I laughed a little. "Hung up to dry and taken down wet," or however that saying goes.

I can't forget to bring Jules's gift. It would not do to be late with a birthday gift. Wednesday afternoon had been a gift from Jules to me. As disconcerting an experience as it had been, Jules knew unless I faced Karen's confession, I could not finish healing.

I'd dealt with the on-going need for forgiveness for my husband, although he'd never apologized—ever. I had to give it to her. At least, Karen had some character—enough to apologize, anyway; a little late, but not too late. Now with final pieces of that puzzle, I could put it to rest.

Seeing my husband in the courtroom made me realize our divorce had been a kind of deliverance for me; although, I hadn't viewed it as such, at that time. He was surely no prize. I wouldn't have had the last fifteen years and met Bill, if I'd remained in that same place. I needed to thank God—even for my pain, and maybe especially.

Turning the faucet of my steaming shower, I started to sing a song I'd heard on our vacation, "I will survive. Hey, hey. . ."

Sylvia and Pierre welcomed me, eager to display photo albums compiled for us. Each page showcased pictures from Christmas and Thanksgiving. Sylvia had used her trusted Kodak instamatic for spontaneous shots of guests.

No one was excluded. Clippings from <u>Baltimore Sun</u> and <u>Baltimore Magazine</u> covering dinner, decorations, and interviews with Mari and Sarah were featured, as well.

"Just wonderful, and so artistically arranged and assembled, too," I exclaimed.

Pierre grinned, and bowed.

Sylvia said, "We wanted you to have them as a thank you for making our holidays so special." She encircled her arm around Pierre, "We hope you'll include us again, if you wouldn't mind."

I hugged them.

Before now, I could not have conceived of my hugging Sylvia in my wildest dreams.

"You're family now. I can't imagine a celebration without you."

Jules sounded the front door buzzer. "Hi," she called, breathless.

"Happy Birthday," we sang, accompanied by Pierre's touting a party horn.

Pierre announced, "Now, ladies, if you will come with me, your spa day awaits."

We followed him through 'The Door.'

I glanced around and noticed questioning glances from other customers as to where we were being taken. I laughed.

Let them have fun imagining what lies beyond.

Chapter 45

Police Alert

Katie

My conversation with Mom, after my tire-slashing discovery, hadn't been nearly as comforting as I'd hoped. Of course, there was nothing she could do about tires or anything else, from North Carolina. *What did I expect?*

I just needed to share my fears with someone who loved me—my mother.

All my disclosure created was confusion for her and more helplessness for me. No one on earth could understand my anxiety but God, of course. I should know, by now, we're essentially alone when it comes to our feelings, in this life. Only God can truly comfort and understand.

Mom was shocked, of course, when I first told her of fearing for my life at Thanksgiving. In fact, she and Daddy thought I'd invented it, at first. After all, Don had been such a nice young man. He was mannerly. He had the means to provide well for her and their boys.

I think they wondered about my sanity.

It was no wonder with the way I looked. I appeared a poorly groomed skeleton—for all intents and purposes, sick. Unfortunately, Don had more than hinted at my not being rational, months before. He'd called them on a regular basis, unbeknownst to me, of course. He'd describe my not acting right: just enough to hint of possible instability— to increase his credibility and decrease mine.

I was never aware of his behind-the-scenes set up. It turned out he'd also called my pastor, our pediatrician, my physician, my ob-gyn, the garbage man and telephone repairman, and notified neighbors at a cocktail party and Jeremy's school, (and who knows who else); anyone in our community to spread news of my unwell state. He could be so convincing, and, of course, being a doctor added to his statements' credibility.

Since I left, those words have also been coupled with my shacking up with a younger man. That only makes me look even more unbalanced; it certainly sheds doubt as to my being a moral and faithful wife—his intent.

Why would he even think of saying that? I'd never lie about anyone, especially someone I loved.

I've given up even trying to figure it out. Plenty of other women in the shelter and in displaced homemakers shared similar experiences. Mine was not unique or isolated.

I learned from my time in counseling, breaking support networks of family and friends, was part of the modus operandi of controllers and abusers. Diminishing credibility and removing all opportunities for a woman's escape, while elevating their own prominence was how most of these men kept control.

In other words: bullying. Having been small, I never knew quite how to deal with bullies, but stay clear of them. Somehow, I'd run so far from them, I'd caught and married one.

Weren't there signs I should've picked up when we dated? I shook my head, wondering, myself, about my own judgment.

I let out a breath.

Now it has sequelled into stalking and slashing tires: another attempt to frighten me into returning or at least giving up. It was working—being frightened, that is.

What could be next on his agenda? Would he go so far as to kill me or take Timmy, (which would hurt me more than death)? I didn't want to guess.

He had money and was part of a network of powerful people. He could arrange to do whatever he wanted, without personally being involved. That was scary. I didn't know who could be my enemy. Lately, I'd become suspicious of everyone, even those I knew were innocent of malfeasance.

I sat, studying my phone. I still had to cancel work, call House of Ruth, and report my loss.

"Police," a male voice sounded from the back door.

I hadn't even called the police yet. *What could they want?*

I rose from my cross-legged position I'd crouched in while on the phone.

"Just a minute, please. I'm coming." I called out.

I opened the door a crack, and purposely left the chain across its opening. One could not be too careful.

"It's Officer Cook, Ms. Ward."

Peering out, I see it is Officer Cook— the one who'd been so kind to Mari after her attack. He was someone I could trust. I almost whooped with joy. According to Mari, he watched Glory's house continually until her attacker was returned to jail. He helped keep her safe.

I withdrew the chain and grinned, "Yes, Officer Cook. Thank you for coming. Won't you come in?" I said, graciously.

He smiled that alluring smile Mari had told me about. I had to agree, he was charming. I recalled someone named Albert Camus describing charm as "a way of getting the answer yes without asking any clear question."

Yes, Officer Cook exuded *charm*.

"I heard about a trespasser on your property. I wanted to investigate about your tires being slashed. Of course, I wanted to make sure you were all right, primarily."

I was glad he'd come, certainly. *How did he know to come, though?*

"I do appreciate your attention, but I have to ask: how did you know about my tires? I haven't had time to report the incident yet."

He blushed slightly, glanced down in a boyish way, and paused, as if trying to frame his response.

"I spoke with Mari." he stammered.

I smiled, noting his shyness when talking about Mari. *He was smitten, all right.*

"How did Mari know? The only person I called this morning was my mother." I added, puzzled by his information.

He shrugged.

Of course, Sarah must have called Mari once she arrived at St. Edmonds this morning. That would make sense. News of any concern spread through our phone lines quickly.

Something in back of my mind was gnawing at me. Something did not make sense. It was early morning, though. I'd had a shock.

Officer Cook rose quickly from the kitchen chair, "I must go. I only wanted to make sure you were all right. I also wanted to assure you I will personally watch your house until this perpetrator is found. You don't need to worry about anything. I will keep you safe."

He patted my shoulder reassuringly, and closed the kitchen door behind him.

I reconfigured our security system and checked locks once more. Hearing a car motor, I glanced out a back window to see his unmarked car back out of our driveway.

I expected a police car. But then I do remember Mari's saying he was a plain clothes policeman.

I never used to notice cars. There was a time I cared nothing about police cars or anything else relating to crime. Now my eyes seem attuned to all kinds of details.

Certainly I have more important things to think of besides that; condemning my ability to be so easily distracted, especially when I had more important details to consider.

It did remind me: I must call police and report my tires. It must be Baltimore County, not Baltimore City. This differentiation could be important. I must have an exact written report to submit to my insurance company for damage claim reimbursement. I knew that much. I couldn't spare an expense of new tires, without assurance of reimbursement.

I'd call now.

I waited nearly an hour for Baltimore County patrolmen to come. It was hard to busy myself in the meantime. I'd cancelled work. I'd called House of Ruth.

I decided to fold clothes and pack. That was far more productive than pacing, for sure.

Although I knew I could trust Officer Cook's surveillance, I couldn't be a prisoner in this house. I'd need to stay elsewhere for at least a week, to throw off any scent. Don was somehow behind all this. At least on Office Cook's watch, Sarah would be safe from intruders, while Timmy and I returned to the shelter, once more.

"Police," came from the front door this time.

Why had Officer Cook come to our back door?

It was partially covered by bushes. One had to go out of their way to even find it. He had been looking for my car, certainly. The important thing now is he's watching our house to keep us safe.

I opened the front door, keeping the chain across the opening as I had at the back door.

Two uniformed officers stood, unsmiling and stern.

"Mrs. Ward, you called concerning an incident involving your car's tires being slashed?"

"Yes, sir, please come in."

I led them to our sitting area, picking up newspapers and laundry as I walked. I'm embarrassed by our clutter. Sarah and I did not entertain at this hour of the morning. In fact, we didn't have visitors at all. Neither of us had time to keep house as we should—not even on our list of priorities, I can tell you that.

"Please describe the situation as it occurred." Officer Shapiro said.

I told of my harassing phone call in the middle of last night. I estimated the time I ventured out to start my car heater. I gave a detailed account of what I'd discovered and how all four tires looked.

I was breathing short breaths, as I'd been aware of doing all morning. I was on the verge of hyperventilating, just recalling my experience, I feared.

"Did you see anyone before you walked to your vehicle?" the other officer asked.

"No sit. It was before sunrise, so it was dark. I wouldn't have been able to distinguish anyone. I park my car in a space under trees, out back. I've assumed it's safer and less visible to on-lookers back there."

"Does anyone else know about this parking area?" Shapiro asked, while writing my last response.

"Not that I know of . . . that's why I use it. I currently have a protective order against my estranged husband. Sarah, the owner of this house, assured me this out-of-the-way spot is less obvious than on-street parking."

They nodded, each recording words as I spoke.

"And your estranged husband's name is?"

"Don Ward. Dr. Donald Ward. He's a dentist."

"Have you seen anyone wandering around back there in past weeks? Persons you have not recognized? Has there been any unusual activity around the back of this house?"

"Sir, when I leave for work in the morning and return at night, it's quite dark. Most days, I'm not here when it's daylight. With shadows from those evergreens, I don't think I'd see anyone if I'd looked. Given traffic sounds, I wouldn't notice noises either."

"May we have your permission to look around outside?"

They each rose from the sofa, simultaneously.

"Of course," I added, trying to be cooperative.

The officers exited the front door as they'd come in. They seemed to spend a long time looking around my car and its graveled space before knocking on our front door again.

"Did you find anything?" I asked, re-opening the door.

"We'd like to ask a few more questions, if that's all right."

"Certainly," I replied, trying to be helpful.

I'd told them all I knew already. I don't think there's anything else I could elaborate on.

"Has there been anyone else looking at your car since you discovered this damage?"

"Not that I know of. Of course, Officer Cook, another police officer, stopped by earlier. I don't know whether he looked around or not. He did come to our back door, though, which is the entrance closest to my car."

"Officer Cook?" Both officers chorused, glancing at each other, with furrowed brows and questioning expressions.

"Yes. He's a friend of a friend. He stopped by just to assure me he'd protect me."

I smiled.

"I don't know an Officer Cook at Baltimore County division. Do you Tom?"

Tom shook his head, his eyes registering concern.

"I think he's an officer with Baltimore City police department." I added.

"Did you call him?" Shapiro asked.

"No, but I think Sarah must've called my other friend. She must've asked him to come." I answered, while trying to make sense of it, as well.

"Do you know that for sure?"

I hesitated before answering. I squinted, looking toward a window, unseeing. I tried to recall details.

"He was here shortly after Sarah left. I just assumed..."

I was puzzled. *What had actually happened?*

Tom, or Officer Shriver, as his name tag read, recorded my words on a second page of a legal pad.

Both stood in tandem and asked, "Mrs. Ward, would you please accompany us to precinct headquarters?

Officers circling this area early this morning apprehended someone acting suspiciously. She was in possession of a tool that's unusual for any woman to carry: something that might be used to do any number of things, but could be used for slashing tires. We may need a formal statement from you."

"Certainly, let me get my coat."

A woman?

Why would a woman slash my tires? It makes no sense.

It's important I go. Some innocent woman may need my statement for her release.

Chapter 46

More Questions

Glory

Who could be calling at this hour? It's only 6:00 a.m.

"Hello?"

"Yes, this is Gloria Harris. Sir, why would she want to speak with me? I see. Yes, I'll need to get dressed. I can be there in an hour. Towson precinct, right?"

"Ms. Harris, I'm Edward Higgins, district attorney. I'm representing a woman who was picked up for questioning this morning."

Still confused, I asked, "Why do you want to see me?"

"The person in question has requested representation, and since she has no attorney of record, she has accepted my services. She was given her right to one phone call. She has waived it in exchange for a visit from you. Are you family?"

"I'm sorry. I don't recall your telling me her name."

"Of course" Mr. Higgins glanced at paperwork. "Her name is Karen Cline-Harris; similar last name, except for the hyphen. I just thought you might be related."

I felt like I'd just been doused with a bucket of ice water. Shaking my head, I asked, "Why, on earth, does she want to see me, did she say?"

Mr. Higgins shrugged, "She did not say. I assumed support from a family member. Since you're not family, I don't know."

I prayed silently, "God, please help me."

I'd hoped I'd never have to speak with this woman again. *What more could she possibly want to say to me?*

"If I speak with her, will she and I be alone, or will you or a guard be present? I am a licensed social worker, but I have no connection with this police department or county government. I am not an objective person. There would certainly be a conflict of interests if there is something you want me to find out. I'm concerned about attorney-client privilege and confidentiality."

"She has been read her Miranda rights. She has given me information I require and she has not been charged with anything yet. I can offer a secure room for your discussion."

"All right, I'll speak with her."

My mouth was dry. I dreaded this. *How in the world did she think I could help her or frankly, wanted to? God would have to give me objectivity I needed to discern facts, and not let our past experience tarnish my perception.*

"Oh, Mrs. Harris, I must warn you: she's dressed in an unusual fashion."

"Let me guess: A knit hat, large sunglasses and a heavy scarf nearly wrapped around her entire face."

"How did you know?"

"I've seen her uniform before, that's all."

Katie

While I waited in the precinct waiting room, I spotted a pay phone. I probably should call Sarah and tell her I'd left home and was now at this police station. She'd left this morning, assured of my being safe in her house all day. *She'd be worried if she called and I didn't answer our phone.*

I searched my bag for spare change. None in my wallet, but there were always coins collecting in its bottom. I proceeded to remove my checkbook, reading glasses, a professional card case, cosmetic bag, several *McDonald's Happy Meal*-toys, pens—with and without caps, gas and dry cleaners receipts, notes with illegible writing, safety pins, bent paper clips, dirty rubber bands, gum paper wrappers and dirt-encrusted life savers. *Gross. When was the last time I cleaned this thing out?*

I was right. Scrunched into both bottom corners was enough change to make a call.

Coins dinged and I deftly pushed buttons of the only number I'd been able to memorize.

"Hey, Ruth, is Sarah there? I really need to talk with her."

"Katie! She told us about your tires. We've been on pins and needles to hear. I won't hold you up, though. Here's Sarah."

When Sarah answered, I explained all that happened this morning. I thanked her profusely for having called Mari about Officer Cook.

I added, "I'm at the police station now."

Silence on the other end of the phone.

"Sarah, are you still there?" I asked, wondering if we'd been disconnected.

"Yes, Katie. I'm sorry. I'm just a little shocked by what you said. I didn't call Mari this morning. She knows nothing about your tires. I feel guilty now that I didn't. I'm glad Officer Cook was there to comfort you, though."

Now I was silent.

If Sarah didn't tell Mari, then Mari couldn't have told Officer Cook. How did he know?

There had to be some good explanation. He probably heard about it on a police walkie-talkie or something. I'm sure Baltimore City and Baltimore County exchange that type of information. Yes, that had to be what it was.

"Well, Sarah, I just wanted to let you know where I am. The police officers will probably escort me back home. Would you be a doll and pick up Timmy after work? I'd so appreciate it."

Chapter 47

Meanwhile...

Sarah

About noon, the phone rang at St. Edmonds. Ruth washed her hands to remove paint she and Sam, Jr. were using to decorate a map of the United States. Its papier-mache mountain peaks needed white for snow, they'd decided—especially those Grand Tetons.

Ruth nuzzled the receiver between her chin and her left shoulder, while she wiped her fingers on a tea towel.

"Hello?"

Glancing around the kitchen and not seeing Sarah, she answered the caller,

"She's not close by. Can I take a message for her? No, it won't be long, I'm sure. She's probably elsewhere in this house—perhaps dressing for work. Let me get a pen and paper.

OK, now whom shall I say is calling? Mrs. Stanofsky, Sarah's neighbor. Very important. Yes, I will give her your message as soon as I can. Thank you."

Gloria

The holding center-part of this police department obviously joined the jail. At least it looked like a jail to me—bars, wired-windows, and all.

Of course, I'd never been in a jail before, so what did I know? This dingy place looked like nowhere I wanted to revisit, for sure.

I was led to what they called a secure interrogation room. I was told Karen would be waiting for me there. A guard and her lawyer would be standing outside the door, should I need assistance.

The coffee given me was now cold, and its creamer tasted decidedly bitter; its bitterness might be coming from the taste of bile in my mouth, though.

Once again, I was doing something I didn't want to do; with and for someone I didn't want to see. I took a deep breath and let it out slowly. Here goes, I muttered, as I pushed the cold metal door knob.

There was Karen, complete with head covering, black sunglasses, a black scarf around lower face and neck, and draped with an oversized black, men's overcoat.

Before it had been brown, hadn't it? The dark glasses had been brown, also. *I remember how mousy and non-descript she'd looked.*

Now her head gear was coupled with an almost floor-length maxi, much too large for her small frame.

She looked much more severe and sinister than I remembered.

She stared at me without words—at least it looked like she was staring at me. With shadowy lens, I really couldn't tell. I turned behind me to see if she was looking at someone else.

No one else.

I waited for a few minutes, allowing her to speak when she was ready. She obviously had all the time in the world. I needed to leave in an hour.

Actually, physically and emotionally, I needed to leave now. The dark spiritual essence of this confined space was oppressive, almost diabolical.

"Gloria" she finally said, "I won't remove my scarf and glasses. They can't make me. No one can."

"Karen, I don't care if you do or don't. Eventually, though, guards may. I can't be sure. Why do you think you need them?"

"Because of something I did."

"Are you willing to tell me what you did, Karen? Is that why you wanted me to come?"

Silence.

I was feeling uncomfortable, even more so than minutes ago. What if she told me something I didn't want to hear, like something illegal? A huge dilemma, and then what would I do?

I'd heard stories of priests and psychiatrists who'd heard someone's confession and were bound by confidentiality of their professions; then, had to carry some sordid tale to their grave, plus bear the guilt of their confessor as well. I was not a priest or a psychiatrist, and I was now glad Mother Superior did not allow me to become a Nun. Even so, this was not a position I wanted.

"I want to tell you all I know so you'll pray for me. I'm cornered—trapped. I'm too ashamed to pray." Karen suddenly blurted out.

"Karen, if you ask God to forgive you—no matter what you've done, no matter how bad —He will; He'll take away any guilt you feel, too. He'll give you a fresh start. All we have to do is ask.

"Certainly, I'll pray for you before I leave. As for your confession, I am not a priest or lawyer. If your confession may incriminate you, your lawyer needs to be here, too."

"No, please don't leave. You're the only person I can trust."

"Why me?"

I remained dumfounded.

"I tried calling Julia, but she never returned my call. Somebody said she was out-of-town. You're the only other person I could think of to ask for."

"Karen, I promise, I won't leave this room until you feel comfortable. However, let me please ask your lawyer to join us, for your legal protection. You need that."

Reluctantly, she nodded her head in assent.

I opened the door.

"Mr. Higgins, please come in. Ms. Harris needs to add something."

Chapter 48

Videos, Anyone?

Sarah

"Ruth, I'm leaving for work now. Is there anything you need from the store . . . groceries, school supplies, whatever?"

"Sarah, my goodness, I forgot all about you."

I shrugged, mystified by Ruth's reaction. "What about me did you forget?" I said and laughed.

Ruth wiped her hands on the paint-covered teatowel, and, running toward the phone, grabbed a slip of paper.

"I forgot to give you this message. It's from your neighbor."

"Was it the Stanofsky's, the retired couple right next door, or the Roseman's across the street?"

"Mrs. Stanofsky. She said it was important. She left her number for you to call as soon as possible."

Hmm, she always says not to worry about anything. She and her husband relentlessly watch our property. She never calls, though.

"Do you think I should call now or just wait and go over there when I go home?"

"I don't know. She sounded concerned. I think you should call now."

I set my coat and tote bag on the counter and pulled up a stool to sit. I was tired. It had been a long night and morning.

"Mrs. Stanofsky? Yes, this is Sarah. I'm so sorry to have concerned you. Yes, my friend's car was vandalized last night. Yes, we're all right, but that's why police were there. Thank you so much for calling to check on us. Excuse me? What did you say? Your security camera may have taped it? Oh goodness, yes. Please. I'm sure police would want to see it. Thank you for your concern."

I set the receiver on its carriage and turned to Ruth, obviously eager for news.

"The Stanofsky's have a video tape from their security camera. Since their back yard joins with ours, it may show the tire-slasher."

"Sarah, Katie may need that right now, do you think?"

"It just occurred to me that Joel may have installed a camera in tree branches back there when we installed our security system. We may have a tape, also."

I'd forgotten all about that camera. I remember its installation. I'd questioned Joel about his hiding it in tree branches, where none of us could reach.

"Ruth, would you drive to the Stanofsky's and pick up their tape, please? You won't be able to get ours—it's hidden high in our Mimosa tree branches. I'll have to figure out how to get that later."

"You and I might not be able to retrieve it in those branches, but I know someone who can." Ruth said eagerly.

I looked at her questioning, but not reading her thoughts.

I shrugged.

"Sam, Jr. A Mimosa tree was his favorite place to play in our Rodgers Forge yard. His little friends would pretend to be GI Joe, with those branches as his lookout." Ruth answered enthusiastically.

"I'll drive to the Stanofsky's and you can follow in your car. I'll go on to work while you get the tapes, OK? Maybe you can deliver them to the police station before Katie leaves."

Katie

I waited for what seemed to be days in the precinct reception area. I purchased coffee from a vending machine, but when my cup was dispensed, it dropped at a slant. Coffee poured out, and splashed on the side of the cup.

There went the last of my change. I wasn't really thirsty, anyway. Just bored and tired.

I'd made my formal statement to the police. They said they'd have paper-work for me shortly to submit to my insurance company. I'd wait all day if I had to. I needed that refund—well, reimbursement minus my deductible. Better than nothing at all.

I glanced up to see two guards escort someone across the hall to a room with a sign, reading fingerprinting and ID.

Poor soul, she must be homeless or something, from the way she's dressed: huge, man's overcoat, nearly touching the floor. Black knit cap and scarf nearly covering her face.

Since my time in the shelter, I'd developed compassion for people who were forced to live on the streets. I've been homeless and helpless and without hope, too.

Poor thing.

Ten minutes later, the same guards led the woman, now handcuffed and without hat, scarf or glasses. I squinted and rose slightly from my chair to see more clearly.

"Oh my gosh. Oh my gosh. I know her." I shouted, not meaning to say it out loud. It just came out, by itself.

Both guards looked around, and the woman covered her face with her hands, trying to hide.

The policeman, who had brought me, looked toward the handcuffed woman and back at me. He signaled to his partner, Tom, who walked to the seat beside me as her guards led her further down the hall, out-of- sight.

"Excuse me, Mrs. Ward. You say you recognize that woman?"

"I'm so sorry, officer, sir. I didn't mean to look at her and say what I did out loud."

My outburst was hardly appropriate. I just couldn't believe it was her.

"Mrs. Ward, you did nothing wrong. Now how do you know that woman?"

"She's my estranged husband's girlfriend. I saw her last month when I was cleaning out my house. I'm really sorry my words may have caused trouble."

"On the contrary: your words may be helpful."

Chapter 49

Teddy Bear Picnic

Katie

I was finally escorted back to Sarah's house at four o'clock. It'd been a long day. I really needed to nap before Timmy came home. The whole day had been too much.

Reconsidering, I really should get packed so we can head to the shelter tonight. Spending another night here was probably not safe.

I'd grab something to eat. I'd had too much caffeine today and not enough food. *I always get really tired and shaky if I don't eat something every couple of hours, even if it's just a cracker or two.*

I wandered into Sarah's huge kitchen and approached her Subzero refrigerator. The inside of this thing was cavernous. Good . . . leftovers from last night's dinner.

I'd never really been in this kitchen alone at this time of day. It was dusk, and street lights were already starting to brighten, but I could still easily see neighboring homes. I closed the refrigerator door, distracted by neighbors parking cars and entering houses.

Through this glass wall's unobstructed view, I could see blocks away. I noticed how evergreen and Mimosa trees separated my car from neighbors' yards. I recalled admiring airy, pink ball-clustered blossoms decorating Mimosas when driving through this neighborhood, countless times over the years. Pretty.

Mrs. Stanofsky's garden path traversed our two properties, winding around those trees and a short hedge.

Such a sweet lady; she'd come that way when she'd deliver a homemade loaf of bread, (a most appreciated gift, after Sarah and I'd been working all day).

Another car was parked further down, nearly to a back alley which entered Kelley Avenue. *Odd.*

Few people knew it was an alley, according to Sarah. She'd always told me to bring my car all the way up to the top of her drive. Since we were single women, we didn't want to give anyone any ideas. We wanted no one to know that we could be alone.

Whose car was it? It was shadowed by trees, and I couldn't distinguish its color. Probably a delivery man for the neighbors, or a repairman, maybe.

I shrugged. I'd go back to my refrigerator hunt.

In moments, I hear a knock from our back door. Gnawing a chicken leg from last night's dinner, I dried one hand and unlocked the kitchen door. I couldn't fasten its chain latch because of the drumstick in my other hand.

Seeing it was Officer Cook, it didn't matter.

"Ms. Ward, I noticed you were out all day. Seeing lights on in your kitchen, I decided to make sure you're all right before I head home, myself," Officer Cook said.

"Certainly, won't you come in? Forgive me for eating. I haven't had much today.

Can I offer you a piece of chicken? It's cold, but really good."

I thought a minute while chewing. *Why was he watching my kitchen?* It's completely surrounded by trees. The other policemen had come to our front door and had exited and re-entered from only the front. *He must not have known that, right?*

"Officer Cook, I so appreciate your taking time out of your workday to watch my house and help me feel safe and secure. How kind of you."

I smiled my most charming smile. I'd learned to hide feelings behind a smile, from living with my unpredictable husband all those years.

He grinned. "That's my job."

"Were you here all day?"

"Yes Ma'am."

"That's odd. I don't recall seeing you here when I left to go to the police station."

He looked at me, eyes wide. Then smiling, but more forced than before, he said,

"You went to the police station? I could have taken you there if you'd asked. I told you I'd be nearby if you needed anything."

"Well, I needed a police report from Baltimore County. Insurance claim, you know. You're employed by Baltimore City, right?"

The more I said, the more anxious he appeared. Drops of sweat formed across his brow. *Something was not Kosher.*

Too many things did not add up. How could he be employed with Baltimore City and spend his day on my property in Baltimore County? Surely his supervisors would not agree to that, would they? I guess they could have a joint arrangement.

What was going on?

I gulped. *What if he wasn't who he claimed to be?* I'd let him into Sarah's house, my present home.

Sarah was not due back until 7:00 p.m. I glanced at the huge cedar floor clock, handmade in Israel. Two hours. I glanced at a weapon in his holster.

I smiled and rose from my chair.

"I need to excuse myself, Officer Cook. Nature's call, you know. Can I show you to the door?"

Officer Cook remained quiet, but his eyes squinted now, and appeared menacing; piercing, with a disingenuous darkness, I hadn't detected that until now. The look seemed familiar; it reminded me of someone...my husband.

I was familiar with frightening experiences. I'd developed an almost a sixth sense for perceiving vibes: sights, smells, whatever signaled danger. Every cell was screaming warnings to my nervous system.

I must be calm so he won't read my fear. That was critical.

I'd read somewhere that vicious dogs can smell and read fear in a human. Fear can trigger an aggressive attack. Having lived with my husband over the years, I'd witnessed that with vicious humans, too.

I must keep my voice even and low. No sudden movements. Keep him distracted with conversation—anything.

"God, please help me as you always have. Send an angel." I pled beneath my breath.

I took a few steps toward the back door. "Officer Cook, I'll see you tomorrow, OK? I'm really tired, and as I said, I must use the bathroom."

If I can just get to the bathroom, I could grab my cordless in an adjoining bedroom. I could call for help.

Before I could move again, he slammed me against the wall; his hand against my throat.

I could not speak. I could hardly breathe.

"Listen," he growled. "Sit down. Do as I say and I won't hurt you. Any sudden moves and you die, you hear?"

I sat, as directed and looked down so he couldn't read my expression. *Who was this man and why did he want to hurt me? Why had he pretended to be someone else, not only with me but Mari? It made no sense.*

I thought my husband had slashed my tires. However, Don was not above paying someone to do anything. I knew that. A policeman was a great cover.

I'm relieved Timmy's still at Day Care, and Sarah and Rebecca are not home yet. If he gets violent, it'll be only me involved.

God please hear my prayer. Send an angel, I prayed again silently.

I sat listening to the tick of the clock, each tick seeming like an hour rather than a minute.

Officer Cook was now pacing, his handgun cocked.

"Where are your son's toys?" He shouted.

Timmy's toys? What could he want with Timmy's toys?

"It depends on which toy, sir. He has some outside and some in his room."

Cook's eyes were wide now, pupils nearly fully-dilated; black as night.

"Stuffed animals."

"They would be in his room. Which one are you interested in?"

He poked me with the end of his revolver. "Show me."

I released a long breath.

I hated going further into this house, away from any exit I might escape. His gun's cold metal reminded me I had no choice. I arose and walked slowly towards Timmy's playroom.

As I flicked the light switch, Cook shoved me aside.

"Where is his bear?"

Timmy had dozens of bears, ranging in size from several inches high to one in the corner which stood nearly five feet. Probably ten or so were what I'd call medium, from 10"-15" high.

Cook ripped a curtain tie-back from the window and tied my wrists. Once I was secured, he raced to the shelf and started pulling off bears. He studied each, discarding most in seconds.

"What are you looking for?" I called, trying desperately to undo my bonds.

"Are there any other bears?" He stared with eyes wide, dark with evil.

"I don't think so."

He searched the top of the closet and finally pulled down a plain, brown, paper-wrapped box. Tearing into it, amazingly, I could see there was another bear.

I had no idea that box contained a bear. I had moved the wrapped box from our house, here. It was stored in back of Timmy's closet at home. I hadn't even opened it to see its contents. No time when I'd packed. I figured I'd open it later. Then I forgot.

How did this guy—this imposter—know what was in the box and I, Timmy's mother, had no idea.

Cook grinned wickedly and stuck the bear under his arm. He shoved me toward the living room and ordered me to sit.

I could feel his gun's pressure against my head. I felt chilled, but I was perspiring profusely. I reminded myself to relax. . . I had to, in order to think. My life depended on it.

"Now I've got what I want, there's really no reason to keep you around." He flicked the chamber. "Your husband told me to get this bear. Then get rid of you and I'd be done."

"I don't understand. I don't know you. Why would he want you to kill me? Why would you want my little boy's brand new bear?"

God, time is running out. If you take me home, please take care of Timmy. Please keep him safe. I prayed without audible words.

I heard the ever so slight sound of his finger slipping off the metal trigger. Either his hand was trembling or sweating. Either way, a distraction could cause him to move. What distraction could I make? Think, Katie, think.

Suddenly, a crash caused me to jump and Cook's gun to move.

"Police! Drop your gun."

The two officers who had been with me most of the day burst through the front door, followed by Sarah, Mari, Gloria, Ruth and Sam, Jr.

"Because he loves me," says the Lord," I will rescue him;
I will protect him. . . I will be with him in trouble."
Psalm 91: 14-15 (Bible, NIV)

Chapter 50

Hello, Hello

It was our regular Friday evening get together, and we decided to meet at St. Edmonds tonight. Lucille had made a delicious fish-for-Friday dinner of catfish, hush puppies, slaw, pinto beans and corn bread, with sweet potato pie for dessert and a bottomless pitcher of Sweet Tea.

"It' bout time I do some real cookin'. I bin layin' down on th'job too long. 'Sides, Sarah bin good, but she can't do Mama's recipes for th'ole basics. No'm,"

Sarah grinned, "I'm not trying, either. I need a night off every once in a while, too, you know. I think I've mastered almost all kinds of cuisine, but I can't do Southern.

Lucille grinned, "Don' none a' us wants you t'try, neither," and she laughed her guttural rolling laugh.

All of us were wilted from this past week's events. Julia had been at an out-of-town conference. She'd flown back to Baltimore this morning– now stunned at hearing Katie's having been held at gunpoint.

"A few days away, and I feel like my whole world has been reordered. Frankly, from the little I've heard, I don't think I could've stood the stress of it, anyway. So, tell all. Don't leave anything out. My life's force demands I hear everything."

She grabbed a piece of chocolate and popped it into her mouth to punctuate her demand.

Gloria said, "Well, I guess if we really must tell you everything, we must go back to the beginning."

Jules pretended to glare, sternly, but she couldn't hide the sparkle in her eye,

"Well, get going then. We don't have all night."

She reached for another chocolate, and positioned to toss it into her mouth.

"Well, Jules, Karen our mystery girl was a major player. You remember her?"

"Of course, how could I forget? She's Charles's ex-wife who destroyed your marriage and reputation, Glory."

She shook her head. She'd hoped they'd heard the last from Karen. Neither she nor Glory were anxious for more encounters with her.

Katie quipped, "Well, her role doesn't end there. Apparently, she'd met Don when he retained Charles as a lawyer. A lot of blanks there, but she's been living with Don and doing his bidding against me. I don't know it all, but she slashed my tires. That was a ploy set up by Don to further frighten me into trusting Officer Cook, alias John Doe."

Jules asked, "Wait a minute, Officer Cook, who was interested in Mari?"

Julia was beginning to think she needed a program to recognize the players. She recalled hawkers at Orioles games; shouting and waving those books as they climbed up and down stadium steps.

Mari answered, "Well, apparently Officer Cook was not who he pretended to be. He was sent to help me (after he heard I'd been attacked), but was really watching who was coming and going from our Roland Avenue house. Apparently, Karen entered as mystery girl at our Tuesday classes to see if Katie was there. She stayed just long enough to figure out we were friends."

Jules blurted out, with eyes wide and mouth gaping, "Really?"

"I think my attacker may have been hired for hunting Katie also, but I distracted him. He was money-hungry, and my attack was really a robbery attempt, like those other women he accosted. I had no cash, so he attacked me in anger." Mari continued.

Recalling that day at the antique shop alerted her to his evil, but he looked malicious. She'd never suspected Officer Cook's chicanery. Unbelievable, in fact, if she hadn't seen him, gun-in-hand, at Sarah's house, she doubted she'd ever be convinced of his fraud.

What a conman.

Katie said, "We'll probably never know all the angles, but Don was paying off Officer Cook. Karen thought she'd get something—who knows what—by doing Don's bidding, Like Mari said, her attacker was in that plan too, until he was arrested. Apparently Don had bought something in the antique store where Tony was a clerk. He accepted Don's offer to do some moonlighting—on the side: perhaps a barter arrangement for dental work or something more clandestine."

Jules shook her head, puzzled, "So how did all this unravel?"

She recalled seeing Cook enter Ward's office the day of her flu shot.

Katie answered, "Officer Cook came to Sarah's house before I could even call police about my slashed tires. I thought Sarah called Mari, but no. In the meantime, Karen had been picked up by police early that morning. I recognized her as Don's girlfriend while I was at the station."

Sarah added, "Our neighbors offered their video tape from a security camera in their yard."

Sam squealed, "And I was the one to climb that tree to get the other video tape."

We chorused, "Yes you were, and police could not have gotten to Katie in time if you had not gotten that tape."

Little Sam bounced and beamed proudly with our acknowledgement of his role in helping police.

He loved being congratulated for his bravery and expert tree-climbing. Lucille promised to bake him a prize cake—a fitting reward. . . and he'd lick the bowl, too.

Mari said, "You didn't tell me. What was on that tape?"

Gloria answered, "Apparently, it showed three silhouettes beside her car in early morning hours. One was obviously Karen, bundled in all her get up. The second was Cook, and the third has yet to be determined. Although shadowy without much contrast due to darkness, Sarah's second tape shows another angle with more details, perhaps even a fourth person. Finger prints on the slashing tool were confirmed to be Karen's, of course."

Jules asked, "Now Glory, how did you get involved in this? After your session with Karen, I thought you'd never want to see her again. You were assured her feelings toward you were mutually distasteful . . .at least that's what I assumed."

Gloria added, "Well, that's what's so odd. Her court-appointed attorney called me. She obviously couldn't ask Charles to represent her or any of his friends. She had no money, which I think is probably what drove her to have an affair with Don. Anyway, because she knew so many lawyers in this area, she didn't trust even an attorney the court provided. She wanted me there to pray for her."

Julia stared, wide-eyed, and silent for a few seconds. Then she added obviously confused, "Pray?"

"You got it. She confessed to slashing Katie's tires, working with Cook and for Don. Charles may even have been involved in some way. She hinted at that, but she didn't actually give details.

"Why she trusted me, I don't know. She said it was because I was kind, listening to displaced women's confessions. Although she never stayed in our room, she apparently listened at the door during each class."

Mari added, "Isn't that incredible?" She shook her head, looking amazed.

"She said she initially wanted to talk with you, Jules, but you were unreachable. So she requested me." Gloria supplied for added clarity.

Questioning glances around our table prompted Julia to answer, "Karen had come for counseling with me this fall. She needed help, but because she'd had an affair with Gloria's then husband Charles, she didn't feel comfortable sharing with Glory, or coming to that class, either."

Oh's chorused from around the kitchen.

Julia continued, "So Don is obviously a key figure here, but why did he bring all the other people into it? I thought he was just guilty of domestic violence, illegal prescriptions, possible insurance fraud and being a classic abuser, as if that's not enough."

Katie looked down, "He wanted to get me out of the way because he worried about what I knew. I think he fears I know more than I do, maybe his drug-use, but perhaps some other illegal activity, I don't know about. He feared he'd be caught, I guess, after he discovered I'd gone to the hospital and his abuse was public. He paid others to work for him so he wouldn't be directly incriminated if something went amiss. And, he wanted that bear. If you want an answer, my father used to say, "Follow the money trail."

Jules made a face, "A bear. . . whatever for?"

The longer she listened, the more complicated this sordid story became. *What else?*

Katie said, "Don bought a stuffed bear and kept it in Timmy's closet, wrapped, so Timmy wouldn't play with it. If Timmy or I had found it, neither of us would suspect it was anything other than a toy. The police found

$100,000 sewn into its tummy. Don hid the money as he probably has done with other assets so it wouldn't be included in our divorce distribution, I guess. It could be ill-gotten gain, also, but apparently there's no proof as yet. He always intended to get that bear before Timmy and I moved out. He didn't think I'd take an unmarked, plain brown, paper-wrapped box with me when I left."

Jules asked again, "So what will happen to all these people?"

Her head was swimming. She needed more chocolate, definitely, and reached for another piece.

Gloria answered, "Karen's only guilty of destruction of private property and trespassing. She was offered a plea bargain in exchange for information and names of who was behind that whole scheme. Although depending on what they discover about Don and Charles, she might later be named as an accomplice, I suppose. I excused myself from the room when she gave that information. That was between her and her court-appointed counsel. I didn't want to know."

Mari asked, "I'm still shocked Officer Cook was not who he said he was. I fell for his lines—hard. He was so handsome and so believable. Being newly widowed made me more gullible, I guess."

Katie answered, "Who wouldn't be fooled? What charm!"

She knew she would've been taken in by his wiles, too, under different circumstances. We were all vulnerable. He was so cute—an evil conman, but irresistible, nonetheless. We all needed to be on guard for wolves in sheep's clothing, for sure.

Gloria said, "Apparently he'll be charged with impersonating an officer. Maybe armed and attempted robbery, also, since he held Katie at gunpoint while attempting to steal the bear."

We were all silent, pondering these circumstances and our future.

Katie said, looking down and fingering her wedding band, "I wonder what will happen to Don."

Gloria spoke, "From what I can gather, there's nothing substantial bringing him in on any of this, at this point, except guilt by association or, as a stretch, an accomplice. He didn't do anything wrong by stashing money in a bear. I don't think there's any proof he broke any law so far, from what I heard. I'm sure they know more than I was privileged to hear, of course. Police are still checking evidence—especially that money in the bear and the videos. We also have to assume he may have been mentioned by Karen or Cook, with their confessions. He's not above reproach yet, I don't imagine."

Katie cleared her throat and stated, "That still makes me a fugitive, I guess."

Gloria answered, "Katie, look how far you've come since you were prisoner in your own home with Don. For that matter, look how far we've all come over past months. God has protected us so far and he will protect us in the future. Plus, we have each other."

We all joined hands confirming our unity and our friendship. We were a team.

We all knew. . . we would survive.

Chapter 51

Go Tell It On The Mountain

Spring, 1993

Gloria

"Honey, has our mail arrived?"
"Have you forgotten, My Dear, mountain mail doesn't arrive as punctually as Baltimore's?" Bill teased, handing his wife her Earl Grey.

If Bill only knew, mail can be slower in Baltimore, sometimes, than here in the boonies.

"Expecting something interesting?' He rubbed his palms together, feigning intrigue.

"Come here," I pulled him onto the sofa, laughing.

"When we returned from our honeymoon, I had juicy letters from the girls, brimming with their latest news. I've heard little lately. I want to know what's going on, that's all. Goodness, I'm sounding like Jules—hungry for details."

"Missing it?" Bill queried.

"Hardly, but I do miss the girls. We were family. I can hardly believe all that's happened over past months."

"Time flies, that's for sure."

Bill sipped his tea, shaking his head with this wisdom.

"So many changes; the best one, of course, is my new husband." I circled my arms around Bill's neck.

"Have you heard news from any of them?"

"Mari moved into St. Edmonds with Ruth, Sam, Jr., Sarah and Rebecca, and I mustn't forget Rags. Sam, Jr. loves Rags. Mari uses the Roland Avenue house as her decorating studio. Her receptionist mans the desk by day, and rents an upstairs room, at night.

"Of course, as you know, Mari manages that house and all the rest of our rental properties in my absence. She's studying about antiques, and her dream is to become an appraiser, eventually.

"What about her son?".

"Tyler's spending the summer with his grandmother in Mississippi, postponing college.

According to the last news I've heard, he'll be taking a course or two from Ole' Miss, which is fairly close to his grandmother's house. He's been in contact with the lacrosse coach at Carolina, who's encouraging him to consider a spot on next season's team. In the meantime, he's helping his grandmother tend her property."

"Huh. Why didn't Mari join Tyler in Mississippi? Tell me again."

Bill was trying to connect. He needed to get it right.

"She still has enormous debt. So she continues to live with Ruth and Sarah, help with displaced homemakers and decrease her debt as much as she can."

"Interesting." Bill refilled his tea.

He'd been in North Carolina, while Glory was in Baltimore, so his mind felt like scrambled eggs when she described it all. He still could barely get all their names straight—the women, their children and respective late or ex-spouses. It was all so confusing.

"Tyler gave his room furnishings to Sam, Jr., who's carefully hung his posters on his wall, placed his comforter on his bed, and his lacrosse goal in the backyard, at St. Edmonds. He wants to be just like Tyler, who's proud and protective, and considers Sam, Jr. his little brother.

I smiled recalling how Tyler and Sam, Jr., both only children and wanting brothers had found one another. The age difference had little effect on their relationship. They were bound by life's trials, as their mothers were.

"Oh, and Tyler's been corresponding with Rebecca. You know, Sarah's daughter?"

"That little girl who struggled with anorexia?"

He did remember that, for some reason. Maybe the medical connection made it easier to associate.

"Yes. This summer, she's returning to the program in Durham, volunteering to help other girls as she'd been helped. Apparently, she loves it there. This fall, she'll start college full-time, on dual-enrollment status with Ruth's teaching at home. She hopes to transfer to Peace or Meredith, small women's schools near Raleigh, in order to continue helping in that program. She's back to a normal weight now. Her hair's completely grown back, and she's blossoming. Sarah thanks God everyday for her healing."

"Wonderful. I'm glad to hear it." Bill answered, trying to connect her past with the present. "She's the one who wants that ancient dark, velvet dress of yours, right?"

"Be careful what and who you're calling ancient. She wants to re-design it into something special. Maybe she can dream dreams with it, as I did when I was a girl. I've given up on perfect dreams, now, since I've got you."

Bill grinned.

"Ruth and Sarah are both enrolled at the college. Plus, Ruth has taken my place as coordinator for DH's, while still caring for Mother and Lucille. With all the girls there and Ruth in control, I know I don't have to worry about Mother or the house—such a relief."

Yes. He concurred. If Ruth weren't taking care of things at St. Edmonds, Glory would still be up there and probably would still not be his wife. Yes. Ruth was his answer to prayer, too.

"What else? " He would get all this straight if it was the last thing he did. These women were family to

Glory. Since she was now his wife, he would count them as family, too.

"Sarah has a weekly TV cooking show, now. She shyly admits it always was her dream, now come true. She, Mari and Rebecca cater parties on isolated weekends. She also manages to help Ruth with the DH's. They're all incredibly busy, but they make a wonderful team, supporting one another and making it all work."

"Sarah is Rebecca's mother, right? I get them confused."

"Yes. Her ex-husband, Joel, has offered to send Rebecca to Harvard to finish college. He thinks it'd be perfect. Sarah's told him there's a new definition of perfect, now. Rebecca and Sarah are perfect just where they are."

"Huh. I didn't know that. I don't remember your telling me any of this."

He massaged his temples.

"Well, I thought I did. So much happened in such a short time, it's all a blur, really. I can't remember what I told you and what I haven't."

"Any news from Julia?"

"I just talked with her yesterday. She's still running around, busy as always. She wants to visit in April to see our mountain blossoms. I can't wait to see her."

Bill pulled her toward him.

The mail came sliding through the slot clattering onto their hardwood floor.

"Would you like your mail, your highness?"

"Please Dear, if you don't mind. I don't want to spill my tea."

"Yeah, right." Bill eased himself off the sofa and stumbled to the door.

"Mostly bills, from what I can tell. Several look personal. They're addressed to you and not me. How is it, when you moved into my house, Dear Wife, all the good letters are yours, and there's nothing for me but bills?"

"Bills for Bill." I laughed.

"Not funny."

"Let's see what we have. Oh, this one's from Ruth." I grinned. "Blah, blah, blah. Oh, she's wondering how our married life is going. What do you think, Honey?"

Bill grinned and kissed my fingertips.

"What's next?"

"Sarah's been asked to cater some big events at Baltimore Country Club. She's excited. Rebecca and Ruth will help serve. Mari's offered to decorate with panache. Mari's business is growing, and its name is Elan. . . French, for panache."

"Huh."

"DH's are going well, but they could use my help"

"Don't even think about it, Glory."

Bill couldn't bear for Glory to leave again. She's here to stay. He could say that, now; she's his wife. Thank goodness.

"I won't. It's self-sustaining now, with God's direction. It'll be fine."

He was glad about that.

"The Wilsons are fine and send their love. Oh, I can't believe it. Sylvia and Pierre join them each weekend for Sunday dinner." I laughed.

How they ever became a part of this group, He'd never know. He tried to recall: Julia rescued them from a beauty salon or was it Glory who found them in a restaurant? Too much. He'd refuse to even try anymore. He'd change the subject.

"Whatever happened with the man who impersonated the policeman?" He interjected.

"Oh, his trial won't be until summer. We must wait to hear the end of that whole episode." I said matter-of-factly.

"How about the girl you used to call the mystery woman? What happened to her?"

"Well, that's where the story gets more interesting. She was charged with vandalizing Katie's car, but apparently there were a lot more things she had against her. Who knows if she learned anything to stay out of trouble? Maybe mercy will guide her in the future, God willing. She was Don, Katie's husband's live-in girlfriend. That's where it gets sticky. Don may be found to be involved, and perhaps even his lawyer, Charles, my ex. It'll take a while for police to sort out all of that."

Bill's eyes were crossing. Maybe he needed an aspirin.

"Here's a note from Julia."

I grinned tearing the flap. I couldn't wait for her visit. I scanned the note.

"Oh, my word."

"Glory, what's wrong?" Bill looked alarmed at my response.

I hesitated before answering.

"I'm just amazed, that's all. Jules was sorting through papers filed in a back office closet.

Although supposedly a secret, she discovered the name of our displaced homemaker's donor.

I can hardly believe it."

"OK, you've aroused my curiosity. Who? "

"Mother Superior. Apparently, she'd kept up with news about me from someone at the college. She was touched by my difficulties. Since, as a nun, she could not accept an inheritance from her parents, she directed their estate proceeds to a trust to help displaced women. I can't believe it."

"But she couldn't have known you'd be directing it, could she?"

I shook my head. *Maybe good had come from my pain.*

I was silent for a moment. Tears brimmed my lids as I considered this news.

Bill held me close, kissed my cheek and said, "Now, what else?"

I tucked Julia's note in my jeans pocket—for later—blinked my eyes, and took a deep breath.

Opening another note from Sarah, I started again, "Everyone's concerned about Katie. Once her divorce came through, she left. She only sent a note saying not to worry. She's safe. She'd write or call later."

At that moment, a tiny knock sounded from the front door. A small face pressed onto glass panes at the side of its frame. Bill rose and unfastened the latch.

"Uncle Bill, can you come out and play? Mommy's too busy."

"Well, well, well."

He scooped the small child into his arms and set him on his shoulders.

"Glory, how about a walk? Is that all right with you, Squirt?"

"Can I have a cookie, too, please?"

"Oh, I suppose you can. Glory, are there any cookies hiding in the big jar?"

"Perhaps. . . unless a little mouse got into them. Maybe Purrfect has eaten them—with the mouse."

The little voice giggled, "No-o-o. Cats don't eat cookies."

"They don't?"

We donned our jackets and headed to our favorite spot. After climbing the hiking trail to the top of the hill, we gazed as far as we could see.

Bill asked our little friend, "Which way is Tennessee? Which way is Virginia? Which way is Georgia?"

He turned from side to side, while still astride Bill's shoulders.

"Want to get down and walk now? Aunt Glory and I are going to rest our tired bones on our bench."

I surveyed these mountains. Crepe Myrtles, Azalea's and Rhododendron's were budding; breathtakingly beautiful here—bright with light and hope, atop this mountain.

God's promise that all things work together for good for those who love Him, breathed through my memory. No matter how awful life's circumstances seem, He works out another way—a second way, a second chance; although sometimes we may not see that final good in life's dark times.

Then again, birds learn to sing in darkness, right?

"Mommy" our little friend squealed.

"Katie, why don't you come for dinner?"

Timmy bounced up and down, "Can we, Mommy?"

She scooped Timmy up in her arms. "Sure. Oh, did you tell Aunt Glory and Uncle Bill your news?"

Timmy grinned, "I don't suck my thumb anymore." He displayed a wrinkled thumb with a batman band-aid wrapping as his reminder. "An' I got on my 'Star Wars' big boy-pants...and...they're still dry."

"How exciting, we must celebrate," we cheered.

I studied the clear, Carolina-blue sky; lit with bright sunlight. I repeated to myself as a reminder: "No more pipe dreams. Take the second right, go to the top of your mountain and embrace second-chance dreams, instead."

"Only if you have been in the deepest valleys, can you ever know how magnificent it is to be on the highest mountain."
Richard M. Nixon

"Every day, somewhere in Maryland, a woman is forced to flee her home to protect herself and her children. She has to walk away from everything that's familiar, be prepared for the legal ramifications, be strong for her kids and somehow start a new life while looking over her shoulder the whole time. For thirty years, we have been there to ensure that no woman or child is ever forced to take that walk alone."

House of Ruth of Maryland, 2008

Acknowledgments

There are so many I could thank for encouraging me to write: loving parents who cultivated my love for books; my wonderful grandmother who tirelessly drove me to the public library almost daily during long, hot summers, my 11th grade English teacher and drama coach, who encouraged me to free my imagination; and professors at University of North Carolina- Chapel Hill, who helped me express my creativity through writing.

Although delayed for decades, it was my relationship with friends, especially the late Barbara McDonald and the late Mary Grace Bergin, which fueled my urgency to create this fictional story. For its process, I thank my son for his patience with his often-bungling, but loving, single mother.

For encouraging my use of computers, printers and other once-foreign technology and devoting many hours of technical support, teaching and unlimited patience, I extend kudos to Computer Clinic: Jim, John and Ishmael. Without their continued support, this book would be unwritten, or hopelessly lost somewhere in cyberspace.

My love to my friends who donated their precious time reading drafts: T. Keats, E. Fulcher, B. Ivie, U. Eitel, C. J. Hedges, S. Fitz-Rhodes, C. Bacon, J. Westefeld, and M. Janus. I thank my editor and dear friend, Carol Givner, who spent weeks helping me fine-tune wording, providing encouragement during times of fatigue, and understanding my message, and the talented staff at Createspace who polished and wrapped it as a paperback. I also thank Jenny Givner, my designer, whose creativity produced such an imaginative cover.

Huge thanks to all the wonderful people who have read and purchased this book. Thanks also for the privilege of donating a portion of these proceeds to the countless women's shelters, nationwide, for their care of women and children recovering from effects of domestic violence.

Lastly, and most importantly, I wish to give gratitude to God, who gave me life as well as the ability to write this story.

Author Biography

Ciby Emrie received her Bachelor's and Master's degrees from University of North Carolina-Chapel Hill, and held a part-time faculty position at University of Maryland for a number of years. She has made several appearances on Maryland Public Television and Maryland Public Radio, while employed with the State of Maryland.

After an extended maternity leave, she chose to become a full-time, at-home mom. Ciby counts her most recent role of single mom as her most challenging and rewarding to date.

Ciby Emrie resided in the greater Baltimore area for over 20 years. Ten years ago, she relocated to the Southeast, and presently practices dental hygiene part-time.

Pipe Dreams is Ciby's first novel. A portion of its sales will be donated to organizations that assist women and their children who have suffered domestic violence.

For information visit her website: www.cibyemrie.com

Made in the USA
Charleston, SC
17 April 2012